GW00494107

The Love Tokens

The Love Tokens

Janet Mary Tomson

PIATKUS

First published in Great Britain in 1994 by
Judy Piatkus (Publishers) Ltd of
5 Windmill Street, London W1

**The moral right of the author
has been asserted**

*A catalogue record for this book is available
from the British Library*

ISBN 0 7499 0258 2

Phototypeset in 11/12pt Compugraphic Times by
Action Typesetting Limited, Gloucester
Printed and bound in Great Britain by
Mackays of Chatham (PLC) Ltd

Dedicated with love
to Roger Collins, Lincoln Albert
Delandro and Rita Seymour
who left this life too soon

Author's Notes

None of the characters in this story is truly real although many of the names are authentic and contemporary to the Isle of Wight setting.

Mrs Carmichael is based on Julia Margaret Cameron, who lived at Dimbola House in Freswhater, Isle of Wight, in the 1860s. She was a pioneer of modern photography. Her next-door neighbour, Alfred, Lord Tennyson, was poet laureate to Queen Victoria. His home of Farringford is now a hotel. He is merely a shadowy figure in the events that take place in this book.

Chapter One

It was the first time in Meg's sixteen years that she had seen a naked man. She came upon him suddenly as she walked along what she considered to be her path, the one that led through the copse and connected the railway site to her grandmother's cottage.

He was standing with his back to her, up to his knees in the stream at the point where a natural dam of willow fronds and silt had formed an icy pool. Meg stopped in her tracks and, hardly aware of moving, shrank back into the shadow of the hazel trees. She could not take her eyes off the white, naked figure in the water.

He was a young man, tall and strong-limbed. A vision of a painting at Hinchington Manor came to mind. It hung in Lord Hinchington's study where Meg went once a week to clean and polish. In the painting beautiful men and women languished beside a pool, their bodies turned in elegant stances, hands held out in gestures of welcome. They were unclothed; only their thighs were obscured by floating lengths of silk or a modest hand. The whole scene was bathed in a creamy light.

The light filtering through the trees in Meg's copse was colder and cast a blue-white hue over the man's skin. Nothing shielded the rise of his smooth buttocks. A chilly wind lifted the coal-black hair hanging down over his neck. His arms from just below the elbow were a rich mahogany brown.

As Meg watched, he turned and she saw the cluster of gleaming black hair on his chest. Water droplets trickled down his sides, following the snake of hair down across

1

his belly to his groin. For the first time in her life she gazed on a man's nakedness, the pit of black hair, the unmentionable organ. She thought suddenly of the proud strutting of a turkey cock.

Meg wanted to run away but was afraid to move. Meanwhile the man was splashing water over his torso, rubbing his hands across his body with workmanlike strokes to remove the grime. He stretched and tossed his shaggy head. Water droplets flew in a crystal arc from his hair and from his groin.

Finally he went to step out of the water. Meg poised for flight but to her relief he moved to the opposite bank. She watched him dry himself briskly with what looked like an old shirt, then pull his clothes over his still damp body. Shivering visibly, he picked up a sack and turned away from her, then strode off, whistling, into the woods.

She stood for a long time absorbing what she had seen, savouring what she had felt. She had not been afraid. His self-absorption had been too complete for him to wish her harm. She could not be sure but she guessed that he was one of the navigators. Everyone said they were vermin, a menace, thieves. Wherever they worked they caused trouble. Meg believed the condemnation so forcefully voiced by her father. Suddenly her certainty was jolted, for, whatever she had previously thought, she had never once suspected that these wanderers could also be beautiful.

It was midafternoon and Meg held out the tea can to her father. As something caught his attention, he pushed it back at her, at the same time reaching for his shovel. His eyes were fixed on the distant river.

'Here comes trouble. Get away home, lass.'

In response she took the can and turned in the direction of home, but her curiosity got the better of her.

'What sort of trouble?'

Daniel Foggarty shook his head impatiently. 'The worst sort. It's that Irisher.' He nodded towards the river. 'He's back again.'

Meg followed his gaze along the newly constructed railway embankment which curved and diminished across the Norfolk mud flats. A hundred yards away she saw a solitary figure moving in their direction.

She glanced back at her father. He and his team of four navvies had stopped digging and now held their spades across their chests like weapons.

'But we're Irish,' she started. 'Why should he – '

Her father interrupted her. 'It's different for us. We've been in this country a long time. We don't steal and cheat. You were as good as born here. Now work's getting scarce, his sort'll sink to any trick to take our jobs, you'll see.'

Meg remained silent. It crossed her mind that fifteen years ago her family had been strangers, like the newcomer, looking to find work anywhere they could, but she kept her opinions to herself. Meanwhile the man continued his steady pace, seemingly undeterred by the sea of hostile faces. The sun suddenly broke from behind a bank of cloud and shone full on him.

Just behind Meg the men moved restlessly. She glanced round to see her father wipe his hand across his mouth and distribute his weight from foot to foot in readiness for the confrontation.

People said she favoured him. She had the same chestnut hair and blue eyes, although by now Daniel Foggarty was losing the rich colouring that had once by all accounts made him the handsomest man back in Killarney. But his face was hard, his mouth a pinched, mean line, and Meg hoped that she would never be like him in nature.

The others jostled behind him and once more she looked ahead. Her heart beat faster. The approaching stranger was now clearly visible. He was a tall man, young, lean, perhaps in his late twenties. Meg swallowed hard. She was immediately back in the copse gazing on his naked body. Her hands began to tremble.

This was not the first time he had come looking for the foreman, although it was the first occasion that Meg had been present. She was overwhelmed by the memory of that other, intimate, shameful time when she had spied upon him.

Her father had recounted his visits before. Always he came looking for work, refusing to believe that there was not something that he could do. Finally they had threatened

3

him with violence if he came near the site again. Now he walked with an easy lope, his hands hanging at his sides. Meg noted with relief that he carried no weapon.

'That's far enough.' It was her father who spoke and the younger man slowed his pace. 'What d'you want?' Daniel Foggarty's voice was belligerent and Meg frowned at him in disapproval.

'I'm wanting to see the gaffer.' The soft lilt of his Irish voice stirred a strange mixture of nostalgia and sweet regret in her. She had been surrounded by Irish voices all her life, wherever they had settled in England, but there was something different about this voice, something pure and unsullied that had her waiting for him to speak again.

'Get away with you!' Foggarty waved the shovel in a gesture of defiance and his friends closed ranks.

The stranger stood his ground. 'It's the foreman I'm wanting. I've no quarrel with you.'

'Well, we have with you. There's no jobs going here. You'd best get out while you can.'

The tall intruder shrugged. 'Well, now, is that the way to be greeting your fellow countryman?' He leaned back on his heels and stretched his long, straight back. 'If you must be knowing, the Company sent for me. I'm a Company man, you might say.' He gave a wry grin.

'How come they sent for you?' Daniel's voice was suspicious.

'It was them that brought me over to this godforsaken country – begging your pardon, ma'am.' He turned towards Meg and for the first time she saw the amazing green of his eyes. His face was long and hollow-cheeked, and there was a sardonic twist to his mouth. Immediately she felt on guard, as if her own experience of life had left her soft and naive and he knew it. To her shame she began to blush and this in turn made her angry, so she stepped forward.

'You'd best go away,' she said.

The stranger pulled a face that conveyed regret and not a little amusement. 'So even the womenfolk turn their backs on strangers here,' he observed.

'We don't. It's just that there's more than enough men here already, and we're not wanting trouble.'

The Irishman nodded his head as if acknowledging the sense of what she said. Before he could reply, however, Meg's father intervened.

'Just get away home, girl. Who do you think you are, interfering in our affairs? Just because you've had some schooling doesn't make you a man.'

'Indeed it does not.' The Irishman nodded appreciatively.

Meg lowered her eyes but made no move to leave. She knew that he was looking at her with that lazy, appraising look that men give to women they find attractive. Her face was hot and she struggled to take control of herself. 'I'll not be having you fighting,' she said, addressing her father but incorporating the stranger in the remark.

'Will ye not now?' It was he who spoke again and she flashed him an angry look.

'There's no sense in it.' Her expression conveyed her contempt for the idea.

'Then I'd agree with you. It's a peaceful visit I'm making.' He looked to Meg's father for some response but the older man's face was grim.

He tried again. 'I'm Brendan O'Neill, from Cork. I worked for three months at Doncaster before moving on here. And where would you be coming from?' The question was met with silence. Brendan O'Neill sighed in exasperation. 'Then damn you, old man. I'm not looking for trouble but I'm not a martyr either.'

Meg studied the stranger covertly. He looked travel-worn in his none too clean cord trousers and leather jerkin. He wore a green kerchief at his neck. She knew that his confident manner was infuriating her father. As she turned to look back at him, his mouth quivered between a cynical smile and raw anger.

'Right, move on.' There was finality in Daniel Foggarty's voice.

'I'm going nowhere until the foreman of this site has told me he doesn't need me.'

'Right. Then by tonight we'll have the cavalry out. They'll rout the lot of you, you and that crowd of vermin camped over yonder.' Daniel nodded towards the encampment that housed the band of itinerant labourers looking to find work anywhere they could.

Brendan O'Neill grimaced as if pained by the foolishness of men. 'Will they mow us all down in cold blood, I wonder? And what about the womenfolk? There are wives and children waiting over there.'

At the mention of the women, Meg felt a tightening around her heart. This man must have a woman: of course he would have. She had no control over the emotion that took possession of her, and she had never experienced it before, but she knew it to be jealousy. It was a moment she would never forget.

One of Daniel Foggarty's gang suddenly swung his spade at O'Neill. It caught him across the shoulders. He swore as he fell and immediately every man closed in on him.

'Stop! In the name of God, stop!' Meg's voice made little impact on the shouting mob.

Although outnumbered, the man was not giving up easily. With uncanny swiftness for one so handicapped by attackers, he suddenly grabbed Meg's father by the legs. He in turn came tumbling down and in a moment Brendan O'Neill had him in a stranglehold.

'No! Let him go!' The impact of Meg's fists made little impression.

'You, mistress, get back. You'll be hurt,' he warned, grunting with the effort of holding one man and fending off four others. Even as he spoke, one of the gang brought his pickaxe handle down with a swingeing blow flat across O'Neill's face. He gasped and a trickle of blood oozed down his hollow cheek. Still he held on to Daniel Foggarty in what looked like a wrestling hold. Meg could see that he was struggling not to lose control.

'Call your men away or I'll break your back.' He jerked hard against Daniel's shoulders to drive home his point. 'I'll not be back. Who in their right mind would choose to work with such narrow-thinking scum?'

'Get back!' There was resignation in Daniel's voice but the hard core of hatred could be seen in his cold blue eyes. As the navvies retreated, O'Neill let Daniel Foggarty drop to the ground with a snort of contempt.

Foggarty's men were stretching injured limbs and dabbing at custs and bruises. Some of them looked shamefaced and did not seem to know what to do next. Surveying their injuries, Meg could not believe that the visitor had done so much damage unaided and against such odds. She regarded him with renewed interest. Unnoticed by him, blood dripped from his face and onto the green kerchief. She had an intense desire to wipe his cheek clean.

'Make sure you and your whores are gone by sunrise,' her father shouted in an unconvincing attempt at authority.

Meg felt her cheeks flush with shame. How could he behave like this, making a fool of himself, treating this incautious man like a dog fox creeping in to steal the chickens?

'By sunup,' Daniel repeated, but Brendan O'Neill only grinned his contempt.

Belatedly Meg went to her father. 'Are you all right?' she asked.

'Of course I'm all right.' He shook her off.

She looked up to see O'Neill watching them. 'Your girl has more wisdom than the rest of you put together,' he said, then turned to walk away. Meg stood up too and moved away from the gang of men. She realised that she was following him and halted, her face hot with embarrassment.

Brendan O'Neill also stopped and now wiped the blood from his cheek. For a moment he stood as if contemplating the skyline, then turned towards her. 'I've seen an old ruin down by the lock. It looks a good place to shelter on a Sunday afternoon.'

For a moment she did not understand his meaning and then, when it dawned on her, her eyes grew large with indignation. She shook her head and he shrugged in response.

'Ah, well, I'll be there anyway.'

The next moment he was disappearing back across the boggy stretch of land in the direction from which he had come.

Meg wasn't sure if she had heard him correctly. She knew the ruin well enough but could he really think she would meet up with a stranger in such a lonely place? Or anywhere else? She shook her head again at the folly. Of course she wouldn't meet him. How dare he even suggest it?

Her father's gang had collected up their shovels and pickaxes and were making desultory pokes at the earth they were supposed to be piling up to extend the railway embankment. Meg retrieved the tea can. As she began to walk back towards the village, her heart was suddenly heavy. She might have some control over what she did but nothing could stop what she felt. With dismay she was forced to admit to herself how much she wanted to see him again — if only just once.

Chapter Two

'Have you heard about the Thorns?' Grandmother Foggarty's crochet hook paused momentarily in midstitch as she pulled a length of wool free from the large cream ball on her lap.

'No?' Meg got up from the stool to retrieve the ball of wool, which had rolled to the ground.

'Well, would you believe it, young Patience is – you know, in disgrace.'

The news was a shock. Meg and Patience had been friends a long while. Sometimes they had laughingly called themselves the Saint and the Sinner, Meg being the self-proclaimed sinner. She wondered how an upright girl like Patience could have been led astray.

Grandmother continued. 'There's been an awful to-do. She was, you know, ravaged by some of those scum at the camp.'

'You mean she was attacked by the navvies?'

Grandmother sniffed. 'Too true. At least, that's how the story goes. Young Patience hasn't named the rogues – it seems there were more than one of them. Can you believe it?' The old lady tutted at the wickedness of modern times.

At that moment the saucepan on the range boiled over. The air was filled with the smell of burning soup.

'Bejasus, look at the time! If he isn't late again!' Grandmother Foggarty crossed herself and looked out at the darkening sky. Meg followed her gaze.

'Shall I go and fetch him?'

'No. Well, you could just walk down there. If you see

anybody going in, ask them to remind Daniel Foggarty he's got a decent home to go to and a meal waiting. Don't you go in there!'

Meg shook her heard. This visit to the Railway Arms to extricate her father was a Saturday-night ritual.

The March evening was overcast and chilly. She reached for her shawl before setting off.

As she walked she wondered if things would have been different if her mother had lived. Meg was an only child and her arrival had caused the death of her mother. It was a heavy burden to carry.

She and her father had been mostly separated as Meg had been in her grandmother's care since babyhood. Daniel Foggarty had followed the railway engineers wherever they had led, preparing the tracks for the great iron engines to crisscross the countryside. It was only the extension of the Sutton le Grange line that finally brought Daniel into the bosom of his family, a restriction that lay heavily upon him.

Sutton had been greatly affected by the coming of the railway. The main line passed within sight and sound of the village street on its journey up the east coast. At one time it had been the cause of much controversy, but that was years ago. Now the village sported a station, red and vulgar, standing within a few yards of the Railway Arms, which in turn stood across the square from St Clement's Church, itself facing the Hinchington canal lock.

It had started to drizzle and the shiny, cobbled decline towards the village centre was slippery after some weeks of drought. The gas lamps from the Railway Arms had been lighted and set a yellow glow across the shimmering path.

Since childhood Meg had been instructed to stay well away from the inn, it being in her grandmother's opinion the resort of the Devil and all his ills. Since her father's return, however, Grandmother had had to swallow her distaste and allow Meg within spitting distance so that her father could be saved from the damnation he was bringing upon himself.

From habit she crossed the road just before the corner, skirting the iron railings that surrounded the cemetery.

Across the square she could hear the sounds of revelry from the public house.

Meg felt her resentment rising. Her father's behaviour of the day before still left her ashamed. It had been no way to treat a stranger. Embarrassed, she tried to push all thoughts of the Irishman away.

Outside the doorway of the inn, women were gathered in groups and she guessed that they were drinking gin. She didn't know for sure but something about their manner told her that it must be so.

''Tis a woman's ruin,' Grandma always said. Meg had never understood in what way but the knowledge was imprinted on her heart like an eleventh commandment: Thou shalt not take intoxicating liquor. Her father's arrival and his weakness in that direction was a burden she and Grandma had to bear, God's punishment on their house for some unexplained sin. Secretly Meg wondered if she were not the culprit and her wickedness lay in being born.

As she drew near to the entrance she recognised Michael O'Grady, one of her father's gang, talking to a woman by the doorway. When she could attract his attention she whispered her message, ashamed of the role that had been foisted upon her.

'Surely I'll tell him.' It was clear that Michael O'Grady had already been inside the inn, perhaps several times. Meg had no great hopes that he would remember her message but at least she had done her duty.

She turned back and skirted round by the hedgerow. As she started to make her way along the narrow lane that led across the bridge and back home, she was aware of footsteps behind her. She began to walk faster but the daylight had almost gone and the ground was muddy from the rain. The footsteps behind her also increased their pace. She tried to ignore them but there was something about their stealth and the measured tread that alarmed her. It took all her willpower not to run. Just as the lane joined the cart track leading up to a farm, two men came abreast of her. With sinking heart she realised that they too had been drinking.

'You're abroad late, young miss.'

She pushed on without replying.

11

'Been to visit your sweetheart, then?'

'I have not.'

It had been a mistake to speak. Immediately they came up, one on each side of her. The smell of gin and stale pipe tobacco made her wrinkle her nose in distaste.

'If you haven't got a sweetheart, why not stop a while, give us the time of day?'

Meg glanced quickly at the speaker and did not like what she saw. He was short but solid-looking and she could see his eyes glistening. He reminded her of a bull terrier. She remained silent.

'Here.' To her horror the terrier grabbed her arm. 'Slow down a bit. Come on, we only want a little kiss.'

'No!' She tried to shake him off but he was frighteningly strong.

'Come on, Jo.' He turned his head briefly towards his companion and the second man, taller, thinner and equally drunk, closed in on her. The terrier had his arms around her, lifting her off the ground while her legs were grabbed from under her.

'No!' She struggled but could not prevent them from flinging her to the damp earth. Immediately their bodies lay heavy on her as they scrabbled at her skirts. The outrage seemed to paralyse her. One man's mouth, foul and cloying, closed over her own. She turned her heard this way and that to avoid the smell of his breath. Thoughts of Patience Thorn and her terrible fate raced through her mind.

As the man who was kissing her released his hold a fraction, she bit him on the ear.

'You little piece of filth!' He struck her across the cheek and her eyes watered with the impact. God help me, she prayed, for she was powerless to stop them.

A moment later there were shouts and the assailants were being dragged away from her.

'Leave her, you bastards!'

She struggled up and dived for the cover of the bushes. Oaths echoed through the still night air and within seconds the two men were stumbling back along the track, cursing the man who now helped her to her feet.

'Are ye all right?'

Meg struggled up, brushing her skirts, and looked up into those green eyes. Brendan O'Neill.

'I'm not hurt.' She allowed him to take her arm because she was trembling.

'You're abroad late,' he observed. 'I saw you outside the pub. I saw them follow you.'

'Thank God that you did.' To her embarrassment she suddenly began to cry as shock and relief caught up with her. Brendan O'Neill untied the kerchief from around his throat and gently dabbed at her tears.

'There, there, you're safe now. A pretty girl like you shouldn't be about alone at night.'

'I got delayed,' she lied between the embarrassing sobs. 'I must get home. They'll be worrying that I'm late.'

'I'll walk with you.'

He too had the smell of gin on his breath but it was sweet, a strange, perfumed fragrance. Fearing that her attackers might not have gone far, she could not protest, and his masculine presence was infinitely reassuring. Meg did not let go of his arm.

They walked in silence. Finally she said: 'I'm sorry about yesterday. My father can't help himself. I fear he really is narrow-thinking.' In his defence she added: 'He's afraid he'll lose his work. It's the first time he's ever had a job near to home.'

She knew that the Irishman was looking at her. 'I hope you weren't hurt,' she added.

'Only a few bruises. And a deal of hurt pride.' He gave a little sardonic sniff.

There was silence again until the Foggartys' cottage came into view. 'Well, this is where I live.' Meg slowed down and halted before they could be seen, unwilling to let either of her relatives insult this man again as, for their different reasons, they surely would. 'I thank you for seeing me home.'

'The pleasure's mine.' They both stood for a moment, then Brendan added: 'I meant what I said yesterday, about the ruin. You know where I mean?'

She nodded but her look challenged him to say more. He ignored it.

'Good. You can think of it as by way of saying thank you.'

13

Meg glared at him, willing him to stop, but he added: 'You're in my debt, princess – and I do want to see you.'

It was impossible to read the message in his eyes. They were at the same time tender and taunting. His whole presence was so compelling that in spite of her grandmother's warnings it caused her to forget everything else. For a moment he moved his face closer and she thought that he was going to kiss her but at the last moment he bowed his head and smiled ruefully.

'I'll be there at two of the clock.'

She did not answer but as he drew back and waved his hand in farewell she gave herself up to the magic he had already woven around her heart.

Tomorrow, she thought. There must be a hundred good reasons to go abroad on a Sabbath afternoon. She knew that she would think of one of them.

Chapter Three

The ruin was little more than three tumbledown stone walls. It had been there for ever — one, maybe two centuries. In Meg's lifetime it had barely changed. She fancied that it seemed smaller only because she herself had grown tall.

In winter sheep huddled inside to find shelter from the biting wind off the North Sea. In summers past Meg had crouched amid the elder sprouting from the earth floor to hide from invading Vikings or packs of wolves in the noisy forms of her playmates. Now she waited with the same sense of anticipation, the half thrill, half fear that heralded the arrival of the unknown.

It was four weeks ago that Brendan had fought on the railway embankment. Twenty-eight sunrises had occurred since the fight and twenty-seven since Brendan had rescued her; twenty-six since she had first come to meet him here at the ruin; twenty-two since ... She could go on counting important events for almost every day since then.

Still the Irishmen and their families were camped in the no-man's-land that separated Over Drayton from her home village of Sutton le Grange. No attempt had been made to evict them. Some of them had turned their hands to labouring on the farms and as there was a seasonal shortage of men they were tolerated. Locally one or two more charitable families had taken them small offerings of tea and bread to help them out. Meg thought sadly that her own family had not been one of them.

There was the sound of cracking undergrowth and she craned forward into the ancient window crevice. The sight

15

of him caused her to pull back again, not wishing to be seen. She was overjoyed, yet as always the feeling was laced with anxiety.

'Meg?' Brendan's softly lyrical voice reached her at the same moment as his body obscured the late April sunlight shafting through the doorway. 'Are you there?'

She nodded as he ducked inside and turned towards her, holding out his arms. 'My lovely girl.'

She could not help herself. She was not even aware of moving but suddenly she was in his arms, pressed hard against his strong body. There was one perfect, magical moment, then he began to lift her skirts.

'No! This must stop.' The panic came from somewhere inside her, too late, illogical but taking control of her.

Brendan pulled back. 'Don't you like me any more?'

'Of course I do.' She could not explain.

He shrugged his disbelief. 'Then have you thought ...?'

Immediately all the conflicting loyalties were back. She looked away from him, gazing through the doorway to a faraway spot where trees, as diminutive as bracken, blended with the distant yellowing hills on the far side of the river.

'I can't,' she finally said. 'I'm all they've got.'

He said nothing but his mouth set in a tight line and his wonderful green eyes were suddenly hard at jet. She wanted to reach up and brush the tangle of black hair away from his brow but he was remote as the moon.

'I want to come,' she said weakly.

He turned his gaze on her, searching her face as if to read the truth. 'Do ye not trust me?'

'Of course I do.' She shook her head as she sought in vain for the right words. 'But I can't just go. If I do I'll leave them alone. They need me.'

'Not as much as I do.'

She wanted to add: 'And that's not as much as I need you', but instead she walked away from him and gazed out through the window recess, looking for something on which to concentrate and calm her crazy need.

Brendan brushed her explanations aside. 'There's no work here, you know that. They're recruiting for the railway further south. Besides, it's time I was away from here.'

16

There was a faraway look in his eyes. 'Come with me!'

He was suddenly urgent and Meg's heart ached. He pulled her close again and she wanted only to abandon herself to him but the cold, harsh reality intervened. Sensing her reluctance, he stood aside.

'I've got money. We could leave some for the old folks and once we're working you can send more.'

'Where did you get that?' She looked at the pile of silver and sovereigns he had drawn from his pocket and now held in his strong, brown hand.

He suddenly grinned, his mood shifting from dark to light. 'Let's just say a horse strayed and I found it a new owner.'

'You'll be hanged!' She could not believe his folly.

He shook his head, laughing her fears aside. 'Is that what you fear? Then never give it a thought, my darlin'. I have a charmed life. Have you not heard of the luck of the Irish?'

A cloud of hopelessness turned her world grey. He was an immigrant, a drifter, yes — and perhaps a thief. In every way he was an outsider. This was not the life that she had imagined for herself.

As if reading her thoughts, he asked: 'Is it a ring you're wanting?'

She shrugged. Even if Brendan did ask her to wed him her father would never give his consent. Not even if — she shut out the other fear.

'What of your family?' she asked to keep that line of thought at bay. After their first meeting, the awkward polite conversation and tense silences, a stronger, deeper need had swept them both along. Thereafter there had been little time for talking.

A terrible doubt still lurked that somewhere there might be a wife or sweetheart. She should have asked at the very first, but she hadn't. Now she knew that, whatever the answer, it would make no difference to how she felt or even to what she did.

He shrugged. 'I have no family. None that I know of. I was orphaned by the Famines.' He made it sound like a joke but she saw the anger behind the cold smile.

'And in this country? Is there no one with you?'

He raised his eyebrows in surprise but said only: 'No one. Here, there or anywhere. There's just me, my love, and I need you.'

She closed her arms about his neck and rested her head against his shoulder but he took her hands and pulled free. When he looked at her his emerald eyes were again diamond-hard. 'You've no idea, have you? Only a fool would bring a woman from the old country over here, beget children in this hostile country of yours.'

'It's not mine.' She did not know where she belonged.

'Well —' He shrugged her answer aside. 'My family weren't as lucky as yours. They starved to death back in Ireland. Yours will do well enough.'

When she did not respond he shrugged again. 'I have to go. If you don't want me hanged for a horse thief I'd better find honest work.' There was again a half-hearted attempt at humour but his face still had that angry set look that had her out of her depth. 'I'll not ask again.'

'Brendan!' She reached out but he stepped back, ducking out into the mellow light. Straightening up, he turned back to face her.

'Think well, darlin'. I'll be leaving on the morrow. I'll call here on my way but only you can decide. Come with me — or say goodbye.'

He stared at her for a long while and she wanted him to hold her again, make it all right. Instead he nodded briefly and walked away.

As Meg walked back, she experienced the aching void of loss which always marked her separation from Brendan O'Neill, only this time it was far worse because they had quarrelled and he was going away. She tried not to think of it but every step took her further away from everything she wanted, perhaps for ever. Clearly it was her duty to stay here with those who had raised her. Obviously she should serve the old and the poor. It would be wrong to abandon herself to life with Brendan, especially outside of marriage. Her deeply religious upbringing made her wonder how she could even consider such a thing and yet — as she came up

18

the path, her grandmother was whitening the doorstep with a pumice stone.

'I'll do that,' Meg said.

With a grunt the old lady struggled to her feet. 'It hurts my knees something rotten,' she replied.

Meg took off her shawl and took the bucket. 'It's a lovely day,' she observed, aware that her grandmother was watching her. She feared that her turmoil must show.

'You haven't heard the news, then?' Grandmother suddenly asked.

Meg shook her heard.

'That poor family.' The old woman seemed lost for words. 'It's the Thorn girl, young Patience. She's been found drowned in the river. They think she couldn't stand the shame.'

Meg's heart lurched and, in spite of the sunshine, she shivered.

'That's terrible.' She could hardly take it in. Dear, pure Patience! After a pause she asked: 'How soon after the . . . attack did she realise that she was going to have a child?' She feared that the tremor in her voice would give her away.

Grandmother shook her head. 'You can't be sure but once you've missed your bleeding it's like as not that you've caught.'

The pumice stone lay on the step beside her. Meg felt as if she were no longer there. A silent barrier had built up between her and the outside world. With sinking heart she heard the old lady say: 'God preserve us from that shame. If ever you did that your father 'ud kill you and that would be the end of us all.'

Chapter Four

Meg and her grandmother went back into the cottage. Meg knew that her future had been decided for her by Patience's fate. Grandmother's pronouncement still hung in the air like a sign. Meg had to join the man she loved: to stay might bring on her family the very shame that Grandma claimed her father would kill her for. Go she must.

Meg was not even sure if she was with child. Her monthly cycle was not something she had ever paid much attention to, but now she thought about it she seemed to remember that it was before the fight that she had last bled and therefore she was late by at least a week. There was no time to wait and find out. If Brendan was leaving on the morrow, then so must she.

Somehow she sat through tea. Her thoughts cut her off from the other two, who ate in their own separate silences. Meg looked from one to the other, balancing her duty to them and her feelings for them, against her feelings for Brendan and the likelihood of disgrace if she stayed.

The continued silence was alive with sound. The sawing of the knife across the round loaf, the rhythmic spreading of marge and jam, the trickle of tea into the cups and the sharp knock as the pot was set back on the china stand were as familiar as a well-loved tune. Her father's chewing, her grandmother's little cough – she would never hear that particular melody again. But she had already made up her mind. It was better to leave than to face a fate like that of Patience Thorn.

For the moment Meg dared not even begin to imagine

what it would be like to share her life with the man she loved. Just to think about it was to court disaster, as if her very thoughts might alert her chance of happiness and cause it to gallop away like a nervous horse.

As soon as tea was over, Meg made an excuse to go up to her room. Looking round the tiny whitewashed box where she slept, she felt her heart grow heavier at the thought that after that night she might never enter this sanctuary again. Every indentation on the rough stone walls was a familiar friend – the shape of a deer by the washstand where a crack had appeared, the impression of a lady above the window alcove which you could see only if you screwed up your eyes and looked in a certain way. She sighed and opened the battered portamnteau that old Lord Hinchington had once thrown out for the gardener to store tools in and Meg had taken home.

She packed the few things she could not do without: her Sunday dress, the spare petticoat and the thick stockings that Grandmother had made her last Christmas. She left her copy of the Bible on the windowsill. No amount of reading the Bible would put right what she was about to do.

At the last moment she allowed herself to take the brooch that had belonged to her mother. She gazed wistfully at it, a small gold bow with a single pearl at the centre of the knot. Had her father given it to her mother as a love token? It was not much of a legacy but it was all she had.

She would have to leave a note, some explanation to ease their worry, but whatever she wrote could only cause pain. She wondered again which was worse – to confess to running away for love or to admit to being a fallen woman and, like Patience Thorn, in disgrace.

Meg thought she heard a movement on the stair and hastily stuffed the case of clothing under the bedstead.

'Meg, are you there?'

'Coming, Grandma.'

Next morning Meg made her regular visit to Hinchington Manor to help in the house. It seemed important to do everything exactly as usual, change into the house shoes kept in the back porch, put on the large, rough hessian pinny and tie her hair beneath a white cap, then sweep and wash the entrance-hall floor and clean the glass panels with their blue and red diamond panes of glass before moving into the house itself to brush and polish, wash and dry.

As the stately grandfather chimed eleven o'clock she went through the familiar routine of fetching the beaker of cocoa that the cook dished out to her at the kitchen door. The kitchen was Cook's domain. Other girls cleaned and scrubbed there; Meg was not encouraged over the threshold.

As was her habit, she took the cocoa into the morning room where she had still to polish the brass fender and the matching companion set. First, though, she sat at the dining table and surreptitiously glanced through Sir Giles's weekly magazines. This was her adventure, her stolen glimpse into the wider world of England and the colonies that at other times would fill each moment of her working hours with fanciful dreams.

She was pleased to find that her favourite magazine was there, the *London Illustrated*. As she opened it, she wondered if this would be the last copy that she would ever see. The thought brought its own bitter-sweet anticipation.

Quickly she lost herself in finding out more about the gentlefolk and their activities: a soirée here, a ball at this great house, a betrothal between two persons of breeding. It was a different world.

With a sigh Meg turned the page and considered an engraving of a large house. It was not like any place that she had seen in real life. She began to read.

The article said that the square central tower of the house was reminiscent of those in Tuscany. The phrase stuck in her mind. She did not know what reminiscent meant and had no idea where Tuscany was but it did not matter. The building, with its jutting wings and ter-races, faced down to the sea and was the most beau-tiful place imaginable. It was known as Osborne and was on the Isle of Wight. It was the country home of the Queen.

Meg read that the monarch's late, lamented husband, Prince Albert, had designed Osborne himself and it was here that Queen Victoria had become increasingly a hermit,

22

hiding away with her shrinking family to the irritation of her ministers.

She closed the paper and thought about a fairy-tale palace on a magical island and a Queen pining away for love. It must be an enchanted place. Her reverie was interrupted by the sound of footsteps in the passage outside and quickly she got to her feet, grabbing the beeswax polish and her buffing pad. She applied herself energetically to the dining table and the footsteps faded into the distance.

As Meg worked, her mind turned from the imagined life of the royal family to the all too real shame of getting into trouble with a man.

My dear Father and Grandmother,
Forgive me but I fear I must leave you. Please do not worry for my safety for I will be in good company. As soon as I am settled I will write to you. I hope to be able to send you regular money to help you along. Do not try to find me.

Please forgive me but there is nothing else that I can do.

Your loving,
Meg

She wrote the note as soon as she got home. While Grandma was down in the orchard paying her respects to the bees, Meg collected her bundle and crept out of the cottage. She allowed herself to glance back once through the open door into the small kitchen. Her letter stared accusingly at her from in front of the jug on the rickety wooden table.

Before her resolve could desert her she drew herself up and turned away, taking long strides which soon turned into running steps. The thought that she might be spotted caused her to run ever faster, as if pursued, and it was not until she reached the shelter of the copse that she allowed herself to slow down. Determinedly she picked her way along the winding path, glancing back nervously now and then. Finally she came out on the other side of the woodland and hurried on down towards her trysting place.

Meg put the portmanteau down just inside the doorway

of the ruin and leaned back against the ancient doorjamb. Her mind was in a turmoil but she would not allow herself to consider any of the dilemmas that jostled for attention. After some minutes, though, one thought began to persist. Supposing she was too late. Supposing Brendan had already come and, not finding her there, had gone away, alone and disillusioned. She hastened back outside to scan the landscape. It was deserted.

She had not for one moment considered that she would go anywhere unless it was with him. Now the gravity of her situation hit her. If he had already gone, then she was truly alone. She could not even begin to contemplate what to do without him. For a moment she turned, wanting to run back home and retrieve the letter, smuggle her clothes back into the safety of her room as if nothing had happened. But already she knew that it would be too late. By now Grandmother would have found the note. Meg was rapidly sinking in the whirlpool of her own worry.

Again she scanned the horizon. At first she could see no one but suddenly there he was, emerging from the copse further down the hill. He carried a sack across his shoulder and was leading a sturdy black pony. The sight of him – his tall, slender body with its easy gait, his tangle of black hair – made her heart leap. She started to run. There was nowhere else she wanted to be, except with him.

At that moment he noticed her and half raised the hand that held the pony's rope. Meg stopped a few yards away embarrassed by the intensity of her joy and relief.

Brendan's face lit up, too. 'There is a God, after all,' he said by way of greeting. 'I prayed for you to come. It was my first prayer since I was a skinny lad back in Cork.'

Meg laughed with relief and pleasure, refusing at the moment to think of the pain that she had left behind for others.

'So you couldn't bear to live without me,' he teased, flinging his bag aside and hugging her to him.

She shook her head, still smiling, secretly wondering what he would say if he knew the real reason that had decided her to come. How could she make him understand the difference between wanting to be there because she loved him and

24

actually coming because her condition made it necessary? It was too complicated to put into words. Besides, she had no idea of how he would view a child.

Arm in arm they walked back up the hill to collect her bag from the ruin. As they went, he bent his head to kiss her hair and she snuggled against him. 'Where did you get the pony?' she asked.

Brendan grinned, clearly in too good a humour to let her questioning trouble him. 'I bought him fair and square from a trader. He's sound and strong. He'll carry you and the bags — and we have a long way to go.'

'Where are we going?'

'To the south coast, near Southampton. They're extending the tracks around there.' He gave a sigh. 'I miss the sea. I can't wait to see it again.'

'Describe it to me.'

There was a silence before he said: 'It's — wet!' With a laugh he kissed her again. 'Come, my darling. I'll show you the sea and a million other things you've never seen before.' He swept her into the air and placed her across the broad back of the black pony. 'Allow me to introduce you. This is my friend Eros. He's the god of love disguised as a horse. He's going to carry you to Paradise and we'll live there together, for ever and ever — just you and me.'

Chapter Five

Meg and Brendan avoided the villages and by nightfall were camped some twenty miles from their starting place. It had been a long haul over rough ground but although Meg was stiff and tired the prospect of a night with her lover cast out all the discomforts.

Brendan chose their resting spot carefully. It was a natural hollow with overhanging branches and a windbreak formed by an ancient thorn hedge. Within minutes he had a shallow indentation in the ground cleared of debris and was piling up dried grass and sticks in a pyramid to start a fire. Meanwhile Meg wandered down to the nearby stream and collected water in a tin can for boiling to make tea. She still half believed that she was dreaming and would soon wake up back at the cottage.

By the time she returned with the heavy can, Brendan was plucking the rich grey feathers from a pigeon.

'Where did you get that?'

He glanced up at her and grinned. 'Never seen one of these?' He pulled a sling from his belt and mimed the action of firing at the nearby branches. 'It's fresh pigeon for you tonight, my love.'

She felt a moment of compassion for the bird, so recently dispatched from this life, and hoped it had not left a mate to mourn. She shivered.

The bird was soon spiked and turning over the gently flickering flames of their campfire. Gobs of fat dripped onto the hot ashes, causing little hissing explosions. Meg sat mesmerised, almost holding her breath to capture the magic of this evening.

'There you are.' Finally the bird was cooked and they picked the carcass apart, nibbling and gnawing at the hot, tender fleh.

'It's delicious! The best I've ever tasted.'

Brendan threw the bones onto the fire, wiped his hand across his mouth and rubbed his strong fingers clean on the cool grass.

'I'll give you something better . . . ' He knelt up and started to kiss her, pushing her gently back into the soft mantle of moss and leaf mould beneath the gnarled oaks. His mouth was sweet and she felt as if some other being had taken control of her, a being without reason, with only the power to feel and accept pleasure.

Brendan's strong hands moved over her body, resting here, caressing there, easing her skirts up, slipping her bodice down until he could bury his face between her breasts. He murmured: 'Tonight we have all the time we could want.' She held her breast to him as if he were her child and when he had taken his pleasure he lay over her, entering her at first gently, then with strong thrusts until she cried out aloud with the excitement of it. Finally he cried too, letting go in gasping jets of anguished release. They kissed over and again until even as their lips still touched they were lost in sleep.

Well into the night the rising insistence of his groin stirred her awake. Still warm from sleep she twisted herself to allow him easy access. The union of their bodies brought a peace she would never have thought possible. 'I love you,' she whispered as he once again unleashed the precious secret fluid into her, but he was already asleep. She snuggled her head against his shoulder and drifted away, knowing that never in the history of mankind had two people loved each other as she and Brendan did.

In total they covered about two hundred miles and it took them exactly two weeks. Each night they slept in the open and the weather was kind to them, keeping them dry and sheltered. There was never more than the merest breeze to

27

touch their tired, love-sated bodies.

They ate well. Brendan had little difficulty in catching birds and an occasional fish, although they stayed nowhere long enough to seek out rabbit runs. He would also disappear into the countryside and return with other prizes, young nettles and scallions. It was the perfect voyage of discovery.

During this time Meg did not bleed and as the days passed she became increasingly aware of feeling unwell. At first she put it down to the rigors of the journey and the constant change of diet, but her breasts began to feel tender and it was only in the mornings, when she first rose from whatever couch had sheltered them, that she felt the nausea. I'm pregnant, she thought. I'm going to have a child. His child. The prospect thrilled and terrified her. She did not tell him.

The arrival at the excavation took her by surprise. After the isolation of their journey it was a shock to be suddenly surrounded by people. Dimly Meg remembered the times when as a child she, with her father and grandmother, had reached some new encampment and sought out the most promising resting place with new neighbours to sum up. Now she felt very much an outsider. She was no longer truly a traveller, no longer truly Irish, no longer a virgin, not yet a wife, soon to be a mother. She pushed the thoughts aside and followed Brendan into the encampment.

He spoke briefly to a couple of men, asking for directions, then sought out the site boss. Meg stood too far away to hear what was being said but noted with pleasure how Brendan stood straight and tall. He would never bow to any superior authority. He is a proud man, she thought, and was suddenly in her turn ridiculously proud of him. With a smile she watched as he came back to where she stood holding the pony by the rope, their belongings piled around her ankles.

'Tis all settled. We can choose a hut over there.'

She followed his gaze to a small jumble of temporary wooden buildings which appeared to jostle each other for space. It was not an inviting sight but she despised herself for expecting it to be any different. This wasn't Sutton le

Grange, and they were lucky to have something already erected. In times past with Father they had had to build their own shelter.

Putting a brave face on her disappointment, she hoisted her portmanteau up and allowed Brendan to take the horse. He escorted her to the line of tenements and after a cursory glance nodded to one of them. 'We'll take that one.'

She ducked through the low doorway into the single room. It was dark inside and smelly from recent occupation. She wrinkled her nose and let her bag drop at her side.

'I'll not be long.' Brendan placed his own sack on the ground and stepped back outside. She wanted to call to him to stay but already he was striding down the road, leading the pony.

With a sigh she looked around her, and started to scrape up some of the rubbish that still littered her new home. She took it outside and stored it on the already sprawling pile at the end of the alleyway between her own row of huts and the parallel line in front. The place still smelled but there was no other means of cleaning it. At the other end of the row of huts there was a tap and she went along to wash her hands before drinking briefly of the chalky water.

From the neighbouring hut a woman poked her head out. She was dark, skinny and weasel-like with greasy black hair and a harsh, thin-lipped mouth. She did not speak but ducked back inside again, which left Meg feeling isolated.

Just when she was beginning to fear that Brendan had gone for ever, she saw him coming back across the debris-littered encampment. He was loaded down with goods, not least a wide horsehair mattress precariously balanced across his shoulder and a deep eiderdown cover held down by his chin. A collection of pots and brushes and a dead chicken dangled on various strings from his waist and shoulders.

'Wherever did you get all that?' Her joy at the sight of him was the sweeter after the fear that he might have abandoned her.

'I've got rid of Eros. We've no need for him and we can't afford to feed him. Instead he's feeding us.'

Meg's heart lurched. Eros, their god of love in disguise, had been sacrificed. It felt like an omen.

29

Clearly unaware of her foolish notion, Brendan was chiv-vying her to sweep the floor with the new broom he had provided while he went back for the rest of his purchases. It took him three journeys and by the time he had finished the little room was filled with such luxuries as a table and two chairs, a rug, a chest and an oil lamp. Fresh vegetables and flour, fat, sugar, milk, eggs and honey were stored inside the little chest to keep them out of the reach of pests. He also deposited a bottle of gin on the chest. 'To clean my throat,' he said as if to ward off any argument.

'Did you get enough from the horse to get all this?' she asked as they gorged themselves on chicken stew.

For a moment he did not answer. When he finally looked at her she saw the quick blink that she already recognised as signifying that there was something unpalatable he wasn't telling her.

'The Company have their own shop,' he started. 'They use their own coinage. You pay for what you have from your wages.'

'But what about the money from the horse?'

Brendan shook his head. 'I told you we couldn't afford to keep him.'

'Yes, but how much did you get for him?'

Brendan shrugged. 'Let's just say he paid a debt for me.'

'What kind of debt?' For a moment she was lost, then a cold tendril of realisation touched her. 'You gambled him away?'

He looked away, raising his eyebrows in a gesture of resignation. 'You win some, you lose some. Nothing to worry about, my beautiful girl. I'll earn enough to pay our bill. Just trust me. You should know by now that I'm always lucky.'

Chapter Six

That night they slept with their backs to each other. Meg still nursed her fury that Brendan had gambled the horse away. It was a double betrayal because Eros, the god of love disguised as a horse, symbolised the essence of their lives together. Not only had he wasted their money but this casual disposal of the horse seemed like a belittling of their union. She had shouted and Brendan shouted back. He drank alarming quantities of gin.

It was terrible to lie for the first time in a real bed and not to touch. His back was stiff and forbidding. She tossed this way and that, trying not to touch him with her knee or arm, yet drawn to the warmth of his body. Finally, in sleep they rolled together and when she awoke his arm was flung across her. She felt a curious mixture of relief and affront but lay there very still so as not to change anything.

Work started at six o'clock. It was barely light and outside she could hear the first risers drawing water and lighting fires. With a sudden jerk Brendan was up and out of bed. He gave a low grunt and moved his head very slowly from side to side as if to relieve the aftereffects of the gin.

Meg got up too but the moment she was on her feet the sickening waves of nausea overcame her. She started to heave and there was nowhere to run. With a groan she fell back onto the bed, everything about her spinning.

'What's wrong?' His voice was sharp, almost impatient, and she fought down the sickness.

'Nothing.'

'You're expecting.' His voice was flat, betraying nothing,

31

but she knew that he was angry. She didn't know how to reply.

In silence he pulled his boots on and made for the door. She noticed with shock that he grabbed the gin bottle and, as he stepped out into the indecently cheerful daylight, took a swig from it.

She wanted to get up but couldn't. If she did she knew that she would be sick, perhaps faint. Instead she lay still for about another quarter of an hour and Brendan did not come back. She could only assume that he had gone to work.

Finally she forced herself into a sitting position and carefully got to her feet. She still felt giddy but gradually the feeling passed and she was able to dress.

When she stepped outside it was to see her weasel-like neighbour chopping wood outside her door.

Meg went to say good morning but thought it would sound foolish so she remained silent. Just as she turned to go back indoors, the weasel woman said: 'You his wife or his woman?'

Meg flushed. 'His woman,' she said. She wanted to add some explanation but weasel woman sniffed and shrugged, her curiosity clearly satisfied.

Again, as Meg turned away, the other woman spoke. 'My man's been here for six weeks. There's work enough for a few more weeks. Where were you before?'

Meg thought quickly, then named the cross-country line that so nearly dissected Sutton. She was too preoccupied with her own troubles to catch what the other woman replied until she became aware that weasel face was staring at her.

'Kathleen Delaney,' she said, clearly repeating her name.

'Oh! Megan F— O'Neill.'

Kathleen Delaney nodded but did not smile as her eyes met Meg's. 'Well, Megan O'Neill, let's be hoping 'tis a peaceful stint. Bad luck has dogged my man ever since Liverpool.'

Again a shadow of unease clouded Meg's already troubled day. 'I'm sure we'll be all right,' she said with an optimism she did not feel.

For much of the day she moped around, then, suddenly pulling herself together, she set to to make a nourishing meal for when her man came home. Her man — the words

32

sounded unreal. Was he her man? Now he knew about her condition he might not stay. He had promised her nothing but the pleasure of his loving. It was a high price to pay.

She heard the distant shuffle of boots across the rough ground and peered out to see the workers in their droves making for the settlement. Her heart began to thump against the dread that he would not return. Her hands trembled as she poked the remains of the chicken and stirred round the newly added carrots, potatoes and fresh parsley. She had never been so vulnerable before.

He was not among the first to arrive. Shadows of dusty, work-worn men passed her doorway in an irregular pattern, at first intermittent, then almost constant and then again in decreasing frequency. Finally, when only a few stragglers remained, the doorway was suddenly filled by his tall, muscular body.

She wanted to run to him but forced herself to wait. In turn he was silent, staring in at her.

'Well, are ye not pleased to be seeing me?'

She looked up and the sight of his quizzical, handsome face had her up and reaching out to be taken into his arms.

'I'm sorry,' she repeated, 'I'm truly sorry.'

'For what?' He kissed her hair before she could reply.

'For being angry – and the baby.'

In response he hugged her closer. ''Tis no matter. Really no matter.'

For a while she was content just to lean against him but inside a voice insisted that indeed it was a matter of great importance.

Finally he pulled back from her and stretched. ''Tis hard work when you've not been used to it,' he observed. 'Our journey's made me soft.'

She smiled and moved towards the cooking pot but he called her back.

'Here, I've something for you. A little "I'm sorry".' He held out his clenched hand and deposited something into her palm, closing her fingers over it. Slowly she opened it to see what she held and revealed a small gold clip. It reminded her of the brooch that had belonged to her mother.

'You don't like it?' he asked.

'Oh, I do. It's lovely.' She did not voice the questions that immediately came to mind — where did he get it and how much did it cost? Instead she kissed him and in response he pulled her roughly to him, raising her skirts to press himself against her.

'Brendan! Not now, it's — ' He silenced her with his mouth and walked with her held tightly against him across to the bed. She lay motionless as he raised her skirts, then with his mouth began to explore her body. Part of her wanted to call out, to insist that this was wrong, but the insistent warm moisture of his tongue roused her into a paroxysm of pleasure. She could only go with the tidal wave of sensation until suddenly she was washed up onto the bank of her own release. He then entered her and took his own pleasure.

'Meg, you foolish girl!' He rolled over onto his back, taking her with him. 'Don't you be worrying about the baby. I'll not desert you.'

She was on a raised plane of feeling that she had never before imagined could exist.

Just as she snuggled her head against his shoulder he added: 'But don't you ever be telling me how to run my life.'

Her breathing stopped and she opened her eyes. For no good reason she thought: Pearls are for tears.

On the little chest her new clasp lay, its cluster of pearls luminescent at the centre of the swirl of gold. In her portmanteau her mother's brooch lay with its pink pearl knot. Had her father given it to her mother on a day such as this? Was her mother then already pregnant? Whatever hopes they might have shared had soon been dashed when she died in childbed.

Meg sat up quickly and pulled her skirts down to her ankles. Aloud she said: 'Do you think that history repeats itself?'

Brendan gave a sleepy grunt, Then, just when she thought he was not going to answer, he said: 'All the time, darling. All the time.'

Chapter Seven

At the end of the month they could not pay their bill at the railway company store. Since their arrival, Brendan had spent thirteen pounds seven shillings in the site shop on household goods, gin and tobacco. His wages for the same period came to six pounds fifteen.

Meg did not realise the gravity of the situation until she went to the shop for some bread. Patiently she waited until she was at the head of the queue and then gave their works number to the storeman.

The man consulted the large ledger that rested on the counter and asked her to repeat the information.

Finally he scratched his head with his pencil and looked up at her. 'I'm sorry, missus, you're not due any more credit.'

She stared at him in surprise. 'But we've just been paid,' she said. It was Saturday and Brendan was even now at the Horse and Coaches with the rest of his gang, easing his throat after the dusty week.

'Well, every week you're getting further behind.'

'By how much?'

He told her the extent of their debt. The man looked not unkind but Meg knew that it would be futile to argue. Stepping back outside into the summer afternoon she began to walk with no direction in mind, anything to get her away and help clear her thoughts.

Of course she would tackle him when she got home but he would either laugh it off as of no importance or resent her interference. Either way he would be drunk and she feared that it would resolve nothing. There seemed to be only one solution. She would have to get work.

As she sank onto the grassy bank where the footpath was obscured by a clump of bushes, Meg suddenly had a clear vision of her grandmother and heard the old lady's words, often repeated when some village crisis had arisen. 'I always vowed I'd do anything to support my family, but not labour on the railways. No man worth his salt would let his woman do that.' Meg closed her eyes.

Sooner or later they would get things sorted out, she was sure of it. If Brendan hadn't been so quick to shower her with all those goods at the beginning it would have been all right. She knew that it had been an act of love on his part, an unwillingness to let her be deprived in any way. It might have been foolhardy but she loved him for it. Dragging herself to her feet, she changed direction and headed for the site.

The foreman was still there even though work had officially finished until Monday morning. Tentatively she approached him to ask about a job. He was an older man, solid and reliable-looking, the sort of man who could be trusted with overseeing his fellow men. Now he looked her up and down and she knew that he recognised her condition although it was too early to show.

'It's hard work,' he observed.

'I know.' She refused to look away from him.

'You'll get fourteen and six a week. And some boots.'

'I'll take it.' With sinking heart she realised that even if all her money went to the shop it would take weeks just to pay off their existing debt — and during that time they still had to live. She would have to talk to him about it.

'You're not working!' Brendan's words were emphatic. The smell of gin on his breath filled the tiny room and his eyes looked bloodshot and unfocused.

'What else are we to do? We have to eat.' She wanted to shake him.

'Are you saying I can't provide for you? Is that what you mean?' His words were slurred and he stood blinking foolishly. Every now and then he swayed slightly and had to adjust his stance to avoid falling.

36

'No.' His state made her angry but she was powerless to make any impression on him. She took a deep breath to speak, then changed her mind. Argument was pointless.

Taking her silence as defeat, he slumped down into one of the chairs. 'Right then. Say no more about. Just leave it to me. I'll sort it out.'

'How?' It would have been easier to say nothing, let him handle it in his own way when he was sober, but she feared that worse might follow.

He turned round, suddenly affronted, cut off from her. Finally he said: 'Don't push me, girl. I'll see to things as I see fit. By Monday you can go back to the shop and it'll all be sorted out. You'll see.'

'How?' She had to insist. Besides, what were they to eat until then?

'I said don't push me! You need to learn you place.' He got up clumsily from the chair, suddenly belligerent. 'I. Know. What. I'm. Doing.' Each word was punctuated by an unsteady shaking of his finger. Suddenly losing his train of thought, he pushed her aside and sank back again into the chair. Meg's anger boiled over.

'Don't you do that to me again!' She hit him with both her fists, pummelling his shoulders in her rage. It did not occur to her that he might react violently and he didn't. He merely grunted as if some insect were irritating him and with a sudden snort hauled himself from the chair and out into the lane. As he went he shouted: 'I'll not be back till I can get some peace! Women!' He walked a few yards and turned again suddenly, hurling abuse at her. Her heart beat so fast that she had to lean against the wall for support.

It was going disastrously wrong. She didn't know what to do. For the moment she could only try to shut it from her mind and carry on normally, whatever that was.

A few moments later there was a tap on the open door. Reluctantly she turned round to see Kathleen Delaney, her neighbour, standing outside. Swallowing back her distress, Meg raised her eyebrows, defying the woman to come any further.

'I couldn't help but overhear.' Uninvited, Mistress Delaney stepped inside, wiping her raw hands on her coarse grey

37

apron. 'Don't let it upset you, child. He's not the only one to be in trouble.'

Meg opened her mouth to deny it. She did not wish to discuss her troubles with this vixenish woman but found herself saying: 'I've never been in debt. My grandmother was that particular ...'

Kathleen Delaney nodded. 'It's all a question of what you're used to. Forgive me for saying it but your man is a wild one, he'll never let a penny rest in his pocket. It's in his blood.'

'Well, in that case the pennies had better rest in my purse. I'll just have to take charge.'

The older woman smiled ruefully. 'I wish you luck, girl. He isn't the sort of man to let you hold the purse strings — or wear the trousers.' She hesitated. 'You wouldn't be wanting my advice, but for what it's worth, I'd think about getting out now, while the going's good — that is, if it's not too late.' She looked pointedly at Meg's belly.

Meg glared at her, aware of her burning cheeks. 'You're right,' she said coldly. 'I wouldn't be wanting your advice. There's no question of me leaving him, ever.'

Kathleen shook her head. 'Well, that's it then, but if ever you're needing my help, you know where I am.'

Meg was so indignant that she did not deign to reply. Alone again, she sat at the table in the gathering gloom and wondered what to do.

He came back after dark, sheepishly creeping in and flinging his jerkin across the table. It took him a long time to unlace his boots and she watched his broad back stretch and bend. In spite of her anger she was intoxicated by the shape of him. Finally he dropped both boots into the corner and turned to her.

'Come here.'

She shook her head.

He shrugged and looked longingly at the beer jug on the chest but did not pick it up. Instead he said: 'I told you I'd sort it out. I've got enough to pay off that piddling debt and more.'

'Where from?'

'A business deal.'

'And what sort of business would that be?' Her heart sank at the thought of another questionable transaction.

'Nothing that concerns you.'

'Brendan, it does concern me.' She sighed, not knowing how to make him understand. 'If you're doing things in my name it matters what it is.'

'Nothing I do is in your name, darling. We're not wed. You're free to disown me if you want.'

She knew that they were in danger of quarrelling again so she tried a different tack. 'Why don't I earn a bit for a few weeks? Just till the baby shows. Then we can pay off our debts, save for something we both want.'

Sitting with his back to her, he did not appear to hear. Finally he said: 'I'm not a good one for settling down. Having a baby to think of is something I hadn't bargained for.'

Meg's chest constricted. He's telling me to go, she thought. He doesn't want us. The price is too high. Aloud she said: 'Does that mean you'd rather be on your own?'

After an eternity he turned round and his green eyes were troubled. He reached out and pulled her close. His head came to rest against her breast. In spite of herself her arms closed about him and her lips touched the crown of his black head. Her body was soothed by his closeness. It was a precious moment of peace.

Into the silence he suddenly said: 'I'm thinking we should marry.'

She felt the relief flood through her. Until this moment she hadn't realised how insecure she felt. Now he was telling her that he meant to stay, for ever. Aloud she said: 'When?'

His head moved gently, snuggling into the softness of her breast. When he sat up, his eyes were frank and unwavering, but she could not see past them into his soul.

With a shrug he said: 'When we're settled. When we know where we're going. There's no hurry, darling. Somewhen.'

Chapter Eight

Meg began work on the Monday. The new line had been laid across a meadow, through a cutting, and now they were approaching the chalky southern hills that stood between one section of track and the other. The only way forwards was to tunnel.

A narrow track had been laid to accommodate small trucks into which the rubble was loaded. The waste was then transported back to the main line where it was transferred to another train for onward shipment further down the line where an embankment was to be erected. No engine was available to pull the trucks so they relied on manpower.

Along with other women, Meg cleared the rubble and carried it in buckets from the site to the train. All day she made the same journey; bending, picking up boulders and stones, filling her bucket and lugging it to the trucks.

At the end of the day she did not know which part of her body hurt the most. Her arms felt stretched from their sockets and her back gave out a low, persistent ache. Every movement caused her to wince, and no amount of stretching seemed to relieve the protesting muscles. Her legs were stiff and she had blisters on her feet.

'You shouldn't be doing it.' Brendan lifted her up and laid her on the bed. Bending down he kissed her feet, tenderly tracing the angry red weals with his lips. 'Just rest now and I'll see to everything.'

Her heart overflowed with tenderness for him. Her father would never have deigned to light the fire or cook food. She was too tired to move but savoured the sight of him as he prepared the meal. When sober he had a grace of movement that stopped her heart.

She glanced at the chest and saw with relief that there was no gin. Perhaps he was economising. If they were careful they could pay off their debts and then she could send a bit home.

She suddenly felt tearful at the thought of how she must have hurt her grandmother. As soon as she did not feel so devastatingly tired, she would write home, assure them that all was well. With the money Brendan had got the other evening he had given the storeman enough to reinstate their credit. Now she could buy a stamp at least.

She rolled onto her side and with a sigh of pleasure thought: When we're wed I can tell them about the baby.

She must have slept because the next thing she knew he was waking her, holding out a bowl of pea soup. 'Eat up now. You've got to keep up your strength.' He rested his hand on her belly and she thought: He'll make a wonderful father.

After he had eaten Brendan got up and stood by the doorway, gazing out into the night. He was still for a long time but she could sense that he was restless. Finally he said: 'I have to go out.'

'Where to?' She tried to fight down the disappointment.

'Just some business.'

Something about the tone of his voice defied her to ask. He came across and kissed her but in doing so he held her arms so that she could not reach up and pull him close. It was as if he was afraid of being trapped in her embrace. All the fears were back.

Don't be long, she thought. Don't be late. Be careful. Don't do anything stupid. Instead she said nothing. Even as he went out she wanted him to offer some explanation, some promise to return soon, but he slipped away as if escaping into freedom. To her shame she started to cry.

The feel of his hands parting her legs and pulling her over onto her back awoke her. For a moment she didn't know where she was but of its own volition her body responded to his touch. Meg turned and closed her arms about him. He lay heavily on her and the air was thick with the scent

41

of gin. She could taste it on his tongue. Now she was wide awake, suddenly tense, unresponsive to his lovemaking. She lay still and made no effort to move with him, even wishing that he would stop, get off her, go away. After a while he did pause and she realised that he was so drunk he was fuddled. He slid from her and grunted as he turned away. Soon he was snoring.

Meg eased herself out of the bed and tiptoed across to pick up his breeches, dropped where he had stepped out of them at the side of the bed. Guiltily she slid her hand into his pockets. Among the jumble of string and dirt particles, farthings and strands of tobacco, she found a tightly folded knob of paper. Carefully she spread it out, going to the window to see what it was by the light of the moon. She studied the ornate black printing and realised that for the first time in her life she was staring at a five-pound note.

'I found it! Holy Jesus, woman, are you saying I stole it?'

Meg stood facing him, not knowing what to think, what to do. He looked dishevelled and bleary-eyed.

'Well, someone must be looking for it. We should take it to the police.'

He snorted in disbelief. 'Do you know what you're saying? That'll pay off our debts. You can have a perambulator for the babe, a proper crib, dress him in lace nightgowns.'

'I don't want any of that. I ... I just don't want any trouble.'

He shook his head as if not understanding her. 'Are you thinking I'm a common thief?' he asked. 'Is that what's bothering you?'

It was her turn to shake her head. He took her action as meaning she believed him.

'Well then, finding's keeping. Anyone with that sort of money doesn't have to worry about losing it. Come on, sweetheart. I'm going to buy you a gown.'

'I don't want one!'

'Not even to be wed in?'

She looked at him and sighed. 'I don't know. I don't know anything.'

'Well, I do. You're not going back to work.'

'But I must.' In spite of the fatigue she could not possibly fail to turn up. It went against everything she believed to be right.

'You'll do as I say.' His voice was final but she fought back.

'I will not! You can't just let people down.' She thought of the other women on the gang. If she did not go they'd have an extra burden of work.

'Meggy, it's the railway company. They don't give a damn about you. You just do as I say now. If you don't ...'

'If I don't, what?' She straightened up to confront him and in the disconcerting way he had he suddenly grinned.

'Then I'll tie you to the bed. Then I'll be forced to ...' He came towards her, hunting, stalking, and she could not help but laugh herself, pushing him away with entreaties to behave. He swept her up into his arms and kissed her long and hard until there was nothing but the magic of him.

Gently he set her down on her feet, 'I love you, so I do.' His eyes were serious now. 'There's been no one in my life like you. Forgive me if I'm a fool. I don't know any better.'

Gently she reached up to hold his face between her hands. She touched his mouth with her own, reverently, an almost religious blessing.

'Please be careful,' she entreated but any doubts were swept away by the wonder of his love.

She spent the morning quietly, her fears soothed by the medicine of his lovemaking. As she kneaded dough to make dumplings, she thought how unworthy she was to be his wife. At times she doubted him, and no good wife would do that.

The dumplings were arranged in white floury balls on the board. She took the lid off the pan and started to drop them in. A sudden disturbance by the doorway made her swing round to see Kathleen Delaney pushing her way in, uninvited again, but her expression halted Meg's annoyance.

'Listen, child. There's a constable on his way. You've still got time, so for goodness sake get out of here while you can.'

43

Meg stared at her in amazement. 'I don't know what you mean,' she started.

'They're after your man.'

'But why?'

'Something's gone missing, I guess — don't ask questions. Just get on your way!'

'I can't.' Meg felt faint with shock.

At that moment Kathleen Delaney was knocked aside and Brendan pushed his way into the hut.

'Quick! We're leaving. Come along, there's no time.' He began to shove things into her portmanteau, looking this way and that as he selected the most valuable.

'What's going on?' she asked.

By way of answer he pushed her towards the chest. 'Take anything worth having. Hurry, woman!'

His urgency rubbed off onto her and she started to push small, light objects into the bag. 'Where are we going?' she asked but he grabbed the bag from her and fastened it, flinging it across his shoulder and dragging her after him.

'God protect you,' Kathleen Delaney called after them, but Meg could not even turn to say goodbye.

'Hurry!' Brendan dragged her by the arm, cursing her for being so slow.

He did not stop until they had put two fields and a wood between themselves and the encampment, by which time Meg was too breathless to say anything. Brendan sank onto a stile and panted, taking in great gulps of air. Meg stood in front of him gazing at him with disbelief.

'You did steal the money.'

He looked up at her speculatively as if analysing her character. His shrug left her feeling that he found her wanting.

'I did not.' There was no strong denial, no raised voice. He sounded tired and disillusioned. Meg was at a loss. Twice he opened his mouth as if to speak, then thought better of it. Finally he said: 'I won it, fair and square. In fact, I won a lot more than that. From the hardware merchant. If I had come straight home I'd have had twenty guineas in my hand. As it was, I went on playing. By that time the shopkeeper had gone. I guess he wanted his money back and that was

44

the only way he figured he could get it — by accusing me of stealing it.'

Meg wanted to believe him. Part of her could only feel aghast that he had held twenty guineas in his hand only to throw it away. Another part of her was appalled that he should gamble at all. She did not understand him. Just as she was going to say so, he added: 'I did it for you. I'd rather die than see you slaving like you did yesterday. I didn't bring you away to reduce you to that.'

'I wouldn't need to if you didn't drink or gamble.' She knew it sounded harsh but she could not help herself.

He looked up at her and she could not interpret his expression. Then he shook his head as if defeated by her lack of understanding.

'Gambling is what makes hope possible. Gin is what makes dreams happen. I can't be any other way.' After a pause he said: 'We were leaving here anyway. I've heard of another job across the water.'

'Back in Ireland?' The idea of leaving the country had never occurred to her.

'No. Across the Solent, there on the Isle of Wight.'

She turned her head in the direction he was staring as if by looking hard enough she might see through hills, across the countryside, over the sea and beyond.

She remembered the piece in Sir Giles's paper, the grand house with the tower, the home of the Queen.

'But have you ever been there? We don't know what it's like.'

Brendan shrugged. 'It's no matter. It'll be a new start.'

'No! We can't just run away every time something goes wrong. It won't solve anything.' She added: 'I know about the Isle of Wight. The Queen lives there. What makes you think there's any work?' Secretly she doubted if such a grand place would have room for ordinary people like themselves.

At her question his face brightened and he turned towards her, suddenly animated, talking eagerly.

'It's the damnedest thing. A group of businessmen have this scheme to build a tunnel. You've no idea how many people go there now. It's becoming the most fashionable resort. The troops are based there and strategically it's important too.'

45

Meg knew that the words weren't his own but said nothing.

'Well, these businessmen have been asking interested parties to put up the money. They're going to tunnel through to a place called Ventnor. I don't know any of the details but there's a gang of men there already.' He hoisted the portmanteau onto his other shoulder and his eyes looked clear and determined. 'Mind you, not everyone's in favour of it. There's local opposition. But you can't halt progress, can you? It's a wonderful thing.'

Meg didn't know whether it was wonderful or not. 'Are you sure there's a job for you?' she asked again.

'Of course I am. I've got the name of a man. He'll put me in touch with the ganger and then we'll be away.'

She felt suddenly despondent. Everything about this had the feel of a harebrained scheme and here they were leaving all that was familiar. She wondered stupidly if they used money on the island, or even spoke English. She really knew nothing about it.

Brendan seemed closed off in a dream of his own. She took a deep breath and shook his shoulder.

'We can't go there,' she repeated. 'It's a royal estate. They won't let us in.'

Now he looked up. 'Oh yes, they will. Trust me, Meg. There's never been a time when I haven't been one jump ahead. Anyway, I truly mean to make a new start.'

Meg looked at him in dismay. She remembered her early life with her father, constantly moving on, never knowing anybody, never belonging. She shook her head but he did not notice. Aloud she said: 'I don't want to keep running from place to place. It has to stop. I just want somewhere to settle, somewhere we can bring our child up in peace.'

Brendan looked suddenly chastened. He stopped and turned to face her. 'I give you my word that once we're on that island I won't ever leave again.'

Meg wanted to believe him but doubts persisted. His strong brown hands closed about her shoulders and he tilted her head so that she was looking straight into his eyes. 'Trust me,' he said again. 'If you had a Bible with you I'd swear on it but before God I'm telling you the truth. Once we're on the Isle of Wight I'll never leave again.'

Chapter Nine

The landscape seemed to have been ravaged by some great marauding beast. Part of the near-vertical hill had been laid bare of its thick protective woodland, and now trucks and carriages, engineers, platers, navvies, diggers, joiners, carriers, horses and engines all jostled around the tunnel entrance like so many frenetic ants. A narrow plateau had been scooped out and on the east side the land dropped away again, tumbling down towards the distant anger of the sea.

Meg's first glimpse of the gaping wound leading into the formidable rock face that was to be Ventnor tunnel gave her the shivers. There was something menacing about the ragged hole – enter here at your own risk.

She felt her fingers tighten about Brendan's arm but he did not appear to notice. The challenge of the work, the feat of engineering required in hollowing out this seemingly impregnable landmass, had made him immune to everything else.

'Where will we live?' She was tired and hungry. Her overwhelming need was to have somewhere to sit down and a shelter over their heads.

'Wait. We'll move on soon enough.' He wandered off to question some of the labourers. Meg remembered when she first saw him at that other excavation. He had been so persistent, yet in the end he had been defeated.

Her thoughts drifted again to her own immediate needs. All the time she felt the eye of the tunnel watching her, malevolently until she wanted to run away and hide from it. She was certain that coming here was a dreadful mistake.

Finally Brendan gave her his attention and there was an

excitement about him, an exhilaration she had not seen before.

'This is better,' he said. 'It'll be a challenge working here. And I promise you I won't get into debt.'

'Or drink too much?'

'Or drink too much.'

'Or gamble?'

He shook his head at her. 'Would you be wanting to put me in a monastery? You must allow me some small pleasure.' With a grin he added: 'Come to think of it, you're pleasure enough for any man.'

She smiled but the tiredness overcame her again and she sighed. He put his arm about her shoulder and hoisted the dusty portmanteau from the ground.

'Come on, princess. For tonight we'll find a room at an inn.'

'Is that where the Company are housing us?' It seemed an expensive and generous gesture.

With sinking heart she saw the now familiar flickering of Brendan's green eyes. He had been lying to her.

'There is no job.' Her voice was flat.

'Of course there is, but nothing's settled yet.' He squeezed her to him. 'Don't be fretting now. I didn't have a chance to talk with anyone before we came away.'

'Then you can't be sure of work?'

'Yes − no.' He shook his head. 'There's jobs aplenty but I have to see someone first.'

'Then let's go back.'

'No! Are you mad, woman? After making this journey? Come what may, we're staying.'

She followed him along the narrow pathway that led down to the resort of Ventnor. Despair threatened to envelop her. Her mind drifted to thoughts of Joseph and Mary looking for their own room at an inn. Had Mary felt this tired as Joseph trailed her around Bethlehem? Had he lied to her about why they had come? At least they had a donkey, and a home to go back to.

They wandered on through the town. Everywhere work was in progress on tall elegant buildings, some three and four storeys high, seeming to crane their necks to see over the steeply descending cliffs. But the new boarding houses perched along the bay were not for the likes of them.

Meg trailed along behind her man. He called at the Crab and Lobster, the Freemasons, the Globe and finally Kent's Tavern, but the answer, although always different, was always the same — too expensive, full up, not suitable for railwaymen, only recommended guests catered for.

Finally Meg flopped down on the low wall fronting a row of modest cottages. I can't go any further, she thought but said nothing.

Brendan stood indecisively in front of her. For the first time since she had known him, he appeared to be at a loss. The silence seemed to last for ages; then, with an intake of breath, he drew himself upright. 'The luck of the Irish,' he said and marched up the tiny path to the cottage door.

A middle-aged woman answered his knock. She was short, rounded and her face was homely. Meg quickly stood up, not wishing to be seen trespassing on her wall. She could not hear what was being said but Brendan was pointing and waving his hands about. The woman appeared to be listening sympathetically. Suddenly she nodded and with a wave of his arm he beckoned Meg to join them. With relief she trudged up the path.

'This kind body has taken pity on us,' Brendan announced, putting his arm around Meg. 'This is my wife, and this here is Widow Galpin.' The use of the word wife brought its own comfort.

'Betsy Galpin,' the woman confirmed. 'Come along in, my dears, you must be fair worn out.'

The cottage was tiny, sparsely furnished and none too clean, but to Meg it was a palace. Gratefully she accepted the proffered seat and a mug of ale. Meanwhile Widow Galpin busied herself poking the fire and boiling the kettle. ''Tissent much of a room but you're welcome till you get settled.'

'Thank you.' Meg smiled wearily at her.

The older woman nodded in response. 'I can get you a plate of stew.'

'That would be like heaven.'

After the meal they retired to the tiny cubbyhole upstairs which housed a simple bed, a chest and a sampler which bore the words 'The Good Shepherd'. A misshapen sheep was embroidered in one corner.

As Meg sank onto the mattress, the springs creaked ominously, but she felt more optimistic. Brendan hadn't really lied to her. She had simply assumed that everything was arranged, cut and dried, the way she liked it. As if reading her thoughts, he suddenly said: 'You worry too much.' She shrugged but could not respond to his smile.

Meg knew he was putting himself out to please her. Listening to his stories, she recognised his ability to charm, to be amusing. It was part of his beauty, the way his long, intelligent face creased with infectious humour. I love him, she thought.

He suddenly jumped to his feet. 'Come on. You asked me about the sea. We'll go and pay our respects to it, tell that old sea god what a fine couple we are, ask his blessing.'

'But it's dark.'

'So much the better.'

She let him pull her to her feet. Outside it was clear and starry-skied. They followed the steep path from the cottage and along the smart esplanade to the pebble-strewn sands. Away to the south, rocky promontories jutted into the icy-grey evening tide. Dusk was falling and there was no one about. As they picked their way around the bathing machines, the enveloping hiss of the waves rose and fell. Together they pulled off their shoes and began to walk hand in hand across the damp shore.

'This is amazing!' Until the boat journey she had never seen the coast before.

'It's amazing,' he echoed, gently mocking her choice of words. 'Come on.' He started to run across the sand, pulling her with him. She protested but kept pace with him. Suddenly sweeping her up into his arms, he changed direction and ran for the water, splashing along in the froth-laced fringe of the tidal limit.

Finally out of breath, he set her down. They began to kiss. His need was urgent and matched by her own. In unison they sank onto the damp sand and she welcomed him into her body. It was another time, another place, a new dimension. Unnoticed, the water baptised their union in rhythmic waves of ebb and flow.

51

Afterwards they lay panting, sated. Then Brendan got up and began to pull what remained of his clothing off, dropping it in a sodden pile.

'Come on, let's swim.'

'No!'

'Yes!' He pulled her up and helped her out of her clothes, dragging her shrieking and laughing into the water. They immersed themselves in the invigorating depths.

'I'll remember this evening all my life,' he said, suddenly serious.

Meg looked at him and tears prickled in her eyes. Apart from the chill of the cool night breeze, another cold touched her. She was afraid that such joy could only mean there was a price to pay.

Gently she cupped his face in her hands and kissed him. When she finally drew away she felt anointed by his love. 'I'll remember this night too,' she echoed. 'I surely will.'

Chapter Ten

The next morning it was raining. Brendan was up before daybreak and ready to leave for the tunnel site. From the bed Meg watched him with sleepy eyes, trying to find the energy to get out of her lumpy nest.

'You're to stay there,' he ordered as she went to throw back the coverlet. 'Mistress Galpin says you're to keep her company until I get back.'

'She's very kind.' She sank back gratefully onto the straw bolster.

'Aye, she is that.' He was struggling into his waistcoat and Meg enjoyed the sight of him, his shirt still unfastened, the black hair of his chest rustling against the rough cloth. Briefly she thought of the evening before but quickly shut the vision out as a renewed hunger for him threatened to overwhelm her. Instead she said: 'I hope you find work.'

'To be sure I will.' He bent to kiss her. 'If I can start today, then I'll stay. You'd best expect me when you see me.'

She kissed him back. As soon as he was out of the door, she snuggled down for a few more minutes of rest.

She must have fallen asleep for the next thing she knew was Betsy Galpin putting a plate of bread and ham on the bed beside her.

'Here you are, my dear. Just you tuck into that. Young women in your condition got to keep their strength up.'

Meg felt suddenly embarrassed, hardly believing that her pregnancy showed. She did not deny it but sat up, still struggling with the mists of sleep. 'It's late.'

'Late enough. Your man must have found work or he'd

have been back.' Widow Galpin stood with her head slightly to one side, studying Meg benignly, then asked: 'How long have you been wed?'

To her shame Meg blushed. She was no good at lying. She had not even considered an appropriate amount of time that would make her a respectable married woman. Already it was too late. Betsy Galpin looked embarrassed and at the same time disappointed. 'You're not wed?' she asked.

Meg shook her head. She felt an uncomfortable mixture of humiliation and disgrace. For a long time Widow Galpin said nothing and when she finally did there was a change to her tone.

'I think you'd best be getting packed. I don't know what my son would say if he knew ...' She sniffed and took a step back from the bed. The plate of bread and ham gazed reproachfully at Meg as if it too disapproved of her shameful status.

'We are getting married,' Meg started. 'It's just that we haven't had a chance.' It sounded such a lame excuse even to herself.

'Well, so you should.' The older woman sighed. 'I'm sorry, gal. It isn't that I think you're a bad lot or anything, not like some of them up there.' She nodded in the direction of the excavation. 'But I'm a respectable widow and being on my own as I am I have to be that careful.'

Meg nodded. She was suddenly too tired to feel anything except the need to get away and find peace. 'I'll just get dressed and go and find my ...' She didn't know what to call him. 'Brendan,' she finished lamely.

'Yes, well, do as you think fit.'

Miserably she struggled into her clothes and collected up the few belongings that they had laid out in the tiny bedroom. Coming down the stairs she did not know what to say. Widow Galpin was pummelling some unidentifiable washing in a large wooden tub on the table.

'How much do I owe you?' Meg had a total of half a crown that Brendan had given her.

Betsy Galpin wiped her hands on her apron and sniffed. 'We'll say a shilling. By rights I shouldn't take anything, it 'ud be wrong to make money out of sin, but, well I need every penny I can get.'

As Meg handed over two silver sixpences, she looked the woman in the eye. No one was going to say that what she shared with Brendan was less than perfect. Aloud she said: 'You might call it sin, but we're more united than any church could ever make us. You can't love to order, you know.' Before her hostess could reply, Meg turned sharply and drew herself upright, walking with all the dignity she could manage out of the cottage and back into the unknown.

Outside she tucked her remaining one and sixpence into her hem where her brooches were secreted, and retraced the steps of the night before. She felt hurt and humiliated; she wanted to shout abuse and cry at the pain but she did neither. Her only thought was to find Brendan and plead with him to come away, take her back to the mainland, even back home. If they were to wed on the way, there would be nothing that anyone could do about it. Even her grandmother would soften when the baby came.

She was halfway between the esplanade and the tunnel when she heard the explosion.

Blasting was a familiar part of excavating any line. She had heard it all her life, and her ear had become attuned to the sound; she could guess the type of charge, the depth at which they were blasting, the magnitude of the explosion. Afterwards she could not have defined what it was but something about this cannonade of sound told her that it had gone wrong. Her palms began to sweat and she quickened her pace until she was running.

As the tunnel site came into view she could see men scurrying in every direction.

'What's happened?' she asked the first man she came upon.

'An accident. In the tunnel.'

'Dear God!' She ran for the entrance but was stopped before she could go inside. 'Whoa, young woman! Don't you know it's bad luck for a girl to go in there?'

'Let go! I must find someone.'

'Who?' The man who held her arm was middle-aged. He reminded her of a more benign version of her father.

'My betrothed. I think he started work here today.'

The man glanced at his companion, who until now had been watching them. Now he looked away. In desperation Meg turned to him.

'Do you know who's been hurt? Is it serious?'

Both men shrugged and pointed towards a small wooden hut near the tunnel entrance. 'You'd best talk to the engineer, gal. We don't know anything for sure.'

She hurried to the hut but it was empty. Around her, people scurried or talked in small groups but no one seemed to notice her. She raised her arm for attention, called out for someone to listen, but it was as if she did not exist.

After what seemed like forever, a horse and gig trotted smartly up to the tunnel entrance and a man in thick tweeds descended from the trap, grabbing a black bag as he went. From his manner and dress she knew that he must be the doctor. Like the others, he did not seem aware of her presence, but when he went into the tunnel Meg stationed herself at the entrance. She would find out the truth for better or worse when he came out.

When he reappeared he was accompanied by two men in dark suits and bowler hats, whom she took to be the engineer and foreman. All three wore sober, shocked expressions. As they hesitated, she took her chance.

'Who is it in there? I must know!'

One of the bowler-hatted men went to dismiss her but the other stayed his hand. 'Who are you?' he asked.

'Megan O'Neill.' She willed him to put her out of her agony.

'Why are you here?'

'My man started work today. I want to find him.'

The men glanced at each other, faces embarrassed. Each seemed unwilling to be the one to speak the awful truth.

'An Irishman?' the doctor asked. 'Young, dark fellow?'

'Yes! For the love of God, where is he? What's happened?'

'I'm sorry, mistress. It must have been quick. There was probably a spark when he tamped the charge home ...'

She did not know which one had spoken. It almost seemed as if someone had blown out the light, slammed shut the door. She was in the dark, silent and alone. Nothing that happened since they left the mainland seemed real. She had a sudden vision of Brendan naked on the beach, his head thrown back with the joy of being alive, teasing, coaxing her into the water. At any moment she would wake up and he would be there.

Somehow they had walked from the tunnel entrance and Meg found herself sitting on a stool in the wooden hut. Two of the men were staring anxiously at her and the third, the doctor, was talking. '... we wouldn't ask but there is no one else who can identify him.'

She looked from one to the other, not understanding. There was now a fourth man present, a police constable. He wore the same grave expression. As Meg met his eyes he reached forward and took her arm. 'Best to come now,' he said. 'Get it over with.'

She followed him back out into the turbulent day, across the rugged ground near the cliff's edge and into a natural alcove where on the ground a grey blanket covered some inert object. She was hypnotised by the scene, the gently rising mound beneath the cover, the edge of a boot visible under the blanket, her awareness of the man's height in spite of his horizontal position.

'Are you ready?' The doctor took her arm and edged her forward. Somebody lifted the edge of the blanket. At first she only saw his waistcoat, the shirt, the curve of his neck and the line of his chin. His head was turned to one side – what there was left of it, for his left temple seemed to have been blown away. Brown, congealing blood matted the hair that gathered around the gaping hole where his ear should have been.

'No!' She screamed her anger at them and everything clouded, silent again, blissfully dark.

'It was him?'

She was lying on the floor now with a blanket over herself. Strange, confusing thoughts of corpses and blankets battled in her mind. The man bending over her held her wrist. He looked familiar. The doctor.

'Matthew Gawthorp, madam. This is a very distressing time for you. In a moment I'll give you something, then take you home, but first the constable asks that you confirm the name of the ... victim.'

She told him. She told him everything. Sometimes she got lost and had to go over it again, making certain that they understood every nuance of her story. The foreman and engineer seemed to have gone. The doctor and the policeman had impassive expressions.

'Are you saying you have nowhere to go?' the doctor asked. 'Where did you stay last night?'

She told him about the inns and Betsy Galpin, about the beach and Brendan going to work. 'He'll be back soon,' she finished. 'I'm sure he will.'

The two men looked at each other and shook their heads. Finally the doctor opened his bag and took out a small blue bottle and a little pad.

'Don't you fret now, young lady. You're going to sleep and when you wake up I'm sure things won't seem as bad as you think.'

Before she faded away Meg could only hear her own derisive laughter.

Chapter Eleven

Meg was by a river. 'Go away!' the old woman shouted. 'My son would kill you if he knew.' The old woman's son stepped forward. Meg saw that it was her own father. She tried to speak to him but he didn't hear. He raised his pickaxe and before she could stop him struck Brendan across the temple. A cavernous hole appeared in his head, big enough to swallow her up. She screamed ...

'There now, that's enough of that!'

Meg struggled to get up but could not move. For a moment she thought she had been buried by the explosion in the tunnel, but as she opened her eyes she saw that the ceiling, high above, was shiny and smoke-stained. She looked down to see why she could not raise herself. To her horror her arms were pinioned to her sides by a strap fastened around the bed on which she lay. She began to struggle.

'That's enough, I say!'

'Where am I?' Meg looked helplessly at her captor. The sight was not comforting. The woman looming over her was large, solid and mannish. She wore a grubby brown apron, the bib of which was strained over her large breasts. Her hair was scraped back and a shabby cap sat askew over the greasy bun. There was no compassion in her eyes.

'You're in the poorhouse, that's where you are.' There was relish in the disclosure.

It took a few moments for Meg to absorb the words. Now she became aware of other beds, other noises, poor souls in torment. This can't be happening, she thought, fighting

59

down the panicky need to struggle. She heard herself ask: 'Why am I here?'

Her guardian sniffed. 'Where else could you go? You've got no home. You're a wicked girl – look at you.' The forbidding form moved nearer and Meg could see the grey whiskers on her pendulous chin. 'Just you behave yourself and I might undo you. If not, then I'll have to put you in the cupboard.' Meg had woken from a bad dream into a nightmare.

'I want to see someone. The doctor, or someone from the railway company.'

The gaoler snorted derisively. 'They won't want to see you. As soon as they discovered you were just a trollop, they washed their hands of you.' She sat down on the edge of the bed, which sagged alarmingly under her weight. 'Means they didn't have to pay no compensation, did they – and him only just started.'

'How long have I been here?'

'Some weeks. You'll have to stay now, till your brat's born.'

Meg stopped listening. She was trying to remember but her imagination was playing such cruel tricks on her she could not begin to understand what was going on. She closed her eyes and concentrated on the voices within. 'Your father would kill you,' her grandmother had said. She wished that he would. She wanted to die, but not here in this terrible place.

Next to her a woman, half naked, was calling on the hangman to tighten the noose. On the other side a crone dribbled over the edge of the cot to which she was secured by canvas straps, the same kind of straps that held Meg fast.

Escape she must and then she would find her way to the sea. That was what she must do, walk out until the cold numbed her and the shifting sands swept her feet from under her, pulling down until she gave herself up to the sea god who had blessed their coupling in the cove at Ventnor beach. How long ago, she wondered. It seemed a lifetime away but was probably only the night before.

Now it was bearable. What a relief to know that there could be an escape from this existence, and one that saluted their last act of love!

As she began to drift away something else disturbed her, something within her but not of her. Meg realised, startled, that it was her baby kicking.

She watched the routine of the institution, taking good care that she did not seem to do so. The door was kept locked and each gaoler held the key in a voluminous pocket in her apron. Over the next few days there were several different keepers. Only one showed any kindness towards the poor souls who were in her charge. Their only crime was in being unable to work, some through infirmity, some because of their simple nature and others, like herself, because they had fallen on hard times. Meg would not allow herself to think about anything else. Brendan was somewhere out there and her only goal was to find him. She knew that he was dead but at the same time it was not true. If only she were free she would be united with him.

'Please, let me have my clothes back.' She looked down at the coarse, grubby gown that enveloped her. It fastened at the back and there were strings on the cuffs which could be used to tie a patient's hands to her sides if she became difficult. Meg did not become difficult.

The kindly keeper looked at her and nodded her head in sympathy. 'I'll see what I can do. The trouble is, if I bring your belongings in here you'll probably lose them.'

'I'll take that risk.'

Meg waited hopefully but shortly afterwards a scuffle broke out between two inmates and her benefactor was otherwise occupied. Reinforcements were sent for and the two howling women were strapped to their beds and subdued with some concoction. They both continued to moan in a horrific duet.

Meg teetered on the edge of despair. She couldn't bear to stay here. She would never let her baby be born into this hell. She wanted to be with Brendan. This place was too terrible even to die in.

To her relief, the next time the kindly woman was on duty she arrived with Meg's best dress and her shoes. 'I can't bring anything else,' she said.

'I thank you.' Meg took a risk. 'How can I get out of here?' she asked.

The woman's expression was regretful. 'You can't, my dear. Best just accept it.' She patted her on the shoulder and moved away.

Carefully Meg felt along the hem of her dress and to her relief found that the brooches were still there. To have lost these tangible links with her mother and her lover would have cut her last tie with normality, set her adrift in hell with no hope of escape.

Finding a dark corner, she hastily pulled off the hated gown and slipped her own dress over her head. It hung loosely on her but at least it gave her back some sense of identity.

She spent the days quietly, biding her time, working on the mindless task of unravelling woollen garments to be knitted up again into stockings or shawls. Sometimes she gazed out on the grounds from a small window through which she could see only when standing. Outside, the countryside was beautiful, with rolling hills. In the distance she regularly heard what might have been a church bell.

'Where are we?' she asked one of her companions, a woman not much older than herself.

'The poorhouse.'

It was not much help. Meg did not know where that was and in any case her geography of the island was limited to the route from Ryde to Ventnor.

Her companion did not offer any further explanation. She seemed closed off in a world of her own. Meg wondered what her story might be but did not ask. The girl had small features and light-brown hair in a wispy bun at her neck, but her faint prettiness was overlaid with a uniform greyness; pallid skin, dull hair and a rough grey dress that might once have been cream.

'Have you got a family?' Meg wondered at her patient acceptance of her situation.

The girl shrugged tiredly. 'If you can call a bastard family, I've got a boy of seven.'

'Where is he?'

'He's hired out to work.'

'Don't you ever see him?'

The mother shook her head.

This appalling thought hit home. Should Meg's child survive, then would this be his future?

'Have you ever tried to get out of here?' she asked.

'To what? There's nothing out there for me.' The young woman gazed vacantly at the blank yellow wall.

'What's your name?'

'Dora.'

Meg felt frustrated by her apathy. 'Is there no one who cares for you?'

'Only Gracie, she sees that I'm all right.'

'Who's Gracie?'

Dora described the wardress who had been on duty the night of Meg's admission. She could not imagine that this hard, hairy bulk of a woman could be kind or caring.

Already the girl had drifted back into her own vacuum and Meg's spirit rebelled at the hopelessness. There had to be some way. The sea beckoned again, huge, all-enveloping, cold and numbing. The sea.

The days continued to pass with the unrelenting boredom of those that had gone before. Only the distress of other inmates punctuated the featureless, drab existence. Meg bided her time and watched.

When the wardress Gracie was on duty, she indeed seemed to show favouritism to the young woman called Dora. She gave her more food, asked after her welfare, occasionally slipped her a bun or a rock cake. Sometimes she would take her into the cupboard at the end of the ward where on that first night she had threatened to lock Meg up. Meg wondered if she gave her more food out of the view of other inmates. Was there a streak of kindness behind that rock-hard façade?

Another thought came to her. This woman was always on the verge of being drunk. Meg knew to her cost that those who drank always needed money. She remembered the one and sixpence in her hem.

The next time Gracie was on duty, the evening started much as any other. Each patient received a bowl of gruel and a mug of watery cocoa. Thereafter they were shepherded in a line to empty the tin pots that held the accumulated slops of the day. As they returned to their dormitory, Meg took her courage in her hands and approached the so-called nurse.

'I want to ask you something.'

The woman's eyes were calculating. She looked Meg over briefly, making her uncomfortable, but she fought down her fear.

'How do I get out of here? I've got family on the mainland, they'd have me back.'

The woman shrugged and nodded in the general direction of the ward around them as she said: 'We'd be glad to see the back of all of 'em. To many by half.'

A glimmer of hope filled Meg but was instantly dashed.

'You'd best get your fine folks to write in on your behalf.'

'They can't. They don't know I'm here.'

The wardress smirked. 'Looks like you're stuck then.'

'Please ... ' Desperation made Meg bold. 'Is there no way? Can't you help me – for a price, that is.'

There was a greedy expectation in the woman's expression. 'What have you got that's worth having?'

For a moment Meg hesitated. To mention the one and sixpence was to risk having it confiscated. She said: 'How do I know you'd get me out if I paid you?'

'You don't.' After a moment of silence Gracie moved closer. 'What have you got that I could want, then?'

The remark was provocative and filled Meg with a strange kind of shame. Her voice sounded distorted as she answered: 'Money.'

'What else?'

Meg hesitate. Her only other possessions were the two brooches. She could not bear to part with either of them. She shrugged, her face turned aside to avoid the woman's too close breath.

'How much money?'

'One and sixpence.'

Gracie looked dismissive. 'I'd want more than that. I'd be taking a risk.'

'I've a piece of jewellery.'

'What sort?'

'A brooch.' A sense of loss twisted in her belly. Her mother's love token would have to be sacrificed.

Again the woman shrugged. Glancing round quickly she met Meg's eyes. There was a touch of hunger in her that was at odds with her gender. 'The money, the brooch – and some of your time?'

Meg frowned, not understanding. Her adversary moved even closer so that there was nowhere to retreat. Meg was forced to stand her ground although every instinct was to back away.

Gracie reached out and raised her chin. The touch of the woman's rough hands made her freeze.

'You're real pretty. I've seen you – you know, when they brought you in. Undressed you myself, I did. You're real beautiful.' Gracie paused. 'I've dreamed about you ever since.' To Meg's shock and disbelief the woman leaned forward and kissed her. The feel of her spiky chin, the smell of stale gin, the pressure from the gaoler's bulky breasts overwhelmed her.

'No!'

'I'll get you out of here. You'd need somewhere to stay for a while. I can look after you.'

'No!'

At that moment all hell broke loose as one of the more violent paupers made a grab at a crippled woman hunched in a corner and tried to strangle her. The guard let Meg go and leaped between them, her fists flying indiscriminately at both attacker and attacked. The noise was deafening.

When peace was restored Gracie came back, pulling down her sleeves. She simply said: 'When I go off duty at seven, you be by the door. I'll take you out. No one'll ask questions. If they do, just say you're working in the principal's house.'

'I . . .' It was Meg's only chance. She had to get out, had to. The thought of being at this woman's mercy filled her with dread but she would have to take her chance.

As the day warders came on duty, Gracie fetched her voluminous grey cloak and moved to the door. She glanced around and, catching Meg's eye, signalled to her to follow. Swallowing down all her reservations she sidled across to the door. She watched transfixed as Gracie turned the huge key in the lock and the passageway was revealed.

'Come on.'

Meg followed, scurrying in the woman's shadow, praying not to be challenged. The corridor was long and dark. Their footsteps shouted out to be noticed, the wardress's long heavy strides, Meg's timid pattering. They turned several times to left and right before reaching the outside door. That too was locked and Gracie rummaged in her skirts before producing another, even larger key which clanked in the lock.

As the door swung open the heaven of daylight and sunlight welcomed them. Stepping out into the glorious dazzle of warmth, Meg draw in a deep breath of unsullied air. In silence they crunched along the path that led across the grass and in the direction of the high brick wall that appeared to surround the entire building. Meg had to fight down every instinct to break into a run.

'Just stay close to me.'

They came at last to an iron gate as tall as the wall. Nearby a man was amusing himself by throwing stones at the shrubs from the doorway of his cubbyhole of a lodge. At their approach he straightened up, stepped out and crossed to unlatch the gate.

'Nice day,' he said to Gracie. She nodded and walked out. Meg followed, aware that he was watching her. She prayed that he would not challenge them.

'Right. Come along then. Let's get on home.' Gracie glanced round and gave Meg a look that conveyed her hunger. She moved as if to put her arm round Meg and the girl's flesh began to crawl. With the merest glance around she darted out of reach and started to run, racing for the bushes that grew some twenty yards away. Once in their shelter she headed off to the right, having no idea where she was going, wanting only to get away.

'Hey!'

Her blood pounded and she fancied that she could hear running feet and shouting. In response she raced even faster, not heeding the brambles that tore at her face and skirts, picking herself up even as she came crashing to the ground, her feet ensnared by creepers.

Finally she could run no further. Her head was spinning

and everything threatened to turn black. Her heart was almost shouting in protest and there was a crippling pain in her left side. Exhausted she sank to the ground, crouched against a hedgerow, hunching her shoulders against the expected assault.

Nothing happened. As her heart calmed and the blood steadied in her veins, she became aware of the silence. Cautiously she looked around. As far as she could see there was only fields. In the distance was a dark shadow that might be a farm building. She swallowed hard and drew a deep breath. I'm free, she thought. Now to find the sea.

Chapter Twelve

Meg was dreadfully hungry. Her feet were blistered and she would have gladly lain down and died where she was, in the middle of a field, but for some crazy reason it still seemed important to end her days in the sea. Unfortunately she no longer knew where the sea was to be found.

Instead she dragged herself up across the next field and towards the woodland that seemed to cap the distant hilltop. As she drew closer she saw that leaves they called bread-and-cheese grew in the hedgerow. She began avidly to pick them, chewing and swallowing the coarse green pith. It did little to stave off her hunger.

She was now on the edge of the wood. Only a few yards to the south there was a pathway. Beyond the path the land fell away, rising slightly and then disappearing steeply until it met the sea. Tears of relief started in her eyes. Turning back she stepped into the gloom of the trees and a few feet away there was a natural leaf-lined hollow. She sank down and gave herself up to sleep.

It had been light when she fell asleep and it was light when she awoke but now it was the clear cool light of morning. The sun, huge and orange, was emering from the sea on the distant horizon. Even as she watched, it came up out of the water and began an imperceptible journey across the vivid blue of the sky.

Meg remembered her feelings about Joseph and Mary when she had followed Brendan into Ventnor. Then she had been tired and disillusioned, trailing behind him towards what had ended in the magical night on the beach. Quickly she shut out the memory of what had happened next. It wasn't true.

Now it seemed that the sun was some sort of sign. She would go in the same direction, follow it like a star along its course. Who knew where it would lead? Getting up and brushing down her skirts, she set off towards what she now knew to be the west.

Coming to the natural meeting place of two hills she sighted a farm. Her instinct was to avoid it but the need for food drove her on. She descended the slope. The central farmhouse was stone-built and with its outbuildings formed a square around an inner courtyard. There was no sign of anybody. Carefully she moved closer. Before she reached the farmhouse there were other barns and cow sheds.

Taking care not to be seen, Meg headed for the first of the barns. Cautiously she peeped inside and, finding no one there, slipped into the dark interior. To her delight there were flurries of chickens disturbed by her intrusion. Within moments she had found a warm egg nestling in the straw. Cracking it open, she let the rich, smooth contents of the shell slide down into her throat. She found another egg, then resisted the temptation to eat more. Too many would only make her ill.

She went from one barn to the next. As she had hoped, the next one housed some milking cows. Her thoughts took her back to a different time, a different place. Some adult, perhaps an uncle or a neighbour, had taught her to kneel down and raise her head, mouth open, to receive the rich, warm jets of milk straight from the cow's udder. The nearest animal was munching hay. Meg approached it and squatted as near as she could, grabbing the plump udder and pointing the teat towards her mouth. She squeezed hard and a jet of milk splashed across her face. With an impatient flick of her head she lowered the teat and the life-giving liquid flowed into her welcoming mouth.

As the day passed Meg kept pace with the sun, stopping sometimes to rest, changing direction to avoid a hamlet, finally reaching a point where on three sides she could see the sea. To the south it stretched crystalline as far as she could see, the merest haze hinting that perhaps land lay in the distance. To the north there was a narrow meandering channel and a darker patch of landscape with the occasional outline of what was probably houses. She guessed that this was the Solent where she and Brendan had made their fateful crossing to the island.

Straight ahead the land continued to narrow as if, at some point as yet invisible, it would become the apex of a triangle. In the distance the sea snaked between a rocky promontory and the mainland coast like a great river. Her resolve strengthening she moved on.

As the sun began to sink back into the sea. Meg reached a high point and stopped once again to get her breath. A little to her left the land fell away to sea level. Ahead chalky cliffs reached up again in sheer walls ending in a solid edifice of green downland. It was almost as if some giant had folded the land in half and, like paper, it had slowly fallen open, leaving an indentation along the fold. It gave her a heady feeling, a kind of welcome vertigo.

Below her a sluggish river dissected the land along the fold from north to south, bound on both sides by wide marshes. The sight of the gently waving reeds reminded her vividly of her Norfolk home. She swallowed back the lump of loneliness in her throat.

The river ended, or started, near to the most spectacular bay she could ever had imagined. No resemblance to Norfolk here. The bay was deeply scooped out of the surrounding cliffs, vivid white, the shingle shelving steeply into the frolicking waves. Out in the bay itself two rocky outposts formed a natural resting place for blinding white, raucous gulls. It was hard to believe there was such a diversity of scenery in so small a space.

Down by the sea a few fishermen's cottages clung to the coast like limpets to a rock. Further on some larger houses staked their claim to a place in this natural wilderness. Meg did not know where she was but something about it − the fishing boats, the spectacular bay, the sheltering marshes − drew her onwards.

She half ran down the incline, resisting the temptation to glance back in case she was being followed. At the same time she continued to scan the landscape ahead, fearing that her arrival might rouse local curiosity.

70

It was as she drew near to the river that she remembered her money. She had been fortunate enough to get away from Gracie with her three coins and her two brooches intact. The relief at the memory of her escape caused her heart to lift. Bending down she raised the hem of her dusty skirt and felt along the border. Her fingers stopped and she counted the five outlines tucked into the material. She let her breath out with a surge of relief. They were all still there.

With a lighter step Meg continued towards the bay. Now that she had money there was less to fear. She was not a vagrant so no policeman could lock her away, and for today at least the coins would feed her.

She had not gone far when she came across a grocery shop sitting at the junction of two lanes. Its bright new brickwork and open door drew her irresistibly. Behind the single counter a middle-aged man in white apron stood, carefully weighing up measures of tea. He looked up from his task just long enough to greet her. His lack of curiosity was reassuring. As the blue packet was filled and the top neatly tucked over, he put it aside and gave her his full attention.

'May I help you, madam?'

The mingled smells of his provisions caused her hungry stomach to twist with need. Keeping a hold of herself, she said: 'Would you have some cheese?'

Without replying he turned towards the large round cheddar on the slab behind him. 'It's been a beautiful day. Four ounces?' He started to cut a wedge before she could answer, weighing it on the scales to his right.

As he held it out, Meg took the plunge. 'What would be the name of this place?' she asked, unable to think of a good reason for not knowing where she was.

The man showed no surprise but answered: 'You're at Freshwater Bay.' When she did not reply, he added: 'Many's the visitor we get these days.' She could only feel grateful to him for not drawing attention to her stained clothing and dishevelled appearance.

'Is there a bakery nearby?' she asked, emboldened by his manner.

'There is. But if it's a small loaf you're wanting, I can let you have one. It's yesterday's so it's cheaper.'

71

Now she smiled at him and nodded her head. Taking her purchases, she left the shop and turned back inland towards the welcoming familiarity of the marshes.

It did not take her long to find the ideal place to rest for the night. A few willow trees grew on a bank and the surrounding reeds could easily be pulled together and bound into what Meg thought of as a nest. With a sense of respite she munched large chunks of bread and cheese and wondered what the morrow would bring. It suddenly struck her that although she had passed within feet of the sea, her determination to make a watery end to her life had at that moment deserted her. So intent had she been on seeking out food that the desire to die had mysteriously been overlooked.

As if recognising her feelings, the baby moved and she rested her hand on the gentle rise of her belly, stilling the small being within.

'All right, my love.' She spoke to this part of Brendan that still remained, feeling that she knew what he was trying to tell her. For the moment at least this was where they would stay.

Chapter Thirteen

Encouraged by the friendliness of the grocer, Meg returned the next day to buy more provisions. She then set out to explore the area of marshland around her temporary home.

After walking for a while she came across a point where the riverbanks were so silted up that it was possible to step from one tussock of marsh grass across to the other side. The opposite bank was lined with trees and, after glancing around to make sure that no one was watching, Meg stepped over to investigate. It was almost as if she had stepped from the mainland across to an island.

The going was hard, for a tangle of vegetation struggled for supremacy around the narrow trunks, but she pressed on, wondering how far before she came out again into open countryside.

She had not gone far before she saw something that stopped her in her tracks. There, straight ahead of her, was a hut. Cautiously she edged closer, fearful that some outcast might emerge and challenge her, but as she drew level with the hut she could feel that the place was deserted.

It took courage to go up to the entrance and peer inside but Meg forced herself to do so. At every moment she imagined a hand grabbing her from behind and had to fight down the desire to run back into the safety of the sunshine. She had come this way for a purpose, and the tranquil atmosphere of the place encouraged her belief that Brendan was there beside her, urging her on, overseeing her journey.

The hut was secret, sheltered and, when she finally dared to look inside, weatherproof. It had probably once been used by reed cutters but that must have been a long time ago. From the overgrown state of the surrounding area and the creepers that half buried the sides and roof, it was clear that no one had visited for many a day.

Meg stepped back outside again and now the place seemed light, even cheerful; she felt suddenly optimistic. There was still a little money. She had already established that there were fish in the river and many times as a child she had netted a dinner for the family. Hazel trees grew in abundance about her, now with sweet milky nuts dropping to the ground. Wildfowl teemed among the reeds. For the time being at least she could feed herself, just until she knew what she must do next.

Having reached this decision, she felt as if a weight had been lifted from her. For the moment at least she could stop running. For no good reason she started to cry.

In the privacy of her sanctuary she gave herself up to tears, wailing and rocking outside the isolated hut, scraping at the dusty earth, flinging her head this way and that and cursing the God who had failed to protect her man. She wanted him. She loved him. She was desolate, lonely, hungry for the touch of him. Her anger was with everything and everyone who had played a part in sending him forth on a journey that had ended in tragedy.

Finally she cried herself out. The sobbing and heaving subsided and she lay back exhausted against the nearest trunk. The sun broke through the canopy of leaves and fell in a shaft onto her new home. She dried her eyes and sat up. It was almost like a blessing.

Meg blew her nose on some grass and, pulling herself together, prepared to go fishing. She had already seen a spot where she could crouch on the bank in the shade of an overhanging tree so that her own shadow would not touch the water. Returning to this place she knelt down, staying very still, and watched. Just below her some roots extended into the water, forming a cove. Nearby innumerable small silver fish moved with the current. Sooner or later one would drift into this temporary pond and then even without a net she would be able to scoop it out. She looked forward to trying again the skill that had once earned her praise.

She kept very still, probably for several minutes. Fish teased her, getting near, then darting away at the last moment. She froze where she was, ignoring her aching knees. Any movement would give away her presence and send out warning ripples across the silver shoal.

'What are you doing, young woman?'

Meg jumped so much that she nearly toppled forwards. The fish scattered in all directions. Turning sharply, she confronted a strange female figure standing a little way behind her. The woman was of middle years, short and heavily built. Her square face was unremarkable except for a wart on the left side of her nose, but her small, alert eyes held Meg's attention. She was dressed in red and her skirts were stained with what looked like dyes. The authority of her voice marked her out as a woman of quality.

Slowly Meg got to her feet, wondering what best to say. Before she could think of anything the woman took a step closer, her head on one side, examining Meg as if she were some specimen she was considering buying.

'I have never seen anyone keep so still,' she observed.

Meg did not admit that she was fishing for fear that she might be trespassing.

The woman continued to study her. 'You have a good face. Fine bone structure. You are young. I could use you.'

'Madam?'

The woman did not explain. 'I want you to come to my house tomorrow. That is, if the light is good.'

'The light?'

Meg waited for her to explain but she merely added: 'I am Mrs Carmichael. I live at the bay. Simla Lodge is the name of my house. Tell them that I told you to come.'

Before Meg could respond, Mrs Carmichael had wandered off down towards the bay, leaving her curiosity unsatisfied.

The next morning was again sunny. Meg washed with care in the stream and took time to dress her long burnished hair. She was glad that the kindly woman at the poorhouse had thought to bring her best dress. It gave her more confidence although if worn every day it would soon become shabby.

She was soon as the bay and it did not take long to find

75

the house called Simla which stood like a sentinel overlooking the high tide. It was a square house, large, bisected by a tall square tower, and ordinarily Meg would not have expected that someone like her would be invited to call, unless as a servant. She hoped that Mrs Carmichael was going to offer her a job but it seemed unlikely.

She entered at the side and on telling the purpose of her visit was directed across the garden to a sheltered corner where Mrs Carmichael and another young woman were carrying out some incomprehensible task. The young woman was standing against a backdrop of yellowing creeper. She held a veil away from her face and was unnaturally still. Mrs Carmichael was spying on her from behind a cumbersome brown box perched precariously on a three-legged stool.

'Hush!'

Meg stopped at the warning while Mrs Carmichael fiddled with her strange contraption. For perhaps five minutes she instructed the girl to remain as she was, not to move a muscle, on no acount to blink, to keep her hand still, to breathe as lightly as a fairy. After what seemed an eternity she suddenly relaxed and the young woman bent forward to ease her clearly aching shoulders.

'Right. Good.' Mrs Carmichael was withdrawing what looked like large glass plates from her box. She rushed them into the nearby shed and banged the door.

Meg looked questioningly at the other girl, who in turn smiled at her.

'What's she doing?' Meg asked.

'Taking photographs.'

'What's that?'

'It's like a painting but it makes a perfect picture of what you look like.'

It was puzzling and did not explain the summons to be here.

'Do you live here?' It was the girl's turn to ask questions.

Meg was not sure how to reply. 'I haven't been here long,' she said. 'I'm not sure how long I'll stay.'

'I was born here, down the bay. My pa's the constable.' The girl sniffed and twitched the end of her nose, the movement incongruous against the elegance of her veil. 'My name's Margery Dore. They call me Margy.'

'I'm Megan O'N – Meg Foggarty.' Meg was aware that in using her own name she had taken an important step. From now on she would not pretend to have been Brendan's legal wife.

'You talk funny. Where do you come from?'

'Norfolk way, but my folks are from Ireland.'

Margy stared at her. 'You ain't half pretty,' she finally observed. 'Mrs Carmichael'll be pretending you're some goddess or fairy or suchlike.'

'Why?'

'She takes her photographs up to London and displays them. Rich folks buy them to decorate their houses.'

It was a novel thought. 'Does she pay you?' To her disappointment Margy shook her head.

'I get a good dinner, though, and sometimes her daughter throws out old clothes. See this dress? It used to be hers.'

Meg was preoccupied with thoughts of work. She would like to stay here in this beautiful place but her condition meant that sooner or later people would ask questions. At the thought of the poorhouse she shuddered.

'You got family?' Her thoughts were interrupted by Margy's question.

She shook her head. 'There's just me.'

Margy gazed at her. 'Looks like you're having a babby.'

Meg blushed and tears pricked her lids. 'I am. My man died. I don't want to go back home.'

'Where you living, then?'

Meg told her about the hut. 'I just need to earn some money,' she finished, refusing to think of the loneliness.

'You could get work with me.'

'What do you do?'

'Tread pug in the brickwords. It ain't much but I get paid. It's hard work, though.'

'I don't mind hard work.' Hope raised Meg up.

'Well, you see the foreman then, come Monday. The place is being sold but we don't never see the boss anyway so it don't much matter who owns it. It's Bill Downer you want. Tell him I sent you and make sure he knows you don't mind

77

hard work. They need so many bricks these days I'm sure he'll take you on.'

At that moment Mrs Carmichael emerged, her mouth pursed with satisfaction. 'I hope that'll be all right,' she said to Margy. She then turned her attention to Meg. 'Now, young woman, I want you to sit over there on the grass and turn your head sideways, then keep as still as you were yesterday.'

Meg followed her instructions. She wondered what these photographs would look like. It would be strange to see herself from the outside.

Mrs Carmichael was struggling with the box again. 'I've only got one plate left,' she complained. 'But that will have to do for today. Do you know anything about photography?'

Meg shook her head and the movement caused Mrs Carmichael to come fussing across, rearranging the drape of her collar, twisting a wisp of hair. 'Don't move, child. Once I expose the plate the slightest tremor will cause a blurring.' As Meg raised her eyebrows in question, the older woman returned to her box and began to explain.

'Do you know what chemistry is? Don't move! I don't want you to answer me, just listen.' She pushed a flattish, oblong box into a recess in her bigger box and jiggled it into position. 'In here is a glass plate coated with collodion. Collodion used to be called gun cotton because if you dip ordinary cotton wool into a mixture of nitric and sulphuric acid it takes on explosive properties, like gunpowder – don't look so apprehensive, I won't blow you up!' Mrs Carmichael bent forward to peer through her box, her eye focusing on Meg. After a few moments she straightened up.

'Now, what I am going to do is let light into the box. Where it hits the plate inside it will react with the chemicals and leave an impression of whatever the light is reflected off. This time it is you.' She peered into the hole again. 'These plates are very delicate and they have to be completely clean. The merest smidgeon of dust and the picture will be marred. Right, child. I'm going to take the cover off the lens and let the light in, so not a movement. Hold your breath and look this way. That's it. Now, not a flicker!'

Meg tried not to screw her eyes up against the sunlight. The small black hole in the wooden box seemed to be staring back at her. She fought down the desire to draw back or swallow. Mrs Carmichael was talking again.

'As soon as the plate has been exposed for long enough, we have to keep it in the dark. If you took it out now you wouldn't see anything on it but once you expose it to light a change takes place. Do you understand this?'

Meg just managed to stop herself from shaking her head. Her neck was by now aching and her knees were stiff.

After what seemed like hours but was probably no more than four or five minutes, Mrs Carmichael straightened up and covered the eye of the camera.

'Right. Come with me, child. I'll show you what I mean.' She struggled to pull out the inner frame of the camera and carried it back across to the shed. Meg scrambled up, easing her aching limbs as she went. There was an urgency about the older woman's movements and she responded to them. Mrs Carmichael hustled her inside with a dire warning not to jar or touch the precious plate.

It took several moments for Meg's eyes to adjust to the dark. In the meantime Mrs Carmichael had opened a door in the top of the carrying frame and lifted out a glass plate with as much care as if it were an eggshell.

When she was ready she lit a tiny oil lamp which gave out a warm yellow light and started to pour a noxious-smelling liquid over the glass plate.

'Proto-sulphate of iron,' she explained.

Meg peered over her shoulder. The liquid covered the plate and drained off into a shallow dish below. Gradually a milky pattern began to appear on the wet plate, growing lighter before her eyes. At first she could not make out what it was but as if by magic she watched a ghostly representation of herself come through, first her white collar and cuffs, then the shape of her face, her darker hair and finally her black dress — only they were the opposite to what they really were; white dress, black collar, pale hair, slightly darker face. She looked round at Mrs Carmichael in disbelief.

'This, my dear, is what is called a negative.' Mrs Carmichael tilted it and studied it critically. 'Mmn, not too bad. There are some little flaws down there, see — those tiny spots – but they could be touched up. Anyway, let's get the plate washed off. See that basin there? Pass it over.'

'What is it?'

'Hyposulphate of soda. It dissolves the salts of silver. Leave them on the plate and the whole thing will eventually fade again. The silver is insoluble in water.'

Meg made no comment. The whole process left her intrigued. By some magic her face had been transferred onto this piece of glass.

Mrs Carmichael sighed and stood the plate up to dry. 'As soon as it's ready I'll varnish it and then we'll make you a print.'

'A print?'

'You don't look like that, do you? The negative is the opposite of what you see in nature; white is black and black is white and every shade in between is represented by its opposite. I'll make you a positive print onto paper. Then you'll see the real you. Only that will have to be later. If you come back on Saturday I'll show you. Are you in service around here?'

'No.' Meg waited, wondering if she might be offered a job, but when Mrs Carmichael remained silent she added: 'I work with Margy – at the brick works.' She knew that just by saying it she had sealed her fate.

Chapter Fourteen

As suggested by her new friend, Margery Dore, Meg presented herself at the brick works at first light on Monday morning.

The site was a sprawling area of diggings, dominated by a central brick-built kiln. Although it was little after six, round and about people were already labouring. Meg looked about her anxiously and to her relief noticed Margy among a small group of women, boys and young children at the clay pit. They were knee-deep in the stodgy pug, treading it methodically to tease out stones and other impurities. The actual brickmakers, four in number, were seated at makeshift benches where, as she watched, consignments of the newly trod pug were delivered to them by the treaders. For a moment Meg forgot her fears, fascinated by the speed with which they packed the clay into the wooden moulds, sliced it off with the ease of a grocer cutting butter and set the newly formed bricks aside to be fired.

'You want summat?'

The voice made her jump and Meg turned to see a middle-aged man approaching her. 'Mr Downer?'

'Aye.' Like the brickyard itself he was grey and dusty. He pushed his hat up on his head and she noticed the shiny line left by the brim, his sparse hair plastered to his forehead.

'I'm looking for work.' Although she was trembling inside, she feared that her voice sounded demanding.

The man did not reply immediately. His curious gaze reduced her once more to a state of anxiety. 'Who are ye?' he asked.

'My name's Meg Foggarty. I'm a friend of Margery Dore's.' She couldn't think of anything else to say.

'You're not from round here?'

Meg shook her head. 'My ... affianced was killed in a railway accident.'

The man did not look impressed. 'There's plenty o' local folk always looking for work,' he replied.

'Please! I can work real hard, and I'm honest and ...' She looked at him in mute appeal.

He stared back at her in silence and when she did not back down he looked away. 'Well, miss, I don't know ...'

Meg leaped on his indecision. 'Just give me a chance. I'll work as hard as anyone here, do anything.'

'You live hereabouts?'

'I've got my own place.' She flushed.

'We – ell.' He still hesitated. 'As it happens, one of our labourers has gone sick today. 'Tis hard work, though.' He looked her over again and Meg held her stomach in, praying that her condition wouldn't show. He gave a sigh. 'All right. For today you can load the kiln.'

The relief was total.

'One and six a day. You'll work till the kiln is full. We want to light up first thing in the morning. You got to load them proper. A good firing's essential. Ben 'ere knows what to do.'

Meg was put in the charge of a small, dark-haired boy of about ten. Obediently she followed his example as the first of the bricks were loaded onto the perforated floor. As she picked up a pile she was staggered by the weight. She longed to divide the load, put them into the kiln one or two at a time, but dared not show any weakness.

'The clamp bricks goes in first,' Ben instructed. 'Round the edges. The facing bricks goes in the middle, to make sure they get the best firing.'

Meg nodded, too breathless to comment. After about half an hour she stood back and looked at the kiln. It still seemed almost empty. 'How many bricks does it hold?' she asked.

'Twenty thousand.'

She groaned inwardly. I can't keep this up, she thought.

Not day after day. Eventually she asked: 'What time do we finish?'

'Soon as it's dark. In summer the brickmakers start at five thirty and work still about seven.'

'At night?'

''Course. They're on piece work, see. They does all right. Trouble is, the rest of us has to work as long as they do.'

It seemed impossible. Already her hands were sore and raw areas were spreading across her palms.

Finally Margery came across to her. 'He said yes, then?'

'For today.' Meg nodded.

'You look fair worn out. Don't worry, I'spect Tom South'll be back tomorrow. Then, all being well, you'll be treading along with the rest of us.'

'I hope so.'

Somehow Meg managed to struggle through the day. She was so tired that going back to her hut she did not even bother to eat but crawled into her makeshift bed and lay exhausted. Tears ran passively down her cheeks. She was too tired to have the energy for crying.

She managed to rouse herself the next morning and make her way back to the site. As she came in, Bill Downer was organising the lighting of the kiln. 'Right, lads, get the temperature up and keep it going from now on. It'll be best part of a week afore we gets this lot finished.'

The coal store was on the edge of the site and already Ben and a man whom Meg assumed to be Tom South were wheeling barrowloads across.

Seeing her, Bill Downer came over. 'You come back then? I didn't expect to see you no more.' He nodded across to where Margy was taking off her stockings and stuffing them in her bodice. 'You can work over there for today. You can be pug boy for old Sam there, on the end. He works fast so you'd better keep the stuff coming. It won't be as hard as yesterday.'

Thank God, she thought. Aloud she asked: 'Does this mean I can work regular?'

Bill shrugged. 'It isn't rightly up to me. The new master's coming soon. From what I've heard Mr Paige likes to do things his own way so we'll have to wait and see. We're all a bit worried, like. If you're lucky he'll take to you.' His eyes came to rest on her belly and he pulled a rueful face. 'If you ask me, gal, I reckon you'd better hope that he does.'

Chapter Fifteen

Bartholomew Paige was in a bad mood. He was not impressed with his lodgings, uninspired by Freshwater Bay, bored with having only his wife Edith for company and disappointed in his clients, who for the most part seemed stuffy and priggish in spite of their reputation as artists, poets and writers.

He had been on the island for two days checking out the property market and its pace of life did not suit him. There was only one thing left to do; get the visit to his new brick works over as soon as possible and go back to the mainland.

'I'm going out on business,' he said to Edith, who was embriodering some frippery by the light from the french windows. He looked at her slight figure and pale, accepting face, and his familiar irritation was back. For the moment he couldn't think of anything crushing to say to her so he merely remarked: 'I hope you'll have changed by the time I get back. That colour makes you look like uncooked dough.'

He picked up his cane and the hat he had recently bought in London from the establishment of a Mr Bowler. Paige strutted outside, reaching into his pocket and glancing at the half-hunter suspended from the heavy gold chain. The gesture was intended to draw attention to his prosperity but there was nobody close enough to see. He decided that although it was four o'clock on Saturday afternoon, there was still time to visit his latest acquisition, which, following the boom in house building, should yield a nice little profit. Having shouted for the carriage that was at his disposal, he changed his mind: he would ride to the brickyard. Viewing the workers from the height of a horse had its advantages. He would look down on then and they had to look up to him, which was how it should be.

Bartholomew rode for about ten minutes, during which time he was aware of the itch in his groin. He wished that he was back at home on the mainland so that he could visit the discreet little house in town where, for a price, any sort of comfort could be bought. He decided that if his business was going to bring him regularly to the island he must make some arrangement.

Riding into the brick works he reined in the horse and watched with satisfaction as a gang of workers carried out the chain of tasks which resulted in the growing piles of orange-red bricks lining the yard.

His eyes turned first to those treading the pug. There were boys and women. His attention was drawn to one young woman who had remarkable deep-red hair. She had a pretty face and a nice body on her. Like all of them, she was smothered in the rough clayey pug, which gave her face a smooth, masklike look. She had her skirts tucked up above her knees to keep them clean as she trod the heavy paste. The sight of her legs stirred Paige's desire. He paid cursory attention to the other females; their arms were bare and one or two of them were quite buxom, but his eyes returned again to the woman with the red hair.

'Who's that?' he asked the foreman.

'Meg Foggarty.'

'And?'

His foreman glanced at him. 'Unwed,' he finally said. 'Lives down in the marshes. Come over from Ireland or some such heathen place.'

Paige noted that her eyes were large and blue, emphasised by the dirt smeared across her face. As she stood up he thought that she looked thicker than he would have expected around the waist. 'Unwed?' he repeated, for confirmation.

'Aye. The poor lass lives in that old reed cutters' hut over yonder. It's not fit for man or beast.'

The brickyard owner splayed out his legs and folded his hands across the small of his back. He dragged his eyes away from the treaders and looked with satisfaction at the rest of his workers. It pleased him that in spite of the heat and the lateness of the hour, when many labourers would be finishing work, his hands were pushing themselves to extra exertions under his scrutiny. He smiled with satisfaction and his eyes returned to the treaders.

'Has that girl worked here long?' he asked Bill Downer, indicating Meg with his head.

'Not long.'

Paige picked up the hesitation in his foreman's voice. 'I won't have riffraff working in my yard.'

'She seems a good worker, sir. I don't know nothin' about her background.'

'Does her family live around here?'

'Not as far as I know.'

Paige caught his breath. 'Tell her to get herself washed up and come to the office in ten minutes.' A plan was forming in his mind.

Meg's heart beat fast but she held her head high and tried to calm herself as she walked to the pump to wash off the day's dirt. She was aware of the covert glances of her fellow treaders and a sense of unease flooded over her.

Mr Paige, the new brick master, wanted to see her and she could not but believe that he intended to send her away. A mixture of fear and outrage swept through her. In an ideal world her condition should not bring so much shame. She wondered how she would survive if she lost her job. Her hand came to rest on her belly. Poor baby, it was not his fault. Had she been a widow they would not be treated so. A tendril of anger with Brendan touched her heart but she pushed it away.

Placing an ancient bucket under the pump, she worked the handle until the pail was half-full and splashed the icy water over herself, kneading out the clay from her skin, hair and clothing. The rough hessian dress clung to her body and she pulled it away, shaking it to remove the worst of the moisture. She repeated the operation three times, then, squeezing her long hair, she coiled it up in a wet knot. The water ran in a cataract across her shoulders.

'I'll not be long,' she said to Margy, giving her a nervous smile.

'You be careful, he looks a bad 'un.' Margy frowned doubtfully.

'I'll be all right.' Meg swallowed down her unease and made her way to the shed that acted as the site office.

At the doorway, the labourers were beginning to line up for their pay. Bill Downer called their names and handed out the wages, two sovereigns here, ten shillings there, sixpence to this child, fourpence three farthings to that. Meg edged her way past them and stepped uncertainly inside.

The first thing she saw was Bartholomew Paige poring over the ledgers on the high, narrow desk that stood beneath the window to catch the light. He did not acknowledge her arrival but as she stood in the doorway she knew that he was aware of her presence.

It gave her an opportunity to study him. He was about forty, she guessed, running to fat. She didn't like the way he looked – his pale, bulbous eyes, his slack mouth bordered by crinkly whiskers, his fleshy nose, his corpulent belly – but, as her grandmother had always said, a shabby purse can hold a pearl.

After several moments Mr Paige straightened up and gave her his attention, looking her slowly up and down.

'Well now, washed up you're quite a pretty little thing.'

Meg leaned back slightly to avoid his breath, and, taking courage, replied: 'I work hard, sir.'

'Do you, now?' He continued to assess her until her face was hot with discomfort. 'My foreman tells me you are not a married woman.'

Meg found it hard to get the words out. 'I came here with my affianced. He was killed, on the railway.'

'Leaving you ...'

She nodded shamefaced, looking at the ground.

Paige did not know whether to believe her or not. It was no matter. His knowledge of her precarious moral position and her need to fend for a child might one day come in useful.

Letting out his breath as if reaching some weighty decision, he said: 'I am a charitable man, a practising Christian. It does not behove me to permit my workers to live immoral lives — '

'Please, sir!'

'But ...' He raised his voice above her plea. 'Our good Lord preaches that we should take pity on sinners. I hear you are living in a hut in the marshes.'

'It doesn't belong to anyone,' she started.

He shook his head dismissively. 'More to the point, that is no fit place for a young woman in your condition.' Again he studied her, his eyes squinting in the shaft of pale afternoon sun that poured through the doorway. The dress still clung to her and his eyes seemed to see through the rough material, resting on her breasts, then her belly, and below. She tried to ease the dress away and shield herself from this sense of exposure.

Paige drew in his breath. 'I expect others will blame me for it, but I am going to give you a chance, Meg Foggarty. As long as you continue to lead a decent life and work honestly, I will allow you, for the time being, to live in a cottage I have just bought.' He came closer again and his shoulder touched against hers as he stood beside her.

'You see that land down there?' He pointed away to the south where a shallow valley nestled between the brick works and the downs. 'Well, I intend to build some houses on those fields. Can you see that cottage over in the dip?'

Meg followed the direction of his hand and looked at the slate roof of a low, cob-built dwelling tucked between two hedges.

Bartholomew smiled down at her and she thought his eyes looked like those of the pike her grandfather sometimes hooked from the river. 'Well, for the time being I have no use for it. The roof and windows will have to be repaired, then it needs someone to live there and keep an eye on the area — I don't want gypsies or tinkers moving in.' He gave Meg a meaningless smile, the merest upward twist of his lips. 'Until I have that cottage knocked down, you can live there, keep an eye on the place.'

'Oh, thank you, sir!'

'God bless you, my dear.' Paige squeezed her arm and for a moment she felt the pressure of his wrist against her breast.

She moved back as far as she could in the narrow space between her employer and the doorway but for a moment longer the contact remained and then his hand dropped to his side.

In the face of Mr Paige's Christian kindness Meg felt ashamed of her thoughts. The touch had been accidental, she was sure of it. It was she who was being wicked, having such an unkind opinion of him. God forgive me. Meg crossed herself out of habit and thought that if she tried really hard perhaps she would become as good a person as her master was.

Chapter Sixteen

Bartholomew felt pleased with his afternoon's work. He rode out of the brickyard at a spanking trot but then reined in, wondering whether to go back and establish exactly where in the marshes his latest prize had her home. After a moment, he thought better of it. No point in being too indiscreet.

For tonight he'd make do with Edith's services although her wooden limbs and whimpering protests did little to inspire him. Marrying for money had its drawbacks. He consoled himself with the knowledge that the next day he would be back at home, where he could creep into the bed of Simmonds, the housekeeper. Simmonds knew the score. She wasn't beautiful like this new Meg or even as pretty as Edith but she had an earthy hunger for sex that pleased him. In the meantime he could postpone the pleasure of possessing Irish Meg and enjoy the anticipation.

An odd clanking noise brought him out of his reverie and he realised that the horse was out of balance. Cursing he stopped and dismounted. One of the gelding's shoes was loose. With a sigh he remounted, changed direction and made for the smithy.

The forge appeared to be deserted. Bartholomew drove the horse forwards and peered inside, screwing up his eyes to compensate for the sudden loss of light. Everything seemed to be black – the twisted swathes of iron, the sooty anvil and hammers lying in confusion on the dusty floor. Only a few coals still gleamed orange in the furnace.

Blast! He ducked back outside, then rode across the yard to the adjoining cottage, which he knew to be occupied by the farrier. Without bothering to dismount, he called out: 'I say, smith!' There was no reply so he shouted again. 'Are you there, smith? I need your services.'

At last the door opened and the farrier emerged. He stood in the doorway, his eyebrows raised as if surprised at the intrusion. 'You want something?' he asked.

Bartholomew felt a moment of irritation. The fellow was young and well built, the sort that women were stupid over. He took exception to his insolent manner. 'Come along, man, I'm in a hurry. I need this shoe fixed.'

'The forge is closed. I don't work after four on a Saturday.'

His audacity shook Paige. 'Well, you'll have to.'

The man continued to stare at him impassively. Just as Bartholomew was about to remonstrate with him, he looked at the horse and his expression changed. 'You'd best dismount. Looks like he's lame.'

Bartholomew slithered from the saddle and held out the reins, but the smith ignored him. Instead he bent down and raised the horse's hoof, examining him carefully. 'Poor old boy, let's have a look at you.' Seeing the confident, strong hand on the horse's leg, Bartholomew had a vision of the smith touching a woman so, caressing, sure of himself. His dislike intensified.

Finally the blacksmith stood up and rubbed his hand across his forehead. 'I'll take the shoe off, then he needs rest.'

'You'll have to re-shoe him, I've got to get back to the bay.'

'Then you'll have to walk. He's lame.'

'Damn it, man! Who do you think you're talking to? I have influence around here. One word from me and you could be out of business.'

'You think so?' To Bartholomew, the smith appeared to smirk. 'Most of the gentry come here. I don't think they're likely to change their minds on your say-so, begging your pardon, that is.'

Bartholomew was livid with impotent rage. He didn't actually know the gentry yet. In spite of taking a house right on the bay he hadn't even caught a glimpse of the famous poet, Lord Tennyson. He did not know how to take charge of this situation. The smith seemed impervious to him, the horse his only concern.

Once the shoe was off, the man straightened up and nodded. 'I'll not charge you. It won't take you long to get home. It's less than a mile to walk. Good day.'

The farrier patted the horse on the neck and walked back into the cottage, leaving Paige standing like some peasant in the yard. He sought vainly for some consolation to soothe his dented pride. As a small act of defiance he hauled himself into the saddle and rode an uncomfortable mile back home. Damn you, smith! When I've made my mark around here, you'll be the first to suffer, he thought, but even to his own mind the threat did not hold true.

Chapter Seventeen

Meg couldn't believe her luck in being offered the cottage. When Mr Paige had gone, Bill Downer came over to give her ten shillings wages and she smiled at him, unable to hide her euphoria.

'There you are lass.' He hesitated. 'You're sure you want to go and live in the empty place?'

'Oh, yes! It'll be much better than where I am.' She did not add that by offering her accommodation, Bartholomew Paige was also tacitly agreeing that she could continue to work. Both her worst fears − of being homeless and penniless − were now allayed.

The foreman appeared about to say something, then thought better of it. Meg felt a moment of disquiet.

'I'll be glad to see you out of that hut. 'Tissent a fit place for a woman, specially in your ...' He didn't finish the sentence. 'My missus has had five and I wouldn't have liked her living like that, nor working so hard.'

'I can't change what's happened.'

'No, you can't girl, and if you ask me it's a danged shame.'

Meg clutched the four half-crowns and made ready to leave. 'It's very kind of Mr Paige to let me stay.'

Again Bill did not reply directly and the sense of unease persisted.

'He is very kind,' Meg repeated.

'Oh yes, he's kind all right.' The tone of his reply did not dispel her unease but, as nothing else was said, she shrugged it off.

It being Saturday, she was glad to finish work early. Margy had to hurry home because the pig had been killed that morning and it was her job to clean the chitterlings. 'I'll bring you in a piece of bacon,' she promised as they parted at the gate.

The sun was shining and its gentle warmth helped to soothe Meg's tiredness. As she walked along the lane leading towards the marshes, she thought about her dream cottage, warm and secure with a garden full of flowers. The baby kicked and she had a vision of herself sitting on a stool by the door nursing it. For the first time she thought of it as being real.

Her reverie was disturbed by the sound of footsteps. She glanced round to see a young woman hurrying after her. Meg slowed down. The girl wore a cap and apron as if she were in service and had not stopped to change. Meg did not know her.

'You Meg?' the girl asked.

'Yes.'

'Mrs Carmichael wants you. Now.'

'I was coming round later.'

The maid ignored her words and tugged at Meg's sleeve. They changed direction.

'What does she want me for?'

'The usual. She's had half the neighbourhood coming and going this morning but she say's yours is the only face that'll do.' The girl sniffed philosophically.

As they reached Simla, the hall and stairway seemed like a thoroughfare with young women and children milling about everywhere.

As Meg hesitated, Mrs Carmichael came in from the garden. She looked harassed and untidy. The strange lace covering she wore over her hair was askew and she had a vivid red shawl flung across her shoulders, the end of which trailed across the floor.

'Right. Off you all go.' Mrs Carmichael began to push biscuits and little cakes at the children. 'See you go straight home now. Help your mothers and fathers.' She piled more sweetmeats into the greedy young hands. Suddenly she looked up and saw Meg.

'Ah, there you are. Upstairs with you, my dear, and Nancy

will show you what to wear.' She indicated the maid.

Meg followed the young woman up the stairs, marvelling at the wide treads and the lofty ceiling. The hallway alone was ten times bigger than her hut and large brass pots stood in corners holding living plants that reached almost to the ceiling. It was like having a garden on the inside.

Meg thought that everything, from the heavy black wood furniture and ornamental rugs to the exotic greenery and burnished wooden statues, must come from the foreign lands she had ready about in Lord Hinchington's shiny journals. She experienced a pang of regret for the safety of her old life as well as a sudden wish to break free from everything, and see the world.

'You got to wash and then put these on. You'd best hurry, she says the light won't last.' Nancy indicated the washstand with its large, flowered jug and bowl. On the bed a filmy dress and veil were laid out.

Meg came down the stairs self-consciously. The dress was flimsy and the outline of her body was clearly visible. She breathed in to lessen the bulge of her belly, but to little effect.

In the garden half-filled dishes, bottles and buckets lay about at random. There was that noxious smell of chemicals again. Mrs Carmichael was pouring water over one of her plates, then she leaned it carefully along with several others against a support in the fading sunlight. She sighed and stepped back.

'Ah, young woman, there you are.' She looked her over critically, which made Meg blush. 'We'll have to have a talk about that,' Mrs Carmichael said meaningfully.

She began laboriously to brush Meg's hair, spreading it out across her shoulders, taking up strands to make into plaits, twisting locks into ringlets about her face. Finally she slipped a lace shawl about her shoulders, pulled down so that her throat was bare. Her hands were small but square and capable and her fingers were stained black with the collodion. She stood back and studied her work.

'That will have to do.'

Meg was supposed to be somebody called Ophelia who was dying for love of a mad prince.

96

'Don't you touch anything now, some of those pots are poisonous.' Meg glanced round her but was grabbed by the chin and her head twisted back round. 'Just look sad and pensive, child, as you usually do.'

'Er, was the "positive" of me to your satisfaction?' Meg used the word hesitantly, uncertain that she understood its meaning.

Mrs Carmichael nodded. 'I've made you a print, yes. It's good, very good. I may exhibit it.' She disappeared under a heavy black blanket and Meg, remembering that she must keep quite still, froze into a statuesque pose.

After what seemed like hours she was allowed to move. As she relaxed her protesting shoulders and turned her head from side to side to relieve the pain in her neck, she was aware that someone had joined them in the garden. A man was standing behind Mrs Carmichael, watching her work. For the merest second Meg thought that it was Brendan and her heart jolted, but when she looked closely she realised that this man was quite different, shorter and thicker-set, with a similar mop of black curling hair but more unruly than her beloved's.

Every now and then he wiped his hand across his mouth and moved from foot to foot as if he was on edge. He was dressed in a strange cape which left his throat bare and gave him the appearance of some storybook character. Meg guessed that he must be somewhere in his twenties. He looked very ill at ease.

'Right.' Mrs Carmichael was rubbing her hands together with gusto. 'You are just in time, Kingswell.'

The man looked down at his clothes and shook his head. 'I look a fool,' he started.

'Nonsense. Have you heard of Hamlet, prince of Denmark?'

He shook his head again.

'How about you, my dear?' Mrs Carmichael looked round at Meg.

She too shook her head, wondering where all this was leading.

'Well, I trust that you have heard of Will Shakespeare?'

This time Meg could say yes and the admission seemed to please the older woman.

'Splendid. You are both to be characters from one of his plays. You, Ophelia, are to appeal to Prince Hamlet for he is your beloved, but your appeal is in vain because he is distraught with anguish. His mother has betrayed him and he has nothing, but disgust for womankind. Come over here now.'

The man came forward reluctantly and Mrs Carmichael busied herself arranging their pose.

'Reuben Kingswell, miss,' he said to Meg as her arm was placed unceremoniously on his sleeve.

'Yes, yes, come on while the light is good. Time enough for names later. You, Meg, turn your head on one side, that's better. Look at him with longing, imploring him to want you.'

Meg could not look at him at all; it was too embarrassing. She lowered her eyes and knew that her cheeks were scarlet.

'You, Kingswell, look away, turn your head, man! That's better.'

Meg was aware that her hand was beginning to tremble as she rested it on his warm, strong upper arm. The intimacy of the pose shamed her and beneath her fingers she could feel that he was tense.

'Not a flicker now, no blinking, keep that head still!' Mrs Carmichael admonished them.

Meg was aware that Rueben Kingswell was cautiously easing his left leg, allowing his foot to slide surreptitiously across the ground. Accidentally his weight came to rest on her bare foot.

'Ouch!'

'No!' Mrs Carmichael threw the blanket aside and burst towards them. 'What is the matter with you both? Can't you just keep still for five minutes?'

'No.' Reuben was stretching and stamping his foot. 'I've got the screws in my toe,' he complained.

'Pah! What babies men are!'

Meg stole a glance at Reuben and began to smile. Catching her eye, he suddenly grinned. His face was transformed – fun-loving, slightly provocative, relaxed, strongly attractive. She looked quickly away, her own face feeling unnaturally hot.

They resumed the pose and this time Mrs Carmichael reluctantly declared herself satisfied with the outcome. 'That's the best I shall get,' she grumbled. 'Right, Kingswell, you'd better get back to your work or you'll be accusing me of depriving you of a living.'

He looked questioningly at Meg. 'Should I walk you home, miss?'

She might well have accepted but before she could respond Mrs Carmichael called her back. 'You, Meg, I want to have a talk with you.'

Reuben Kingswell acquiesced with a regretful expression. He said nothing but his eyes held Meg's for just a second longer than was necessary. They were a light hazel colour, and alive with curiosity.

As soon as he was out of hearing, Mrs Carmichael said: 'Winter's coming. What are you going to do about the baby?'

Meg shook her head.

'It's a crying shame. The man should be made to marry you.'

'He's dead.'

Mrs Carmichael was silent. She walked ahead of Meg into her little hut and proceeded to repeat the developing process that Meg had witnessed on the previous occasion. Over her shoulder she said, 'How are you going to manage?'

'I'll be all right.' Meg secretly feared that she wouldn't.

After an age, Mrs Carmichael continued: 'When are you due?'

Meg did some hasty calculations and realised that it must be very near to Christmas.

'I will be on the mainland for a few weeks or I might have had you to stay here.' Mrs Carmichael lit the little lamp and was holding it up to look at her visitor. The scrutiny made Meg feel uneasy. For a moment she thought of Gracie at the poorhouse, her solid mannish build, her hungry eyes, but there was no threat here, only concern.

Mrs Carmichael sighed. 'Something has to be done. Apart from anything else, I'd hate to lose that face — you are one of the most interesting models to have come my way. Look, here is your likeness.' She retrieved a single sheet of stiff paper, about nine inches by seven, and held it out to Meg.

Taking it, she gazed in wonder on her own face, gently tinged with golden brown, looking straight back at her. 'It's magic.'

'Science, my dear.'

Meg glanced up and finding the older woman's small, shrewd eyes still upon her, looked away again. 'I'll be moving, into a proper cottage soon,' she said, with more confidence than she felt.

'I'm glad to hear it. That hovel's not fit for a beast. Here, come and hold this plate. It needs to be immersed in water and when you've rinsed it, move it along to the next bath. It has to be absolutely clean.'

Meg was relieved to have something to do. She laid her print carefully aside and bent over the shallow bath, crinkling her nose at the acrid smell.

'If I just have enough food — ' she started.

'I shall arrange for food to be sent to you every week.' Mrs Carmichael was wiping her hands on her shawl, evidently not for the first time. 'When you move you must let me know where. There are some spare blankets and clothing here as well. And ...' She reached into her voluminous, dusty skirts and searched in a pocket, finally producing a sovereign which she held out with fingers, blackened by the developing fluids. 'You are to take this for anything else you need. And don't hesitate to get the doctor. I will pay.'

'Thank you, ma'am. You're very kind but I can't accept.' Tears welled up in Meg's eyes.

'Nonsense, child.' Tilting her head to one side, the older woman added: 'You should find yourself another suitor. With your looks there can be no shortage. Only be more careful in your choice this time.'

Meg shook her head. 'I lost the only man I could ever love.'

For a moment they were both silent. Then Meg said: 'Mr Paige has agreed that I can live in his cottage in return for looking after it.'

'Paige from the brickworks?' Mrs Carmichael looked sceptical; then, as if thinking better of it, her expression became noncommittal. Finally she said: 'Be careful. You may not be a maid but you're still very young.'

'Is there something wrong with Mr Paige?'

Mrs Carmichael pulled a face. 'I would be doing the man a disservice if I said that there was. Just call it my suspicious nature.' She paused. 'Anyway, the safest thing is to think of a suitable marriage. Loves comes from doing the right thing, marrying for the right reasons. You'll not stay single all your life.'

I will, Meg thought. To my dying day I shall remain faithful to the most wonderful man that ever lived. That stupid moment when she had mistaken Mrs Carmichael's visitor for Brendan had shaken her up, brought back all those old feelings. She wanted Brendan back with such intensity that suddenly she could hardly bear to breathe. She knew that she must get away before she lost control. Aloud she said: 'When I have my new address I'll let you know. And thank you for the print.' Keeping her face averted so that her anguish should not show, she took her leave.

Chapter Eighteen

Pressure of work kept Bartholomew Paige busy on the mainland for several months but he was determined to visit his brick works again before Christmas. The foreman seemed reliable enough but Bartholomew was never happy unless he had control of things himself.

Besides, he had another reason for wanting to go. Almost as soon as he had left the island he had regretted not having made arrangements to visit the Irish girl just once. His head told him that his caution was sensible. After all, it was important to protect his good name. On the other hand, if he had acted immediately he could even now have the pleasure of remembering what it was like to possess her. Her pregnancy was only a minor inconvenience. The thought stirred his desire and he daydreamed about what it would be like to have her.

'Will I be coming with you?' Edith broke into his reverie.

'No, you will not. You may follow me over in a few days.' Much as he would have preferred to be without his wife, there was merit in being seen as a happily married man and he still had his reputation to establish across the water. Once he'd wormed his way into polite society he could safely leave her behind.

As Edith passed by, he grasped her by the wrist. 'I want you to arrange a musical soirée here before Christmas. It had better be a good show. Just make sure you invite everyone who matters and do things properly, I don't want to be embarrassed.' As he spoke he squeezed her arm tighter until she winced with pain.

'Something wrong, my dear?'

Edith shook her head, tears glistening in her doelike eyes, and he smiled as he let her go.

He left for the island the following morning, being driven from Winchester by Jennings, his coachman. The sea was quite rough and there was some debate about whether a crossing was wise. Bartholomew did not relish the idea of seasickness but neither did he want to kick his heels in Lymington, so he insisted on hiring a boat and several strong young men to row him across.

The rhythmic sway soon upset his stomach. In spite of the strenuous efforts of the men, the boat seemed to make little headway and he began to regret his rashness. The water looked black and angry and he could not swim.

At last the tide turned and they were washed up to the jetty. As Paige stepped onto dry land his legs were like jelly. He threw some coins at the men, ignoring their complaints that they would need a night's lodgings and hired a gig to drive him the four miles to Freshwater.

It was still blustery but he was glad to see that it was not raining. His seasickness gradually subsided. As they were nearing the village, a strange figure suddenly stepped out from behind some bushes and into the road in front of the carriage, arms waving to stop them.

'Drive on!' Paige said to the coachman, but the stranger was blocking the road and the man halted.

'Good. I'm so grateful. I would welcome a lift to the bay.'

Bartholomew was surprised to find that the person was a woman, albeit neither young nor pretty. From her voice, however, she was someone of quality, so he opened the door and raised his hat to her.

'Bartholomew Paige, ma'am. You seem to be a long way from home.'

'Mrs Hay Carmichael.' The woman struggled across to the gig, carrying an assortment of strange boxes. Ignoring his proffered hand, she pushed them at him. 'Take care of this, it's my dark box.'

Bartholomew piled the equipment on the floor and helped her aboard. 'Photography, how interesting,' he said.

'It is. I've just been to that brick works. There are some remarkable-looking children there, poor little souls.'

'The brick works?'

'Yes. Nice fellow, the foreman. Kind. I gather the owner's no good. He treats his workers like cattle. Anyway, I'm in a hurry, got to get back before the plates dry out.'

Bartholomew felt his face flush. 'Who did you say you were?' he asked to cover his confusion.

'Mrs Carmichael. We have a house at the bay. Next door to my dear friend, Tennyson.'

Bartholomew felt the excitement mount. 'I've always wanted to meet him,' he said hopefully.

'Alfred can't abide the public.'

He felt chastened but did not give up hope. 'It gives me great pleasure to escort you home,' he said. 'I would welcome an opportunity to see your photography.'

'You would? Who did you say you were?'

He hesitated. 'Just a visitor to the island, on business.'

He dropped his passenger off at the entrace to her house and in spite of a hint or two was not invited in. Never mind; now that he had made her acquaintance he'd find some way to take advantage of it.

He was troubled, however, by the unfair way in which the woman had described him. It was vital that he should be respected. As he reached the lodging house where he regularly stayed, he vowed that he would make every effort to put that right. Regretfully he realised that any ideas of visiting the Irish whore in her new cottage had better be delayed.

'What you gonna do for Christmas?' Margy asked as she and Meg stood near the brazier that burned in the brickyard. It was 1 December, a blustery day, and thoughts of the break from work loomed large among the workers.

It was a question that Meg had been avoiding. Work had only just began on the cottage and her dream of settling into her own place, attending morning church, then eating beef and plum pudding, became increasingly unreal. 'I'll be all right,' she said.

'Well, Mam says if you're on your own you're to come and stay.'

'I couldn't.'

''Course you could. Anyways, you're to come for tea today.'

In spite of the fact that her father was the village constable and therefore the guardian of local morals, Margy showed a touching interest in Meg's life quite unhampered by disapproval. She herself had never been further than Yarmouth, four miles away, and their house was far too small for her large family of brothers and sisters. Time and again she dragged Meg home with her for a bite to eat or to play a game with the children.

The cottage was even smaller than the one that Meg had shared with Grandma Foggarty and far dingier but the family were close and happy. Warmth came not from the small coal fire but the cluster of bodies. Now she found herself sitting on the bench between Ruby and Nell, two of Margy's younger sisters, waiting for tea. Margy and Florrie and Mrs Dore were slapping slices of jam roly-poly onto plates.

Margy's mother was shapeless and washed out but had the air of one to whom nothing would come as a surprise. Just having somewhere to come eased Meg's burden of loneliness. In the past weeks she had cried herself dry and now only a vacuum remained.

'When you due?' Mrs Dore shouted over the babble of young voices.

'In a few weeks.'

'About the same time as me then.'

The news came as a complete surprise. Mrs Dore was so round that there had been no noticeable change in her since Meg had first arrived in the village. 'It'll be my thirteenth. I lost two.'

Meg's helping of pudding arrived in front of her and she tucked in hungrily. The older woman's matter-of-fact tone reassured her. As she looked up, Margy took her seat at the end of the bench and started to shovel her roly-poly away. Grandma Foggarty would have chided anyone eating in such a manner but Meg thought it did not matter. It was her friend's loyalty that was important. It ensured her acceptance by the rest of the brick workers and without this she could not have survived.

105

'Say you'll come and stay for Christmas. It'll be fun,' the other girl said, her mouth full of suet pudding. 'We can sing carols and play charades. Do say you will.'

'Perhaps.' Meg gave her a sudden smile. 'I'll never forget you.'

'You going somewhere, then?' Margy looked alarmed.

'No. I just meant . . .' But she could not explain.

'Meg, you should go to church.' After tea Margy walked part of the way home with her friend and now, as they made ready to part, she took up her familiar plea. It was a request that Meg regularly denied.

'You know I can't. I won't have them all staring. Anyway, there's no Catholic church nearby.'

'Well, there's a church and a chapel. Don't make no difference. You should go. People understand about your man being killed but if you never go to church they'll think you're a bad girl.'

Meg did not reply. Since she had run away with Brendan she had been neither to confession nor to Mass. She felt so angry with God that she wanted to turn her back on Him, but every now and then a fear learned in childhood came to torment her. If she were to die right now she would surely go straight to hell, and yet there was no point in asking for forgiveness for something that she did not regret.

Margy would not let the matter drop. 'Why don't you go to the service tomorrow? You can ask the minister if he'll christen your babby when it comes.'

'No. I don't want to. Besides, he isn't a priest.'

'That don't matter. S'pose your babby died? It won't be one of Jesus' lambs if it ain't baptised.'

Meg sighed. Sometimes her friend seemed little more than a child, and yet her arguments struck a chord. Even if Meg did have a quarrel with the Almighty, she knew that her son's soul was another matter. She wondered if God might not get his own back by harming the baby in some way. You are a bully, she thought, thinking of the heavenly Father.

Perhaps Margy was right. She should not deny her baby a decent baptism. Looking at Margy's anxious face she knew that she was defeated.

106

'All right, I'll go. But I'm not promising anything.'

The girl smiled at her. 'That's good. The vicar'll be pleased to see you. He's a good man — well, he must be, mustn't he, otherwise he wouldn't be the vicar. In fact, everyone in the village is nice really, except Mr Paige perhaps, I don't like him much.'

'He's all right. He's been kind to me.' Meg let her friend ramble on. 'Are you coming to church then?' she finally asked.

'I can't. I've got to help Mam.' As Meg went to protest her own unwillingness anew, Margy added: 'But I went last week, and I'll go again at Christmas. Honestly, it's your turn.'

'All right! I've said I will.'

Chapter Nineteen

The following morning Meg dressed demurely and fastened her hair beneath a blue bonnet that had belonged to Mrs Carmichael's daughter Julia. Meg knew that the blue emphasised the colour of her eyes and contrasted pleasingly with her deep russet hair.

At the idea of going to church she still felt a fraud, for her own faith was destroyed, yet she missed the comfort of belief. Life had seemed less complicated when it was possible to see every event as part of God's purpose. Perhaps today she would find a way back.

She walked up from the river and along the narrow causeway that led to the beautiful old church. It was a clear, sunny day, warmer than usual for the time of the year. She stopped to admire the flat expanse of silver water and the mudflats where myriad birds sang their own hymns. She stood there until she realised that the bell had stopped tolling and she was late. She almost ran the last hundred yards and passed swiftly through the graveyard and into the building.

The service had not started and the air was alive with subtle movement; a hat adjusted here, a Bible opened, a whispered conversation. The first person Meg recognised, on glancing down the row of pews, was Bartholomew Paige, seated near the front. Viewed from the back he enamated an air of prosperity. At his side a neat little woman in a dove-grey suit glanced round at him rather as a cowed dog might watch its master, seeking out signs of displeasure. The realisation that he had a wife shocked her. Until this moment she had viewed his as an entity complete unto himself.

The minister was already at the altar and as he turned he stopped and stared at Meg. She smiled uncertainly at him, and his face took on an expression of indignation. Sensing that something was happening, other members of the congregation turned round and Meg found herself faced by a sea of hostile eyes. She felt sick with embarrassment. Nearby somebody whispered loudly: 'Look, it's the Roman whore.'

Meg felt her anger rise. She wanted to turn and run but if she did so she would never be able to show her face in the village again. It crossed her mind that as long as she kept out of their sight the good people of Freshwater had tolerated her, but to parade herself here overstepped their bounds.

Her eyes were beginning to water and she felt that she could not stand there a moment longer. She had to get away. There was nothing else to do. People were still looking and whispering. There did not seem to be a kind face in sight.

She was suddenly aware that someone seated near the back of the church had risen from his pew. As she stood almost paralysed with shame, he came across to her, his boots echoing against the stone floor. Nodding towards her, he held out his arm, indicating that she should follow. She recognised him as Mrs Carmichael's Hamlet although now dressed in a Sunday suit. He escorted her firmly back to the pew and nodded to her to sit down. Gratefully she did so, seeking escape in an attitude of prayer, eyes tightly closed, hands clenched together to still their trembling, ears refusing to hear the muttering that still buzzed about her. Gradually the rest of the congregation settled down and the minister, turning his attention away from her, began the service.

When Meg felt sufficiently calm she sat up straight and stared defiantly ahead. She was determined not to let them see her confusion. The thought of asking this minister to baptise her child was now ridiculous.

After a while she glanced round at her rescuer. Disconcertingly, again she had imagined that it was Brendan come to her aid. Why did she keep making this foolish association? It threw her into a turmoil. This man looked quite different, his skin was darker, and when she caught a glimpse of his eyes she saw again the light, speckled hazel. There was an easy confidence about his manner which had the effect of taking away her own self-assurance.

He turned his head and nodded to her. Quickly Meg looked away and her cheeks felt hot. This man now knew that she was an outcast. She willed the service to be over. As the congregation rose to sing the first hymn, she wondered with disdain what had been God's purpose in subjecting her to this humiliation.

Reuben Kingswell was rarely present in the congregation. He preferred the Nonconformist chapel but he came now and then because the forge need the local patronage. Churchgoing was in any case not high on his list of priorities, but not to be seen at prayer could well brand him as a godless man, which he was not. He knew too that an outward show of goodness could belie what went on inside a person.

The scene that had just taken place proved this point. Here was this lonely, defenceless woman from across the sea and when she came into God's house, for whatever reason, she met with reproof. He glanced at her and the sight of her fine profile and the courage with which she conducted herself filled him with conflicting emotions.

Looking away, he scanned the rest of the congregation. In the middle rows were those who considered themselves a cut above the working men. One such was the new owner of the brick works. Although he spent precious little time on the island, his reputation had already spread: greedy, grasping, not the sort of man to leave alone with your sister. Reuben heard the gossip while he was shoeing the horses. He turned his lips down in derision.

The sermon commenced and as he stretched his legs he touched the skirt of Meg Foggarty. His senses were heightened by her closeness and the sweet smell of herbs that emanated from her dress. He closed his eyes momentarily and breathed in slowly to absorb the perfume.

As the sermon got into full swing he let his mind wander. After the service he would walk the half-mile to the forge cottage and have dinner. It would be cooked and delivered by Mrs Cheke from along the road. Boiled mutton, potatoes

110

and dumpling, then gooseberry tart. His stomach rumbled.

Reuben considered himself fortunate in having completed his apprenticeship with such a good master. What was more, Amos was now in his seventies and forced by poor health into retirement. Reuben's thoughts digressed as he considered what a shame it was that the poor old boy was getting so addled, but every ill wind blew some good. As a result, at twenty-four Reuben was already recognised as the village smith in his own right. In addition there was the bonus of his master being a widower and childless.

'When I goes, the forge is yourn,' old Amos was often heard to say. He had even had the foresight to write it all down in front of witnesses before he had become so muddled. Reuben was grateful to him.

The sermon droned on and his mind drifted to what he would do with the cottage when once it was his. He would have the pump moved inside and then build a proper hearth. All the walls would be white-washed and perhaps he would even build on a little lean-to where there could be an indoor sink. Yes, and he'd put in a kitchen range. Thinking of the possibilities was a pleasant way to pass the time. The vicar's voice hardly intruded.

The young woman's perfume was suddenly in the air again, bringing him back to the present, making him aware of her disturbing closeness. He studied her covertly. She worked at the brick works although she looked more of a lady really, not delicate but somehow noble. She stood tall and straight and her lovely blue eyes were on the minister. She seemed angry with him as if she disagreed with everything that he said. He averted his eyes from the sight of her distended belly. The village folk had not time for strangers and little compassion for one who had fallen by the wayside. He thought cynically that they might be more forgiving if she was less pretty.

Reuben didn't realise that he was staring at her again until she turned her attention from the minister and glanced at him. There was challenge in her expression and quickly he looked away. Swallowing hard, he hoped that she hadn't read his thoughts. They were the sort that should never be expressed in a church.

'You got any ideas about a wife?' This was a question

that old Amos asked him regularly. Reuben wondered why he should think of it just at this moment, then, looking back at Meg Foggarty, he knew.

Bartholomew Paige had arrived later than he preferred for the morning service, so that already many of the common sort were in their pews. Round and about other carriages and coaches were arriving. The wealthy folk of the village were helped down by their drivers or grooms, left to walk only a few yards to their devotions. Bartholomew chivvied Edith so that they could get inside quickly and find a suitable pew where he could watch the gentry and be himself noticed. He looked forward to the day when they would have a pew of their own.

Just outside the doorway some of the poorer people were putting on their boots to go in to the service, being unwilling to wear them out on the rough roads. He strode past them, not deigning to look in their direction, and accepted a hymnal without thanks.

At that moment Lord and Lady Tennyson arrived. The congregation stood as a sign of respect and Bartholomew got his first glimpse of the famous poet. He looked older than he had expected and shabby. The discovery disappointed him but he reasoned that no doubt it was because he was an artist. Poets and painters were always bohemian.

Lady Tennyson by contrast looked very respectable, dressed all in black with a bonnet that almost obscured her pointed, sallow face. She held herself erect and on reaching their pew immediately sank to her knees in earnest prayer. In the Tennysons' wake came a retinue of would-be poets and admirers from across the water who shuffled into the pews behind and followed Emily Tennyson's example. Only her husband sat, his eyes downcast, presumably also in prayer. Bartholomew had attempted to nod in their direction but unfortunately they did not appear to have noticed him. He was sorry to find that the Carmichaels were not there or he would have introduced himself after the service.

There was some sort of disturbance going on at the back of the church. He tried to ignore it, poking Edith who had glanced timidly over her shoulder, but after a while curiosity got the better of him. As he looked round he saw Irish Meg standing alone at the back of the church, her head thrust forward like Joan or Arc.

He looked back quickly, not wishing to be seen by her or associated with her predicament. 'It's the Roman whore,' someone whispered. Gazing at the minister, Bartholomew saw that he cast a cold, accusing stare at the sinner. People began to whisper and there was a rustle of movement. Bartholomew could not prevent himself from taking another quick look and was less than pleased to see the smith from the forge walk up to Meg and invite her to sit next to him. Paige's face grew hot and rage and jealousy suddenly coursed through his veins.

At last everyone seemed to be settling down again. Bartholomew opened his hymnal at the correct place and raised his head to where he imagined God must be, somewhere above the altar. He began to sing loudly to the Twenty-Third Psalm, enunciating each word with particular care. Anybody watching would see at a glance that he was a good Christian.

At his side Edith was singing in her trembling, reedy little voice. He noticed as he glanced sideways that her hands shook and the discovery irritated him. Without moving his head, he reached out with his foot and pressed down on her toes. She struggled to suppress a squeak of pain and he carried on through the psalm with renewed vigour. The knot of jealousy continued to tighten under his ribs but he consoled himself with thinking of what he would do to the girl when she was safely under his patronage.

'For ever and ever, Amen.'

As the service finally drew to a close, the parishioners filed out, the gentry leaving first while the rest stood in respectful silence. The minister was busying himself with those who mattered and Meg followed Reuben outside. They stood in the midday sun, breathing in deeply, enjoying the warmth.

'May I see you home?'

He almost blurted out the question and she shook her head, thinking that she could never let him see where she lived, but added: 'I won't forget what you did for me in there.'

''Twas nothing.'

She shook her head again. 'But it was. You don't know how I felt at that moment. I thought they might stone me.'

He shrugged philosophically. 'They could do, too.'

At that moment the new brickyard owner and his wife passed them. Paige held his wife tightly by the elbow and she was almost running to keep up with him. As they passed he glanced in Meg's direction. The look was swift but all-enveloping and she blushed uncomfortably under his scrutiny.

'Arrogant, jumped-up ...' Reuben did not finish the sentence but glanced quickly at Meg. 'I'm afraid I've no great liking for that man.'

'So it would seem.'

He looked at her and in contrast to Paige's arrogant stare there was kindness in his steady light-brown eyes. 'Don't you let these folk upset you. You're worth more than the rest of them put together.'

'You think so?'

He flushed and she guessed that he was embarrassed by the show of feeling. Again there seemed to be nothing to say. Finally Reuben took a step or two back. 'Well, I'd best be going.'

'All right.'

He halted and nodded indecisively. 'Well, goodbye then.'

'Goodbye.'

Still he hesitated; then, with a shrug of his shoulders, he turned and walked away. Meg watched him saunter along the graveyard, his hands now in his pockets. As he left it seemed as if the warmth went with him. She watched until he was out of sight, then, suddenly aware that she was alone in this unfriendly place, she began to hurry in the same direction.

Chapter Twenty

The foreman of the brick works had done his work as instructed and on 17 December Meg stood for the first time in the kitchen of her own cottage. As soon as she was alone she closed her eyes and breathed deeply to absorb the pleasure of her new situation. She had given up hope that it would ever happen.

The cottage was not large but it had one sizeable room with sufficient space for a table, two chairs and a sideboard. When the time came there would be a place for the baby's crib in the fire recess.

Going up the narrow stairs she discovered that there was a single bedchamber large enough to hold a bed and perhaps a chest of drawers in addition to the baby's cot.

Back downstairs Meg ran her hand along the old whitewash of the rough wall and looked at the powdery film on her hands. It was grey with age and she resolved to paint it very soon. This was a new life for her and she intended to have a clean start.

The relief in having a decent shelter was so great that for a while she simply sat on the rickety old stool that had been left behind by the last tenants and stared into space. Then she set to arranging her few precious belongings. These had mostly come from Mrs Carmichael, who, at the end of every photographic session, insisted on sending her home with something else. Now the place looked like home.

Taking a bucket and brush she set to work to scrub the floorboards even though it was a Sunday. Her grandmother would be shocked to see her working on the Sabbath, but then she'd be shocked about a lot of things. It was weeks since Meg had thought of home. Now she had a sudden vision of her own small room back in Norfolk, and longed to be back there. At the time her life had seemed hard but now she would have given anything to exchange her present loneliness for the simple peace of her past existence.

Meg worked until it grew dark. When she squatted down to light a fire, she noticed that the fire basket was broken. She would have to get it fixed. For tonight, best go early to bed. Her back was aching, a dull gnawing low down, and she felt exhausted.

It was a relief to lie on the bed even though the mattress turned out to be hard and lumpy. Tendrils of pain were creeping across her belly, nothing much but warning pulses of discomfort. Meg shifted her position and closed her eyes. She shouldn't have worked on the Sabbath.

For a while she must have slept for the next thing she knew it was quite dark. As she lay wondering for a moment where she was, her belly suddenly seemed to be stretching as if she were on the rack. The pain increased into a crescendo of intensity, then mercifully died away.

Oh, my God! The baby's coming. She tried to sit up but the pain started again and she could only draw her knees up and writhe as if wrestling a python.

Meg wanted someone to be there, anyone. Between the pains she called out, hoping that somebody passing would come to her aid. Through the bedroom window she could see a navy velvet sky. There was silence.

She didn't know what to do. Nothing was ready. She began to scream to relieve the agony and the silence. The pain went on for hours in great undulating bursts of agony. Now there was no respite, only the bludgeoning insistence of the hurt. Her breath came in gasping bursts. She was pushing as if to expel her very insides, twisting this way and that to rid herself of the torment.

'No! she cried out as the struggle reached a climax. 'No-o-o!' There was a rush of feeling, a sweeping along of emotion, and the tide of pain began to ebb. In its place the sense of wellbeing was tangible. There on the bed, cushioned between her thighs, the tiny, grasping, blind infant murmured. Meg

116

heaved herself up onto her elbows and reached out to cradle its head. 'Oh, my little love.' She saw that it was a boy and tears of relief and gratitude bathed her. Gently she drew the child up onto her breast and covered him with the blanket that had been cast aside during her labour.

In spite of the exhaustion there was one more thing that she knew she must do. With trembling hands she felt for her shawl and managed to unravel enough of the wool to tie off the baby's cord. Her fingers were cold and she could not stop shaking. Somehow she managed to separate the child from the lifeline that had sustained him during those long months in the womb. Now, to her relief, she felt the rhythmic rise and fall of his chest, listening to the snuffly intakes of breath. In spite of herself, her last thought before sleep overcame her was: Thank God!

As the first light licked through her window, Meg was aware of a movement against her, not like the insistent kicking of before, and it was a moment before she remembered what had happened.

'Declan?' She raised the baby up and he whimpered, his small face moving aimlessly, seeking comfort in the gloom. Strands of damp, black, curling hair cushioned his crown. Tenderly she held him to her nipple and he began to suck. Anxiously she searched his face for signs that he resembled his father and to her joy she was sure that he did. Now in one sense Brendan would always be with her. 'It's all right, my love. Mother's here.'

Afterwards she got up and changed the bedding, then managed to wash herself and the babe. She felt dizzy and nauseous and had to fight to stay on her feet. The sun lent a little warmth to the room but she found that she was shivering. Again she remembered the broken basket downstairs. Meg had to admit that she badly needed help but she was too frail to leave the cottage to find it.

The only thing left to eat was part of a stale loaf. It was so dry she thought it might break her teeth but then she discovered that there was still a little souring milk in the crock and soaked the crust until it was edible. She slept again.

When she awoke Meg began to wonder if anybody would

ever find them. There was no food, and she felt too weak to fetch water from the pump. We could lie here and die, she thought, cradling the baby to her. Nobody would miss us. She was so tired that the idea of slipping into an endless sleep was not unwelcome. Some distant memory of Freshwater Bay came to her. Such a long time ago she had planned to drown herself but had not done so. Had she survived only to come to this?

'Yoo-hoo Meg, are you there?'

The sound of Margy's voice reduced her to gasping sobs. 'I'm here! Please get some help.'

Margy gazed at the scene with kind, bovine eyes. 'Oooh! Ain't he lovely?' She touched the babe carefully on the cheek.

'He is, but we haven't got anything to eat or drink. Will you go to Simla Lodge and tell them what's happened?'

''Course I will.' Margy seemed stunned by events. 'It was Bill Downer what sent me. He wondered where you were.'

Meg nodded. 'Tell him I'll be back to work as soon as I can. Just give me a few days and I'll be right as rain.'

Margy nodded. 'The master was asking after you too.'

'Master?'

'Aye, Mr Paige is still here. He's going in a few days. He came round the works this morning. He wants another thousand bricks a week. Don't know how we'll do it.' Margy sniffed. 'He wasn't pleased to find you weren't there. Do you think he'll sack you?'

Meg shrugged but the sinister thought clawed at her. 'You tell them I'll be back soon,' she repeated.

'Well, get some sleep,' Margy urged. 'I'll get the things you need. Nothing to worry about now.'

In spite of the new fears, Meg could not stay awake and when she finally came to again it was to find a bowl of stew on the chest beside the bed. Margy was nowhere to be seen. After she had eaten, Meg made her way shakily down the narrow stairs, Declan cradled in her arms. She could not be separated from him; she wanted him there, safe, both night and day.

Downstairs milk, bread and cheese were in the scullery and blankets and linen piled on the kitchen table. From their quality she knew that Mrs Carmichael had had them sent over. There were even binders for the baby's stomch and squares to keep him clean. She could not stop herself from weeping tears of weakness.

In spite of the mended roof and windows, the cottage still felt cold and draughty. Meg began to shiver. It was then that she noticed a stack of logs and kindling piled by the chimney breast. How good Mrs Carmichael was! Pulling out the broken fire basket, Meg piled sticks crisscross on the floor of the fireplace and finally coaxed it alight. Without sufficient draught to draw it, it was a feeble fire, but better than nothing. She discovered with misgivings that it took an age to heat even a small amount of water. As soon as she was well enough she would take the fire basket and get it fixed.

The next few days seemed to pass in a haze of sleeping and waking. On the third day, having fed Declan around midmorning, Meg must have dozed off for something jolted her into wakefulness. For a moment she lay blinking, trying to work out what time of day it was. Then she heard a sound at the bottom of the stairway. It was only the slightest creak but she froze, knowing that somebody was there, waiting.

'Hello, Meg Foggarty, are you at home?'

Although it was months since their meeting she immediately recognised Bartholomew Paige's voice. Her heart began to pound and she swallowed hard to calm herself.

'I – I'm coming,' she called, hastily scrambling out of bed and looking around for her clothes.

'Should I come up?'

'No!' Quickly she pulled her skirt on over her nightgown. For once Declan lay sleeping in his crib. She tiptoed over and picked him up before making her way down the stairs, wrapping her shawl about them both for warmth and protection.

Paige was standing in front of the empty fireplace, legs apart, hands clasped one over the other on the handly of a shiny cane. He looked confident, virtually impregnable. Meg had to remind herself that he was a kind man who looked after his workers. His cloak was fastened at the throat with what looked like a gold

119

buckle and his boots had the soft, cosseted look of good leather.

'Well now, I hear that you have a son.' He peered at the baby held close to his mother's bosom.

Meg nodded.

'Splendid. I merely called to see that you had everything you need.'

'I thank you, yes.' She longed for somebody to light the fire, boil a kettle and make her a hot nourishing drink.

'Good.' He was still looking at the child. 'I have never been blessed with an heir. Perhaps some day ...' He wandered across to the tiny window and peered out into the increasing gloom of the afternoon. He had to duck his head to see under the eaves and the action left Meg feeling small and vulnerable.

'Some day,' he repeated.

In spite of telling herself that everything was well, the room seemed alive with Meg's tension. She would have liked her employer to go but could not offend him. She felt weak and had no energy for social pleasantries. He was now studying a china cat on the mantel shelf which Mrs Carmichael had given her and gave a little grunt of dismissal.

'Right. I imagine it will be a week or two before you are ready to undertake your duties?'

She was aware that her hand was at her throat as if physically calming the breath that came in too fast bursts. 'I fear it may be longer than that, sir.'

Sensing his disappointment made her feel inadequate. What did other women do in such circumstances? 'I am keeping an eye out, sir. I'll be very thorough,' she said, thinking of the responsibility of keeping vagrants at bay.

'I'm sure you will, my dear.' He seemed to find the remark amusing. After a pause he added: 'I fear I'm leaving on the morrow. I just wanted to be sure that everything was going ahead as planned.'

She nodded uncertainly.

'Good. Well, next time I come I'll be able to watch you at work.'

Still she remained silent, not understanding what he meant.

120

There was a familiarity about his manner that made her uncomfortable.

'I can't tell you how I am looking forward to that time.' He came over and, lifting her chin, suddenly kissed her on the lips. She tried to turn her head away and push him back so that he did not crush the baby but the gloved hand was strong and determined.

'Mr Paige, please! I hardly think ...'

With a little laugh he let her go but held her gaze. She thought again that his pale eyes were fishlike, unfeeling. She began to shiver.

'Forgive me, my dear. I am presuming too much at such a time. Say that you pardon me.'

'Er ... yes, but I think you should go.'

'Right then.' He patted her paternally on the shoulder. 'Just you get back to bed. Take special care of yourself now for I really want you fit and well.'

As he turned towards the door, Meg closed her eyes, but the expensive pomade that oiled his hair lingered in the air. Suddenly she felt very lonely indeed.

Chapter Twenty-One

Meg spent the period of Christmas lying in. From her bed she could just see out of the small, deeply recessed window. The mornings were clear and crisp and the sun cast a gentle light into her room. As the days wore on the light faded and the room became darker and colder. She kept herself and Declan warm by wearing every article of clothing she possessed and staying deep beneath the blankets.

Daily Margy came to visit, bringing small tokens of food and snippets of news. Her friend's loyalty created sunspots in the otherwise unrelieved gloom.

'Mam's been confined.'

'She has?'

'Aye. Another girl. Can you imagine? That makes ten of us and two nippers.'

'Are they well?'

'They're both fine. Like pigs in muck, Pa says. Mam says to tell you to drink porter. It's good for the blood.'

'Tell her thank you.'

On Christmas Eve Mrs Carmichael herself arrived along with a servant laden with parcels. The older woman stomped up the stairs uninvited to the bedroom and looked about her. She made no comment but clearly the cottage was better than she expected.

'You have everything you need, my dear?'

'Thank you, ma'am. I'm well cared for.'

'Good.' Mrs Carmichael was peering into the crib, tutting at the sleeping form of Declan. 'What a beautiful infant! As soon as you are well I will have to photograph you. What a perfect Madonna and child!'

Today Mrs Carmichael had on one of her oriental dresses, made from material she had brought back from the east. It made her look like a Gypsy, wild, untidy, unconventional. Only the straight carriage of her sturdy body implied a pride in herself. She began to unpack some of the packages that the servant had placed on the floor beside the bed before retreating to wait outside.

'What do you intend to do now that you have the child?'

'Why, go back to work.' Meg was surprised by the question.

'At the brick works?'

Meg nodded.

'It is too hard for a feeding mother.'

This was something that Meg feared herself, but she did not say so. 'I am sure that Mr Downer will find me something lighter.'

Mrs Carmichael shrugged sceptically. 'How long do you intend to stay in this cottage?'

'Until such time as Mr Paige needs to demolish it.' Hoping to change the subject, she added: 'Having your own front door is something very precious.'

'As long as it is your door and not ...' Mrs Carmichael did not finish. 'Anyway, I wish you the very best for the new year, Meg Foggarty. If the sun shines next week, bring the youngster over and we'll take some pictures.'

'I will, thank you.'

To her embarrassment Mrs Carmichael bent over and kissed her. 'You're such a brave young woman.'

'Happy New Year, Ma'am.'

As the visitor left, Declan started to cry and Meg opened her gown and placed him at her breast. His eyes were closed and his small fists clenched and opened with pleasure as he drew the milk into his mouth. Meg traced her finger along his cheek, gently cradling the tiny head in her palm. The beginnings of Brendan's black waving hair tucked into the curve of his neck. Brendan. The void of loss opened.

She wondered again about the need to have the baby

baptised. Anything to stop her thinking about the man she loved. Since her ordeal at the church she had tried not to think about the whole question of religion and worship, but now she found her mind drifting back to Mrs Carmichael's 'Hamlet'.

There was really no reason why his opinion should matter, but it did. In spite of her humiliation in front of the congregation he had treated her with courtesy and she drew some small comfort from the knowledge. She had a vision of those warm hazel eyes so candid that they seemed to expose his every thought. It was hard to imagine that he could be devious or sly.

As they had stood outside the church, several people had approached him and asked for his services during the coming week. He had greeted each one with a friendly word, suggesting a time when they should call. It had not occurred to her to ask but now she found herself wondering what he did for a living. Whatever it might be, he was clearly very popular.

Her eyelids began to droop. The next thing she knew, Declan was crying and she realised that she must have fallen asleep with him still at her breast. He felt cold and she cuddled him into her shawl. Great waves of tiredness overcame her. She stretched and blinked. Come what may, she would have to go to the brick works next morning. Stay away any longer and there might be no job to go to. That would spell disaster.

The air had turned colder but Meg got out of bed and made her way shakily down the stairs. In spite of the fatigue she felt that she should get a little exercise in preparation for going out the next day. Her first thought was to warm the room and then remembered the broken fire basket. She was fed up with not being able to light a proper fire nor easily heat water. It would have to be fixed as soon as possible, which now meant waiting until after work the following Saturday.

The idea of a week of labouring increased her exhaustion. Tucking Declan into the crook of her arm, she dragged herself back upstairs. Her last thought before falling asleep again was of Bartholomew Paige and his wife standing side by side in the church. One thing was certain, no matter what the future held she would not allow herself to fear the brick master in the way that his wife surely did.

Chapter Twenty-Two

It was late on Saturday afternoon before Meg finished her first week back at the brickyard. Bill Downer had been as kind as circumstances would allow and Meg had spent her time sorting out the different types of bricks ready for the wagon to take them to the river for shipment to the mainland. It was still exhausting work but she had survived better than she had dared hope. She had even mastered the knack of feeding the babe while she worked, tucking him into her shawl so that he could suckle undisturbed by the rhythmic movement of her piling the bricks.

Finally it was four o'clock on Saturday and people were filing out of the yard. There was a sudden spring in the way they walked. The rest of the afternoon and all day Sunday would be theirs. Meg followed behind, grateful for the chance to rest before another week was upon them. She had remembered to bring the broken fire basket with her and hoped the smith would not have finished work for the weekend. She knew that his workshop was down by the brook but had never seen the man himself.

As she approached there was an ominous silence inside the workshop. She stood uncertainly in the yard, wondering what she would do if no one was there. Cautiously she peered through the open doorway. Although the embers glowed inside the forge, there was no sign of anyone. Meg came back outside and looked around, then walked round to the back. She could not believe the sight that greeted her.

In spite of the cold, in the yard behind the forge she came upon the smith washing off the soot and grime at the pump. It's him. She thought in amazement. It's Hamlet! The discovery threw her into confusion.

His head was bent forward under a cascade of water and he rubbed his face and hair vigorously, spitting out the water that had trickled into his mouth. Straightening up, he shook his black head and a spray of droplets splashed across the brick floor of the yard. Meg was back in another time. A sudden, heady vision of Brendan bathing in the woods immersed her. She was out of control and wanted only to run away.

Realising that he had company, the man hastily wiped his eyes with his fingers and turned to face her. For the moment Meg was bewitched by the sight of his white skin beneath the coal-black dust from his fire. His body stirred a suppressed hunger in her, aroused in that past existence whenever Brendan had dowsed himself at the end of a day's hard labour. She could not control her shaking.

Reuben Kingswell hastily fastened the top button of his cord trousers and pulled his braces back over his naked shoulders. His shirt was a sodden heap in the rivulet of water still running from the pump. He seemed oblivious to the cold.

'Can I help you, miss?'

She struggled to seem calm. 'I need to get this fixed. Quickly.' The request came out as haughty and demanding.

He reached out and took the basket, examining the broken pieces.

'Shouldn't be difficult. I can soon weld them together.' He looked back up at her. 'How soon is "quickly"?'

'Well, I can't heat water properly for the baby until it's fixed.' She was blinking fast to control her nervousness.

'In that case I'd better see what I can do.'

He signalled to her to follow and led the way back round to the forge.

'But you've just finished for the day,' she observed, now feeling fractionally calmer.

'Can't have the little one with no hot water.'

She felt a moment of gratitude towards him. His manner was easy and comfortable. The embarrassment subsided.

As she watched he began prodding the coals with a long

127

iron poker and then briefly squeezed his leather bellows into their mist so that they burned bright again. He was long-backed with wide shoulders, muscled by the constant swinging of the heavy hammers against the molten metal. He placed the broken parts of the basket into the furnace to heat them.

'You live nearby?' he asked, raising his voice to be heard above the roar of the fire.

'In the cottage by the green.'

'Oh, aye.' He hammered rhythmically. 'You there on your own?'

There was no insinuation in the question. 'Yes, with the baby,' she answered immediately.

'You a widow?' he asked.

To her consternation Meg blushed. 'I was never wed,' she answered shortly.

He turned his head and gave her a brief nod. 'I've never been wed.' His words seemed intended to ease any embarrassment she might feel.

She found herself explaining. 'My ... betrothed died. An explosion when they were blasting.' She said the words but still did not believe them. Fortunately Declan, who was now awake, started wriggling to be fed.

'It must have been hard for you.'

Meg shrugged. 'There's no explaining these things.'

'You must be angry.'

She nodded, grateful for his understanding.

'Damn!' He suddenly swore and leaped back from the fire as if stung.

'What's wrong?'

'It's only a spark.' He was examining his chest.

Meg came forward and regarded the reddening patch of skin. Already an angry blister formed a crescent shape above his right nipple.

'Let me fetch some salve.'

'There's no need. It's nothing.'

Realising how close she was to him, she stepped back, her face reddening, although whether from embarrassment or the heat of the furnace she was not sure.

'It's my fault. You wouldn't be working without a shirt if I hadn't interrupted you.'

128

He shrugged. 'It's no matter. I'm used to a few burns. See?' He held out one of his strong, grimed hands and she noted the pale scars crisscrossed on the darker skin.

The intimacy seemed suddenly to impinge on both of them and they fell silent. Meg looked at the baby and Reuben turned back to the whitening bands of iron that formed the fire basket.

'I'll just straighten this out,' he murmured and, turning his back on her, proceeded to work with vigour on the damaged article.

Finally the basket, newly assembled, was set to cool.

Reuben put his irons aside and wiped his hot forehead. He looked in need of another wash and Meg enjoyed the smell of his fresh sweat.

'How about a cup of tea before you go?' he offered. Already he had placed a large black kettle over the fire and it was beginning to sing.

'Why, that would be welcome.' Meg relaxed as she watched him put a pinch of tea between his fingers and thumb into an old china pot, then pour the steaming water onto it. A battered jug with a little milk was on the shelf at his side and he divided the contents between two tin mugs, adding a spoonful of sugar to each.

'Best part of the day,' he observed. 'I have my tea once a day. It's my luxury, that and frying up bacon here on the fire.' Looking up at her, he added: 'One of these days you must come to breakfast. I'll pick you the finest mushrooms over yonder and fry you the tastiest rashers you've ever had.'

Meg suddenly laughed. His manner and his quaint country way of speaking entranced her. Her spirits were lifted. Declan chose that moment to start to cry and without thinking she unfastened her bodice and began to feed him. Reuben looked away and she sensed his embarrassment, which in turn discomfited her. It seemed such a natural thing to do, as she would have done with Brendan, only this wasn't Brendan but a young unmarried man.

'Do you have a sweetheart?' she asked, not allowing herself to be shamefaced.

In response he grinned. 'I've had one or two. Nothing

129

serious, though. I always say, why pick just one flower when you can smell the whole bunch?'

Meg laughed. 'There's something in that, but there's something special too in having one "flower" that's just yours.'

Reuben nodded. 'I expect you're right.' He was looking directly at her now, meeting her eyes, and then he laughed again and turned away to pour the tea.

They sipped in silence and as soon as her mug was empty Meg put it aside and, turning her back, fastened her dress.

'I must go.'

'You're very pretty.'

She ignored the statement and Reuben bent to pick up the fire basket. 'Are you sure you can manage this?' he asked.

'Of course. I carried it here.'

'Aye, but then it was in two pieces. Now it's just one.'

She laughed at the crazy logic and he grinned at her, handing over the basket.

'How much do I owe you?'

'Nothing.'

'But I must pay.'

'You must?'

When she nodded he added, 'Well, in that case you owe me the pleasure of your company for breakfast on the morrow.'

She shook her head.

'You can't?'

She could think of no good reason other than the panic that his invitation engendered.

'You afraid I might poison you?' he asked.

'Of course not.'

'Then ...?'

Meg inclined her head to show that she had no answer.

'Then you'll come?'

'I've said I will. I always pay my debts.'

'But you aren't in debt to me.'

His face was suddenly serious and she was afraid that he could see her fears, her doubts. She wanted to be away. Without saying goodbye she turned and started to walk away, holding tight to her two loads.

130

'See you in the morning,' he called after her.

She did not reply but as she found safety again in the solitude of the country lane she had a vision of his face. Both of her burdens seemed suddenly lighter.

Chapter Twenty-Three

Next morning the smoky smell of bacon greeted Meg even before the smithy was in sight. The knowledge that Reuben Kingswell was cooking for her was bittersweet and recognising this was not without its dangers. She had to remind herself that she could manage alone, did not need a man for help or comfort.

Meg hesitated, wondering if it would not be best to go back home. She stood in the lane, the crisp light of the January sun, bathing herself and her child. The smell of the food and the thought of seeing the smith again, even if only once, was an indulgence she could not deny herself. She walked on.

It being Sunday morning, Reuben was not in his working clothes. In spite of her anxiety, the sight of his clean hair and scrubbed face brought a smile to her lips. Swallowing hard, she walked into the forge.

The furnace was not alight and he was cooking over a battered bucket filled with glowing coals. The black frying pan sizzled and spat as he turned it this way and that, pushing the contents about with a poker.

'It is clean,' he said, seeing her eyeing the implement.

She smiled.

'Here, there's a place for the babe.' He indicated a box lined with old sheeting that he had placed just inside the door.

'Thank you.' His thoughtfulness took her by surprise and she put the sleeping baby down.

She stood and watched him for the sheer pleasure of it.

There was something endearing in the way a man carried out a domestic task. The finesse of cutting and peeling and cleaning took on a clumsier but more practical aspect.

With a smile of satisfaction he ladled the mushrooms and bacon, a black-specked egg and greasy browned fried bread onto a plate and handed it to her along with an unpolished knife and fork.

'They need cleaning,' he apologised but she shrugged it aside.

Perched on a bench with the plate balanced precariously on her knees, she ate hungrily. The flavours were so mouthwatering that she knew this was a meal she would remember.

'Are you going to church today?' he asked with the merest hint of sarcasm.

She shook her head. 'How about you?' She made an effort to push the memory of the last visit away.

'Not me. I'm not comfortable with all those good folks.'

They both smiled, acknowledging kindred spirits. After a while he said: 'I wondered if you would like to come with me up over the downs. I could show you the countryside.'

'Won't we cause a scandal — walking out instead of attending church?'

'Will we?'

There was suddenly an infectious excitement between them.

'All right!' She felt the childlike enthusiasm for adventure returning. For today at least she would put her fears aside.

Reuben began to pack bread and cheese, some apples and a jar of beer into a sack. It was hardly the time of year for a picnic but the day was clear and the ground would be hard and dry. He hoisted the bag onto his shoulder and insisted on carrying the baby.

They walked in silence, the man laden like a donkey and Meg for once unencumbered. It occurred to her that since Declan's birth she had always had a burden to carry and the rare freedom seemed symbolic. Watching Reuben striding ahead, unconcerned about his load, also seemed like an omen.

Shaking off the fanciful notion, she picked up her skirts

and ran to catch up with him, puffing as the ascent through the wooded foothills steepened.

Emerging at the top, they both paused to get their breath.

'It's beautiful.' she said as they gazed across the breathless descent of the downs towards the sheer cliffs. 'Beautiful.'

Reuben turned to the right and started another ascent towards the brow of the hill.

'Are we allowed here?' Meg asked, suddenly feeling exposed by the isolation.

He shrugged. ''Tis private land, it belongs to Lord Tennyson, but I come here often. No one minds if you do no harm. Come on.'

'Wait. I can't go so fast.'

He slowed his pace to accommodate her. As they reached the brow of the hill he stopped and lowered his sack to the ground, Declan still tucked into the crook of his arm. He looked down at the baby, then held it out to its mother. Meg took him with an awkward smile.

'See there.' He pointed. 'That's where the old beacon burned. If ever there was danger it was lighted. It warned of the coming of the Armada.'

She gazed at the spot.

After a moment he said: 'It didn't warn me.'

'Warn you about what?'

'About you.'

'Me?'

He nodded. 'I haven't stopped thinking of you since I saw you in the church. You've invaded my heart.'

To her relief he suddenly laughed and she joined him. She could not cope with the feelings, his or hers, not yet. At the same time she knew that she wanted him to care. The knowledge scared her.

They picnicked near the beacon and then wandered back the way they had come. When they reached the village he insisted on seeing her home.

As they walked up the path of the cottage she was aware of his curiosity.

'You've landed on your feet. How did you manage to get this?'

Her heart began to beat uneasily. 'I'm looking after it.'

He pulled a wry face but said nothing.

Taking Reuben into the cottage, she bade him be seated while she lit the fire in the newly mended basket, ready to boil a kettle. All the time he was looking around, his shrewd eyes noting everything. She had the feeling that he could see right into her.

After a while he got up and went to stand by the window. 'Who does the cottage belong to?' he asked.

'The brickyard owner.'

'Who's that then?'

'A man called Paige.' She guessed what he was thinking and did not know how to justify herself.

'I'm using the cottage just until it is pulled down,' she said again lamely. 'Keeping an eye on things.' He did not reply.

When the kettle had boiled and she had made him tea, he continued to stand at the window.

'You need some help around here. The garden's in a fair tangle. I could give you a hand.'

'Thank you.'

'I could paint in here too.'

She bowed her head, not wanting to commit herself into his debt.

'Who looks after you?' she asked.

He told her about old Amos and Mrs Cheke.

It was already late afternoon and he announced his intention to leave. She wanted him to go to avoid his searching questions but she wanted him to stay because his company was warm and enveloping.

'Thank you for a lovely day.'

He grinned wryly. 'It's been a good day for me too.' Suddenly serious, he added: 'I hope there'll be more, or do you have some other commitment?'

'No.'

'I wondered about the brick owner – Paige, you said.' After a pause he asked: 'That's the stocky, arrogant fellow with the mouse of a wife?'

Meg nodded.

'Well, you be careful. It's none of my concern but I

135

wouldn't like to see someone I . . . liked . . . get too involved with the likes of him.'

'I'm not!'

He nodded but there was disbelief in his eyes. With a shrug he opened the door, saying: 'When I have time to spare I'll come and dig the garden.'

'That's kind. But I must pay you.'

With the already familiar grin he replied: 'You can cook me breakfast then, every day if you like.'

With a wave of his hand he was gone, leaving her to interpret the remark in whatever way she chose. She let out her breath with a long sigh and leaned back against the doorpost. Already she wanted to see him again but this feeling was dangerous. It only led to hurt and loneliness. In the shadow of this knowledge came the vision of Bartholomew Paige. Sooner or later he would return and then she feared she would have another debt to pay. Paige would not be content with breakfast.

'I can't.' She said the words out loud. Whatever her intentions had been before today, and she had not allowed herself to think them through, she knew now with certainty that she could never become Bartholomew Paige's mistress. What she did not know was where the decision would lead her.

Chapter Twenty-Four

When Meg came home from work the next evening Reuben was already there, digging relentlessly among the tangle of plants that had once been a vegetable patch. She was tired and sticky, her hair and clothes stiff with the hated pug, but her heart lifted as she saw him.

He did not look up and she leaned back against the gatepost and shifted Declan to her other shoulder so that she could watch him work. Finally he saw her and raised his hand in greeting.

'I didn't expect to find you here.'

'I knocked off early,' he said, continuing to ply the spade with a rhythmic thud against the hard earth.

She glanced towards the house, thinking now of washing and changing her filthy gown.

As if reading her thoughts, he added: 'There's water drawn in the pitcher. Nice and fresh. I've set the fire too.'

'You are good.'

He shrugged. Suddenly throwing the spade aside, he said: 'Here, give us the babe. You have five minutes to yourself.'

For a moment she hesitated, unwilling to let the child go, but seeing the honesty of his expression she finally held her baby out. To her shame his kindness brought tears to her eyes. She turned quickly away so that he should not see.

Inside she stripped off the rough fustian dress and began to bathe away the dirt. The water splashed across the flagstones and trickled out under the doorway.

Finally she was clean and as she went back outside it was

137

to see Reuben leaning back against the apple tree, talking and cooing to the child. Again her heart did strange things.

He gave a smile, including her in his amusement with the baby.

'He's a bonny boy.'

She nodded and took him back.

'I'll get us something to eat. You must be hungry after all that digging.' She gazed at the newly turned plot of earth.

'We'll have some veg in there,' he replied. 'Set you up for the year.'

Again she felt grateful. This is becoming a habit, she thought, but one that she did not want to break.

There were eggs and spinach and potatoes. It did not take long to prepare and she set out two plates and a board of bread and marge on the scrubbed table.

Reuben tucked in hungrily. She watched him covertly, the way he held his knife, the way he broke hunks of bread and put them into his mouth. At other meals now long past she had watched Brendan often enough.

As he finished eating Reuben carried his plate across to the sink and swilled it under the pump. The sink was one of the few modern installations.

'We'll have to get you a range.' he called above the swish of the water.

'And some gas lighting? And a grand privy?'

'And running water and your own carriage.' He joined in the game.

Meg smiled. 'You're very domesticated. How is it you help so much?'

He wiped his hands on his trousers before filling the kettle and placing it on the trivet over the fire.

'My old mum had sixteen young 'uns – and my father died when I was twelve. I saw the way she had to slave to keep us all clean and fed.'

'She had one good son at least.'

Reuben shrugged. 'Not really. She died when I was fourteen and by then I was serving my time with old Amos. I lived in – well, I had to, to make room at home for the rest.' He looked away from her. 'I suppose I still feel guilty because I was lucky. There was only Amos and his wife and

138

she made a fuss of me. She didn't have any children of her own. I did go home every other Sunday and work in the garden, though, chop wood and that sort of thing.'

He gave a little grunt, dismissing his reveries. 'And how about you, then? Where did you grow up?'

'In Norfolk, with my father and grandmother. My mam died when I was born.' The thought of an orphaned childhood prompted her to pick up Declan and hold him close.

'My gran brought me up. I was to go into service in a big house. I used to work there most days but just then – well, I met Brendan. He was leaving and I just went with him.'

'That must have been an adventure. I've never been off the island. I guess I'm not a wanderer.'

Meg shrugged. 'Brendan surely was. He never settled anywhere for long. He used to say that when he finally found his feet, we'd ... get wed.' She hesitated over the admission and wondered how much difference it would have made if they had been married.

Again, as if tuning into her thoughts, Reuben said: 'It might have been easier for you to be a widow.'

She nodded. 'It might, indeed.'

They both fell silent and the intimacy of the room suddenly became oppressive.

'I was looking out for some hens,' she observed, to break the silence.

'I'll find you some.'

'You're going to do a lot for me.' She smiled at him.

'Maybe.' Getting up, he arched his back to stretch the aching muscles. 'That'll depend.'

'On what?'

'On what it is you want.'

Meg shook her head. 'Just at the moment I don't know what I want. I'd like to stay safe. Declan doesn't have a grandmother to bring him up.'

'Then perhaps you should find him a new family.'

She did not reply and could not meet his eyes. When she remained silent, he said: 'Do you really think you need the brick master?'

Her face reddened. 'This is his cottage and I've got nowhere else to go.'

139

'Maybe not.' He moved towards the door. 'Seems to me you've had one mishap, been unlucky. I think perhaps you've got a choice now.'

'I have?'

'Most women want to be decently wed.'

'They do? And who am I to wed, then?'

In the disconcerting way he had, he suddenly grinned. 'Well, if you can't capture some rich chap, then perhaps you should settle for someone poor and common, like a handsome young smith.'

'I don't know any young smith who would want me.'

He raised his eyebrows and beneath the joking manner there was a seriousness.

Carefully she added: 'You don't know me.'

He shrugged his shoulders. 'You don't know me − yet.'

'Reuben − don't hurry things.' The past was coming back to haunt her, and the future also threatened; Paige, Reuben and his expectations. She was afraid.

He was looking at her questioningly. 'I don't understand you. My life's been ordinary. I can't promise to understand but I'll try. Do you want to tell me what it is that worries you?'

Meg shook her head. After a while she changed the subject. 'I have to go to Simla tomorrow. Mrs Carmichael is illustrating some book. Can you imagine, she wants me to be in it − my picture, that is.'

'Who better?' Like Meg, he seemed relieved to change the subject.

She said: 'She asked me about you. She needs a man to photograph.'

Already he was shaking his head. 'Not me. Once was enough.' As an afterthought he added: 'But I suppose I should be grateful. If it hadn't been for that Hamlet fellow, I wouldn't have met you. By the way, in the story, did he marry Ophelia?'

Meg shook her head. 'She drowned.'

At Simla Meg sat for two long hours while her picture was taken. As a reward for her patience, when Mrs Carmichael had finished she showed her how to remove the plates to

140

process them and how to prepare some more.

'Where do you buy these?' Meg asked, lifting the heavy glass from the camera.

'I have them specially made, diamond-cut, and then I prepare them myself. Now, you've seen me develop them but if you wish you can prepare your own plate and take an image of your little one.'

Meg nodded and her palms felt dry. This was a complicated process and she was afraid of making a mistake.

'The very first thing you must do is to wash the plate until it is perfect. The slightest blemish, even coughing on it or leaving it in a damp atmosphere, can damage it. I've had some soaking for several hours in that solution there – nitric acid it is, so be careful with it. It will have destroyed any impurities so your first job is to wash it thoroughly in water and then dry it with a clean cloth.'

Meg nodded and followed the instructions. When the plate was shining she held it out, but Mrs Carmichael shook her head. 'It may look clean but there is always some residue. Before you can prepare it, give it a good polish with ammonia. Here you are.'

Meg crinkled her nose at the acrid smell and blinked back stinging tears. 'That's horrible,' she remarked.

'Horrible but effective, my dear. Now, this is where you start the preparation.' She handed Meg a cumbersome bottle.

'What's this?'

'That's the collodion.' The heady smell of ether pervaded the tiny shed and Meg breathed deeply. She felt quite light-headed.

'The solution has to be perfect. I've drained it so that there is no sediment and now it's a question of coating the plate and not leaving any smears or drips.' As she spoke, Mrs Carmichael deftly tipped the plate in every direction until the surface was entirely coated. The excess liquid dripped into the bath below. 'Keep it moving,' she advised. 'As you'll see, a surface film is beginning to set. We don't want the faintest ripple. It has to be completely smooth.'

Gingerly Meg took over the task of rocking the plate.

'Good.' Mrs Carmichael studied the plate and said: 'Now

141

you immerse it in the silver bath – that's right. That's nitrate of silver. That is what sensitises the plate. Good girl. I think you have an aptitude for this.'

Meg flushed with pleasure and tried to recall everything that she had been told. Meanwhile the plate had taken on a yellow hue and Mrs Carmichael declared that it was ready for the camera.

Once it was rested face down in the carrying frame, they hurried back out into the garden where Nancy the maid had been entertaining Declan. Under instruction Meg inserted the box into the camera and then bent her head to peer through the spyhole. The upside-down world of Mrs Carmichael's glass house and Meg's sleeping child was revealed.

In the meantime Mrs Carmichael rummaged in a corner and produced a large piece of card upon which were the images of Meg and Reuben Kingswell.

Meg's surprise at the faithful image was mingled with the memory of that crazy afternoon when she had rested her hand on the stranger's arm and implored him to love her. Her face grew hot.

Their heads were close together and she had to admit that she did look beseeching. Reuben on the other hand, had turned his face just a fraction as if to shake her off. Only his eyes betrayed his embarrassment. She studied him. His face, half in profile, was powerful, the sort of face to inspire confidence. His mouth, slightly parted, revealed his regular teeth. His thick black hair framed his head and, thinking of his presence, his voice, his humour, Meg felt a moment of pure pleasure. The discovery confused her.

'Now to compose your photograph. Choose you subject and plan your own setting.'

Meg thought how wonderful it would be to see Declan recorded in a picture. Besides, he was sleeping peacefully, so she needn't worry about getting him to keep still.

Cautiously she followed her teacher's instructions. She was half afraid to point the camera at her son in case it did him harm but she told herself not to be foolish and went ahead. Through the lens she could see the sleeping babe, his head tilted to one side, a piece of silk wound about his naked limbs.

'How much does a dark box cost?' Meg asked.

'I can't say. Several pounds. Mine was a present from my daughter. I have had it for some time now but they are making new ones every week. There are special photographic depots in most towns now.' Mrs Carmichael sniffed and puffed out her bosom, a mannerism that Meg recognised as meaning 'let's get down to business'.

At last the photograph was revealed. Slowly the likeness of the sleeping babe emerged upon the blackened plate. 'It's beautiful! It's a part of Declan captured for ever.' In spite of having witnessed it, Meg was still amazed by the process. It struck her that every mother in the village would want such a picture of her child.

Mrs Carmichael declared herself surprised and pleased with the result. 'We'll make a contact copy of your picture onto paper.'

'Is it just ordinary paper?'

'It's been specially treated with chloride of silver, then egg white.'

'Egg white?'

She thought she was being teased but Mrs Carmichael did not play jokes. The older woman ignored her surprise and helped her to transfer the image. 'The albumen gives it a nice shiny quality,' she explained. 'Sometimes I find it hard to remember whether I am developing photographs or making meringue.'

Meg laughed but her amusement gave way to disbelief as she watched the photographic process reversed so that the pale areas of her negative were replaced with a dark image on the albumen paper as light was allowed onto it. She resisted the impulse to say that it was magic or miraculous, knowing that Mrs Carmichael would once again remind her that it was science.

'There.' The picture was beautiful. In the very centre, his body arched gently, his small fists clasped, his head tilted to one side, was her son. It was ...

Mrs Carmichael insisted that she take the treasured portrait home.

'Oh, thank you!'

The older woman inclined her head. 'I hear you are getting help from the blacksmith.'

Meg hesitated, unsure whether it was an accusation. 'That's right.' She felt suddenly defensive and defied even Mrs Carmichael to criticise.

Instead her mentor said: 'He's a good-looking young man, don't you think?'

Meg looked away. 'Good looks aren't everything,' she observed neutrally.

'Of course not, look at me.' The older woman paused to study another of her plates, tipping it towards the light to see if there were any flaws before continuing. 'I have the mixed fortune of having more beautiful sisters but it has not prevented me from finding fulfilment. I have a dear, devoted husband and lovely children.' She looked up before adding: 'And I have a skill that lets me mingle with the famous and the beautiful. Mr Herschel, Mr Garibaldi, Lord Tennyson, Mr Watts, they all succumb in the end.'

Meg regarded her large, square, pendulous face with affection and Mrs Carmichael smiled at her. 'Good looks are a pleasant bonus.' Suddenly serious again, she said: 'Have you given any more thought to your future? It's time you left that brick works.'

'I can't.'

'Why not?'

Meg struggled to find the words. Finally she said: 'Mr Paige owns my cottage. If I leave the yard I won't be able to live there any more.'

Mrs Carmichael's expression was guarded. 'Do you mean that he has a hold over you?'

'No.' Meg was aware that she did not know exactly what the truth was.

'Well, I'm pleased to hear it.' The older woman sighed. 'Perhaps at some time in the future I will have a vacancy for a maid.'

Before Meg could comment, her benefactor said: 'Come along, child, you don't want to labour in that brick works all your life, do you? You do have a choice.' Her eyes suddenly sparkling, she added: 'Perhaps you should marry your smith.'

'He's not my smith, ma'am.'

'He could be. He was quite a firebrand when he was a youngster.'

'In what way?'

Mrs Carmichael shook her head. 'Perhaps I shouldn't be telling you this, giving away secrets he'd rather keep.'

'Is it something bad?'

'Of course not.' Mrs Carmichael held out the picture of Meg and Reuben. 'Here, take this with you. I meant what I just said about your choices. You are young; if you can't decide between finding other employment or having a husband, why don't you try both?'

Chapter Twenty-Five

At first, Reuben came once or twice a week to help with Meg's garden, but gradually, as she came home hot and dusty from work, it was to find him there more and more often. After about a month, she realised that he was visiting her every day.

She was anxious about what was expected of her. Religiously she cooked him a meal and offered to mend any tears or holes in his clothing, but still this did not seem to be payment enough. While accepting the food, he declined to let her do anything else for him.

'You've got enough to do for yourself. Mrs Cheke will always do my mending – any that I don't do for myself.'

'But I feel I should repay you.'

His expression became serious, as if covering up some deep emotion which should not, or could not, be voiced. 'Just let me come here. I enjoy it, every moment.'

She began to let his presence wash over her. The soothing pleasure of his caring, the looking after that had been denied her for so long, was sweet enough. For the time being she did not allow herself to think further.

On Sundays he called as well, dragging her out into the countryside to share his joy in the familiar landscapes. It was comforting, uncomplicated and yet wrought with potential danger. Sometimes she felt as if they were poised before a treasure house. There was joy in the contemplation of it and yet neither of them suggested that they should actually go inside, help themselves to the wealth of pleasure that was there for the taking. Who knew what the price would be?

Yet, in spite of all her intentions, it was becoming a habit. He was becoming a habit.

His holding back was a reassurance. It gave her confidence and self-respect. He did not come just to take pleasure from her body, indeed he had not so much as kissed her, yet perversely his self-control left her aching to be touched.

The weeks passed in a haze of work and sleep; spring came and blossomed into summer. As Meg came home on the first Monday of July it was to discover that her hedge had been cut and some beans and rhubarb picked. She smiled to herself.

'Come and see.' Reuben came round from the back of the house, wiping his hands on his trousers, automatically taking Declan from her. Holding her by the wrist, he pulled her along with him. 'There, see that? You've got a Christmas dinner laid on.'

A large white goose was exploring its newly erected pen.

'Oh! But that's months away.' She turned to him and laughed but her smile faded as the hunger for him surfaced. 'You're very good to me.'

'You know why.' He did not take his eyes from her face.

Meg looked away, her need for him fighting with the fear. She stood so for too long and his response was to step back. She knew that he was hurt.

'Right, well, I'd best be going.'

'But aren't you going to stay for a bite to eat?' He always did, always. The thought of his leaving in anger caused cold fingers of fear to tighten around her heart.

'Perhaps I come here too often. Perhaps you're afraid of the talk.' His voice was cold.

'Are people talking?'

He shrugged. 'No doubt they do. My "interest" in this place has been mentioned by some of my patrons.'

She did not know what to say. A barrier of resentment seemed to have grown up between them. He was within reach but she could not touch him. She didn't know if she would ever be able to, if she dared.

'I was going to do dumplings.'

'The way to a man's heart . . .'

Suddenly he was all right again, joking; he wasn't going to

leave. As she turned into the cottage to wash and then begin to cook, she wanted to skip with relief.

They ate in near silence, just the occasional small talk to fill the empty moments. As usual it was Reuben who cleared the table while she fed and settled Declan. Everything was back to normal, the way she wanted it to be, only she knew that it wasn't. Nothing stayed the same. She was suddenly frightened again.

She made a tentative remark about the brick works, anything to break the tension.

'Is that what you're set to then?' he asked. 'Working there for the rest of your life?'

Meg's breathing seemed suspended. There was no pretending that everything was the way it had been before. The time for playing at friendship was over, she knew it.

Aloud she said; 'I've managed to cope with the job so far. If I can make a success of this, then perhaps I can better myself. People might stop treating me like an outcast.'

He shrugged. 'Is that your ambition? To win the approval of the villagers? You think that by working hard you will become respectable?'

It was her turn to shrug. For once she wanted him to do something, break down all the barriers, tell her what to do. She stole a glance at him and was frightened by the cold, hard expression on his face. He was not looking at her.

'Will you come tomorrow?' She did not know why she asked. She had never done so before.

He did not answer and she moved closer to him. He stood with his back half towards her and she longed to reach out and touch him, take him in her arms, but she was both scared he might push her away, and afraid he might hold her close.

Finally he said: 'I want more than this. Some day I want to get wed. If that isn't what you want you'd best say so now.'

Slowly he turned towards her and there was longing in his eyes. In spite of herself she reached out her arms. Then he was holding her, kissing her, swaying against her as if he would lose himself in her being.

'I love you,' he murmured against her hair and before she could answer he buried her mouth beneath his own.

She gave herself up to it, did not resist the intimacy of his body pressed hard against her. But suddenly an ominous, chilling memory from the past caused her to freeze: Brendan lying dead, not even beautiful but disfigured, charred. She pushed him away.

'What is it?' He reached out to hold her again but she backed away, shaking her head.

'No,' she said simply.

'No, what?' He waited.

She could not answer.

'You don't want me?'

'Yes.'

'Then you want to wait until we're wed?'

Again she shook her head.

'Then what?'

Finally she said: 'Please, Reuben, it's no good. There's no future with me.'

'I don't understand. I ... hoped you cared for me.' When she could not reply, he added: 'Are you waiting for your master to return?'

For a moment she did not know what he meant, then he added: 'His foreman thinks you're his mistress.'

A vision of Paige made her shudder. He had not returned to the island since he had come to the cottage after Declan's birth but some time soon he surely would. Aloud she said: 'I'm not. Perhaps I could have been, but since I met you ...' She didn't know what to say.

'Have you slept with him?' His voice was low and cold. She suddenly felt that he did not know her at all.

She was about to deny it when the anger seized her. 'And who are you to be asking me these questions?' she suddenly stormed.

'Aye, who indeed?' He grabbed his hat and lifted the latch. As he pushed his way clumsily out into the cold night, he shouted: 'Don't forget to feed the goose.'

'Reuben! When will I see you?' Her call met with silence. He had already gone.

Left alone, Meg hugged herself to drive out the pain. She didn't know what to think, what to feel. Life without Reuben would be empty and desolate. She wanted his smile, his support and – yes – his body. She ached with emptiness.

Meg leaned her head back to ease the tension in her neck and sighed. It was no good. Her fear of losing him was so great that she would rather send him away herself than let fate play another cruel trick as it had done in taking Brendan.

Interlocking her fingers, she squeezed them tight together to strengthen her resolve. I've got Declan, she thought, and Margy and Mrs Carmichael. I've got the cottage and a job. I'm a very lucky woman. Her inner voice scoffed at her foolishness. What was the point of it all with no one to share it with? What in life could compensate for a warm body next to hers at night, a strong loving man to protect her? Her anguish overwhelmed her.

She hardly slept. Next morning she dragged herself to work and somehow struggled through the day. Declan was grizzly and Meg guessed that he was teething. She rubbed the gold of her brooch along his gums. Pure gold was said to ease the inflammation. For a while she stood looking at the lover's knot, the delicate tracery and the way the metal seemed to fold and intertwine. The small luminescent pearls glistened as if with unshed tears. She thought that there were plenty more to come.

After work, as she walked back to the cottage, she hardly dared look into the garden in case he was not there. Quietly she pushed the gate open and crept along the grass verge so that she should not be heard. Everything was ominously silent. She peered hopefully in through the back door but the kitchen was empty. Declan began to struggle so she sat him on the sacking which served as a doormat. He propelled himself across the flagstones on his bottom, making baby noises.

Meg went quickly back outside and forced herself to walk to the bottom of the garden. The goose hissed at her but otherwise there was silence. He had not come.

She collected the eggs from the hen run and went back indoors. 'Mama'll boil you an egg,' she said to Declan. 'Soft-boiled.' All the time she was thinking. Please let him just be delayed.

When the babe had eaten a little of the egg yolk, Meg held

him to her breast and rocked him. The movement eased her own pain, releasing the anguish with each movement. Soon Declan's eyes closed and leadenly she carried him upstairs and placed him in his crib. He was almost too big for it but for the present there was no other bed.

Downstairs she tidied up automatically and carried a few scraps out to feed the poultry. As she was scraping it into the run, she heard the gate click. Her heart somersaulted and it was several seconds before she could bear to turn round.

'Am I welcome?'

She gazed at him, noting the questioning look on his face. It was all she could do to stop herself from running and flinging her arms about him. 'I thought you'd deserted me,' she said by way of reply.

'Yes, well, that isn't very easy to do. I'd like to have a talk with you.'

Silently they walked around the garden. As they did so he stopped to pull up a weed here, break off an overhanging twig there. This is his garden, she thought; he made it. She didn't know what the admission meant.

Finally he said: 'I'm sorry for what I said, about your master. I ... I just feel jealous of any man who is part of your life. I know it's not true.'

Meg remained silent. Tonight she would choose her replies carefully. She only knew that she didn't want to lose him.

'I've been thinking. When old Amos dies I shall have a cottage of my own. In the meantime I haven't got a place to offer you a home.'

She waited.

'I can't bear the thought of you struggling at the brick works. There's no need.' He turned towards her and took her hand. 'Let's get betrothed. I won't hurry you into anything but there's no need for you to go on working. I'll rent a cottage somewhere and you can live there.'

She didn't know what to say. What he was offering was everything that she wanted and yet the fear still remained.

'People would still talk, you coming to visit, and us not wed.'

'Is that what is worrying you?'

'No.'

151

'Then what?'

She couldn't tell him, not about Brendan and the fear of losing people. There weren't any words to explain.

'Then would you rather stay here? The next time the brick master visits the island I could see him and arrange to pay him rent. That way you could carry on living here but you wouldn't be beholden to him.'

The air was charged with uncertainty. Meg didn't know if they had reached an agreement or not. Their eyes met and he said: 'Tell me you don't care for me and I'll accept it — but I don't think you can.'

Still she didn't say anything. Her mind would not work fast enough to think of all the implications. Again her only thought was that she did not want him to go.

'I can't explain,' she said at last. 'I'm so afraid of ...' She could not bring herself to say 'being hurt'. Tears started to prickle along her eyelids. Taking a deep breath, she said: 'I don't want to live without you.'

'Meg!' He pulled her to him and began to kiss her. His mouth seemed to breathe life into her, lift her out of the abyss of fear that held her fast. She closed her arms around him and wished that she could lose herself in his very being. She was aware of the hardness in his groin and did not draw away as he pressed closer against her but eventually he stood back.

'I'll not ask you to do anything wrong. God knows how much I want you but I'll not have them counting the months until our first baby's born. We're going to do it right, you and me. Hold our heads up high.' As an afterthought, he said: 'Don't make me wait too long.'

She shook her head, smiling tenderly at him; then, suddenly serious, she said: 'What about Declan?'

'What about him?'

She shrugged. 'If we have children of our own ...'

He pulled her close again. 'You foolish girl. Don't you trust me? As far as I'm concerned Declan's my first-born. Don't you have no fears about that.'

She rested her head against his shoulder and cool ripples of happiness bathed her. She thought how pleased Mrs Carmichael would be. Marry your smith, she had said — he was such a firebrand when he was younger.

Meg opened her eyes. 'What did you used to do when you were younger?'

'In what way?'

'Mrs Carmichael called you a firebrand.'

He grinned at her. 'I used to be good with my knuckles, always getting into fights. But that was the beer. When I'd had a few too many ...'

She felt herself tense against him and he looked down at her. 'What's wrong?'

'I could never share my life with a man who drank, or gambled.'

He raised his eyebrows, perplexed at the way things were going. 'Have you ever seen me drunk — or even drink?'

Slowly she shook her head.

'Well, you won't. That was a long time ago. You're afraid of me? That I might do that?' He didn't look as if he could believe it.

'My father was always in the pub. Brendan drank all the time, and gambled. That's why we ran away, to the island.'

Reuben hugged her close. 'Then it's an ill wind, my love. If you hadn't taken up with a tippling, gambling traveller, you would never have been here in my arms. I thank God that you are.'

With a great sense of relief, she let her head rest again against his shoulder. For the first time in a very long time, she began to think that there was some purpose in life after all.

Chapter Twenty-Six

Meg would not have believed that it was possible to feel so happy. The morning after Reuben's proposal of marriage he arrived at the cottage just as she was leaving for work. She watched him dismount from Ginny the mare, loop her reins over the fencepost, leap over the gate and come hurrying along the garden path, whistling. The very sight of him made her want to laugh with joy.

'Come here.' He took her hand and led her down into the garden. 'Stand there, under the apple tree. I've got something to say.'

Meg waited. Her face felt warm and relaxed by the constant smile on her lips.

Wiping both hands across his mouth and preparing himself as if for some major event, Reuben sank onto one knee.

'Meg Foggarty, I want you for my wife. I want you to have this as a token.' He reached out for her hand and pushed a slim gold keeper onto her finger.

She looked down at it in amazement. The slender ring was carved with interlinking loops like the links in a chain.

'It goes on for ever,' he said, 'round and round. No breaking it. For ever.'

It fitted perfectly and she thought: This is an omen. We're meant for each other. Leaning forward she kissed the crown of his head as he still knelt before her. His hair smelled of wood and smoke and a special manliness that was his alone. He nestled against her breast and the gentle pressure of his face filled her with warmth. For a long peaceful time she stood there, just holding him. She never wanted the moment to end.

Finally he got to his feet and kissed her, swinging her round until she laughingly protested. She yielded herself up to him willingly, safe in the knowledge that whatever happened he would protect her.

'It's lovely,' she said, turning the ring on her finger.

'A lovely ring for a lovely girl. I must go; farmer Attrill's bringing his team round at eight and I still have shoes to make.'

'Reuben – you don't mind if I carry on living here?' The doubt was back in her mind. She had to be sure.

'I've already said. If you think that's all right, then that's the way it'll be.' He held her eyes and she knew that he was looking for some reason why she should ask. She did not know the answer herself.

Reuben kissed her again and she watched him walk up the path, then ride along the lane until he disappeared from sight. With a sigh of satisfaction she collected Declan and left the cottage a few minutes behind him.

At the brick works she told Bill Downer of her intention to leave.

Bill nodded his understanding. 'Why, I'm sorry to hear it in one way but it's no more than you deserve. Young Reuben'll take good care of you, I'm sure. He's a decent chap.'

Meg hesitated. 'Reuben'll talk to Mr Paige about the cottage, but, in the meantime, do you think that it's all right to stay there?'

'Why, yes, of course. I can't see no harm in it.'

'Thank you.' She felt relieved. Everything seemed to be working out.

Margy was starry-eyed at the news of Meg's betrothal.

'Oo, our Meg, you are lucky! He's the handsomest man in the village – but then you're the prettiest girl.'

'I'm not!'

'You are! And just look at that ring. You can see 'tis real gold.'

Margy tilted her head as if she had suddenly thought of some snag. 'What will Mr Paige say when he hears you've stopped work? He likes you.'

'He doesn't. Anyway, Mr Downer's going to tell him and

Reuben'll sort everything out as soon as the master makes his next visit.'

'You sure he won't mind?'

Meg shook her head and spread her hands out as if to prove the point. 'Instead of me living there free he'll be getting a rent. Whatever could he have to mind about?'

The day passed quickly for Meg, absorbed in happy thoughts, and, after leaving the brick works, she set out to walk the half-mile to Simla. She chose to go by the path that skirted Farringford, the home of Lord Tennyson. She liked this route because there was always something happening.

As she slipped through the narrow gate that gave onto the lane, it was alive with weekend pilgrims jostling for position in the hope of getting a glimpse of the famous poet. Many had travelled by train just for the day, crossing on the steamer as part of a special excursion. Others had taken rooms nearby and patrolled the perimeter of the estate in the hopes of bumping into their idol on one of his outings.

Meg had to push her way past a group of earnest young people standing near the entrance to the house. The men supported themselves on malacca canes and their sisters, sweethearts or wives sheltered from the unusually fierce sun beneath parasols. The girls paid her little attention but she was aware of appreciative glances from the men. It increased her sense of wellbeing. There was a rumour that Lord Alfred was expected to leave shortly for the bay and the air was tingling with anticipation.

Several young men had climbed into the elms that surrounded the estate and were scanning the garden in the hopes of spying Lord Alfred among the shrubbery. Young women clasped volumes of his poetry in the hope of obtaining the famous man's signature, and one or two were reading aloud for the delectation of those nearby. Meg guessed that they would all be disappointed, for, according to Mrs Carmichael, Lord Alfred had a positive terror of being approached by his admirers. If he left Farringford it would either be before dawn or after dusk, in disguise or by the new bridge that took him across into the wilderness behind his home.

The entrance to Simla was a few hundred yards further

on and, still smiling, Meg skirted the elegant frontage and went round to the servants' entrance. She knew the maid, Mary, who answered her knock, as another of those who acted as Mrs Carmichael's models. The girl looked refined, even majestic, but when she spoke her accent was broad and rural. 'She's got company. His Lordship's visiting from up the road.'

Meg thought of the hopeful apostles who waited in vain. Aloud she said: 'It doesn't matter. Please give her a message. Tell her that Meg Foggarty has left the brickworks and is now betrothed to Reuben Kingswell!'

Mary grinned. 'I hope you'll be very happy.'

The weeks passed peacefully. Instead of going to the brick works, Meg presented herself at Simla Lodge most working days. Mrs Carmichael was now busily illustrating Lord Tennyson's latest work and was pleased to have her model available at a moment's notice.

Mr and Mrs Carmichael were shortly going on an extended visit to their son who lived abroad, but, before they left, the mistress of the house was preparing to take some pictures to an exhibition in London. Standing in her garden studio, she pored over each print in an agony of indecision. Among them were portraits of both Meg and Declan.

'What do you think, this one or that?'

Meg studied them critically. 'I like that one best. The children look like angels. How do you get their faces to shine out of the shadows like that?'

Mrs Carmichael drew in her breath. 'It's a question of lighting. I cover up some of the panes in the glass house so that I can direct the light where I want it. You may not have realised it but when you took that likeness of your son you arranged him in exactly the right place. If you had turned him round his face would have been in the shadow.' After a pause she added: 'I think you have a natural flair for composing a picture.'

Meg felt pleased with the compliment. She went off to the well for more water to wash off her patron's latest batch of plates. This was one of the worst jobs, drawing up bucket after bucket until her arms screamed in protest and her shoes

157

were wet with slopped water, but it had to be done.

'I want these to last for ever,' Mrs Carmichael said fancifully. 'They are my small claim to immortality – they and my children.' She picked up another picture of Meg and Declan. It was hazy, slightly out of focus and rather underdeveloped, but that gave it an ethereal, almost religious quality. Mrs Carmichael grunted with satisfaction. She looked across at Meg. 'I'm glad you're getting married. This is one of my favourite portraits but – ' She hesitated. 'While you are neither a virgin nor a wife it is rather difficult to show it. Everyone who has seen it so far has wanted to know more about you. It's a good job your smith has come to his senses. When do you plan to wed?'

Meg frowned, wondering what Mrs Carmichael meant. 'Did Reuben tell you he was going to propose to me?' she asked.

'The other way round. I told him to get on with it. Men are such dunderheads.'

The disclosure left Meg feeling uneasy. She would have been happier if Reuben had come to his own decision without any prompting from this all too forceful lady.

'I don't know,' she said in reply to Mrs Carmichael's question. 'We haven't called the banns yet. At the moment we've nowhere of our own to live.' To forestall any advice from her patron she quickly added: 'One day Reuben will own the forge cottage but not til Mr Mew – ' This sounded callous, as if she wanted Amos Mew dead, so she corrected herself: 'We'll probably wed soon. Reuben is going to talk with Mr Paige about renting my cottage.'

Mrs Carmichael did not appear to have heard, but just as Meg was turning her mind to something else the older woman said: 'We're going back to Simla, where we had our plantation. My son farms there now. I doubt if we'll be back within a year.' She straightened up and gave a little grunt of discomfort as if her back were troubling her. Her face became serious and she hesitated before adding: 'I wouldn't be so sure about the cottage. If you want my advice, don't start counting your chickens. You might be wiser to look somewhere else. If you'll forgive the bad joke, I can't help thinking that Mr Paige is something of a bad egg!'

Meg felt herself begin to blush. She remembered Paige's kiss and felt that in some way she must have been to blame. Perhaps she had encouraged him, given him the wrong idea. Anyway, he had apologised.

She was touching up a negative of a rather beautiful young woman who had recently been a guest of the Carmichaels. She was a lady, not a working girl like Meg. Her breeding showed in the confident way she held herself and the cut of her dress, but the picture was marred by the too fine reproduction of her freckles on the negative. Painstakingly Meg was darkening each minute spot with a pencil so that when the print was made the tiny blemishes would be no more.

'Mr Paige is all right,' she said. 'He is a decent Christian. I'm sure he'll understand about me leaving his employ, and I'll still look after the house.'

There was a pause before Mrs Carmichael replied: 'You think so, my dear? Then I very much hope that you are right.'

Reuben was just finishing for the day when Mrs Carmichael walked into the forge.

'Ma'am?' He raised his hat and waited for her to speak.

'Kingswell. You may have heard that my husband and I are leaving the island. Mr Carmichael is going on Saturday but I'm staying for a few days to tidy things up. On the way to the steamer I want you to come with me as far as Whippingham to look at a carriage horse. It is Lord Alfred's birthday on the 6th and I want to surprise him. I shall then be travelling straight on to the mainland from Cowes. You can arrange for the delivery.'

'Yes, ma'am.'

'Will you come then? Good. Remember it's a secret. Not a word to anyone.'

'Of course not.'

As Mrs Carmichael left, Reuben took off his leather apron and turned his mind to other things.

He began to wonder about old Amos. Just lately the old man seemed to be getting more muddled. Some nights he got up at two in the morning saying that he had to go to work, and other days he had difficulty in remembering who

159

Reuben was. Reuben sighed. He'd have to ask Meg to keep an eye on his master while he was away with Mrs Carmichael. He didn't want anything to happen to him.

He went to the door and looked out into the sunset. Meg would be at the cottage and he felt a tremor of warmth at the thought of seeing her. He noticed someone lurking outside the forge, a dirty, shabby creature, hardly more than a girl. She looked half starved and as he had bread and cheese left from his nammet he held it out to her. She did not move but stared at him with wide, vacant eyes.

He called out. 'Here ye are. Don't be afeared.'

She remained where she was and he thought that perhaps she was deaf and dumb. She looked daft, too. After he damped down the fire he made a point of leaving the food just outside the door where she would see it. Poor lass. He suspected that she slept in the forge at night but he couldn't see that it did any harm.

Chapter Twenty-Seven

Since the start of the year, the pressure of his business enterprises had taken Bartholomew Paige abroad. It was his first taste of foreign travel and in many ways it was satisfying, but during his trip he had found to his surprise that thoughts of Meg Foggarty intruded even in the most diverting situations.

As soon as he arrived back in England, his first thought was to go to the island and visit her. He stayed at home just long enough to have his linen washed and to check on his business affairs.

'You needn't unpack my things,' he said to Edith. 'Just check that my special bag is replenished and get my clothes laundered.'

'Yes, dear.'

Paige didn't give Edith the satisfaction of saying where he was going. He liked to keep her guessing. She picked up his special bag and took it upstairs. He always kept it packed ready with emergency supplies in case he was called away. All his pills and potions, a change of linen, collar studs, brushes, cuff links, writing materials, they were all there. There were even spare bullets for the gun he had bought especially to take abroad to America. He thought to himself with some relief that at least he wouldn't need the gun on the island. Renegades and robbers were mercifully scarce.

He set out on his journey on the following Friday. On the steamer he was able to think about the days ahead, and particularly about Meg. Unless his memory played him false she was an exceptional girl. She had the perfect combination of qualities; good looks, good health and poverty. Paige had come to a novel decision.

When he reached the island he had his luggage conveyed to the guesthouse at the bay and made his own way to the brick works. He felt quite ridiculously excited, like a young boy looking for his first sexual conquest. Using the pretence of visiting the proposed housing development, he would arrange to see Meg that very evening. His whole body was alive with the anticipation.

As he arrived at the site, he saw Bill Downer over by the kilns. The foreman stopped what he was doing to come hurrying over. Paige glanced covertly around but could not see Meg. He thought that later on he would set her up permanently in the cottage, but for the moment it was best that she continued to labour at the brick works. Until he had established his reputation locally he could not risk a scandal. With an added frisson of pleasure he thought that what he had in mind for Meg would definitely require her to stop working.

'Mornin', Mr Paige, sir.' Bill Downer doffed his cap and Bartholomew made a few cursory enquiries about production and any problems. He listened impatiently to the man's account and as soon as he decently could he asked: 'Where's that Irish girl?'

'Meg Foggarty, sir? She's not here.'

'How, not here?' He felt alarm and disappointment rising.

'Not here at the brick works. She's given up working, sir. Gotten engaged to the blacksmith. She's still at the cottage, though.'

Paige felt his face grow hot with rage. 'You mean she's still living in my cottage but not working?' he asked, trying to keep his voice level.

Bill Downer looked uncomfortable. 'Young Reuben wants to talk to you about paying rent.'

'He does, does he? We'll see about that. Get me a horse.'

Bill Downer sent one of the men to the livery. As Bartholomew waited, he silently fumed. The minutes seemed like hours. Finally the lad returned with a handsome bay mare and Paige snatched the reins.

162

'If you're looking for a horse, sir, I should have a word with young Reuben,' Bill suggested helpfully.

'With young Reuben.' Paige gave a snort of anger and pushed his foreman aside. He struggled into the saddle and drove his heels into the mare's sides. They cantered briskly out of the yard in the direction of the cottage he had so generously supplied for the Irish slut. His heart thundered in his chest and his fists clenched with barely suppressed outrage.

After they had gone about a quarter of a mile he slowed down, partly from breathlessness and partly to assess the situation. The feeling of betrayal gnawed at him and at first he thought he would go in and physically throw her out, bag and baggage, but as he pondered further he realised that there was no need to change his plans after all. In fact, now he thought of it, the last thing he wanted was to hand her over to the upstart smith. If 'young Reuben' thought he was going to have her, he had another thought coming. The decision made him feel better and a certain sense of pleasure came from knowing that he could thwart the blacksmith's dreams.

By the time he reached the cottage he had worked it all out and was almost cheerful.

Friday was not one of Meg's days for going to Simla Lodge. She was quite relieved to be able to spend the day cleaning the cottage, putting onions up on boards to store for the winter and salting runner beans.

Declan amused himself by crawling under the apple tree to pick up small green fallers and put them into her basket. In his own small way he was always trying to help. She would throw them away later.

Picking up her child, she went back indoors and started to make a pie for Reuben when he called round later in the evening. He had been called away to shoe a horse at Swainston Manor, some six or seven miles away, so he would be late.

The sun was beginning to get low in the sky and when the pie was cooked, Meg went outside to unpeg the washing from the rope that stretched from the cottage to the apple tree. As

163

the wicker laundry basket began to fill, she heard the gate click. She turned round, thinking that Reuben had got back early, but to her dismay she saw Bartholomew Paige coming down the path by the side of the cottage.

Fighting down her instinct to run away, Meg continued to take the clothes from the line. She pretended not to have noticed him.

'Miss Foggarty. You look nice,' he greeted.

In spite of knowing that he was there, she still jumped when he spoke. Picking up the full basket, she rested it across her hip, hoping that the gesture would imply that she was busy and not to be detained. Ignoring it, he leaned back slightly and looked her over as if assessing a good horse.

'You look very well.'

'We were hoping to speak to you,' she started.

'We?'

Meg felt herself blushing. 'I'm to be married, to Mr Kingswell, the blacksmith. I hope you don't think I've been taking advantage of your kindness. I am still keeping an eye on things here, and my ... fiancé will settle any overdue rent.'

'Will he now?' He began slowly walking around her, still looking her over as if she were something he was considering buying. Declan crawled across to her and held out his arms to be picked up. This forced Meg to put down the linen basket again.

'Well now, my dear. It seems that we have some sorting out to do. Allow me.' Bartholomew picked up the basket and preceded her towards the cottage door. 'I hope you are going to show me round?'

Her heart was beating fast. She longed to say that Reuben would be along at any moment or suggest that Paige came back at another time when she knew that Reuben would be there, but she remained silent.

Paige put the basket down on the table and settled himself in one of the two kitchen chairs that he had supplied.

'Come and sit down, my dear. We have to have a little talk.'

Reluctantly Meg slid into the other chair, still holding Declan close. She knew her son's normally large blue eyes were clouded with suspicion as he stared at their unwelcome visitor.

'It seems as if we need to get this question of payment sorted out,' Paige began.

'Reuben ....'

'The arrangement, my dear, is between you and me. I'm not looking for a few paltry shillings from your smith. Just put that child down, will you, and I'll explain what I have planned.'

Meg continued to hold on to Declan her mouth dry with tension. Paige raised his eyebrows expectantly but when she didn't move he gave a gesture of dismissal and leaned back.

'Right then, Meg Foggarty. You of all people must know that life for the working class is hard, especially for a young girl who has, shall we say, not kept herself as she ought to.'

Meg went to protest but the look on his face froze the words in her throat.

'Now then. I'm sure, like the next person, you would like a life free from poverty. In fact, who wouldn't welcome a life of luxury? Can you imagine what it would be like to have everything you wanted?'

'I've got everything I want here.'

Ignoring her, Paige continued: 'You may have heard that my poor dear wife is unable to give me children. That is a sad situation for a man in my position. I am rich, you see, but I have no flesh and blood to leave my estate to.'

Meg continued to watch him, stiff with apprehension.

'You are a beautiful young woman, but I expect you know that. There is more, though, something of quality about you, not like these village girls.'

'Mr Paige –'

'Which is why I have reached a very serious decision.' He sat back with his hands on his knees, looking at her. 'We know that you are capable of having healthy children, the little lad proves it.' He reached out and patted Declan's head; the child turned away, burying his face against Meg's bosom.

'Lucky little boy,' Paige observed. As Meg went to move

165

out of the chair, Paige raised his hand to stop her. 'I have decided that you, my dear, are to have the honour of bearing me a child, or even several children.'

'No!'

He did not acknowledge her cry. 'In return I'll find you somewhere else to live, a palace compared with this. In fact, you can have pretty well anything you want.'

'You must be crazy!'

His eyes narrowed. 'That's a foolish thing to say. You haven't thought about it. I'm offering you a lady's life, and my child, our child, will be raised like a gentleman.'

'No!'

'Tut-tut, Meg Foggarty. I thought you had more sense.'

'Please leave or I'll tell my fiancé.'

'That would be really silly. You don't seem to have grasped what I am saying.' He got up and came to stand close to her, his hand wandering down across her shoulder to rest between Declan's cushioned face and the rise of her breast. His touch disgusted her and she struggled to get up but he stood too close. 'I'm afraid I'm not asking you, dear girl, I'm telling you. I've waited a long time for this.' His voice suddenly hardened. 'If you care about your little bastard here as much as you pretend you do, then you'd better reconsider.'

'Get out! Touch one hair of my son's head and I'll kill you!' She turned her back on him to shield Declan from his touch, her entire body trembling with fear.

He gave an artificial little laugh. 'Oh, Meg, you are a foolish young thing. I don't want to hurt him. I just thought that if you won't take pity on me and give me a son of my own, then I might be driven to take yours.'

She couldn't believe what he was saying. 'You couldn't, you can't!'

Still blocking her retreat, he slid his hand into her bodice and cupped her breast. 'Come along now. Come on upstairs like a good girl. I won't hurt you.'

Meg flew to her feet, catching him off balance, and put the table between herself and him. 'Get out!' she repeated. 'I'll tell the constable if you threaten me.'

Calmly he walked around the table as she retreated. He had to raise his voice to be heard above Declan's screams. 'It's no good. You still haven't heard what I've been saying, have you? Who is really the father of your child? Such a fanciful story about your fiancé being killed. People don't believe it. They'll know why I took you in. After all, I couldn't have my son and his mother destitute, could I?'

As the implications of his story hit home, Meg found it difficult to breathe. 'Please,' she said. 'I'll leave the cottage. We'll pay you anything I owe. I'll find somewhere else to live.'

'Not with my son, you won't.'

'He isn't −'

'Who'll believe it, if I take him away for his own good? After all, the child is in moral danger, living with a known whore.' He closed his hand around the back of her neck so that she could not move. 'It's no good your so-called fiancé saying he'll take you in. I shall simply claim what's mine − my flesh and blood, as it were. Now if I had a genuine son of my own, then I wouldn't need to be bothered with this one, would I?' As he spoke, he wrested Declan from her and held him high. She screamed in protest and the babe yelled with fright as Paige swayed him to and fro. 'Mustn't drop him,' he said quietly.

'Give him back! I'll do anything, whatever you say, only don't hurt him, don't take him away.'

Paige held him out. 'That's better now. Just you pop the little chap down somewhere and come along upstairs with me.'

Meg crouched in the corner of her kitchen and hugged Declan to her. The bile rose in her throat and she felt sick with disgust. She had made one last-ditch attempt to run away but Paige had been too strong for her. Now she shut her eyes to keep out the memory.

It had been quick. Unable to drag her up the stairs, he'd thrown her to the kitchen floor and taken her there while she fought and screamed. All the while Declan, roughly pushed aside, had sobbed hysterically.

Concern for her babe had partly obliterated the horror of what was happening. When it was over Paige had struggled to his feet and brushed his clothes down.

'There, now. Such a fuss! Next time we'll have more time, arrange things better.'

'Get out!' She had scrabbled for her child and tried to reassure him, rocking him to her with little whispers of love interspersed with her own sobs. She wanted to run away but there was nowhere to go.

'Remember,' Paige said as he opened the door, 'do anything foolish and I'll be back for the boy. If necessary I'll get an order from the court.' Meg glared her hatred at him. He put on his bowler, then raised it again in farewell. 'Good night, my dear. Not a word to your smith, now. I'll make sure he doesn't trouble you again. And sleep well. I'll be back on the morrow.'

Meg was immersed in black despair. Nothing that had happened before compared to the horror of this. There was no way out. She had betrayed Reuben and now she felt dirty, used, violated. She might lose her child. With growing terror it dawned on her that she might once again be with child, this time by a man she hated and feared.

Declan finally fell asleep against her breast, giving in to exhaustion. Even in sleep little sobs still escaped him. Wearily Meg dragged herself to her feet and slumped into a chair, still holding him close. She thought she heard a footstep and her heart jolted in case it was Paige returning. Then for a wild moment she thought it might be Reuben, but as the reality of her situation dawned on her anew there was only hopelessness. How could she face him after what had happened? Where would she find words to explain? What use would he have for someone else's doxy?

She remained sitting in the chair, Declan sheltered in her arms. It was the longest night of her life. In her mind she went over everything that had happened since her arrival in Freshwater Bay, seeing it in a new light. Now she could not believe how foolish she had been, how stupid and naive not to have seen what Paige intended. Mrs Carmichael's words and Margy's reservations also pointed to the same thing. Meg alone had not seen it. Worst of all was the knowledge that Reuben had expressed his doubts about Paige and she had ignored them, secretly accusing him of jealousy.

Reuben – what was she to tell him? How could he forgive

her? Surely there could be no marriage now? Even if he still agreed to the wedding, Paige had threatened to intervene.

'Then other doubts assailed her. Had not Mrs Carmichael said that her portraits of Meg and Declan were her best work? The only reason they weren't exhibited freely was because of Meg's past. She was a fallen woman and as such not fit to be recognised by decent people, least of all as the holy Madonna. Mrs Carmichael was used to getting her own way. If she wanted Meg wed so that she could parade her photographs without embarrassment, then she was capable of pushing Reuben into marriage. Was it possible that he was marrying her not out of love but for some reward? Nothing was what it seemed.

Meg tried to clear her mind but thoughts chased each other like moths round a candle, fluttering and pushing for attention until they were roasted by the fierce heat. One by one her burning thoughts destroyed her.

Protectively she held Declan tight and he grunted in his sleep. Remembered cries of 'Bastard' and 'Roman whore' added to her anguish. Above all, there was one terrible truth. No matter what, she could not fight Paige's threat to take away her child. In despair she thought that she did not even know where Brendan O'Neill's body lay, so how could she prove that he had even existed, let alone that he was the father of her child?

Paige was powerful and selfish. He might toss Declan away as an unwanted kitten. Like Mrs Carmichael, Paige was used to having his own way and as long as he knew where Meg was he would not let her go. She knew with certainty that her life at the bay was ended.

Chapter Twenty-Eight

Reuben returned late from Swainston. Although it was nearly dark he rode on past the forge and continued in the direction of Meg's cottage just to let her know how he had got on. She'd be wondering where he'd got to.

'Get going, you bitch!'

Reuben stopped and listened in surprise. He had been about to enter the copse and now from amid the trees he heard the thwack of a stick and a squeal of pain. He moved forward cautiously to see what was happening, parting the bushes to reveal a man astride a bay mare. The animal was taut, refusing to pass a gate, and as Reuben watched the rider drove his heels viciously into her sides. 'Get on!'

She began to back away and the man's anger seemed to explode. He brought his crop down across her rump with all the force he could muster. The mare leaped forward and another squeal of pain escaped her. In response to the blow she seemed to become rigid.

He began to hit her again and again, kicking her unmercifully. Finally she reared and he came tumbling to the ground, still clutching the reins. Now his fury burst from him and, still holding the whip, he laid into the terrified animal, beating her about the head and legs while she shrieked with fear and pain.

'You bastard!' Reuben leaped from Ginny, his mare, and gripped the man's arm so hard that the reins slipped from his grasp. He gave him a suffocating blow to the belly which had him flattened on the ground.

'You evil bastard! How dare you treat a horse like that?'

With shock he realised that the winded man was the brick master. A moan of pain and outrage escaped his adversary but Reuben turned away.

'Easy, my beauty. There, there.' He moved cautiously towards the horse and her white eyes began to calm. 'Hush, my love.' He had hold of her bridle now and was running his hand down her neck. 'There, my lovely gal.'

Suddenly he felt a stinging blow as the man brought his crop down with all his force across Reuben's back.

'That'll teach you to interfere with your betters!' He swung the whip again, catching Reuben across the arm as he was in the act of turning towards him. 'And just you keep away from the Irish bitch.'

The horse had pulled away and Reuben crouched as if stalking a prey.

'You've used that whip for the last time,' he promised, his anger boiling over. With a leap he was upon Paige, holding the offending crop and tearing it from his hand.

'Right, you arrogant son of satan! Now you can find out what it's like to be horsewhipped.' Holding Bartholomew by the throat, he laid the whip across him while he yelped with pain. 'Never. Ever. Do. That. Again.' He punctuated each word with a blow from the crop, then, straightening up, threw it into the bushes.

Breathing heavily from his exertions, he suddenly registered what the man had said. 'What has Meg Foggarty to do with you?'

Paige struggled up, wincing and pulling his shirt away from the whip lashes. His eyes gleamed with malice.

'She's my property.'

Reuben swallowed down his anger. 'You leave her alone,' he said. 'Go near her and I'll do for you.'

The older man straightened himself and puffed out his chest. 'No good you getting notions about her, mister. She's mine. Paid for. Go round there again and I'll have you publicly disgraced.'

Reuben's fists were taut balls of frustrated fury. 'You harm her and you'll have me to answer to,' he warned. 'We're betrothed.'

'You think so?' Paige gave a derisory sniff as he moved

171

a safe distance away. Awkwardly he bent down to retrieve his stick from the undergrowth. 'Be warned. The girl's in enough trouble already. You go near her and you'll live to regret it.'

Before Reuben could answer, Paige made a show of straightening his coat and brushing down his crumpled trousers, then strutted away.

Margy hated to walk home alone through the woods in case a wolf or a Gypsy should chase her. Her worst fears were therefore confirmed when, passing through the copse between her grandmother's and her own cottage, she heard raised voices. Her first instinct was to turn and run but then she thought that this would attract attention so she froze for a few moments before creeping forward to peer in the direction of the noise. The sight that greeted her caused her mouth to drop open.

Reuben the blacksmith was holding Mr Paige by the shirt collar and striking him across the back with a whip. She could not hear what Reuben was saying because of Mr Paige's squawking but his face was dark with anger. She strained her ears and thought Reuben said: 'Go near her and I'll do for you.'

At this Mr Paige started to shout back; 'No good you getting notions about her, mister. She's mine. Paid for.'

For a moment Margy thought they must be talking about a horse, then she thought she heard Reuben say: 'We're betrothed.' She realised with astonishment that they were fighting over Meg.

Paige was struggling but now they were coming closer and Margy began to stumble hastily away. She had no wish for either of them to know that she had been a witness to this extraordinary scene.

As she skirted round the clearing, tripping in her haste to put a safe distance between herself and the two men, she wondered if she should tell her father.

Bartholomew walked painfully back towards the bay. As he went he swore that he would not rest until he had driven his hated rival into ruin.

172

Shored up by plans of revenge, he managed to stumble the half-mile back to his lodgings and to slip in unnoticed. The last thing he wanted was to have prying busybodies asking questions.

In his room he struggled out of his muddy suit and bathed his cut and bruised body as far as it was possible to reach. There was a mirror behind the washstand and he looked critically at his puffy face. He'd have to say that he had walked into a door.

All the time his anger simmered. No man had ever insulted him in such a way. He'd fix the interfering swine once and for all and make Meg Foggarty pay.

Remembering the salves in his portmanteau, he dragged it out from beneath the wardrobe and opened it. Taking out a pot of comfrey, he dabbed it gingerly on his bruises. The stinging was marginally better.

As he was in the act of putting the jar away, he noticed the bullets nestling in a velvet pocket in his case. For a moment he gazed at them, then took one out and fingered the dull metallic case. As he rolled it comfortingly between his fingers a plan began to form.

After the fight Reuben hurried in the direction of Meg's cottage. He was afraid for her safety and wanted only to reassure himself that she was unharmed.

As he passed through the darkening woodland that lined the road between her home and the bay, he saw the runaway mare. She was standing with her head lowered and even in the gloom he could see that she was trembling. She looked a picture of misery. He approached quietly, talking to her all the time. He caught her trailing rein and she took one reluctant step forward, then, after a moment of resistance, began to follow him. He turned back towards home so that he could see to her injuries before calling on the woman he loved.

For tonight he would keep the mare in the compound with Ginny, his own workhorse. Next morning, once he was sure she had no serious injury, he would return her to the livery stable where she had been hired. He recognised her as he did all the horses in the neighbourhood. Sometimes he joked that he knew the horses better than the people. Anyway, he would make sure that the owners of the stable knew just what sort of man had hired a horse from them.

Lighting an oil lamp, he tied her up outside in the yard and set to work to bathe her wounds. She was a lovely mare, fine-boned and with a silky coat to protect her sensitive skin. Again he thought of fine, handsome Meg and his heart ached.

He worked long and hard until the horse was settled. Thinking of her helped him not to think about the other thing but he could not keep his mind away from it for long. What was Paige up to? Although Meg had lived rent-free in the brick master's cottage, Reuben knew that she wasn't a loose woman. Yet she had come to the village with a child and no husband.

He shook his head as if to throw off the train of thought. Some other being seemed to be asking the questions to which he did not want to hear the answers. What reason could the brick master have for saying what he did unless he and Meg had some arrangement?

For the first time Reuben felt doubt, wondered if he'd been a fool to have some romantic notion that Meg had been wronged. He probed the wound of his own suspicion and winced at the pain. It rocked his world. He had never felt as he did about a woman before and the knowledge made him angry with her.

It was now approaching midnight and too late to even think of going to the cottage. Besides, he was also anxious to see that Amos was all right. Any change in routine confused the old man even more. He gave a heavy sigh of fatigue, remembering that at first light he was due to leave with Mrs Carmichael to look at the driving horse for Lord Tennyson.

As he walked leadenly into the cottage, he saw that Amos was asleep in the downstairs room where he lived out his life. Reuben felt relief and tried to console himself with the thought that all would be sorted out when he got back home the next day. Meanwhile the time between now and then stretched like a desert and, try as he might to be optimistic, a terrible fear clutched at his heart.

Chapter Twenty-Nine

The next morning Meg was at Yarmouth at first light waiting for the ferry. She had no idea of the sailing times and found that it was another two hours before the steamer was due to leave. For a while she stood on the quay, the water lapping only a few inches below her. She felt exposed and cold and it would have been easy to slip into the grey swirling sea beneath and give herself up to it. Only Declan, laying in innocent trust against her shoulder, held her back.

The morning threatened rain and there was a pervading chill in the air, heightened by a sharp offshore breeze. Meg's clothes were damp from dew. Looking round she spotted an upturned rowing boat drawn up on the wharf and, making sure that no one was watching, she crawled underneath to find shelter. As Declan snuggled into her warmth and finally slept, she tried to make some sensible plans for her future.

The belongings she had managed to bring with her were few and chosen for sentiment rather than practical use. In spite of everything she still needed this tangible link with the past. It was all she had.

Already her courage was threatening to desert her. The choices were stark. Before coming to the island she and Brendan had been near Southampton. But navigators moved around swiftly, to suit the convenience of the new rail-crazy industrialists. If she went back there she could not rely on finding anyone they had known, and in any case they could not afford to take her in. Nor could she bear to visit the place where she had shared her life with Brendan. That would bring another kind of pain, another reminder of the capriciousness of fate.

Her second choice was to go home to Norfolk, but how could she face a family that would throw up their hands in horror at the prospect of two more mouths to feed? Even worse was the knowledge that she might be carrying another bastard child.

She remembered the Catholic Father at Sutton le Grange. Even as she pictured her return, the very idea of the priest presuming to lecture her on sin hardened her heart. What did he know? His God did not live in the shantytowns of the labouring poor. His God did not know about love and desire or blackmail and fear. That God's place was in the country where the peasants were blinded by superstition.

She dismissed the third option even as it forced itself into her mind. The Freshwater cottage was the only home of her own she had known. It was there that Reuben had worked for her, shared her dreams, asked her to be his wife. Two days ago it had represented everything that she wanted. She wanted only to be back there but now it had become the lair where Paige waited to destroy her.

She thought cynically that if Reuben had not loved her she would have coped with Paige well enough. Her role as care-taker and paramour would have become just another work contract. Although it offered no security of tenure, no fixed wages, no guaranteed days off, she would have understood the conditions of service and been prepared to carry it out.

In harsh, cold terms Reuben offered much the same. He would take care of her in return for her being there, in return for exclusive rights to her. But for her there would be a price to pay in feelings, in wanting him, in valuing him, in depending on him. That was a blind alley that ended in a brick wall labelled PAIN. She crouched lower to peer out from under the boat at the steamer drifting in the distant haze. Better the pain she made for herself than one that would be inflicted upon her, she thought.

Finally the paddle steamer was tied up alongside the jetty. Still there was a long delay as several bullocks and five horses were in turn bullied and persuaded to stumble down the ramp and into the hold of the vessel. Evan as she watched, Meg

176

knew that her life was no freer than theirs. Here she was being driven aboard by circumstances outside her control, by one man who wanted to own her and another who wanted to love her. Did her future look more hopeful than that of the lowing creatures that careered in panic around that slippery enclosure in the belly of the ship? She doubted it.

That same morning Bartholomew Paige was up before daylight and left the house with the stealth of a burglar. In spite of the cold, damp weather he did not risk putting his boots on until he was outside the gate and then he travelled practically at a run to reach Reuben Kingswell's forge without being spotted.

It was still dark when he arrived. Looking around to make sure that no one was watching, he tiptoed inside with pounding heart. He saw to his satisfaction that the fire in the forge was already laid, a few crisscross sticks over some straw and a mound of coals. Bartholomew fumbled in his pocket, taking longer in his haste but finally extricating half a dozen silver capsules. For a moment he looked at the bullets, hesitating, then, making up his mind, he pushed them carefully in among the coals, making sure that they could not be seen. With a sigh of satisfaction he crept back outside, wiping his hands on the smith's apron which hung by the door.

Scuttling across the yard, he secreted himself in the shadow of the bushes and prepared to wait. Every nerve jarred within him and he fought to calm his pounding heart. He feared that he could not tolerate the tension of this vigil. Now that he had set things in motion he longed for the satisfaction of revenge. When those bullets went off they would blow the smith's face away.

The sky began to lighten. At last the cottage door opened and a man came out, beating his hands against his upper arms for warmth. Bartholomew held his breath as he watched, and his eyes grew wider.

Old Amos Mew hobbled towards the forge. Bartholomew was rooted to the spot. The old man was mumbling to himself and weaving a painful path across the yard. He went inside and after a moment Bartholomew saw the flare of light as Amos ignited the fire.

'I say!' Bartholomew called out, but the sound of the flames in the cavernous forge and Amos's increasing deafness left him unaware of his visitor.

The next second it happened. The blast rocked Bartholomew where he stood. There was a blinding flash and the air was showered with sooty cannon balls of coal, tumbling in every direction. The sound seemed to be delayed but when it came it appeared to lift the roof off the forge. As Bartholomew stared, paralysed by shock, the roof was back where it belonged and he knew that he must have imagined it. Slivers of paper curled and climbed skywards and a dusty haze blacked out the frosty morning sun. There was silence except for the odd cracking of hot embers. As he stared, an orange glow began to illuminate the back of the forge.

'Old man!' Paige found his feet and raced into the blackening gloom. It took several moments for his eyes to adjust to the dark caused by the dust. Screwing them up, he stared desperately around until he saw the hazy shape of the elderly smith on the floor. At the back of the forge, flames began to lick hungrily about the wooden supports. Hastily he grabbed the old man by the waistcoat and dragged him outside.

'Old man!' He shook him hard, slapping his face to rouse him, but Amos Mew was beyond recall.

Moving in a daze towards the bushes, Bartholomew retched violently and at that moment there was another explosion. He remembered nothing more.

When he came to, the first thing he saw was the kindly face of Constable Dore. The shock of what had happened flooded in upon him. He closed his eyes again to buy time. It needed some quick thinking to explain his presence.

Finally he looked up and accepted a helping hand to get to his feet. Glancing surreptitiously again, he saw that the body of Amos had been moved and things tidied. He must have been unconscious for some time. At the memory of the explosion he felt sick and shivery but his main concern was what to say.

'You all right, Mr Paige, sir?'

'Such a shock,' he said guardedly. 'I called to enquire

after a mare Mr Kingswell was minding.'

'You did? You don't know where he is, then?'

'I'm afraid not.'

The constable looked troubled. 'A bad business, what with poor old Mr Mew and the young girl.'

'Young girl?' Paige started and his heart rate increased.

'Reuben's fianceé. She must have come here early for some reason. I s'pose you don't know where her little lad is?'

As Paige slowly moved his head from side to side, the policeman added: 'We think old Amos had managed to crawl outside but the girl – we found her body at the back of the forge under the debris. She's . . . unrecognisable.'

Mrs Carmichael and Reuben set off at first light in her carriage with Reuben's mare trotting along behind so that he had transport back when their business was completed. The carriage had been piled high with trunks and boxes. Often Mrs Carmichael liked to drive herself but today she sheltered inside, squashed into one corner of the gig. Reuben sat in the open and urged the carriage horse on. The air was damp and cool and as yet no one seemed to be on the road.

At first they made good progress but just the other side of Newport things started to go wrong. The roads were worse than usual and the carriage suddenly hit a rut with such force that the wheel came off.

It took Reuben two hours in relentless rain to put it back on. He kept looking out for other travellers to come to their aid, but the road remained deserted. No one in their right mind would be out on a day like this. By the time they set off again, Mrs Carmichael was beginning to fret lest she miss the afternoon steamer.

To add to their troubles, when they arrived at the farm where the horse was for sale, no one was to be found.

'This really is too bad,' said Mrs Carmichael. 'I haven't got time to wait and if I don't make the arrangements now I shall be off the island and on my way to India.'

Reuben went to look around. He located what he presumed to be the horse in a loosebox and went inside to have a look at her. He checked her over thoroughly. She was a good-looking animal but her feet were bad and he shook his head.

'My advice would be, don't buy her,' he said. 'Those feet'll be nothing but trouble.'

Seeing Mrs Carmichael's disappointment, he added: 'I'll keep my eye out for another, if you like.'

She sighed. 'Thank you, Smith, but no. When we come home next year. 'I'll bring Mr Tennyson something then.'

He drove her the rest of the way to the steamer and watched from the shore as she boarded. While porters were stowing her belongings on board, she returned to the quay to say goodbye.

'Thank you, smith, for all your help. I wish you well in your marrige. You both deserve happiness.' She looked away and her face was suddenly sad. 'I regret that I won't be here to witness the ceremony, but I shall think of you all.' She hesitated and her eyes glistened. 'I'm very fond of Meg. Take good care of her, won't you? I didn't say goodbye to her. There are so many partings and they are all painful.'

'I'll take care of her, ma'am, you can be sure of that.' Reuben took the two sovereigns that Mrs Carmichael pushed into his hand. 'Have a happy life,' she called as she boarded the boat.

'Safe journey, ma'am.' He waved to her and turned away. With a sigh he mounted Ginny for the return journey. It was a long ride back and he was feeling cold and tired. There had been a brief respite from the rain but before he had gone a mile it started again.

He was still about eight miles from home when darkness fell. The journey which should have taken a few hours had lasted all day. For a while he and Ginny struggled along the unlit lanes but twice the horse stumbled in the hidden ruts, slipping and sliding as she went, and he thought that to go further would be foolish. The rain was falling in unrelenting sheets. He went on just as far as the next barn and bedded himself and the mare down for the night.

There was some hay in the barn but he was wet, cold and hungry. He lay listening to the rhythmic sound of Ginny's crunching. Sleep would not come. He worried about Meg, what she must be thinking. He worried about

Amos, wondering what he had been up to during the day. He even worried about the vagrant girl who slept in the forge and who would be waiting hopefully for scraps of food.

Chapter Thirty

By the time Meg reached Lymington the weather had turned colder and it started to drizzle. Despairingly she looked back towards the island but it was hidden in thick grey fog, almost as if it had been obliterated from her life. She turned back and gazed forlornly along the marshy expanse before her.

Panic began to mount as she wondered where they would lay their heads that night. Even worse was the thought that without regular food her milk would dry up and with nothing else to feed him little Declan would certainly be doomed. She almost got straight back onto the ferry, only she could not face Paige's glee and, far worse, Reuben's possible rejection. She went on.

They spent the first night in a barn just outside of Beaulieu. The accompanying farmhouse did not look welcoming and the distant sound of barking dogs had her on her guard, fearing discovery at any moment. The good thing about the barn was that it was dry and wind-proof within the thick stone walls. Unfortunately, apart from a few pieces of rusting machinery, it was nearly empty; no hay to sleep on, no apple store to raid. She went to bed on the hard earth cold and hungry.

In the morning Meg was still wet and dishevelled, which made the prospect of finding work even less likely. Her limbs ached and she felt exhausted. It was hard to face another day. Drawing up her courage, she stilled her empty stomach with icy water from the animal trough outside the door and crept thankfully away from the farmstead.

As soon as she reached the next town, she began the

depressing task of knocking at doors. One after another the fortunate occupants of the rows of houses at which she called turned her and her child away.

The weather was still cold and rain began some time in the afternoon in an angry, pounding burst. Meg shielded Declan as best she could inside her sodden shawl and stared hopelessly along the next gloomy street. There was little chance of shelter here. Summoning the last of her energy, she began to trudge out of town. Another barn seemed to be her only hope.

To keep her mind from utter despair she decided upon an experiment. As she walked she sent up a challenge. 'God, if you really exist and care about us, then grant us a place to lay our heads; somewhere warm and safe. This is your last chance.' If tonight they died of exposure beneath a hedgerow in this alien countryside, then at least she would have had the satisfaction of disproving the Almighty's existence.

Paige was in a turmoil. He walked back shakily from the smouldering forge to his lodge house, refusing the constable's offer of an escort. It was all too much. Try as he might to ignore it, the fact remained that he had killed Meg Foggarty.

He wondered how the girl could have been so stupid as to go to the forge. The thought that she had visited Reuben sent pangs of jealousy and alarm surging through him. Would she have told the smith about what had happened the evening before? Even worse, had she confided in the constable's daughter, assuming that was where she had left her brat? Did the police now know of the incident that had taken place at the cottage?

Bartholomew tried to phrase his story but he was hard put to find a suitable word to describe what had actually taken place between him and his lodger the night before. Try as he might, it was difficult to pretend that she had been merely coy. He consoled himself with the thought that all women put on a show of reluctance.

It suddenly dawned on him that Meg's brat would now be an orphan. He could indeed now carry out his threat to have the child, but what would he do with a bastard

183

boy from the railways? He had no interest in the child if he couldn't be used as an instrument of blackmail. Paige sighed. His first priority must be to get his story straight, make sure that he was above suspicion. He wondered what Kingswell would tell the police. They seemed concerned that the smith was nowhere to be found.

Bartholomew's route took him near to Meg's cottage. He was about to make a detour to avoid the scene of his last encounter with the girl when another thought occurred to him. Supposing there was something at the cottage which would throw suspicion onto him? Reluctantly he changed direction and made for her home.

The door was unlocked and he went inside, trying not to look at the place where he had taken her. The room felt abandoned and cold. He shivered. At that moment he noticed something on the table. His heart pounding, he picked up a folded sheet of paper. He read:

Dear Reuben,
Forgive me. I cannot stay. There are no words to explain so please do not try to find me. Much as I would wish it otherwise, there is no future for us. Do not think badly of me. You will always remain in my heart.
    Meg.

Bartholomew was about to screw the letter up but he had a better idea and placed it carefully back on the table. He knew that the constable was coming shortly to his lodgings to take a statement and would no doubt visit the dead girl's last abode. His mood lightened and with sudden clarity he saw the way forward. Let him come.

At first light Reuben left the barn and continued his journey back to Freshwater. The ground was waterlogged and in many places boggy but at least they could see where they were going.

Above everything he wanted to see Meg. She must be worried sick by now, wondering where he was. Their enforced separation of the last two days had put things back into perspective. He didn't give a damn what Paige had said; of course Meg was above suspicion. The best thing was to find another cottage and get wed quickly, away from the brick master's evil influence. The thought of holding Meg in his arms and being her husband warmed him. No more waiting. He wanted her now.

As he completed the last few hundred yards towards the forge, he was deep in thought. Only at the last minute did he look up to see if there was any sign of Amos. The sight that greeted him froze him to the spot. In a daze he slid from the saddle and took a few steps towards the burnt-out shell that had been his forge.

'Amos?' he called out as he turned to the cottage, racing up the path and pushing the door open. The place was still.

Reuben ran down the path again and, grabbing Ginny's rein, leaped astride and pushed her on towards Meg's cottage. His heart was thundering and wild thoughts of disaster crowded his brain. As the cottage came into sight he looked out anxiously for Meg, wanting only the hear the truth.

He lifted the latch, hurried into the kitchen and was amazed to be confronted with the solid shape of Constable George Dore.

'George? Whatever's going on?'

The police officer's expression confirmed Reuben's worst fears.

'Amos?' he asked. To himself he thought: I should never have left him. I should have known he'd have an accident.

'Where have you been, son?'

'With Mrs Carmichael. I got caught out last night, couldn't get back.'

George Dore's face remained grave. 'Why did you do it?' he finally asked.

'Do what?'

'No good pretending, lad. We know.'

'Know what? Is Amos dead?' Reuben felt his alarm rising. 'I know I shouldn't have left him so long but I thought Meg would have – '

'Why did you kill her?'

Reuben could not answer. He stared at the policeman in disbelief. 'What are you talking about? Where is Meg? Where is she?'

185

'We think you know.'

'For God's sake, George! What has Meg got to do with this?'

'Mr Paige told us about the letter and you having the bullets.'

Reuben's knees suddenly gave out under him and he sank onto the edge of the table. 'I don't know what you're talking about,' he repeated. 'Where's Meg?'

'She's dead, son, along with old Amos.'

'No!' He was shaking his head, refusing to hear the words. 'Where is she?' he repeated.

'There's nothing to see.'

He didn't know what the man was talking about. At any moment he was sure that she would walk in and explain what was happening.

George Dore took his pad and pencil from his tunic pocket. 'I've got Mr Paige's statement here. And I've got the letter.' He held out a single sheet of folded paper to Reuben and shook his head regretfully. 'I know you cared for her, son, but to kill her because she was leaving you ...'

'You're crazy.'

'No, I think you're crazy. You deliberately asked Mr Paige for bullets, then put them into the forge to destroy the evidence. Did Amos catch you out or did you think if you killed him too you could have the cottage to yourself?'

'I ...' There was nothing to say. It was a nightmare and he couldn't wake up. 'Where's Declan?' he suddenly asked, but the constable continued to talk in riddles.

'You tell me. What have you done with him?'

With tense fingers Reuben unfolded the single sheet of paper and began to read. The words might have been in a foreign language for all the sense he could make of them.

'I'm afraid you'll have to come with me.' The older man straightened up, pulled his tunic into place and cleared his throat. Loudly he announced: 'Reuben Kingswell, I am arresting you for the abduction of Declan Foggarty and the murder of his mother, Meg Foggarty, and also of your master, Amos Mew.'

186

Chapter Thirty-One

After walking for more than an hour, Meg was almost too exhausted to put one foot in front of the other. It was dark now and although the rain had ceased, a keen wind blew in her face, making the going harder. Her path took her up a seemingly unending slope. By now they were back out in the countryside and there was no sign of village or farm. Declan had long since given up his pathetic whimpering and lay mute within the folds of the cold, wet shawl. As Meg was about to abandon herself to die in the shelter of a ditch, she made out the low, shadowy outline of a building on the crest of the hill. She realised that it was on a crossroads and therefore probably an inn. Somehow she increased her pace.

Dragging herself closer she saw that the building was isolated, small and tumbledown. The hazy moonlight was just bright enough for her to see that the thatch hung in tatters and several rotting boards replaced long broken window panes. Above the door an ancient sign creaked in the wind. She could barely make out the words but finally deciphered them with the help of the painted illustration as saying 'The Bear'. Although it looked abandoned, she knocked at the door before pushing it open on rusting hinges and peering inside.

Two candles flickered in response to her arrival. They enabled her to make out a low-ceilinged, bare and dusty room with a rough table and chairs, drawing their light from the small fire burning in the grate.

She jumped as a figure moved in the shadows. The landlord, seated on a settle to the side of the grate, was in an equal state of decay, his grey lanky hair in neglected wisps, more gaps than teeth in his slack mouth and the stench of stale gin on his breath. He regarded her in silence.

Meg had two shillings. 'How much is a room?' she asked with sinking heart. For an eternity he eyed her.

'Are you alone?'

Meg was surprised by the educated tone of his voice.

'I'm widowed. I'm on my way to my family.'

Gin Breath digested this slowly. Meg could almost see his brain at work, so slow were the thought processes.

'It will cost you nine pence,' he finally announced. His voice was slurred and he blinked owlishly, the better to focus on her.

'Let me see it first.'

He shrugged. 'Top of the stairs, first on the right.' He did not bother to move.

She hesitated for a moment, then climbed the rickety steps, worn away by thousands of tired feet. Reluctantly she pushed the door open to reveal a dark cubbyhole. There was one iron bedstead with a flat mattress and a grubby-looking bolster. Meg summoned all her resolve. This must be better than subjecting the child to another night outside, but her heart quaked.

Downstairs Gin Breath was dishing up something that resembled stew. In spite of the unsavoury atmosphere, Meg's mouth began to water.

'I'll take the room,' she said shortly. 'Do you sell supper?'

Gin Breath was looking at her again and she felt nervous and vulnerable. She longed for Reuben to be there.

Finally he said: 'It looks as if you could do with a good dinner. Here.' He passed the plate over and Meg accepted, suddenly unable to contain her hunger. As she ate he watched.

'Nice baby.' He was looking at Declan. When she did not reply, he said; 'I had a son once. I don't know whatever became of him.'

He held the jug of gin towards Meg but she shook her head, not wanting to encourage familiarity.

'Go on.' He pushed the jug at her again. 'There's no

charge. I get tired of drinking alone.' With unexpected intuition, he added: 'There's a bolt on the inside of your door. Nothing to fear.'

Meg drank then and enjoyed the warmth of the spirit coursing its way into her belly. Breathing deeply, she allowed herself to relax a little, creeping closer to the fire.

'You look exhausted,' Gin Breath observed. 'You have far to go?'

'I don't know yet.'

He shrugged and took another slurp of the gin. 'When I was a young man ...' A long, complicated story followed and Meg forced herself to listen although by now she was dropping with fatigue. She got the impression that he had lived in a vicarage once, but thought that she must be mistaken.

No one else arrived at the hostelry and there appeared to be no servants. The thought that she was alone with her ill-favoured host filled her with misgivings.

Well, he won't murder me, she consoled herself, fortified by the drink. She wondered at the madness of her situation. She had run away on account of what Reuben would think and what Paige would do, and now here she was with a dissolute drunk. The irony, or perhaps it was the gin, suddenly made her snort out loud.

Gin Breath looked at her with piggy, unfocusing eyes. 'You're a fine-looking woman, you shouldn't travel alone.'

Meg stiffened, but he merely added: 'Get you to bed, you look as if you need some rest.'

Gratefully she hurried up the stairs and bolted the door. The gin had stopped the cold eating into her bones, but instead she felt strange, floating, out of touch with her surroundings. As she lay in the narrow bed she wondered whether or not her prayer had been answered.

Whether it was the gin or her arduous day, she slept soundly. It was already light when she awoke. She lay for a few moments wondering where she was. When she remembered, the thought of another day such as the one before chilled her heart.

However, she got up and tidied herself before going down the stairs. There was no sign of Gin Breath but some bread and cheese and a tankard of small beer were on the table. There was also a note scrawled in shaky, thick pencil on a yellowing piece of paper. 'Take the Donkey. He's yours.'

'She looked at it with a frown of incomprehension but ate the food. Still there was no sign of Gin Breath so she left nine pence on the table and went outside. The first thing she saw, tethered to a ring in the wall of a rickety shed in the yard, was a large white donkey. Her eyebrows shot up in surprise.

'Take the Donkey.' She could not quite believe in Gin Breath's kindness but nevertheless she went over and untied the animal. Hitching up her skirts, she scrambled onto its back and found to her delight that it was quite biddable.

As she was about to move off, a shower of rain broke overhead. Hunching over her child, she enveloped Declan in her still damp shawl and kicked the donkey forward'. At that moment the innkeeper emerged from one of the dilapidated outbuildings.

'Are you leaving?' he asked.

Meg nodded. 'Thank you for your kindness.'

He merely shrugged, staring at her with glassy-veined eyes. Finally he said: 'The child will get wet.' When Meg did not reply, he added: 'You are planning to go far?'

Meg hesitated. 'I don't know.' He had asked the question the day before and her answer had not changed.

Gin Breath continued to stare at her. After a moment he said: 'This place has gone downhill a bit.'

This was an understatement but Meg said nothing. She made to push the donkey forward.

Gin Breath shuffled his feet awkwardly on the ground. 'I'm a fair cook,' he said. 'It's the other things I can't seem to get round to – the cleaning and such like.'

The expression on his face of loneliness and near desperation made her ask: 'What is it you're thinking?' The idea of remaining in this squalid place filled her with dismay but she seemed unable to stop herself.

'I couldn't exactly pay but I would feed you. There'd be a roof over your heads.'

Meg started to shake her head but she suddenly thought of Paige pursuing her and trying to take her back. He'd never

190

find her in a godforsaken place like this. The donkey gave a sigh, reminding her of the man's generosity. 'Well ...' She hesitated. 'Perhaps I could stay for a day or two, just to give you a hand to get the place cleaned up.'

'You could?' Visibly his spirits lifted.

Meg dismounted in a daze. What am I doing? she asked herself. This was madness and yet there was nothing out there to go to. 'Just for a day or two,' she repeated, 'and then I really must leave.'

As the rain cleared and the sun came out, Meg discovered the extent of the task that she had taken on. The Bear was in an advanced state of decay and any attempt at cleaning must have been abandoned years before. She could not help contrasting it with the cosy warmth of her recently deserted cottage and she longed to be back there cooking for Reuben, waiting to hear his voice, to see his smile. With an effort she drove the image away and set to work. She found a bucket in the outhouse and filled it from the pump in the yard.

Back inside the inn it was chilly and damp and she insisted that her host light a fire in the taproom so that there was somewhere warm to put Declan while she worked. He did so without protest and then offered to go out and collect firewood while she made herself busy. She was glad to see him go.

Once alone she started with the kitchen, flinging the rush mats outside, unearthing a dusty box of soda and heating water on the decrepit range. She grew quite hot systematically scrubbing floors, walls and tables, sending bucket after bucket of blue-black water swirling down the elderly drain until it clogged.

'You'll have to clear this,' she called to Gin Breath when he came back, as the culvert began to overflow.

The man was obliging. When not carrying out her instructions, he stood and watched as if mesmerised by the transformation that was taking place. 'It's a miracle,' he kept repeating. 'I think you've been sent here by divine providence.'

'Nonsense.'

Meg moved on to clean the snug and was glad when Gin

Breath went back off into the kitchen. Above the sound of her own labours she could hear him banging pots around. The homelike noises made her think of Reuben again and all the pain came flooding back. What had he thought when he read her letter? He would feel betrayed and let down. The knowledge tore at her but nothing she could do would change things.

Leaning back against the newly washed wall, she felt momentarily dizzy and her third fear possessed her: Don't let me be pregnant.

'Come and eat. You'll make yourself ill if you keep working like that.' Gin Breath's timely call took the edge off her fear. She was hungry, that was all.

Meg ate some smoked ham and swilled it down with ale. She reasoned that this morning she had earned it. All the time her host watched as if recording just how much she consumed. He nodded approval at each mouthful.

'How long have you been here?' she asked to distract him from his surveillance. He gulped down a lump of ham. The sound of his chomping grated on her nerves. It was hard to equate the educated voice with this shambles of a man.

'I was born in London. Would you believe that my father was a bishop?' He gave an ironic little sniff. 'I even considered the church myself, but then I went into public service.' Meg waited. She was about to get up and clear the plates when he said: 'Things can go badly wrong in life. I went to India. I was married.' Again he was silent, remembering. 'Winifred, my wife, was a handsome woman – not unlike you. We had a child. I thought that would make her happy, but ...'

'I'm not a replacement wife,' Meg warned.

He looked at her and showed his broken teeth in what passed for a smile. 'I wouldn't expect it. I'm hardly a catch, am I? How old do you think I am?'

Meg hesitated. She guessed he was about sixty but cut off ten years to be on the safe side.

'I'm forty-two,' he corrected. 'I've let myself go, being on my own.' He sighed and reached for a jug of gin and immediately Meg was transported back to the railway hut, with Brendan's bottle on the shelf.

192

'You don't need that.' She looked away, unnerved by her own temerity. To her relief he did not pick it up.

He said. 'Having someone in the house makes all the difference. Travellers don't stop here any more but once this was *the* place to change horses. We used to cook good meals. People used to come from miles around.'

'We?'

'I had a partner, a business arrangement. He left when he realised that we weren't making money any more.'

'Perhaps it could be like it was before – ' Meg stopped herself but Gin Breath was already in agreement.

'Aye, perhaps it could. With the right person to help me.'

She started shaking her head but the thought of a roof over her head and good food, a sense of purpose and a safe place for Declan made the offer difficult to refuse outright.

'If you ever come near me I'll kill you.'

It was his turn to shake his head. 'My dear, there's nothing to fear from me. I want a housekeeper, that's all. Just someone to stay here, and perhaps a customer or two to make it all worthwhile. What do you say?'

'I don't know.' She tried to think of the alternatives but there didn't seem to be any. Finally, in the face of his hopeful expression, she gave a sigh. 'All right. We'll give it a try.'

He nodded, letting out his breath in relief.

'What's your name?' he asked.

She told him. 'And yours?' She could not continue to think of him as Gin Breath.

'I am Arthur Watts. Please call me Arthur and, if you permit, I'll call you Meg.'

Meg shrugged to show her indifference but as she cleared the greasy plates from the table and returned to her scrubbing, she realised that she did not really mind at all.

As the days went by, Meg's fear that Paige might seek her out began to fade. Yet, in spite of telling herself no one knew where she was, a lingering worry remained. She kept Declan close at all times, which was no longer so easy now that he

193

could pull himself up and make his way around by clinging on to anything within reach. At a crawl he was positively speedy. Every now and then Meg would lose sight of him and panic would seize her. 'Declan!' she would scream, knowing relief only at his answering burble.

Frequently she found herself going to the window just to make sure that no one was coming. The road past the inn remained empty.

On the eighth morning since her arrival, she awoke to find that she had started to bleed. The discovery lifted another cloud. Now she knew that she was not carrying Paige's child she could begin to distance herself from him. In fact, the more she thought about it, his threats to take Declan were probably empty gestures, yet a fleeting memory of his voice or the image of his fleshy body would suddenly set her trembling and she knew that she could not take the risk. She must remain where she was.

By now she had thoroughly cleaned the downstairs rooms and two of the bedrooms in the inn. Only her own and Arthur's remained. She shied away from entering the land-lord's room. She did not want to know about him or trespass on his territory and equally she did not want him to come into hers. As she tried to move her bed, however, she discovered that it was propped up on some heavy boxes. No matter how hard she tugged and heaved, she could not dislodge them, so reluctantly she had to ask him for help.

Arthur puffed his way up the stairs and began to pull at the trunks. His face went scarlet and for a moment Meg feared that he might suffer from apoplexy, but he was clearly very strong and finally the boxes slid roughly across the wooden floor.

'My wife's clothes and things,' he said. 'Silly really. I should have thrown them out long ago but ... ' He didn't continue.

Meg remained silent and he looked around the room as if seeing it for the first time. Finally his eyes came to rest on the two photographs which Mrs Carmichael had given her.

'What's this?' He went closer and screwed up his myopic eyes the better to study them.

'They're photographs.'

'Why, that's you!' He stepped back and his face was animated by the discovery.

'They were taken by Mrs Carmichael. She's a lady, a friend of Lord Tennyson, the poet,' she added in case he had not heard of him.

He was still shaking his head in wonder. 'She did these herself?'

Meg began to tell him about the dark box and the developing and fixing. As she talked she was back in the garden at Simla, lugging furniture and bottles in and out of the glass house. Nostalgia threatened to overwhelm her.

'They're amazing,' Arthur said.

'It's science.'

He continued to scrutinise the prints. 'Who is this babe?'

'Declan.'

'And the young fellow?'

'Just the local blacksmith.' Her eyes were drawn to Reuben's cloaked figure, the strong profile, the soft curl of his hair. She knew her face must betray her feelings.

Apparantly unaware of her turmoil, Arthur continued to register his interest. 'Do you know how to make pictures like these?' he asked.

Meg hesitated. 'I might do. With enough light, and if I had the right equipment.' She tried to remember each process.

Arthur was looking at her with renewed respect, rather as if he had discovered that the cat could talk. He chewed the knuckle of his thumb as he considered the possibilities.

'Could you take an image of me?' he finally asked.

'Not without a dark box. And some plates, and the right chemicals.'

'Where could you get them?'

Meg shrugged. 'I expect that there is a photographic depot in Winchester or Southampton. It would cost a pretty penny, though.'

'How much?'

She considered. 'Well, the camera would cost at least five pounds, then there's the plates and the paper and the collodion, to say nothing of a good ground lens. I don't suppose you'd get any change from ten guineas.'

Arthur looked thoughtful.

Now that the inside of the Bear was spick and span, Arthur Watts hired a team of men to restore the exterior. During the next months a carpenter replaced the rotting window frames, a painter whitewashed the grey-green walls, a thatcher replaced the perished reeds and two unemployed men came to tidy the garden. The place began to look revitalised.

Soon two travellers stopped at the inn to ask for a meal and stabling for their horses. Meg and Arthur scurried around to make them welcome and they went away saying they were well satisfied. 'Didn't know you were here,' one of them said. 'I'll pass the word.'

This was encouraging but at the same time Meg felt uneasy. Now that the inn was attracting customers, it would be more difficult than ever for her to leave. Then there was the risk that someone would come there and recognise her. What if the word got back to Paige that she was hiding out? He'd come hurrying over to take Declan away! Nervously she fingered Reuben's ring, twisting it around her finger.

She shut out the thought and tried to concentrate on washing the yellowing linen she had found in the former Mrs Watts's trunks. It was of fine quality and would look well on the tables in the snug.

To keep her mind from her own fears, she wondered what Arthur's wife had been like. He had offered Meg her dresses and although she had immediately declined, she was amazed by what she found in the boxes beneath the bed. Furs, evening gowns, beaded gloves, satin shoes. What sort of life had she and Arthur led? From their size, Mrs Watts must have been very tall and slim. Meg pondered on Arthur's marriage and the fate of his wife and child.

Soon, however, her thoughts drifted back to her own dilemma. It was no good worrying about the future. She decided to say that she would stay until New Year. If Paige discovered where she was, then it was just as likely that Reuben would find out too. For a while she immersed herself in the dream of Reuben coming to take her home, forgiving her for what had happened, telling her that

Paige was dead. The dream stilled her worst fears. As she wrung out the tablecloths she thought: there's still two weeks to go until New Year. Anything might happen before then.

Chapter Thirty-Two

The cell had dark-green, damply shining walls and a stone-flagged floor long since worn uneven by the anguished pacing of feet. Reuben sat on the hard, narrow bunk and gazed around him. An oil lamp flickered on the small deal table and, apart from a tin chamber pot, a thumbed copy of the Bible was the only object in the room.

Reuben's arrest had come as such a blow that he was still unable to take in the consequences. Because of the nature of the crime he found himself shipped across to Winchester to answer the charges.

His position seemed hopeless. Incarcerated as he was, he had no opportunity to challenge the charges or even discover exactly what they were. As far as he had been told, he was accused of stealing Declan, killing his master to gain possession of the cottage and also of having murdered Meg.

Meg! He was plummeted again into despair. She couldn't be dead. What would she have been doing in the forge at the crack of dawn? He remembered his anger with her following Paige's insinuations and hated himself for his disloyalty. Now he would never have a chance to make it up to her.

In the face of all that had happened, Reuben began to welcome the idea of being condemned to death, but some sense of injustice niggled at him even in his darkest moments. He knew that Paige was implicated and felt that, whatever the outcome of his trial, he could not rest unless the brick master was exposed for the fraud he was.

'Tell me who accuses me,' he demanded of the policeman who came to question him – not a local constable like

George Dore, but an officer from the crime squad.

'A Mr Paige claims that you asked him to sell you some bullets he had with him left over from his foreign travels.'

'It's a lie! What would I want with bullets? I haven't even got a gun.'

'He said you used them to cause an explosion. In his statement he says that you told him you wanted your independence and that you were tired of playing nursemaid to your master.'

'It isn't true. I – I loved the old man.' Reuben struggled to control the break in his voice.

Untouched, the officer added: 'Then there's the letter.'

'What letter?'

'From your affianced. Saying she was going away.'

'I never saw any such letter, not til George Dore showed it to me – afterwards.'

'After what?'

'The ... accident.'

'Well, the prosecution have it now. Anyway, we think you did see it. We think you couldn't face the idea of her leaving so you took her to the forge and blew it up, hoping to make it look like an accident.'

'Damn you! I love her ... I loved her.' Reuben turned angrily away from his tormentor, pacing this way and that as if to escape from his pain. Finally he said: 'I wasn't even there. I'd gone with Mrs Carmichael to look at a horse.'

'You have any proof?'

He shook his head. 'She's gone away.'

'Where to?'

'India, or some foreign part. I don't know.'

The policemen smirked as if to imply how convenient her absence was. He asked: 'Who else saw you?'

Reuben's heart hit rock bottom. 'No one. It was a filthy day. When we went to look at the horse there was no one there. I didn't come back that night because of the weather. I slept in a barn. No one saw me. When I got back I found ...' He could not go on.

The policeman straightened up as if to confirm that that was the end of the interview.

'How long before I come to trial?' Reuben asked.

199

'Some time yet. These things don't happen overnight.' As the officer waited to be let out of the celll, he said: 'I shouldn't be in too much of a hurry. After all, it doesn't look very convincing, does it? We have a letter from your sweetheart saying she's leaving and a man is willing to swear you had the wherewithal to cause the fire. You had a motive in wanting revenge on your sweetheart and something to gain from the old man dying. In the meantime you can only say you weren't there. All in all, it doesn't really look very hopeful. Not very hopeful at all.'

For a few weeks after the tragic deaths at the forge, Bartholomew Paige remained at his lodgings in Freshwater Bay, ostensibly overseeing the brick works. He feared that if he left too quickly it might cause suspicion, so he promptly sent for Edith to keep him company, as any happily married, respectable man would.

The fact that Meg had died as a result of his actions weighed heavily upon him. He had had such plans for their affair, and persuaded himself that she would bear him a child. He sighed regretfully and comforted himself with the thought that it must be God's will. Perhaps another, more suitable girl was waiting just around the corner.

Amos Mew's death did not disturb him. He pardoned himself with the knowledge that the man was old and had been near to death's door in any case. He had merely hastened the old man on his way. In fact, he reasoned that he had probably done him a favour by saving him all that lengthy lying around waiting to die.

Fear of discovery had been Paige's immediate concern, especially with Reuben's suspicions, but this had now subsided and to his relief the smith was safely locked up in Winchester gaol awaiting trial. So far as he could tell, no one else suspected. Now the only mystery was what had become of Meg's baby. The only person she ever trusted with her brat was Margy Dore and the girl denied having seen it.

'It is such a tragedy,' Edith said for the upteenth time. 'If you hadn't been here to help the police, no one would have known what happened.'

Bartholomew looked at her suspiciously, wondering if she was hinting at something with her observation.

'How do you mean?' he asked.

'Well, if Mr Kingswell had killed his poor master and that young woman some other way, no one would have known it was he. It's only the fact that he asked you for the bullets that shows he's guilty.'

'And the letter,' he pointed out. 'Still, it's a good job I was here then.' Secretly he worried how many other people might have come to the same conclusion. He thought back over all his actions and calmed himself with the knowledge that until that fateful evening there had been nothing to link him to Meg Foggarty except Christian charity. It was a comforting realisation.

Bartholomew knew that he would return to the island in the new year to arrange for the sale of Meg's cottage. He preferred to do that when Edith wasn't about. She asked so many inane questions. Secretly he thought he might sell the brick works too, make a clean break with the island. After all, it hadn't brought him much luck.

At last he felt that he could safely go back home and be ready at hand for whenever the trial took place. It was convenient that it should be held in his home town of Winchester – almost an omen, really.

That morning before his departure for home he visited the brick works one last time just to check that all was well. As he rode into the yard, the first person he set eyes on was the constable's daughter, Margery Dore.

'Hey, you! Come here,' he called.

She left what she was doing and came over. He could see the suspicion on her face, the unwilling pose of her body. She was a plain girl, thickset, of no sexual interest to him.

'Has your father found out what became of that baby?' he asked, assuming an air of concern.

Margy shook her head and tears began to well up in her eyes. She said nothing.

'A sad business,' Paige ventured. 'A terrible thing is jealousy.'

'Reuben didn't do it. We all know he couldn't do a thing

201

like that.' There was spite in her voice and she was looking at him with glistening, hostile eyes.

'No good ignoring the facts, young woman.' Paige began to feel uncomfortable under the force of her scrutiny. Could Meg have said something to her? He knew they were thick as thieves.

Margy twisted the neck of her dress in anguished fingers. Finally she said: 'My pa don't believe it neither. He thinks there's more to this than meets the eye. If Meg was leaving, something must have happened to frighten her. Someone.' She was glaring at him now.

His heart began to thump uncomfortably and he swallowed back the urge to shout: 'You're fired!' After a moment he said: 'If your father's right, then I shall be the first to offer any help I can.' He sighed regretfully before adding: 'Sadly, I know what I know. Young Kingswell did express his frustration with his lot, and he did ask me about the bullets — but there, I shouldn't be discussing this with you before the trial.' He reached out and patted her plump, resentful shoulder. 'Just you tell your father that Bartholomew Paige is as anxious as anybody to get to the bottom of the mystery. I'll help the law in any way I can.'

He walked across to see Bill Downer, but all the time he could feel Margy's eyes boring into him. I've got to be careful, he thought with dismay. That young woman may be stupid but she is the policeman's daughter. She could be dangerous.

Chapter Thirty-Three

It was not until Arthur Watts got drunk on New Year's Eve that Meg realised what a transformation had taken place in him. He had dramatically cut down on his consumption of gin and had taken to regular washing and shaving. His hair was trimmed and each Sunday he even changed his shirt. His eyes had lost the glassy, unfocused look that Meg first remembered and she thought that he seemed taller, younger and not without self-respect.

Tonight the fire positively roared up the chimney in the tavern, creating sinuous tongues of orange light on the yellowing walls. Holly and ivy, now brittle and dulled by dust and thirst, festooned the picture rails, and guttering candles peeped into every cranny of the snug. Two travellers seated at one of the scrubbed tables, replete after their gigantic meal, toasted each other diligently in brandy. The room was bathed in warmth and good will.

As Meg finished clearing the table, she heard Arthur come in through the back door. The hinge squeaked and the wood dragged across the stone pavings. It was a sound that was now familiar, not unlike the creaks and bumps that had once been part of her life in Grandmother Foggarty's cottage. Until that moment Meg had not realised how much at home she was.

Arthur came through to the tap carrying something wrapped in sacking. It was large, square and flat. Meg looked round and raised her eyebrows.

'It's for you, a gift.' Seeing her frown, he added: 'Well, a gift for the Bear really, just to show appreciation for what's been done.'

'Meg wiped her hands on her apron and took the offering. Laying it on the table, she unfolded the cloth to reveal a framed print. She raised it towards the candlelight to get a better look. The picture depicted a blacksmith's forge. In the foreground a fine bay horse with a docked tail was in the process of being shod. A pale donkey peered from behind the horse, watching the proceedings.

'It reminded me of Blanco,' Arthur observed, following her gaze.

Meg nodded, but her eyes were drawn to the figure in the forefront of the painting, a sturdy smith in the process of shoeing the bay mare. The sight of him made her heart lurch. He was a rather plain, pudgy man, stocky rather than muscular, but the association of ideas had her back at the forge, enveloped in the heat and glow, immersed in the presence of that other smith, young, strong, with a face that caused her heart to beat with longing.

She looked quickly up at Arthur, wondering why he should have chosen this of all pictures. Every day it would remind her of what she had left behind.

'You don't like it?'

'It's good.' She gave him a tight little smile. 'It'll brighten up the tap no end. Shall we put it there, over the mantel shelf?'

Arthur nodded and she could see that he was pleased.

The travellers called out that it was nearing midnight and a new year was upon them. Meg condescended to take a sip of brandy to wish 1868 welcome. Declan was asleep up in her room and Arthur was poking the fire with stabbing imprecision, brought on by his inebriated state. He seemed impervious to the resultant burst of sparks that threatened to sting him. As Meg watched, a realisation occurred to her that she had repressed until now.

Whereas her presence had had a dramatic effect on Arthur, she had not succeeded in changing Brendan's habits at all. In fact, if he, like Arthur, had lived to be forty-two, the chances were that he would have been in the same drunken state as Gin Breath had been when she first encountered him.

For the first time she began to wonder if losing Brendan was such a terrible tragedy after all. If things had continued

204

as they were during their brief liaison, by now they would have been homeless, penniless and outcasts. And what of Declan? He might well have died. It was a devastating thought.

Meg accepted another brandy. 'Happy New Year!' Her thoughts left her numb. She could no longer ignore the fact that her confidence had been totally crushed while Brendan had been her lover. Otherwise she would surely have viewed Rueben's friendship in a different light. After all, what had there been to fear in the offer of love from someone so honest and kind? The fear was in her own lack of judgement, a suspicion that Reuben's strong physical appeal could not by its very nature be combined with true love and loyalty. Must all good-looking men be rogues?

She suddenly pictured Reuben so clearly that she could almost have touched him; his wry grin, the compassionate hazel eyes, the way he moved, laughed, the way he had kissed her. The need for him submerged every other feeling.

Her hand came to rest on the familiar outline of Brendan's brooch. Silently she unfastened it and crushed it in her hand. The sharp point of the pin drove into her palm but she did not flinch. Declan apart, if she were to weigh up the pros and cons of having encountered Brendan O'Neill, the balance had to come down firmly against. I regret you, Brendan, she thought. She continued to crush the brooch as if she could exorcise one hurt with another. I regret you for your failings and myself for my weakness. As a love token she no longer had any use for his brooch.

With a sudden movement she threw it into the fire. It fell between two glowing logs and was quickly enveloped in streaky orange flame. Tears began to trickle down her face. Goodbye, Brendan, rest in peace.

She sat for a long time gazing at the blue flames round her cremated brooch, then quietly left the bar.

Declan's regular, slightly snuffly breathing greeted her as she tiptoed across her room.

'May I come in?'

The sound of Arthur's voice caused her to jump.

'I didn't mean to frighten you. You disappeared and I

205

thought you might be unwell.' Arthur peered cautiously round the door.

'I'm all right.'

'Good.' His mouth was half open and Meg looked at his ill-shaped teeth. He swayed slightly and steadied himself by grabbing the bedpost.

'I'm just going to bed,' she said, but he did not move away. She had no fear of him but there was something about his presence that forced her to pay him attention.

After an awkward silence he turned and looked at the two photographs propped up on her mantel shelf. Meg could not stop him but it felt like an intrusion into her most private feelings.

Finally he said: 'Who is he then, the lad's father?'

She shook her head and knew that she was blushing.

Arthur shrugged. 'You were sweet on him?'

She did not reply.

There was another awkward silence before he said: 'I ... I've got something else I want you to have.'

'What sort of something?'

'Come with me.'

He led her across the narrow landing towards his own room and she followed reluctantly. At the doorway Arthur stopped and looked sheepishly at her. 'You'll think I'm foolish but ever since I saw your pictures I've thought, well ...'

Eyebrows raised, Meg stopped just inside the door. The room smelled stale, and she wrinkled her nose.

Arthur crossed to the cluttered chest of drawers and pulled out a slim book. 'Here. Have a look through this and pick out what you need.'

He held it out and Meg took it, tilting it towards the light so that she could see. She read the words: 'Chartwell and Slugg, Every Requisite in Photography.'

She looked up astonished and Arthur nodded encouragingly towards the book. 'It's their sales catalogue. They've got everything in stock. All you have to do is choose, then we'll get it.'

'But ...'

'Don't skimp now. I want you to have the best.'

Her eyes raced over the advertisements, pages of cameras,

columns of lenses, lists of chemicals ready prepared for use.

'But ...' She knew there must be some snag.

'Go and study it, then.' Arthur followed her back across the landing. At the entrance to her room he shuffled from foot to foot as if to get in touch with her mood. 'Is it all right?' he asked.

'All right? It's ...' She was lost for words.

Arthur broke the silence. 'Meg?'

She had half turned from him and now looked back over her shoulder. He seemed ill at ease and avoided her eyes. At last he said: 'You promised you'd think about staying. Have you made up your mind?'

Meg shrugged. She did not want to think about it, not now. Suddenly the offer of the camera felt like a bribe. 'I don't know,' she replied. 'Is that why you're giving me this?'

'No! No.' Arthur looked hurt. 'I wouldn't dream ...' Finally he asked: 'Would it make any difference if we were to wed?'

The question took her so much by surprise that she stared at him open-mouthed. 'I ... I ...' There was no answer.

He looked away, then back at her with his pale, pathetic eyes. She felt a wave of affection for him but could not bear to raise his hopes or to hurt him. At last she said: 'Arthur, I can't marry you. I can't marry anyone, but thank you for asking.'

He nodded and with a little sniff took a step towards the door. He said: 'This doesn't mean you have to go, does it?'

'No, it doesn't.' She wanted to shut him out, just look at the catalogue in peace. 'I must get to bed. We'll talk about the camera in the morning.'

He nodded and withdrew. In a moment she could hear him lumbering down the bare wooden stairs back to the snug.

Sinking onto her bed, she pulled the guttering candle to the edge of the washstand and thumbed through the catalogue. She had no idea there was so much to choose from. Her eyelids grew heavy. Climbing into bed she pulled the eiderdown tight up to her chin. She thought about Arthur at length. Always she was prepared to be suspicious, to defend herself from his acts of kindness, but behind the shabby façade she was coming to recognise a gentle, middle-aged man whose only failing was in being lonely.

Just as she was dozing off she heard him come back up the stairs to bed. 'Make a list,' he called from outside the door. 'We'll go to the depot in the morning.'

Next day they presented themselves at the premises of Messrs Chartwell and Slugg. The shop had tinted glass windows behind which was a tantalising display of photographic equipment. Engraved into the windowpane were the words: 'Joseph John Chartwell, Medical Chemist; Joseph Montrose Slugg, Manufacturer of Photographic Apparatus.'

Meg pulled down the heavy brass handle and somewhere in the back a bell tinkled to announce their arrival.

Mr Chartwell, or Mr Slugg, emerged. 'Sir, madam, how can I be of assistance?'

Arthur looked at Meg and she felt herself flush. 'I want a camera,' she said, not quite believing what she was saying.

'Does madam have any idea what she wants?'

'I like the sound of this one, in your catalogue.' She pointed to a page and Mr Slugg (or Mr Chartwell) read aloud: 'Double-bodied, folding, Spanish mahogany camera: French-polished, one body working inside the other so that the focus may be adjusted to the greatest accuracy by means of an endless screw. Designed to take photographs of size nine by seven inches.' He looked up. 'A good choice, madam. May I hazard a guess that you have experience in this field?'

'A little. How much?' she said.

'That one comes at five pounds and ten shillings.'

She caught her breath at the thought of such extravagance. 'Er ...'

'I can supply you with the best in lenses, three and a half inch diameter, hand-ground.'

'And that would cost?'

'Two guineas, madam.'

Seven pounds twelve shillings already! She looked round at Arthur but he was still nodding his encouragement.

'Now then, we can offer you negative collodion, six and

208

sixpence a pint, and a very superior negative varnish at the special price of three and sixpence.'

Eight pounds two shillings. She started to shake her head.

'It's too much.'

Arthur signalled to Mr Chartwell (or Mr Slugg) to continue. 'It's for me as much as you,' he said to Meg. 'Just think, you can photograph all our customers.'

Thus encouraged, the shop proprietor offered her a quire of excellent albumen paper for a mere seven and sixpence.

Eight pounds nine and sixpence.

Various other items were added to the growing list.

Finally the camera was brought from the back room for Meg to examine. She felt a tremor of excitement as she looked at the highly polished wood and the warm glow of the brass fittings. It was smaller than Mrs Carmichael's and lighter to move, and it came in a smart case lined with blue velvet. Inside there was space for a lens and plates and other paraphernalia.

The whole came to twelve pounds nine and sixpence. Meg fought down the excitement by guiltily considering the expense. As Arthur produced two large white notes and three sovereigns, Messrs Chartwell and Slugg promised to deliver the consignment to the Bear within the day.

The next morning being cold but clear, Meg took her new camera out into the garden of the Bear. Carefully she set out her photographic equipment on old sheeting so that it should not get dirty. With the thoroughness instilled in her by Mrs Carmichael, she had washed and sensitised the plates and now they were ready for the exposures.

To her amazement, Arthur came out wearing a black frock coat and stovepipe hat. The coat strained somewhat across the middle and to hide the bulge he kept his hands folded over his belly. His shaggy grey hair hung down untidily and gave him rather a rakish appearance, but he could no be persuaded to take the hat off.

'Where did you get those clothes?' Meg asked as she heaved the camera up onto the tripod. This was an improvement on Mrs Carmichael's and there were grooves into which the camera could be fixed. Sometimes at Simla it had looked as if the whole thing would collapse.

Arthur seated himself on one of the wooden benches next to an upturned beer barrel that in summer served as a garden table. 'I wasn't always as you see me now,' he said, brushing some fluff from his lapel.

Something about his bearing and the quality of his voice suddenly reminded Meg of Lord Hinchington, from the manor near her Norfolk home. It dawned on her that this man had fallen very low indeed.

'Right,' she said, dismissing his past life. 'I want you to look at me and keep very, very still.'

Arthur wriggled about for a moment, then took up his chosen pose. His back was very straight and his chin was tucked in as if his head was merely balanced on the top of his neck.

'Try to relax a bit, and no talking.' Opening the aperture to let the light in, she kept chattering to deter him from moving. 'Right, now you may relax.'

When Meg had finished, she looked around the garden wondering what else to photograph. It occurred to her that she could take a picture of the Bear. It would make a very good advertisement for the inn. When she told Arthur, he said: 'I've thought it all out. You can have your own workplace, over there in the barn. We'll get it fixed up the way you need it. From now on you can take pictures and sell them. I'm sure they'll be as popular as hot-cross buns at Easter.'

Meg had some moments of anxiety in case she could not remember the developing process, but when she had finished, the portrait of Arthur Watts and the picture of the Bear were better than she dared hope. She wondered if they might not be even better than the pictures taken by Mrs Carmichael.

Arthur was impressed. 'Fancy that!' he exclaimed. 'I do believe we have an artist in our midst.'

Meg worked hard all morning and after dinner sat by the fire and thought about her future. Her success with her photographs left her feeling very positive. She began to ask herself why ever she was hiding away. Now it seemed foolish and cowardly. It was time to get in touch with Reuben. What

210

could the brick master do to her now? She was miles away and she owed it to Reuben to let him know that she was safe. It was just a common courtesy, after all, designed to put his mind at rest. There was no reason for him to read anything more into a letter. She tried to deny it but in her heart of hearts she wanted some link with him, however tenuous. Now that her future was looking secure, she could at least afford to write and tell him that all was well.

For a long time she thought about it but the right words would not come. Once she drafted the perfect letter in her head but at that moment the brewer called and by the time he left she had forgotten it again. Arthur was going into town the following morning so before going to bed she made haste to pen something, even though it did not say what she wanted. She had to act now while the decision was fresh. Decisively, she put the finished letter on the mantel shelf.

When she arose the next morning it was already daylight and Declan was standing on a stool by the casement, chattering to the starlings that wheeled in front of the inn. Sleepily Meg stretched and climbed out of bed. As she dressed, thoughts of yesterday came back to her and she remembered her temerity in writing the letter. Today she knew that she would tear it up.

Descending the stairs, she listened for Arthur, but everything was silent. 'Arthur?' There was no reply. Still plaiting her hair, she pushed open the back door and looked across the yard. The donkey cart was missing. Barefooted she padded across to the shed where Blanco spent his nights and checked that he was gone. Then she went back inside and forced herself to look on the mantel shelf. The letter was not there.

Meg went about her day's work in a trance. Inside, her stomach churned. When Arthur returned later, she asked: 'Did you see my letter?'

'Oh yes, I posted it.' Seeing her dismay he added: 'It wasn't sealed, but as it was addressed, I thought you would want it dispatched.'

'Thank you.' She wondered if Arthur had read it but guessed that he was too much of a gentleman. Now her heart was thumping unnaturally. She wanted Reuben to write to her, yet she was afraid that, sooner or later, the truth about her and Paige would come out. What would she tell Reuben if he asked why she had left? Far worse, how could she bear it if he did not care enough to ask?

Chapter Thirty-Four

As soon as New Year was past, Bartholomew Paige decided to go back to the Isle of Wight and arrange the sale of his property. He made enquiries about the island solicitors but then decided, to be on the safe side, that he would use the regular family firm. He placed his island properties in the competent hands of Draycott and Simpson with precise instructions in how to dispose of them, and breathed a sigh of relief. Now his connections with that ill-starred place were as good as severed.

He stayed for two days, during which time he paid a last visit to the brick works and also to Meg's cottage. So many hopes had been pinned on these ventures and now they were all dashed. It was in sober mood that he suddenly felt the need to have a final look at the forge, just to allay any anxiety that there might be something that he had overlooked. He had heard that the mainland police were coming over and they were a different kettle of fish to the likes of George Dore.

No one was about and he surveyed the blackened shell of the building with a certain reverence, knowing that he personally had instigated so much damage. The place wsa so devastated that clearly there was nothing left to attract attention. He wondered if the baby's remains were somewhere in the burnt-out ruin. Perhaps the police hadn't looked properly. At the same time he could not bring himself to go too close. He shuddered.

Instead he wandered across towards Reuben's cottage. The garden was looking overgrown and the windows were thick with grime. He thought with satisfaction that there would be no bride coming back to cross this threshold.

As he was about to open the gate, he heard somebody come up behind him. He turned to see the postman, who had stopped by the hedge and was rummaging in his bag.

He seemed to think that he owed Bartholomew an explanation. 'I've got a letter here, to young Kingswell. I supposed I'd better give it to the police.'

'I am on my way to see George Dore,' Paige said quickly. 'If you give it to me, I'll take it with me.'

The postman looked uncomfortable. 'That's more than my job's worth, sir. I'm not allowed to give letters to people in the street, even if they are addressed to them personally.'

Bartholomew swallowed down his irritation. 'In that case, I'll walk along with you.'

They went in silence and all the while the brick master wondered how he could get a glimpse of the letter. It might not be important, but he had a feeling about it.

As they reached the police house, Bartholomew wondered whether to offer to take the letter inside, but decided against it. He did not want to arouse suspicion. Reluctantly he stood back and let his companion in first.

A bell jangled somewhere in the house, but nobody came to investigate. Seizing his chance, Bartholomew said: 'There's no need for you to wait, old man. Why don't you just leave it on the desk?'

The postman hesitated for a moment and then nodded. 'I've got another letter here, for George.' Carefully he placed them on the counter that separated the entrance from the rest of the office. 'Will you make sure he sees them?'

'Of course.' Bartholomew forgot himself to the extent of raising his hat, in his anxiety to hurry the man out of the building. At last the door closed, causing the bell to tinkle again. Quickly, Bartholomew seized the letters and stuffed the one addressed to the blacksmith into his pocket. He just succeeded in replacing the second letter on the desk when the constable came in from the back room, carrying a garden rake.

'I'm so sorry, Mr Paige, sir. I didn't hear you.'

'No matter, constable. I just called in to see how your enquiries are going. Any news of that baby?'

214

George Dore shook his head and made a tutting noise of regret. 'Not a sign. Such a bad business.'

'It is indeed. Well, I won't delay you, I know you are a busy man.'

Paige made his escape and hurried back to his lodgings. As soon as he was inside he pulled out the envelope. To his surprise it was postmarked Winchester. The coincidence that it had come from his home town registered for only as long as he was breaking the seal.

The address written at the top in firm strokes was that of the Bear Inn just outside Winchester. Paige had not been there for several years.

The letter itself was very short. As his eyes skimmed over it he saw that this was some sort of plea from a girl who was sweet on the blacksmith. He sneered in disdain.

It was not until the very end that his mouth dropped open in disbelief.

Declan misses you greatly. There is much more that I would like to say, dear Reuben, but it is best that we do not meet again. Hard as it may be for you to understand, I remain your true friend.

In sadness,

Meg Foggarty

A pulse began to throb in Bartholomew's neck and his hand ached as he crushed the paper in his palm. The little vixen! She was still alive! Panic threatened to overwhelm him. He tried to think of the implications but his thoughts were too confused. One thing was clear, no one else must know.

He thought how fortunate it was that the postman had come along just when he did. Clearly, someone up there must be looking after him. With this comforting realisation, he unscrewed the letter again and looked at the date. It had been written only two days before. With a sigh he tore it up and pushed it under the kindling in the newly laid fireplace. Whatever happened, he had to cover his tracks. The little slut had crossed him once too often. Tomorrow he would be back on the mainland and, no matter how long it took, he'd make her suffer for this, just wait and see!

*

Reuben, sitting in Winchester gaol, had been unaware of the passing of 1867. Every day in prison was the same; dreary, monotonous and barbed with sudden terrors as the thought of his trial and its outcome forced its way into his mind.

Faced with the prospect of swinging at the end of a rope, he could not eat. Anyway he had nothing to live for. Meg had died horribly and without her there was no future. He wished it was all over − trial, sentence, execution.

'When am I going to court?' he asked his warder. He was a gruff man but not unkind.

'Can't say.' The warder plonked Reuben's bread and cheese on the bunk beside him. 'There's quite a backlog of cases. Crime's one of the few things that's on the increase.' He gave a snort as if he had made some clever remark and looked quizzically at Reuben. 'I shouldn't worry about it, young feller me lad. If you're lucky you'll die of old age first.'

In spite of her intentions, Meg could not stop herself from looking out for the postman, but her letter to Reuben was greeted with silence. She deeply regretted having written it for in so doing she had allowed herself to hope and once again she knew the hurt of rejection.

Meg tried not to think of him but it was impossible. Now it was clear that he despised her, did not think her worthy of even the most cursory note. It left her feeling ashamed and abandoned. In the privacy of her room despair claimed her and she cried, twisting the keeper ring on her finger in a paroxysm of anguish. The very presence of the ring bore witness to what she had so nearly had and now lost. Declan lay asleep in his crib, blissfully unaware of the misery around him.

After a while she chided herself for being so ungrateful. In most ways she had everything that she could want. In the short time since Arthur had given her the camera, she had photographed several families. More had made enquiries. Although her studio was incomplete, she had hung up some of Mrs Watts's curtains and stood her subjects before the drapes, or sat them in rows, with children perched on knees and a proud father resting a patriachal hand on a wife's shoulder. Best clothes were worn, infants were bullied into stillness, older sisters blushed, young men stuck their chests out. This modest success made Meg feel proud.

In addition, she had plans to make calling cards for the more well-to-do. Each card would be inscribed with details of the owner, his business or connections, or perhaps the announcement of the times a lady would be at home to visitors. A photograph of the owner or his premises would grace the front. As long as she did not think of the past, these plans sustained her.

Meg knew that she owed everything to Arthur. In the face of his kindness, how could she be so ungrateul as to lie abed and cry? Arthur deserved better than that. She didn't know what she would do without him.

Drying her eyes she set herself to work, taking the eiderdowns and bolsters out into the yard so that they could have a good airing in the early sunshine. After a while she sat on one of the garden benches and gazed across the meadows towards the church spire. She became lost in thought.

'Mistress!' Her daydreams were interrupted by the arrival of Jed Thomas the carter. His anxious face had her immediately on her feet.

'What's the matter?'

'I'm sorry, m'm. It's the innkeeper. He's been took with a seizure.'

Meg felt her heart jolt. 'Is he bad?'

'Very bad. We found him down by the gate. We've brung him back in the wagon. I do think he's . . .'

Meg ran to the kitchen of the Bear. The room seemed engulfed in darkness after the light of the garden and it took a few moments for her eyes to adjust to the gloom. When they did, the first thing she saw was Arthur laid out on the scrubbed kitchen table. He was completely still and as she reached out to touch his hand she knew that he was dead.

'No!' She drew back and closed her eyes, unable to face the sudden loss.

'There, missus. Don't you fret. The doctor and the vicar 'as been summoned.' Jed Thomas held his cap awkwardly in his hands, twisting the rim. 'He didn't suffer,' he offered.

Meg was too numb to think beyond the practicalities. Her

217

mind went off at a tangent. Did Arthur have a plot in the churchyard? Was there a family? Was he church or chapel? She grasped at anything to avoid thinking about her loss and what would now happen to her and Declan.

Afterwards she could remember very little. The doctor and the vicar must have called; the village policeman certainly did. He asked questions that she could not or did not want to answer. When they left she closed all the curtains as a sign of respect, then washed the body and dressed Arthur in his frock coat. She carefully trimmed his straggly hair and placed his hat beside him on the table that continued to act as a bier. Gone was the seedy disreputable drunk. Instead he looked at ease with the world, comfortable, serene.

Now she cried, great gasping sobs for Arthur and herself, for dead Brendan and lost Reuben, for the mother she had never known and the grandmother she had deserted. She was washed away in a tide of pain. It was only Declan's howls of protest that drew her out of the deluge. As he clung angrily to her she smoothed his black, gently curling hair and wondered where his life would lead. If she had to die in the attempt she vowed to make sure that his path was smoother than her own.

Her night was disturbed by tangled dreams and waking moments of disbelief. The room seemed alternately stuffy and cold. Finally sheer exhaustion overcame her and she escaped into a shadowy sleep.

She was disturbed by a persistent thumping somewhere in the vicinity and started awake to register that somebody was hammering at the front door of the tavern. Still half asleep she stumbled from her bed, dragged on her clothing and cautiously opened the door. The person standing there was clearly somebody of importance and she was painfully aware of her uncombed hair and tear-reddened eyes.

'Mistress Foggarty? Emmanuel Simpson, of Draycott and Simpson.' He did not offer his hand – or elaborate, and surreptitiously she tucked her bodice into her skirt as the stranger walked past her into the snug. She offered him a seat and stood politely waiting for some explanation, trying to collect herself.

218

'I represent Mr Watts,' he started. Meg stared at him blankly. Apparently he recognised her confusion for he added: 'I am Mr Watts's solicitor. As you may be aware, he left very precise instructions about his estate.'

Meg shook her head and sat on the bench opposite the solicitor. He was straight-backed and his nose wrinkled slightly as if he found his surroundings less than pleasing. His grey waistcoat sported a discreet diamond stud that flashed in the light of the new easterly sun.

'Well, Mr Watts has a son whom we believe to be in London. He has settled a sum of money upon him.'

Meg nodded and waited for her own position to be spelled out. She wondered how long before she would have to leave, bracing herself for the blow.

Emmanuel Simpson added: 'There are no other relatives.'

'I see.'

She went to stand up, assuming that the interview was at an end, but Mr Simpson continued: 'Just one moment, Mistress Foggarty; there are other matters to discuss.'

She sank back like a reprimanded child. 'I'm sorry.'

'Now. This brings us to the bulk of Mr Watts's estate. He has left very precise instructions. You, madam, are the main beneficiary. There are, however, certain conditions which I believe are included to protect your son — it would seem that Mr Watts was very fond of the boy.'

Meg was in total confusion. From the solicitor's expression she wondered if he suspected that Declan was Arthur's child. She wanted to explain but there was nothing to say. Instead she gazed at him, her eyes unblinking. He shuffled his papers.

'Right. The property and his money are left personally to you. The instruction is, however, that you sell this place. Mr Watts wished you to set up in business on your own account, somewhere more central, Winchester perhaps. He had great faith in your talent as a photographer.' He paused to let Meg digest what she had so far heard.

'It was Mr Watts's contention that once you have established your position, no matter what else the future holds, you will always have a certain independence.'

Meg began to shake her head. 'It is all so unbelievable,' she started. 'I had no idea.'

Mr Simpson acknowledged her remark, his face professionally impassive. 'I should tell you,' he said, 'that you will receive something in the region of seven hundred pounds, in cash that is. Then, when this place is sold, I would guess that you may have a total of around thirteen hundred pounds.'

It was too much to assimilate. Arthur could never have had so much money. Surely there was some mistake and soon somebody would come along and tell her that she must leave. Meanwhile Mr Simpson stood up and brushed his coat down somewhat pointedly with his pale-grey glove. 'Well, madam, I shall of course be in touch. Is it your wish that we act on your behalf to sell this property?'

'Er ... please.' She had no idea how to begin.

'And perhaps in the purchase of suitable premises for your little enterprise, when you have had time to think about it? In that case you will be hearing from me.' At the door he turned and bowed stiffly. 'My condolences, ma'am. I sympathise with your loss but wish you well for the future. I am sure that you deserve every success.'

'Mr Simpson — how did Mr Watts make his money?' Meg flushed at the indelicacy of the question.

The solicitor bowed his head in thought. His hands were crossed neatly over the handle of his cane and he looked calm and assured. 'Mr Watts spent some time in India. At one time he was governor of a northern province. Good day to you.'

'Thank you. I understand.' She didn't.

Meg stood at the door and let the solicitor's visit and all its implications wash over her. In a daze she picked Declan up and mounted the narrow stairs to her room. While the babe bounced energetically on the bed, she sank down and gazed into space.

Eventually she got up and automatically began to tidy. Above the tiny fireplace her two photographs still rested on the mantel shelf. She gazed at them, remembering that first meeting with Reuben in the garden of Simla and that moment in her child's young life when he slept naked on the grass. The visual images helped her to recapture the feel of the time in a way that few other things could. The portrait of Arthur was in his room. She had not found the courage to look at it yet – the loss was too recent, the pain too new – but she was thankful that the picture existed. How else could she be sure of keeping his image alive.

Now she walked across the landing and hesitantly pushed open the door of the room that had been his. There was little to see. The jug and basin on the aging washstand were of good quality. Here and there piles of clothing lay across the backs of chairs. The bedstead had brass knobs that needed polishing.

Meg wandered across to the dressing table, noting the tortoiseshell-backed brushes, the silver cuff-link box. Here were clues to Arthur's past. She pulled open the top drawer and among the handkerchiefs and collar studs were a few yellowing invoices. Beneath these was a folded wad of flimsy paper, well thumbed, held together with what looked like a woman's diamond clip. Carefully Meg opened it, hating the feeling of prying into Arthur's life, although recognising that it would fall to her to clear out his belongings.

She went to the window and turned the letter towards the light, then started to read.

The Hill Station,
Kashmir
Arthur,
By the time this reaches you, Gervaise and I should be on the boat for England. I am of course aware of the scandal that will have greeted our departure. Believe me, I would not have inflicted such pain and humiliation upon you if there had been any other way. I am also painfully aware that when we arrive in England, Gervaise will have no choice but to resign his commission. This grieves me greatly.

I hope that you will try to understand. In one way I did love you, or perhaps I should say, do love you. What has happened to me, however, is beyond my control. Perhaps in the fullness of time you will find such a passion, then you will understand.

When we reach England, I shall take Roderick to stay

221

with my parents. He is young and will soon forget India and our troubles. Papa would like Roddie to go to his old school, and I hope that you will agree. I know that you will miss the boy, but for his sake it might be better if you try to forget both of us.

My earnest wish is that your career should not suffer on account of my foolishness.

Please find it in your heart to forgive me. I would ask you, do not try to find me.

Your unfortunate and erring wife,

Winifred

Meg folded the letter carefully and put it back into the drawer. She thought of Arthur's sad, gentle expression. What must he have felt when his wife ran off with a soldier? She could imagine the pain and loneliness, but guessed that there was another, searing blow to someone in his position of authority. How people must have gossiped!

Now she forced herself to look at Arthur's portrait. He looked benignly down at her, his head tilted slightly to one side, his eyes betraying a mixture of amusement and pride. Meg pictured how excited he had been that day, not unlike a small boy.

She remembered then his bequest. He wanted her to go to Winchester and be a photographer. It would be just the place to attract the right kind of customers. With a sigh she said to the spirit of Arthur that shone so brightly from his image on the mantel shelf: 'You're right as usual. As soon as Mr Simpson can arrange it, I'll move there.'

Chapter Thirty-Five

Meg did not attend Arthur's funeral. From the moment his body was removed from the inn, she closed her mind to the reality of his loss. Left alone, she sat on the bench near the window and took in every detail of the room; the low beams, the smoke stains on the walls and ceiling, the pewter pots that hung on nails above the chimney place and the uneven paving stones of the floor. In the hearth the ash was cold and dead. Never again would she open the doors of the Bear and welcome visitors into this room to warm themselves over a glass of porter or to eat a good baked mutton pie.

With a sigh she got up and went back into the kitchen. Painstakingly she penned a sign in large letters on an old piece of card, which she pinned to the front door: CLOSED DUE TO BREEVEMENT. Going back inside, she locked the door.

She looked around, wondering what to take with her. She knew that she would leave most of the things behind. Anything she wanted of Arthur's had to be personal; the print of the bay mare, perhaps some of the bed linen she used for herself – and, of course, her photographic equipment.

As she folded the blankets that had been on Arthur's bed, she wondered if she might be cursed. Brendan had died horribly in an explosion, cut off in the prime of his life. Reuben, wonderful Reuben, had offered her his world and in return she had laid herself open to disgrace, leaving him with the shame and humiliation of being abandoned.

Finally there was Arthur, dear kind Arthur, who had asked nothing of her and, just when he was beginning to enjoy life, was struck dead in one wretched moment. Any man with whom she came into contact seemed to be doomed. God, if he existed, must surely hate her. Angrily she thought: I won't give Him another chance to hurt anyone. Never again will a man get close to me. As Grandma Foggarty used to say: 'The Lord thy God is a jealous God.' Meg hardened her heart.

When the solicitor next came to see her, he brought some documents for her to sign.

'I don't think I want a profession,' she said, looking at the incomprehensible script; then, after a pause: 'Sometimes I don't think I want a future.'

Mr Simpson maintained an impersonal expression. After a suitable length of time he said: 'It was Mr Watts's wish, and perhaps you should think of your child.'

Feeling inwardly dead, Meg took up the pen. It really made no difference to her one way or the other. Something had switched off inside her and it could never be turned on again.

After he had completed the paperwork, Mr Simpson gathered up his documents and piled them back into his case. Standing up, he bowed correctly to Meg and moved to the door, but as he lifted the latch he turned. 'I'm sorry to see you still so distressed, ma'am. If it is any consolation, Mr Watts himself told me that you had brought sunshine into his life. He knew he was dying, you know.' Again he paused before adding: 'If you don't mind my saying so, I think you prolonged his life. In fact, you are the sort of person to bring happiness into many lives, begging your pardon, that is.'

Meg looked disbelievingly at him, fighting to keep the treacherous tears from her eyes. 'Do you know what became of his wife?' she asked, to divert her thoughts from Arthur's last days.

'Mr and Mrs Watts had some marital difficulties. She died, of cholera, before she could leave India.'

Meg said nothing. She thought of Winifred Watts and her soldier. Whatever their daydreams, they had not been fulfilled.

With a nod of his head, Mr Simpson saw himself out of the back door.

In the tavern everything seemed still and quiet again, almost suspended, as if it was waiting for Meg to go so that it could renew its old way of life. One day soon someone else would fill the place with warmth and life.

Only Declan's gentle breathing broke the silence as he dozed on the settle. In the strange way that grief is sometimes followed by the merest glimmer of hope, Meg thought: Although life has been cruel, what I shared with Brendan, Reuben and even with Arthur was not all bad. With each of them there had been some happiness, taken and given. The burden of guilt eased.

'Mumumum,' Declan called insistently, clambering from the settle and pulling at her skirt. He thrust a wooden brick into her hand. She smiled as she took it. There was really no choice, she had to go on. For herself life might seem to be over but it remained to bring joy to Declan, see to it that his life, whether long or short, had its fair share of sunshine. She sighed and threw off her fears. Now it was up to her. For Declan's sake her photographic studio would have to be a success.

'I've got some news for you,' the warder said as he brought Reuben's breakfast. 'They've set the date for your trial. It's due to start on 21 March.'

'Good,' said Reuben, pushing the mug and bowl aside. 'The sooner it starts, the sooner it will all be over.'

Mr Simpson, of Draycott and Simpson, took Meg to view possible premises for her photographic emporium. She wandered around the rooms apprehensively, unwilling to have to make a decision, but gradually the suitability of the place filled her with a sense of excitement.

The shop consisted of an upstairs kitchen, sitting room and bedchamber. Downstairs, one large, square room would serve very well as a studio, and a convenient cupboard could easily be enlarged to make a dark area for developing. The whole was part of an ornate brick terrace that already housed a glover, a haberdasher, a provision merchant and a purveyor of fine teas. It was quite centrally located and seemed the perfect setting.

Going through to the back, Meg discovered a small yard that included a privy. There was also a tiny patch of grass that would make the ideal place for Declan to play in safety. The spring sunshine bathed the whole in white afternoon light.

The contract was signed on a Thursday and Meg moved in on the following Saturday. It had cost her one hundred guineas, which left her over two hundred pounds in cash, so she could afford to wait for a suitable purchaser for the Bear.

Standing in the shop, surrounded by boxes, Meg considered her studio. There was much to be done and for the moment she couldn't decide what to concentrate on first. The studio needed to be well lit and decorated in such a manner as to provide a suitable backdrop to her customers. This would mean buying new furniture, carpets and curtains. Never before had she had the wherewithal to indulge in such a spending spree. It filled her with a mixture of pleasure and guilt.

On Mr Simpson's recommendation, a very capable girl called Carrie was hired to help with the domestic work. At fourteen, Carrie had already had plenty of experience in cleaning and childcare, two skills which Meg welcomed. She was a rather plain, straightforward girl, who reminded Meg in some ways of Margy. For this reason she warmed to her new servant and knew that she would trust her with Declan's wellbeing.

Meg gazed out of the window and turned her thoughts to advertising. If the place was to succeed she would have to make some effort. A sign would need to be painted but in the meantime she thought she might publicise her skills by displaying photographs in the window. By now there were many to choose from but her first thought was of those early works, two of her own and the one that Mrs Carmichael had taken.

Idly she wondered where Mrs Carmichael was at that moment. What tragic times had passed since her patron had left the country! She sighed. How surprised Mrs Carmichael would be to find that Meg was now a rich woman and a successful photographer in her own right.

*

Bartholomew Paige was greeted just after breakfast by a messenger. The man handed him a folded, sealed document and he opened it to find an official summons to attend the criminal court on 21 March. The first day of spring, he thought. It felt like a good omen.

He had not told anybody that Meg Foggarty was still alive for he had no wish to cast doubt upon Kingswell's guilt. The identity of the dead woman was of no concern to him.

'I wish that you weren't involved,' Edith said. 'Suppose there is a mistake and you are misunderstood?'

'How, misunderstood? If I tell the truth, what can go wrong?' Paige sighed as one who is long-suffering and has been hard done by. He explained his position to Edith as to one of low understanding. 'I was an innocent bystander, but a witness none the less. I could have pretended that I knew nothing but that would not have been public-spirited.' He gave Edith a withering look. 'An old man and a girl lost their lives because of this crime. I can't stand back and let the villain off scot-free now, can I?'

'What sort of girl was she?' Edith asked. He thought there was an edge of suspicion to her voice.

'How should I know? I doubt if I ever set eyes on her.'

Edith looked troubled. 'That's odd,' she ventured. 'Jolliffe says she worked in your yard.'

Paige alerted himself to the danger but his first feeling was one of irritation. Stupid woman, had she no more sense than to enquire after such things? She should know by now that there was an area where any sensible wife would turn a blind eye. Aloud he said: 'You are very foolish indeed if you think I know every trollop who works for me.'

Edith muttered something and when he asked her to repeat it she merely shrugged. Damn the woman! He might be wrong but he could have sworn that she had said: 'Only the pretty ones.'

Chapter Thirty-Six

Reuben's trial started at ten in the morning. Although he was given a legal man to speak on his behalf, he had no real interest in the proceedings. He sat bareheaded in the dock and studied his hands, wondering at how soft and white they had become. The good honest grime of his life in the forge had long since gone.

The judge was seated on a dais at the far end of the courtroom, like a vulture perched in the highest branch of the tree, black and hunched, his head shrunk into his neck. He surveyed the scene before him through hooded eyes. The boredom and lack of interest on his face did not bode well.

One by one jurors were brought forward and sworn in. As each man stepped up, Reuben's lawyer enquired if he had any reason to doubt the man's impartiality. He hadn't. He didn't mind much one way or the other.

Finally the charge was read. It seemed very long but what it boiled down to was that Reuben had deliberately got hold of some bullets and put them in the forge with the express purpose of blowing up old Amos and his own beloved Meg. None of it made sense. How did Paige know that the explosion had been caused by his own bullets? If Meg was dead, where was Declan? Surely, God forbid, anyone killing the mother would also have disposed of the child, although to what purpose he had no idea.

Reuben did not voice his doubts to anyone, least of all his lawyer. He wondered idly what the villagers at home must think of him and what they would do now for a decent farrier.

He hoped that someone had returned Paige's injured horse to the livery stable.

He was surprised to see Constable Dore from Freshwater in the court. Soon the village policeman was called to the witness box and he looked very uncomfortable as he recounted his version of the events of that morning. Once he caught Reuben's eye and gave him a regretful took. Reuben acknowledged him, then looked away. He had no wish to be part of this, at least, not until the next witness was called.

'You are Bartholomew Ebenezer Paige?'

'I am.'

At the sight of Paige something in Reuben seemed to explode. This was the man who had said that Meg was his property, paid for like so much merchandise.

'You evil bastard! What did you do to her?' He made a leap for the well of the court where the witness stood.

'Kingswell!' One of the guards grabbed at his wrist but he evaded him and lashed out at the hypocritical face of the hated brick master.

The blow made contact just to the right of Paige's fleshy mouth, narrowly missing his nose. Within seconds Reuben was overpowered, his hands forced behind his back and handcuffed.

'Take the prisoner down,' the judge ordered.

He was hustled away to the cells.

Now he was oblivious to everything except the hatred he felt for the man who had employed Meg. For the first time he began to suspect that jealousy was the root cause of the charges against him and that the only evidence came from his enemy. Reuben knew that he hadn't killed Amos or Meg, so who had? What a fool he had been not to see the obvious!

'I want to go back to the court,' he said to the warder.

'Don't know if the judge'll let you.'

'I just want to hear what he says.' He meant Paige.

'Your man will put your case.'

Finally the lawyer appeared at the door of the cell and Reuben was allowed back into the proceedings, his hands securely fastened to the court officials who stood on either side of him. He raised his eyes slowly to focus on Paige, who was now in full spate.

229

'You are saying that the prisoner actually told you what he intended to do?' Reuben's man asked.

'Not exactly, no, but he confided in me that he was fed up with being nursemaid to an addled old man. If I recall his exact words, he said: 'I'm young, I want to taste life. Once I'm free this will be mine.'

'I see. What did he mean by "this"?'

'Why, the forge and the cottage. And the girl. He planned to wed Meg Foggarty, but she wouldn't have him until he had a place to offer her.'

'It's not true!'

'Silence!'

Reuben's lawyer waited for the noise to die down before he asked: 'And how did you come to give him the bullets?'

Paige looked shamefaced. 'I didn't actually give them to him.' He looked at the jury to engage their understanding. 'He bought them from me, insisted on paying. He said he was getting a firearm but couldn't get hold of any ammunition.' Paige hesitated. 'I must admit it sounds very suspicious now but at the time I really believed him.' He embraced the whole of the courtroom in his honest stare, looking for support.

'Ask him why he killed her!' Reuben shouted.

'The prisoner will be silent!' The judge glared at him but Reuben had eyes only for his hated enemy.

'M'lord, may I say something?' Paige asked unctuously.

'You may.'

'Poor Miss Foggarty was a stranger in the village. She had had a bad start, made a mistake, had a child out of wedlock, don't you know. I am a Christian, I believe in forgiveness and in helping the poor.' He looked around the court again. 'Ask my dear wife,' he finally said. 'She knows that this is my way of practising my religion.'

'Your wife is in court?' Reuben's man asked.

'No, sir, but she could be summoned.'

'I don't think there is any need.' It was the judge who interrupted.

Suddenly Reuben felt exhausted. He knew that it was hopeless. Nothing he could say and no one he could call upon could prove his innocence, any more than he could

230

prove Paige's guilt. Meanwhile the cross-examination of Bartholomew Paige continued.

'How well did you know Mr Mew, the blacksmith?' Reuben's man asked.

'I did not know him at all,' Paige said truthfully.

'And when did you last see Meg Foggarty?'

'Not for some months,' he lied.

Now the evidence moved on to the letter that Reuben was supposed to have received from his dear Meg. They said that she had written to say she was leaving him. Part of him wanted to see the evidence again but the thought of reading those words was too much. If she had really meant to leave he was in the dark as to why. Right now he couldn't bear to look on her handwriting, or face the fact that she was gone.

With a shake of his head he slumped down onto the bench in the box. Paige had it all worked out and the judge believed him. The jury believed what the judge said. It was cut and dried. Reuben felt so tired. Now he just looked forward to the day when he could go to sleep and not waken to the nightmare that had gripped him for the past terrible months.

When the jury retired he was taken down to the cells again. He refused anything to eat or drink. The guards stood silently at the door.

'You never know,' one of them said in an attempt at optimism.

The jury didn't seem to be gone very long before Reuben was summoned back into the courtroom. Around him there was tense anticipation but he could not share those feelings. As the crowd rose for the judge's entrance, he thought: Please, God, just get it over.

Paige left the court on top of the world, the words of the judge circling round in his mind.

'Reuben Kingswell, you have been found guilty of the murders of Amos Obadiah Mew, widower, of Freshwater in the Isle of Wight, and of Meg Foggarty, spinster, recently of that village. We find that you did maliciously and with premeditation cause them to be killed. You will be taken from this court and on a date to be appointed you will be taken to a place of execution and there-be-hanged-by-the-neck-until-you-are-*dead*!' Pleasure bubbled up within him.

As he called a cab and settled himself inside, he thought that as soon as Kingswell was dead, there would be nothing to stop him from putting his original plans for Meg into action. After all, even if she did discover how her fancy man had died, it would be too late. As long as she believed that she had been the cause of Kingswell's actions, she would be like putty in his hands. Guilt in other people was a wonderful thing.

Paige wondered how long it would be before the sentence was carried out. Suddenly he felt impatient, not wanting to wait another day to have her in his power. Some time soon he might wander along to the Bear Inn, just to have a look. There would be no need to go in, unless ... He gave a little grunt of longing. There must be something he could do.

'Hurry, man!' Paige called to the cab driver. He felt so good that when he got home he would spend a very satisfying hour or two with his housekeeper and after that, why, he'd still have energy left to torment his wife.

In fact, he was so much on top of the world that before going home he decided to make a detour to the offices of the gas company. Instructing his driver to wait, he strolled inside and spoke to the clerk.

'I want to have gas lighting installed in my residence,' he said.

'Certainly, sir. If I can just take a few particulars ...'

Paige enjoyed giving his address and details of what he required. As the interview came to an end, the clerk asked: 'How soon were you wanting this to happen?'

'Why,' said Paige, 'as soon as possible.'

The next morning, on the pretext of a business visit, he set out for the Bear, still ebullient at the prospect of the future. His shock was therefore savage when he arrived to find that the place was empty. For a while he simply stared in disbelief. He could not believe his ill fortune. The Irish bitch might be anywhere.

As it started to rain and he was about to abandon all hope, he noticed the 'For Sale' sign. The sale of the property was in the hands of his own solicitors, Draycott and Simpson. He started to smile.

232

Chapter Thirty-Seven

No sooner had Meg opened her studio doors to the public than she found herself in demand. At first she could not believe that anyone would patronise her, actually pay for her pictures, for there was so much that she did not know. But the good people of Winchester had much that they wished to record — births, weddings, comings of age, betrothals. Some people came merely for the novelty and before long her *cartes de visite* were the latest rage.

Each working day she opened her doors at nine o'clock and closed them again at five. Whether or not she was busy with customers, she worked religiously at her art, and with the help of Carrie, her life ran smoothly.

One lunchtime, as she was about to close the studio for her hour's break, the bell above the shop door tinkled. Meg was about to ask the caller to come back later, but the sight of the large, flashily dressed man made her hesitate. He did not look the sort of person who would expect to be sent away. For a dreadful moment she thought that it was Paige and felt weak with relief when she saw that it was not.

He asked: 'Are you Mistress Foggarty?'

The sound of his voice took her by surprise. He spoke English but with a strange flattened accent, drawing out the words. She had not heard the like before. Slowly she nodded.

'I saw your name on the sign outside.'

She did not take her eyes from him and he continued:

'Randolph Vine, ma'am — W-E-I-N.' He spelled out his surname as if from habit. Meg had never heard it before.

Still she remained silent, unsure of what he wanted. He held out his hand and shook hers, bowing as he did so.

'I've been looking at your pictures, in your window. They're good, ve-ery good.' His voice was appraising and he nodded his head as if to confirm what he had said.

'I thank you.'

Mr Wein came into the studio and looked around, almost in the manner of one who was thinking of buying the place. 'You took all these yourself?'

'I did.'

'Ve-ery good.'

'May I ask where you come from?'

Randolph Wein smiled. 'All the way from America, ma'am.'

'America?' She had never met anybody from there before. 'Such a long way,' she ventured.

'It is indeed, and I was amazed to discover this little shop on my first day in your city of Winchester.' He drew in his breath before continuing. 'I run a publishing house, print a daily journal, magazines.' He paused. 'A good magazine is always on the lookout for stories. A lady photographer – I thought I might feature you in one of my issues.'

Meg shook her head in disbelief. Looking around him again, Mr Wein placed his hat on a table and hung his cane over the back of a chair. 'Meanwhile, if you have the time, ma'am, I would like you to take my portrait.'

'Er, of course.'

He settled himself in a chair and looked expectantly at her. 'Nothing fancy,' he said, 'Just a really good head and shoulders.'

Meg's hands had begun to tremble. She felt as if she were on trial. Memories of Lord Hinchington's *London Illustrated* magazines flashed through her mind, with their exotic places and important people. Did this man really mean that he wanted to write about her?

As she set to work, Mr Wein watched her every move, assessing, considering. 'Your husband is in the same line of work?' he asked conversationally.

'There is just myself and my son.'

234

'I'm sorry. Widowhood must be a difficult state for a lady.'

Meg made no comment. She had no wish to discuss her private life. She felt so much out of her depth that she wished Mr Wein would go. He continued to watch her and she grew increasingly hot.

'I've never felt the need to marry,' he announced. 'I guess you could say I'm married to my job. Just now I'm looking for people to come and work with me, work for me. I've got the best publication this side of the Rockies.' He bent forward and took something from the bag he had placed on the ground, then held out a periodical to her.

Meg took it. The name of the magazine was *The American* and the cover featured a full-page illustration of a strange man.

'Cherokee,' Mr Wein said, pointing to the wide-faced, dark-skinned man with a magnificent feathered hat. He was like nothing Meg had ever seen.

She looked up. 'Does he live in America?'

'He sure does. Now, though, I'm looking for some English stories. You have a beautiful face, ma'am.'

Meg blushed.

'I shall be in England for a week or two and then sail home.'

'Fancy that.' Meg worked quietly, preoccupied by the exciting world glimpsed through the illustrations in *The American*. There were lots of questions she would have liked to asked but she refrained from doing so. Instead she finished her work and asked Mr Wein if he could call back the next day to see the results.

The Amercian stood up and brushed the knees of his trousers to remove undetectable hints of fluff. He picked up his hat and raised it before placing it at a jaunty angle on his head. 'With pleasure, ma'am.' He hesitated and looked into the shop window again. 'You've really got me quite excited, you know. If the picture comes up to my expectations, well ...' He smiled. 'Let's just wait and see, shall we?'

The portrait of Randolph Wein had to be special. His manner convinced Meg that her success or failure as a photographer

235

might be judged by this man's reaction to her work.

She touched out the hints of grey in his hair and erased the tiny wrinkles around the eyes, then she toned the picture with a mixture of gold and silver, using all her skill to gauge when the shade was just right. When she was satisfied that it was just sufficiently dark to allow for natural fading, she made a contact print onto albumen paper and stood it in a prominent spot so that she could look at it. She was quietly proud of the result.

'Man,' said Declan helpfully.

'Yes, man.' Meg gave him a cuddle. 'The man's coming back soon so you be a good, quiet boy.'

When the American walked into the studio, he was wearing a pale-grey suit and matching hat, shoes and gloves. He looked unreal, a character from a book illustration such as the works of Mr Dickens that Meg had glimpsed at Hinchington Manor. Immediately his eyes were drawn to his likeness.

'We-ll!' He walked over to it, nodding his head in approval. 'Ve-ery good.' For a few moments he continued to study it, then he gave Meg his verdict. 'Ma'am, this is even better than I hoped.' He regarded her as if seeing her for the first time. His eyes were appraising, approving.

'Ma'am, would you do me the honour of dining with me this evening?'

'I can't – I'm sorry, the babe.' She looked down at Declan, who was eyeing Mr Wein with interest.

'I'd forgotten, you're a widow. Do you not employ someone?'

'There's Carrie, but ...' She had never gone out in the evening before, never left Declan. The thought of doing so seemed irresponsible.

He pursed his lips thoughtfully, then tapped the floor with his cane as if to underline that he had come to a decision. 'Nothing to worry about. If you don't trust him with your girl, I'll arrange for somebody to come from my hotel – you need have no fear, they only employ staff of the highest calibre. It will be someone of the utmost reliability.'

'I don't know ...' Meg had never been out to dine. Part of her was panicking, wondering what she should wear. From habit she thought that she should refuse but then reminded herself that she was beholden to no one.

'Leave it to me,' he said. 'Be ready at eight of the clock and I'll send a nurse and a carriage.'

'No, there's no need.' If she was going to leave Declan with anyone, then it had better be Carrie. He would be frightened by a stranger.

Mr Wein shrugged. 'Perhaps your girl would like a night off herself?'

'No, really.'

'As you wish.' He gave the picture one last approving look and turned to leave.

'Aren't you going to take your portrait with you?'

Randolph Wein smiled. 'Give it to me tonight. Over the next few days perhaps you'll tell me all about yourself, explain to me something of your craft, so that I can write it all up.' As he passed by the table he dropped a sovereign onto it and observed: 'Money well spent.'

'Really, I'd rather you didn't pay for the portrait ...'

'At eight o'clock then.' Ignoring Meg's protest, he left.

Meg put on her pale-grey silk dress with the slim skirt and the back gathered into a bustle. The bodice was tuck-pleated and fine pink velvet ribbon was threaded through the lace collar. She knew that it suited her well and hoped that it would not look out of place wherever they were going.

Declan was already asleep and she anguished over the wisdom of leaving him, but Carrie brushed her fears aside.

'You just go an' enjoy youself ma'am. Declan's all right along o' me.'

Meg nodded, trying to suppress her foolish qualms. 'I'll not be back late.'

The cabbie drove her to Mr Wein's hotel. Large white gateposts guarded the entrance and the drive curved round to an imposing pillared doorway. Meg swallowed hard as the horse crunched to a halt and the driver jumped down and opened the carriage door.

As she stepped onto the marble platform at the bottom of the steps leading to the entrance, Randolph Wein came hurrying down to meet her.

'Mistress Foggarty! I'm so glad that you are here. Allow me to present you with this small token.' He held out a single flower, swathed in ferns and held together with a pin. 'For your dress.'

'Oh! Lovely.' Never had anyone treated her so like a lady. He ushered her into the hotel, across a marble hall with exotic runners and pots of fern and aspidistra. The gas light from the chandeliers gave out an orange glow and the distant smell of roasting meat was mixed with the honey fragrance of beeswax.

They entered a reception room furnished with several large dark leather chesterfields and matching chairs. Meg accepted the invitation to sit down and pinned the corsage to her bodice.

'What sort of flower is it?' she asked.

'An orchid.'

They dined in another huge, brightly lit room at a table for two. The linen was heavy and patterned with silver threads. Silver claws held the matching napkins and the cutlery was ornate and heavy to hold.

'I've never been to a place like this before.'

Randolph glanced dismissively around him. 'It is really quite impersonal. After a while you find it lonely.'

He signalled to the waiter, who took his order and returned moments later with a crystal decanter of rich honey-coloured wine.

'A glass of madeira. It will warm you, make you feel relaxed.'

Meg sipped the liquid cautiously, liking the sweet cloying taste.

'Drink up.'

Hot onion soup was ladled from an elegant tureen into matching bowls and served with hot bread. Meg waited to see how Randolph held his spoon before starting herself.

The evening passed quickly and they talked nonstop. Randolph told her about his family, how his father farmed two thousand acres, how they had a town house in New York, how his sister had married an Italian count. A glittering world unlike anything she had known was painted for her.

At first Meg said nothing. Her life in Norfolk and on the

railway, then as a pug treader in the brickworks, seemed a thousand miles removed from this fascinating man's. After a while she told him about Mrs Carmichael.

'I know of her. Her work is the subject of much disagreement. Some think it is gifted and others that she has no talent. What do you think?'

'I think she is an artist.'

He smiled. 'But a poor shadow compared to yourself.'

'Oh, no!'

'Oh, yes. You really are exceptional – and beautiful.'

She flushed. 'I should be going.'

He pulled a wry face but acquiesced. 'I shall accompany you home.'

'There's no need ...' She began to feel nervous, not knowing what she had agreed to in accepting this meal. Memories of Paige came back – did she give men the wrong impression?

As if sensing her unease, her host said: 'I assure you I am a gentleman, Mistress Foggarty. I shall escort you home and then leave forthwith. But I hope you will allow a lonely foreigner to call on you again?'

Meg smiled gratefully at him, and nodded.

As they drove the mile back to her house, Meg leaned back in the darkness of the carriage and wondered what would happen next. She felt safe now and the wine had done its work.

'Please don't get down,' she insisted as they drew up outside her shop.

He shrugged. 'Am I being banished?'

'It's late.'

'It is. May I call on you tomorrow?'

She spread her hands as if to say that she did not mind.

'Good. Until tomorrow then.' He reached out and touched her fingers but did not try to kiss her. 'Sweet dreams, Mistress Foggarty. Sweet dreams.'

Chapter Thirty-Eight

The morning after dining with Randolph Wein, Meg awoke to hear hammering at the front door. The new experiences and the thoughts these had inspired had kept her awake until sunrise. Now she hurried down the stairs, tripping in her haste, her heart thumping unnaturally in protest at the disturbance. Over the nightgown she wore only a shawl, so she pushed the door open only the merest fraction. There was nobody there.

She was about to close it again when she noticed something on the step. Opening the door just wide enough to bring it through, she carried a large basket of flowers into her studio. She drew back the heavy green chenille curtains to let in the sharp daylight. Blinking, she turned back and stared mystified at the basket.

Blooms of lilies and irises filled the wicker frame. Blue, white and gold stood out boldly against the green backdrop of fern. An envelope was attached to the handle of the basket by a ribbon. Bending down, she opened it carefully, her hands clumsy with suspense. Inside was a card.

Thank you for a perfect evening. Regrettably I have been called to Town today but please, I beg of you, would you make yourself available to go upon a little excursion on the morrow?

Please don't disappoint me. I will call at ten of the clock on Wednesday morning.

Your admirer,
Randolph

*

Meg placed the card on the table, breathed in deeply and hugged herself. Her blood began to pound in her temples. Never before had anybody sent her a bouquet of flowers or invited her on a mystery outing.

The euphoria reminded her of that first walk on the downs when Reuben had carried Declan and told her that she had captured his heart. For a moment the magic of that day threatened to eclipse the present, but she told herself that this was different. Randolph was not courting her. He had travelled the world and knew how to compliment ladies, not that she was a lady, although he had the knack of making her feel like one.

Carelessly she put positive collodion onto her negative plate and ruined it. Luckily the photograph had no particular importance but now was clearly not the time to be working.

The hours between that morning and ten o'clock the following day seemed more like a week. In the evening Meg lit the fire in her bedroom and washed her hair over the basin. She soaped it thoroughly, then took particular care to rinse it well, using four jugs of water. As she towelled it dry, she chided herself for her vanity, but some inner sense of self demanded that she make the most of her assets. It was no good denying that her deep-chestnut hair was remarkable and an innate vanity made her want Randolph Wein to admire it.

In spite of his energetic manner and healthy male exuberance, she did not find him attractive. There was a padded softness about his body that bordered on plumpness. In a few years he would be overblown, like Bartholomew Paige. Perversely her mind turned again to Reuben. His body had a natural muscular energy that would stay with him into old age. Hunger for him gnawed at her.

Meg had no idea what to wear. Her wardrobe was limited to two work dresses, one brown and one black, an outdoor dress in grey with tiny black flecks and a full flounced skirt, and the afternoon dress that she had worn on her previous outing with Randolph. She settled for the outdoor dress, which had a matching lined cape. After all, he might be taking her out into the countryside, perhaps to take photographs.

241

The carriage drew up on the dot of ten.

'You're sure you'll be all right?' Meg asked Carrie, doubtfully. On the last occasion Declan had slept through the evening, oblivious to the fact that his mother was not there.

'Course we will, m'm. We'll go out and take some bread and feed the ducks.'

'Ducks,' said Declan and began to bounce up and down.

Meg smiled her relief. Looking around, she saw Randolph standing in the doorway watching them.

'Mistress Meg.' He raised his hat and bowed. 'I hate to hurry you but we must leave.'

'Where are we going?' She tied the strings of her bonnet and looked round for her gloves.

'You'll find out soon enough, but in the meantime we have a train to catch.'

Randolph had reserved a first-class carriage. Inside the seats were upholstered in dark-brown moquette and white antimacassars protected the headrests. The smell of engine oil and coal fumes invaded the carriage but did not detract from the air of luxury.

Randolph closed the carriage door and heaved on the heavy leather strap to pull the window shut. Now Meg felt cocooned in a different world.

'Sit there, dear lady. That way you won't have your back to the engine.'

She sat down and removed her gloves, looking out of the window as the guard paraded up and down to check that all was well. After a few moments she heard the piercing shriek of a whistle and with a rumbling, chugging jolt the train started to move.

Fleetingly she remembered that day long ago when she had loaded stones into barrows to level the ground for a new railway track. Then she had not envisaged ever travelling on a train herself. Now it felt as if that life had belonged to some other person, a poor, ignorant Irish girl.

'Was your visit successful yesterday?' she asked to break the silence.

'Successful enough. I had to arrange some travel documents.'

242

Meg did not ask when he would be leaving. The thought of his departure filled her with a curious mixture of regret and relief.

'Where are we going today?' She did not want to think about the future.

'To London. A little treat for both of us. We are going to the theatre, then out to tea and then home again.'

'The theatre?'

'The Princess's. We are going to see a little melodrama.'

Something else she had never done. Aloud she said: 'I'm not sure if I'm appropriately dressed.'

'My dear.' He reached across and took her hand. 'You look perfect.'

Randolph had hired a box. Sitting next to him, Meg gazed down at the auditorium, now packed with people. They were squashed together so tightly that latecomers could reach their seats only by being manhandled over the heads of those already seated. A hubbub of noise rose and fell like waves on a shingle beach.

Looking around, Meg saw two ornate balconies and from these there appeared to be tier upon tier of seating diminishing into the roof. The distant ceiling domed into the very heavens. The red plush of the seats and the matching carpeting fitted Meg's idea of luxury. The whole was lighted intermittently around the walls in a backdrop of yellowing husky gaslight.

'Are you comfortable?'

She nodded, too overwhelmed to speak, and studied the rich plum velvet of the curtains with their central pattern of leaves, topped by a crown. Now and then the curtain moved as some unseen figure on the stage made last-minute adjustments.

Now the musicians began to tune up until their random notes attracted the attention of the audience and a hush fell across the theatre. The conductor rose from his seat, tapped twice upon his music stand and, to the strains of 'Rule Britannia', the leaves on the curtain split asunder as the drapes parted to reveal the stage.

Meg found the play engrossing. The story was so sad. Nell, a poor but honest girl, was left alone to care for

243

her ailing mother. Her father had been killed in mysterious circumstances. Now they had no money to pay the rent and Despard, the evil landlord, threatened to throw them all into gaol unless Nell agreed to marry him. Poor Nell. She wanted to protect her family but her heart belonged to handsome Jack who had gone to London to seek his fortune. As the weeks passed and the day approached when they were to be thrown into gaol, Nell finally agreed to sacrifice herself for the honour of her family.

Don't do it! Meg crushed her gloves in her hands and was immersed by the ghosts of Paige and Reuben.

Suddenly it became clear that the wicked Despard had killed Nell's father so that he could steal her away. Kneeling at her mother's bedside, Nell prayed to be forgiven for her sins and waited for Despard to come and claim her as his bride.

There was a knock on the door, so loud that Meg jumped in her seat. Involuntarily her hand shot out and grasped Randolph's sleeve. He took her hand and covered it in his. Onto the stage came not Despard but Jack, returned from his adventures and loaded with riches. He was very handsome, with rich golden hair and a powerful, passionate voice.

'Where is the love of my life?' He had come to claim his bride. Even as he began to tell Nell that it was Despard who had killed her father, the villain himself arrived armed with a pistol and threatened to shoot Jack if he did not let Nell go.

'Never!' Jack put up his fists to fight.

In order to protect her love, Nell threw herself in front of him at the very moment that Despard fired and poor Nell fell dying to the ground.

'Have no fear,' she whispered as Jack knelt beside her, clasping her hands. 'I am called to heaven to sit with my father. No woman could have a greater honour than to die for love.'

As the curtain came down Meg pulled her hand away from Randolph's and surreptitiously wiped her tears. She dwelt on the noble spirit of Nell who had died for love and been honourable until the very last. If only her own past had been so pure!

She was still distracted as they dined at a little teahouse

near the Strand. The memory of the play kept coming back to occupy her thoughts.

'A penny for them.' Randolph wiped his lips on his napkin and laid it aside. His plate was now empty except for rich buttery blobs from the three muffins he had consumed. 'You don't seem to be hungry.'

'I keep thinking about Nell. What a wonderful person she was!'

Randolph smiled and Meg suspected that he was laughing at her. 'Would you sacrifice youself for a man you loved?' he asked.

She looked away and he leaned closer and patted her hand. 'I'm sorry. You are remembering your husband?'

'I wasn't wed.'

He was silent. 'I beg your pardon. I simply assumed.'

'My then betrothed was killed in an accident, on the railway.'

'I'm sorry. So many people are struck down when they cross the lines.'

She shook her head. 'He was a navigator, an Irish navvy. He died in a tunnelling explosion.'

'I see.' He was silent.

'After my child was born I became betrothed to someone else but ...' She couldn't explain.

After an age he asked: 'But you're free now?'

'Free?' She wondered what that meant. Although Reuben's keeper still circled her finger, she could hardly consider herself engaged.

'You aren't betrothed to anybody?'

'No. Does this mean you won't be writing about me now?'

'My dear, I want to know everything about you. Everything.' Randolph snapped his fingers and a waiter came over. 'The bill.' He kept looking across at Meg as if assessing her anew.

'I'm not what you thought,' she said.

'How do you know what I thought?'

She shrugged.

Back on the train they sat on opposite sides of the carriage and Randolph tried manfully to make conversation but Meg knew that he must be disappointed in her. Probably he could not wait to get her back home, say good night and goodbye. His next words therefore caught her totally unawares.

'This must sound quite unreasonable but I don't have time for niceties. I – I've never met a woman quite like you before. I want you to consider coming to the States. If you wish to practise as a photographer then I'll set you up in a studio – or, if you would find it more acceptable, you could come as my wife.'

Meg stared at him, silenced by his proposition. What was he offering here – a job, marriage, another proposition like Paige, a new life like Reuben? 'It goes round and round, for ever, no breaking it.' That was what Reuben had said about the gold keeper. Today, in the company of this rich, exciting man, she had thought of Reuben at every turn. She was not free.

'I'm sorry. I'm flattered but ...'

'You need more time?'

She bowed her head.

'In that case I'll wait. How long do you think you need?'

'How can I say? Perhaps for ever. I don't think there's any point ...'

'I'm not a man to accept defeat easily.' He sat back as if something had been settled. Grasping her hand, he said: 'In the meantime, may I see you again?' With a quick smile, he added: 'If you let me call on you, I promise not to mention my proposition.'

In the face of his boyish enthusiasm, Meg agreed.

Chapter Thirty-Nine

Two weeks after his trial, Reuben was notified of the planned date for his execution.

'You'll be leaving here on 15 June,' his informant said euphemistically.

'Good.'

The man paused. 'Is there anything you wish to have seen to? Any arrangements?'

'None. Yes – I want to make sure my horse is cared for. I'd like her to go to Jo Attrill or Alfred Cheke. They'll treat her well.' At the thought of the world outside the gaol, a tornado of hurt threatened to engulf him. 'Do you have to stay in here?' he asked the warder sharply.

'It's usual. We don't like leaving ...' The man appeared to have difficulty in thinking of an appropriate word and finished lamely: 'It's not good to be left on your own.'

'It's what I want.' The warder made no move to leave and after a while Reuben asked: 'Where is she buried?'

The man replied as if reading out a statement: 'The victim was interred in the graveyard of All Saints' Church in Freshwater, on the Isle of Wight.'

Reuben shook his head. Poor Meg, that was the last place she'd have wanted her remains to lie. 'I'd like a headstone on her grave,' he said. 'I'd like to word it myself.'

'They'd never let you.'

Before Reuben could say anything else, the warder added: 'And don't ask if you can be laid with her cus you can't. Felons aren't allowed on hallowed ground.'

Reuben shrugged. 'It makes no difference to me. I have

no hope of resurrection. I only hope that once you're dead you can really rest in peace.'

Margery Dore had not had a good year. The news of Meg's death and Reuben's subsequent trial was followed by another setback. Before Mr Paige disposed of the brick works he sent word that the staff was to be reduced, and Margy was one of those singled out for dismissal.

The loss of income was a blow but even worse was her sense of failure. She had worked at the brick works since the age of thirteen. It was all that she had known.

It was therefore a wonderful surprise when she was summoned by Mrs Gosden, the housekeeper who remained in residence at Simla Lodge. Although Simla had been virtually closed up since the Carmichaels went to India, from time to time members of the family would visit. Before each arrival there would be a housekeeping frenzy as everything was dusted and aired and some life breathed back into the villa.

For Margy the visit of Mrs Carmichael's daughter Julia with her rich merchant husband and friends was a godsend. She was offered a chance to work in the kitchens. It would only be for a month but it restored some of her confidence.

Margy thought Julia Norman was beautiful and secretly hoped that she would have some more dresses to throw away. Since Mrs Carmichael had left the island, she had missed the hand-me-downs.

On the day of their arrival Margy was sent into the garden to pick lily-of-the-valley which grew in profusion on the bank that separated the house from the lane. It was a good time to daydream.

As always, her thoughts drifted to Meg. She still could not believe that her friend was dead. Meg had been so beautiful, so special. Surely God had not meant to wipe out such a wonderful person? Her trust in the Almighty faltered and her train of thought switched to Reuben. At the memory of him Margy's heart gave a lurch. Although it had always been impossible, she had once nursed a foolish fancy that Reuben would fall in love with her. She had never really expected it to happen and of course it never had. She was so plain and simple and Meg was bright and beautiful. As she sang that hymn in church she always associated it with Meg.

When Reuben had declared his intentions, Margy had felt no envy of her friend. It had been as it should be, the handsome and beautiful united in love. They would have had such perfect children. She sighed. No doubt there was an ordinary, plain chap somewhere who would one day take a fancy to her. Who could understand these things?

When she went back into the house it was to find that Miss Julia had summoned the entire staff to the drawing room.

'I have a letter here from Mrs Carmichael,' she announced. 'In it she tells us such interesting news and she mentions many of you so I thought I should read it aloud.'

The staff shuffled in anticipation and Julia cleared her throat before commencing.

Margy listened spellbound. Mrs Carmichael described the Indian Simla and its plantations in detail. It sounded very exciting. She talked of elephants and tigers, and how Mr Carmichael had been struck low with a fever but was making a recovery. She asked after Mary and Hilda, her maids, and Mrs Gosden. She sent snippets of advice to her gardener for the care of the rhododendrons and azaleas that they had brought back on previous visits. Margy thought the letter was the most exciting thing that she had ever heard.

As Miss Julia came towards the end of the letter, her voice faltered.

'Er ... "Tell young Kingswell that as soon as we get back I will still want that horse for dear Alfred. I appreciated his company to the steamer even though our expedition was unsuccessful."' Miss Julia gave them all a regretful look before carrying on.

There was a little more but Margy was puzzling over what she had just heard. Had not one of the mysteries been that Reuben was missing on the night of the accident, and had he not said that he was with Mrs Carmichael? She screwed her face up, wondering if the letter had any significance. She wondered if she should mention it to her papa.

The next day being Sunday, Margy went to church twice with the rest of the servants at Simla Lodge in the make-shift iron building that Mrs Carmichael had had specially converted to save her friends the long haul up to the parish church. Afterwards Margy worked hard preparing food and fires for the visitors at the house. It wasn't until after supper that she managed to slip out, only to find that her father was in Newport on business. She hung around impatiently, sorting out the mountain of socks that her mam gave her to put into pairs.

When at last George Dore came home he declared himself to be stiff and tired. 'A bite to eat, then bed,' he said to his wife as she helped him pull off his boots, then to Margy: 'Get us a mug of ale, there's a good lass. Shouldn't you be at work?'

Margy hastened to obey. Soon she would have to leave or she would be in trouble with Mrs Gosden. As she handed the tankard over, she took the plunge.

George listened attentively, his official face on. From time to time he nodded and grunted to show that he was paying attention. When Margy finished, he leaned back and took a deep ponderous breath.

She waited impatiently for him to pass sentence. Finally he expelled his breath and said: 'You were right to tell me, girl. There was some question of Reuben being with Mrs Carmichael but no proof.' Slowly he sipped the ale and wiped the froth from his moustache onto the back of his hand. Again he pondered before saying: 'I s'pose the letter might be used as evidence but what you just told me really don't make much difference. Mrs Carmichael ain't actually here to confirm it and anyway, I wasn't going to say nothing, but the sentence'll be carried out pretty soon. I reckon it would take something more than that to change it now.'

As Margy began to snivel, he patted her hand. 'Don't take on so, girl. I reckon that, one way or the other, since he learned young Meg was dead Reuben don't want to go on anyways.'

The news of the imminent execution made Margy go cold and she looked at her father, willing him to tell her that it wasn't true. Instead he began noisily to eat his bacon pudding. Between mouthfuls he said: 'Don't you fret. What will be will be. Whether Reuben's guilty or no, he's got nothing to come back to − no forge, no wife.' He shook his head and tutted at the shame of it. Wiping up the juice from the pudding with his bread, he popped the last piece into his mouth and chomped thoughtfully, then reached for his pipe.

'I know I'm right, you take my word. Reuben don't want to go on. You just get along back to work and put it out of your mind. In these cases it's best to let the law take its course.'

Paige was feeling decidedly uneasy. He was beginning to regret that he had approached his solicitors and discovered the present whereabouts of Meg Foggarty. It would definitely have been more sensible to have waited until the smith was hanged, and then dealt with things himself.

The unexpected arrival of his friend Randolph Wein from New York had made him careless. When Paige had been in the States, Wein had been an excellent host, taking him to some pretty interesting places. The fact that Bartholomew was abroad, and therefore it was unlikely that news of his exploits would get back to England, had enabled him to have a very good time. Ve-ery good, he thought, remembering some of those American girls, and echoing his former host's intonation.

As a result, when Wein showed up just at the end of the trial, Bartholomew had made the mistake of telling him more than he should have done. Of course he made no reference to the little 'accident' at the forge, but he had let slip his interest in Meg, and his earnest desire to get her back again.

Randolph had caught on immediately. 'It sounds as if the girl has landed on her feet, Bart, come into a small fortune.'

'I don't know about that. I − I wouldn't want her to find out that she is supposed to be dead. That farrier deserves all that he gets.'

'And you want her back where she belongs, eh?'

'I do.'

'If it would help, I could call round and sound her out, see if she suspects anything.'

Now it seemed that Wein had been seeing a great deal of the girl − too much. It was unlikely that he would succeed in seducing her where Paige had failed, but Bartholomew was still jealous of the time the American was spending with her.

251

He wondered what his motives were – lust, avarice for the inheritance that had come her way, or just a plain desire to achieve something that Paige had not? He thought that perhaps it was time he took matters into his own hands.

Outside he could hear the regular pounding of a shovel as men from the gas company prepared the way for the pipes. Trenches were being dug, holes drilled and pipes laid outside the Paige household. The gas had already reached as far as the house across the street so it was a comparatively straightforward exercise to extend the service.

'Once the work is complete we'll have a little soiree,' he said to Edith, who was embroidering a chairback cover. Her heart sank. His little entertainments always meant a lot of anguish for her.

'I thought we could ask the chief constable and his lady, and perhaps the head of the council.'

When she didn't reply he picked up a book from the table and threw it at her, knocking the sewing from her hand. 'Pay attention when I'm talking to you!'

'I'm sorry, dear. I did hear what you said.' She bent down and picked up her embroidery, trying to ignore the pain in her arm. Fighting to keep the tremor from her voice, she asked: 'Were you thinking of asking anyone else?'

'No.' He sounded suspicious and she blushed.

'I just wondered.'

'And what did you wonder? Did you have one of your trivial little acquaintances in mind?'

'Oh, no. I was only thinking about the numbers, the work.'

Bartholomew's eyes narrowed. 'Yes, it does make a lot of work, doesn't it? I tell you what – why don't we invite that silly brother of yours and his even sillier wife? They seem to think you're married to some sort of peasant.'

'I'm sure they don't – '

'And we could invite our solicitor, couldn't we? That is, if it wouldn't make too much work?'

'No, dear.' Edith lowered her eyes so that Bartholomew should not see the blush that entered her face whenever Mr Simpson of Draycott and Simpson was mentioned. Instead she asked: 'Would you like to arrange a date?'

252

'How about 1 June? That's the beginning of the month we'll have something to celebrate.'

'We will?'

'Certainly we will. That is the month that murderer meets his just deserts.'

'Oh, Bartholomew! Don't you feel pity for the poor man?' Too late she realised that she had fallen into the trap.

'Pity? You think I should feel pity for a man who blows up an old blacksmith and a young woman in cold blood?' He leaned forward and pinched her arm just where the book had hit it. 'No, my dear. I don't feel pity. I rejoice in the fact. For once we'll have the pleasure of seeing that justice is being done.'

In spite of herself she gave a squeak of pain and he sat back in satisfaction, his eyes gleaming malevolently. Edith tried to continue with her sewing but her hands were shaking too much. Knowing that he was watching her, she tried to imagine that she was digging the needle into him.

Miraculously the trembling stopped.

Chapter Forty

Meg had been working hard all morning. To her relief, Randolph had neither called round nor sent a message, and she hoped that now he knew more about her, he had changed his mind. Even though the prospect of foreign travel was exciting, she had no wish to go with him to America. Neither did she wish him to write about her. She did not know why she suddenly felt so apprehensive about him. In spite of his charm and generosity, he always seemed to be putting her under pressure. It would be better all round if he stayed away.

It was past the time for something to eat and Meg thought she would close the shop. Carrie was out visiting her mother who was sick, so it was good to have a little time to herself. At that moment the bell tinkled.

'I'm sorry, I'm cl – ' Her voice faded and her heart leaped with shock as her visitor came into the studio. She began to shake her head and back away. All the time she thought of Declan lying asleep in the other room.

Bartholomew Paige took off his hat and bowed with the courtesy that any gentleman would show to a lady. 'My dear Meg, you've had us so worried.'

'Go away from here! How did you find me?' Her sense of being in control ebbed away.

'Meg, Meg.' He stood with his head bowed, penitent. 'I found you through Draycott and Simpson, through the sale of the Bear. We share a solicitor, it seems. Don't I deserve a warmer greeting than this?'

'Please, please go away!'

He gave a little laugh. 'I know I behaved badly. Please find it in your heart to forgive me. I know now that little plan of mine was foolish and I had no right to force it on you.' He looked repentant, imploring. 'I really do care about you, you know.'

She could only shake her head and will him to leave. She felt powerless to move.

'Just say you forgive me and I can sleep in peace.' He looked a picture of remorse.

Meg remained silent. The past was tumbling back upon her, all the fears and horrors of that night, the loss of Reuben, her own shame.

'If we could just be friends ...'

Suddenly she found her voice. 'You and I could never be friends. Just get out.' Her voice started to waver and she saw Paige flush. His eyes narrowed. For a moment he appeared to be thinking and then, as if making up his mind, he nodded his head.

'As you say, my dear. Before I leave, though, in case you haven't heard, I feel I should acquaint you with one or two unfortunate facts.'

Meg leaned back against the wainscot and tried not to listen.

'I don't know if you are aware but that smith you were so fond of, he's about to meet his end.'

'I don't know what you're talking about.'

'Reuben Kingswell. He committed a murder.'

'I don't believe you.'

Paige raised his shoulders in a gesture of indifference. 'Believe it or not but in a week or so he'll be gone.'

'How? Who ...?' He was talking rubbish.

With a magnanimous air he slipped off his thick worsted cloak and laid it across the back of a chair. 'It's a long story, but from what we can gather he killed his old master so that he could inherit the cottage and the forge.'

'That's nonsense. Reuben wouldn't hurt anyone, least of all his master. He loved old Amos. Where is he?'

Paige shrugged. 'It doesn't much matter where. He had a woman friend too, murdered her.'

'You're mad.'

255

'I may be mad, my dear, but I don't go around killing people who get in my way.'

The very mention of another woman tormented Meg. She could give no credence to the rest of Paige's story but the thought of Reuben with a sweetheart tied knots of jealousy in her stomach.

'I must go and find him.' Meg grabbed her shawl as if she meant to leave at that very moment.

'No!' Paige stayed her with his hand. After a moment he said: 'It wouldn't be wise. You see, there were other suspicious circumstances, too complicated to explain. The fact that you ran away ...' He left her to draw her own conclusions.

'I didn't have anything to do with it. I didn't even know!'

He nodded his understanding. 'I know that, but ... Supposing, just supposing you were arrested, what would become of your babe?'

Meg moaned. The implications of what he was saying were too much to cope with.

'I beg you, don't think of looking for him,' he said. 'For your own safety, it's best to remain here.' He reached out to pat her on the shoulder but she swung away from him in disgust.

'Don't touch me! You've done enough damage already. As God is my witness ...'

Bartholomew gave her another understanding nod. 'I don't blame you for what you're saying, my dear. You are upset. I shall leave now but one day soon I'll come back, just to see if I can help. Just remember what I've said and remember that I will always be your friend.'

'I don't want to see you again, ever!'

Paige acknowledged her remark and looked pointedly around the room, taking in her surroundings. 'You've done very well for yourself. Have you found someone else to befriend you?'

'Not in the way that you mean. This is all mine, honestly come by.'

He persisted. 'Forgive me, but I can't help feeling that now, of all times, you need a man to support you.'

256

'I don't! Anyway ...' She stopped herself from saying more.

'Ah.' He nodded as if understanding her new situation. 'One hears of such terrible things, confidence tricksters, preying on lonely women. There was a case recently of an American ...'

Meg felt her cheeks darken.

Paige smiled, the merest twist of his lips. 'Anyway, I don't wish to frighten you.' With a bow he backed away. 'Just so long as you are alert to the dangers. Goodbye, my dear. Until the next time.'

As the door clicked shut, Meg was swallowed up in black despair. Her first instinct was to seek Reuben out, but Paige's warning of the threat to Declan was too serious to ignore. Besides, Paige might still try to claim the babe for his own. She hugged herself and paced the room.

She wondered who the other woman could have been. Was it possible that Reuben had found another love so soon after she had left? And was it true that poor old Amos had died?

Finally there was the brick master's last warning. Could it just be a coincidence that he should mention an American confidence trickster? The more she thought about it, the more the description fitted Randolph Wein. Did Paige know that she was seeing the American? She had a terrible feeling that everything she did was known to him. She pushed the bolt home on the door and leaned back against it.

The only thing she knew for certain was that she wanted to run away.

Bartholomew was satisfied with his afternoon's work. He had achieved what he set out to do; let the girl know she couldn't escape and then tormented her with the knowledge of what was about to happen to her fool of a lover. At the same time, if Wein had any dishonourable intentions in visiting her, he had planted enough suspicion to scotch the American's plans.

He arrived home in a buoyant mood to discover that the work on the gas installation was finished. The engineer was in the process of explaining at length how to light

257

each appliance and how to turn it off again. Edith had dutifully lined up beside Simmonds, the housekeeper, to hear the instructions.

'Now pay attention,' Bartholomew counselled. 'This stuff can be dangerous, you know.'

The representative went through the process several times, pulling the chain down so that the gas went on, lifting the glass funnel to expose the mantle, holding a lighted taper to it until the gas ignited, then replacing the dome and adjusting the flame by pulling on the chain.

'That's quite straightforward, isn't it?' Bartholomew asked the two women. He squeezed his wife's arm with just the merest hint of menace and caught Simmonds's eye long enough to give her a knowing look.

Simmonds gave a shrug and looked bored. Edith nodded doubtfully and chewed her lip. The new innovation terrified her. She couldn't abide mechanical things.

After dinner Batholomew announced his intention to retire early to his study, where he had some work to complete.

'Make sure that I'm not disturbed,' he said to Edith as she placed her fork and spoon neatly together on her pudding plate.

'No, dear.'

Simmonds came in to collect the dishes. Edith pretended not to notice but she could not help observing how Bartholomew's eyes followed her around the table. The girl was really quite coarse but she had the sort of magnetism that seemed to attract gentlemen.

For a moment Edith felt a twinge of indignation. She sat up straight and said: 'The pudding was cold, Simmonds.'

'I'll tell cook.'

Bartholomew made a show of wiping his mouth and tossed his serviette aside. 'When you've finished all you have to do down here, you can bring me up a whisky,' he said to the housekeeper.

'Certainly, sir.' The woman tossed her head coquettishly and Edith drew in her breath. Before she could say anything, her husband looked at her and added: 'Simmonds can sort some documents for me as well. If we're not finished by ten o'clock, you can put out the lights and go on up to bed.'

Edith went to protest but he was already out of the door. Her heart beat fast as she thought of them closeted away together. Tears of humiliation threatened. Don't think about it, she comforted herself, it's of no account. Instead she cast her thoughts back to the evening of their soiree and glanced at the jardiniere, where the fine aspidistra that Mr Simpson had brought her as a gift was planted. A warm glow embraced her; she sighed and wondered when she would see him again. Sadly, as far as she knew, Bartholomew had no more legal work to bring his solicitor to the house.

She tried to read and then to sew but could not concentrate. All the time the discontent niggled. As soon as it was time, she put her things away and prepared to retire for the night. With sudden alarm she found herself face to face with the dreaded gas appliance. Now what was it the man had said? She pulled the chain down uncertainly and the light gutted, so she quickly pulled it up again. Which way should it be? Reaching up uncertainly, she pursed her lips and blew out the rebellious flame ...

As the day of the execution drew near, a barber was summoned to Winchester gaol to shave the prisoner.

'Fine head of hair you got here, mister.' The man snipped competently at Reuben's black locks.

'You want it?' he asked drily. 'Soon I'll have no use for it.'

'P'raps there'll be a reprieve.'

Reuben pushed aside the tin pot holding a ladleful of stew that represented his supper and stretched out his legs. He suddenly longed to walk somewhere, up over the downs at Freshwater. He'd sell his soul for a lungful of fresh air. 'I'm not afraid of dying,' he said. 'It's staying alive that takes courage.'

The barber opened his cuthroat razor and began to scrape it across Reuben's cheek. 'You may have a point there,' he said. 'But you never know what's around the corner.'

Chapter Forty-One

Meg was so distressed by the morning's events that she did not notice when the clock struck two. Shortly afterwards somebody tried the door. Her heart leaped and for a terrible moment she thought that it might be Paige. Peering cautiously around the curtain, it was to reveal not him but Randolph Wein.

At first she was not going to let him in, but in the face of his persistent knock, she finally unbolted the door.

'Meg? Whatever is the matter?'

She shook her head, eyeing him distrustfully. At that moment, Declan came toddling out of the living room, newly awake.

'Hello, young fella,' Wein moved towards him.

'Don't touch him!'

The man swung round in surprise. 'What is it? Have you had some kind of shock?'

Meg screwed the material of her skirt into a tight ball, and faced her unwelcome visitor. 'I know all about you. You are nothing but a confidence trickster, preying on lonely women.'

He laughed out loud. 'I don't know what you're talking about.'

'It's been in the papers.'

Wein looked genuinely puzzled. 'What papers? Show me.'

'I was told ...'

He still looked nonplussed. 'Who's been telling you such things?'

Meg moved this way and that, her anguish mounting by the moment.

'My dear girl, whatever is it?' Ignoring her protests, Wein took her arm and led her to a seat. 'You cannot say such things about me without an explanation.'

'I've had bad news. Somebody I used to know is to be – hanged.'

'Ah.'

'It seems that I might be implicated.' Now she looked at him for understanding. 'I haven't done anything. I ran away because – '

'Why don't you tell me all about it? Everything. That way I am sure it can all be sorted out.'

After a moment the whole story tumbled out, a jumble of facts and explanations, Brendan, Reuben, Paige, Arthur. Meg could no longer hold it back.

Randolph sat back on the table and regarded her. 'This man Paige violated you?' he asked. 'Threatened to take your child away?'

She nodded between the now choking sobs.

Wein sighed. 'Was it this Paige who told you I was a confidence trickster?'

'He warned me about an American who preys on women. I thought ...'

The American's face darkened with ill-suppressed anger. 'I think I should tell you a thing or two. I read your English newspapers. I have read all about this case of the blacksmith. There seems to be something important you don't know, something your Paige didn't bother to tell you – the girl the smith was supposed to have murdered is you.'

Meg could hardly take it in. 'Are you sure?'

'They mentioned a woman bearing your name.'

She sat deep in thought, then looked up to meet the American's eye. 'If you knew that, then why did you never mention it to me?' Her suspicions were now back.

He shook his head to dismiss the question, his face still taut and brooding.

Meg stood up. Slowly she said: 'You know Bartholomew Paige, don't you?' When he did not reply, she continued: 'I don't know what's been going on but I would ask you to go now, and not return. I don't understand anything – about you or about him – but if you don't leave me alone I . . . I'll call the police.'

Wein appeared to force down his anger. 'I meant what I said about marrying you . . . ' he started.

'Please go.' Her voice was cold as frost.

He came close to her and she fought down her sudden fear of him. 'Please.'

He snorted and stood back, now displaying his true feelings. 'Paige is a bloody fool! If he had kept his mouth shut I would have got you back for him – after I'd finished with you.' He sniffed again, eyeing her with derision. 'You're such a little innocent. You believe everything a man tells you. You might be pretty, dear lady, but you're nothing.' After a pause he asked: 'How much are you really worth?'

'Worth?'

'How much did your last lover leave you?'

Meg gasped with disbelief. 'You disgust me! Get out!'

Wein made for the door, bumping into Carrie as he opened it. To Meg he shouted: 'Women like you deserve all you get!'

Carrie came in, looking in surprise after the hurrying man, then at her mistress. 'I'm sorry I've bin so long, ma'am. Me mum's real bad. I'm afraid I'm goin' to have to go home and help her. I'm awfully sorry.'

Meg sighed. 'It really doesn't matter. I'm going away from here anyway. I doubt if I'll be back.'

Not knowing where Reuben was to be found, Meg decided that the best thing to do was to go back to the island. The thought of Margy and her family, and the Carmichael household, stirred up a longing for them all. These were genuine people, honest and caring. She knew that she could trust them.

Quickly packing a few things, she left the studio and hired the first cab that she could find. She offered the driver half a sovereign if he would drive fast to Southampton.

'Where you wantin' to go?' he asked.

'The Isle of Wight.'

262

He nodded and within minutes they were leaving Winchester at a spanking trot.

The journey seemed to take forever. They stopped only once to change horses but Meg did not allow herself the luxury of a meal. It was early evening by the time they reached Southampton, only to discover that there were no further sailings until the next morning. Meg had to accept that she could not reach the island before the following day.

She paid the driver off with a sense of failure, knowing that Reuben's release would be delayed for another day. Every hour must be a torment to him. Adding sixpence to the price, she told the driver: 'Give the horse a good feed.' He had earned it.

She could have taken a room at a hotel but something prevented her. She had money but no luggage and she did not feel that she belonged in the world of travellers and guests. This was the world of the Randolph Weins. Instead she found a lean-to down near the jetty and curled up with Declan snuggling to her for warmth. It reminded her of that other journey when she had set off from Yarmouth to start a new life. Now she had the feeling that she ws going full circle.

The first steamer sailed at eight and she was aboard early. Sitting on the wooden bench on the upper deck with the spray brushing her face, she watched the mainland recede into hazy morning light.

The gentle rise of the waves stilled her tension. Soon they would be back on the island. She had never thought to visit it again but as the low, wooded coastline came into focus, she realised that she loved it.

It was Mrs Dore, Margy's mother, who answered Meg's knock. The sight of Meg caused her to back away in alarm and cross herself to ward off the impossible.

'Mrs Dore, it's me, Meg. Don't be afraid. There's been a terrible misunderstanding.'

'Lord save us!' Mrs Dore breathed deeply and stood back to let her pass. 'You've given me such a turn. They said you was dead.'

'I just heard about it yesterday.'

Margy's mother let out her breath between her teeth.

'Oh, Meg, where have you been? Did you know that Reuben ...?'

'I only found out about that yesterday, too.' Meg described her encounter with the brick master.

'I knew that Paige was a bad lot,' said Mrs Dore indignantly. 'Surely they'll let Reuben go now they know you're safe? We all knew he couldn't hurt a hair of your head.'

'Where is he?'

'Why, he's in gaol, in Winchester.'

'Winchester?' The irony made her snort with disbelief. 'I've just come from there.'

'He's due to be − you know − on 15 June.' Mrs Dore could not name the unmentionable but then her face brightened. 'But now you're safe there's nothing to worry about. What a miracle!'

Meg agreed. It only remained for her to go back and present herself and then it would all be sorted out. 'Where's Margy?' she asked.

'At work. At Mrs Carmichael's folks'. She don't work at the brick works no more. Paige sacked her.'

That was another injustice that Paige should pay for, Meg thought. Aloud she said: 'I'll go and visit her.'

'You'll find her at Simla. Leave the little lad with me, he can play with young Archie.'

Meg suddenly kissed Mrs Dore's plump apple cheek. 'I love you,' she said.

It took Margy about an hour to recover from the shock of finding that her friend was alive.

'It's a miracle!' she kept saying. 'You're risen from the dead.'

'I'm not. It was a terrible misunderstanding.'

Margy continued to shake her head in wonder. 'Look at you − such smart clothes! It's a miracle.'

'Margy, do you know anything at all about what might have happened to old Amos − or this young woman?' She found it difficult to acknowledge that there had been somebody else in Reuben's life.

Margy shook her head. 'We thought the gal was you.'

'Well, I must go straight back to Winchester and tell them

264

that I'm alive, but I'd like to know everything there is to know.'

'Well ...' Margy told what she knew, her witness to the fight in the copse and what Mrs Carmichael had said in her letter.

'Do the police know this?'

'I told Pa, but ...' Margy flushed. 'He seemed to think that Reuben didn't want to live. He thought it might make things worse if I told them what I've just said. Besides, I was frightened I'd have to go to court.'

'Oh, Margy! What you know might have saved Reuben's life. It doesn't prove that he didn't do it but it shows that he might not have done and that's what they rely on, isn't it, reasonable doubt? If I hadn't found out ...'

'If you want me to, I'll say it all.'

Meg gave her friend a hug. 'With luck, when I tell them the truth that will be the end of the matter, but in the meantime it's best to have all the proof there is. I need to speak to Miss Julia. I should ask her for that letter.'

Margy scooted off and soon returned with the present mistress of the house.

'Can I be of help to you?'

Julia was not like her mother, being refined, pretty and very aware of her status. Meg feared that she was exceeding her place in requesting this interview, but then she remembered her smart clothes and the money in the bank and, more than anything, that Reuben's life was at stake.

'I need to borrow the letter that Mrs Carmichael sent to you from India,' she said. 'In it she mentions Mr Reuben Kingswell. What she wrote might help to save his life.'

Miss Julia raised her eyebrows in surprise and rustled her skirts, which had become tucked up in the buckle of her house shoe.

'I am afraid you cannot have the letter,' she replied after a moment. 'My father has been ill and my housekeeper had a foolish notion that the letter might carry infection. I regret that she took it upon herself to burn it. Now, if there is nothing else ...'

Meg shook her head and accepted her dismissal. Her heart felt heavy and the nagging fears closed around her. Perhaps she should ask Miss Julia to come to the prison herself and repeat what the letter had said, but in the face of the other woman's indifference her courage failed her. She could only hope that her own testimony would be enough.

Margy saw her to the door of Simla Lodge.

'Where you goin to stay?' she asked. 'Mam'll put you up.'

'I'm not staying.' She hesitated. 'Do you think your mam'd look after Declan for a day or two? He's with her now. He seemed to like your Archie.'

''Course she would. Oo, Meg, do be careful. You might be in danger. You ought to get the police to find out the truth, that's what they're trained for.'

For a chilling moment Meg thought of Paige. He had warned her not to make herself known, suggesting that she might in some way be implicated. She wondered how he knew so much and if it was not he who had something to hide. The memory of his face, the cold eyes and the greed, made her sick to her stomach.

Looking up to find Margy watching her, she forced a smile. 'Don't you worry. I'm not in any danger. I've only got to tell the truth and it will be sorted out. Really, Margy, there's nothing to fear.' She gave her friend another hug and turned her back towards the village.

As she walked through the half-forgotten lanes she soaked up the sense of home and safety. This place gave her courage, a sense of belonging. One day she would come back. Straightening her shoulders and preparing to say her farewells to Mrs Dore, she thought: Now it's all up to me.

Chapter Forty-Two

Now that Meg was travelling alone she made haste to return to the mainland. On the journey she tried to plan what she should do and say when she reached the gaol, but every time she ended up in confusion.

She had no idea what to expect. Would they let her see Reuben and would they believe him when he confirmed that she had once been his betrothed?

The thought of seeing him brought its own anxieties. What were his feelings towards her when she had run away? Did he think she had known about the killings and abandoned him to his fate? Even worse, perhaps the authorities would dismiss her story as untrue. Then she remembered that she could always call on her solicitor, Mr Simpson, to identify her. The thought of his calm, professional support eased her worst fears.

Back in Winchester she went straight to the gaol. The building exuded a cold, immovable presence and in spite of the early sunshine she was shivering. Taking all her courage, she walked up to the huge solid forbidding door and banged upon it.

'Ma'am?' The prison warder who answered her knock looked at her in surprise.

'There's been a mistake,' she started. 'Mr Kingswell. He's being held here. He's supposed to have murdered me, but I'm ...' She ground to a halt.

Her mutterings were met with silence. Making a huge effort, she said: 'My name is Meg Foggarty. I have been out of touch with what is going on. Yesterday I learned that I was believed to have been murdered by Reuben Kingswell.'

'You're Meg Foggarty?' The man registered amazement. 'You'd best come on in.'

Her escort conferred with another man on duty. Meg could not hear what they were saying but they kept glancing over at her before resuming their discourse. Coming to some conclusion, they both approached her.

'You have proof of who you are, ma'am.'

'No. I –'

Again they looked questioningly at each other. 'Another crank?'

'I'm not! I'm Reuben's fiancée. Why don't you ask him?'

'He'd say anything to get out of here.'

'What would prove to you who I am?'

After a moment's thought, one of them said: 'Where's your nipper, then?'

'Declan? He's been with me but I've just come from the island. I've left him with Mrs Dore, she's the constable's wife.'

To her relief, she seemed to have hit on the right answer. Now there was a sense of urgency in the way that they hustled her along low corridors, finally stopping outside one of the many identical cells.

'Let's see what your "fiancé" has to say, then.'

One of her escorts unlocked the door, which clanked noisily as the catch flew back. Hesitantly Meg went to follow the guards inside, but they stopped her at the doorway.

'Just wait here.'

She raised her eyes to take in the gaunt, hunched figure sitting by a deal table.

'Stand up, man. This lady has come to save you.'

The prisoner moved his head away slightly but did not oblige. He seemed immune to what was going on about him.

'Come along. Up with you.' The guard prodded him and he swung round. At that moment Meg saw him full-face, the hollow cheeks, the tired hazel eyes, the straight nose. He raised his eyes to hers and something happened to his expression. Suddenly his eyes grew large and he grabbed the edge of the table as if for support. He leaped up and began to back away, shaking his head.

'What is this? What sort of trick is this?'

At the sound of his voice Meg gave a little wail of anguish. She pushed past the guards and held out her hands towards him.

'Reuben! I didn't know until yesterday. What have they done to you? I'm not dead – did you really think I was?' She felt dizzy with shock.

He sank back into his chair and continued to stare at her in disbelief.

Meg's eyes were riveted to the condemned man. With an effort she turned to his gaolers. 'We were ... betrothed. I ran away.'

'You're the one he's s'posed to have killed?' There was incredulity in the question.

'I believe so.' Even as she spoke, Meg could not believe that her beloved had been reduced to the half-stranger who sat before her.

'Reuben?' she said again.

As the warder went to move towards him, the prisoner suddenly flung out his arm, sending the tin mug on the table clattering across the floor. His eyes blazed with hurt and anger.

'Get me out of here!' he shouted. 'Now! Take me out there.' He nodded towards the courtyard and got up, starting towards the cell door, dragging the warders with him. As the men struggled to prevent him, he swung round to face Meg, shouting: 'Haven't you tormented me enough? What did I do to make you treat me this way?'

Meg gazed at him blankly. Had he lost his sanity? After all she had just gone through, she had expected a different welcome.

In the face of her silence Reuben suddenly pulled away again, dragging his captors with him. He cried: 'For pity's sake let's get it over! Take me now, this very minute, take me to the gallows and let me swing!'

Nothing that had happened to Meg before compared to the chaos of her emotions as she watched Reuben, her

269

lover, a condemned man, fighting to make his way to a premature death.

His two gaolers quickly overpowered him, dragged him struggling back to the cell and threw him onto the narrow bed. Then they locked the door and led her back along the corridor, her mind numbed.

'Now, Mistress Foggarty, sit you down. This is clearly something of an ordeal for you. Are you saying that you are the same Meg Foggarty who was engaged to Reuben Kingswell, and whom he supposedly murdered?'

She looked at the man's greying sideburns, in which nestled scurfy flakes of skin. His face was florid and dry.

Somewhere, a long way away, she heard herself say: 'I was engaged to Reuben, yes, but he could never murder anybody.'

The two men glanced at each other. One of them said: 'The fact remains, mistress, that he did. It may not have been you but there was a young woman in the forge, apart from Mr Mew.'

At this, Meg threw off the numbing shock as outrage took over. 'You're not still saying he killed old Amos? Never! Reuben would never hurt his master. It's unthinkable.'

Florid Face regarded her impassively. 'Did Kingswell have any other lady friends?' he asked.

'No!' Meg felt a surge of jealousy at the thought. She closed her mind to the vision of Reuben with someone else.

'Why did you run away?'

Meg was almost too ashamed to admit what had happened, but in her confusion she could think of no substitute for the truth. She kept her eyes down and when she spoke her voice was expressionless.

'He raped me.'

'You're saying that Kingswell raped you?'

Meg frowned at their stupidity. 'No, Bartholomew Paige.'

Again the two men looked at each other. 'How well do you know Mr Paige?'

'I used to work for him.'

'Did your fiancé know about this "rape"?'

Meg shook her head. 'That's why I ran away.'

270

'Did you know that it was Mr Paige who was chief witness at the trial? He swore on oath that Kingswell bought bullets from him with the express purpose of blowing up the forge when old Mew lit it.'

Now Meg knew it was a lie. 'Amos Mew wouldn't normally have lit the forge any more. He was old and confused.' As an afterthought, she added: 'Why would Reuben want to harm him?'

'To get possession of the cottage so that he could get wed.'

She snorted. 'That's rubbish. He – we were hoping to rent Mr Paige's cottage.' Tears threatened as she remembered her conversation with the brick master. 'Reuben didn't know, but when Mr Paige discovered that we were betrothed, he threatened to take my child away.'

'Why should he do that?'

She blushed. 'He wanted me to be his mistress. It was his way of getting what he wanted.'

'Were there any witnesses?'

Through her brimming tears she scowled at him. 'Of course not. You don't make threats like that in public.'

The officer nodded at the truth of this, but added: 'Then it's your word against his.'

Meg's shoulders slumped in defeat. Her word would hold very little weight compared to that of a man like Paige, a pillar of respectability. The thought of facing him again made her cringe with fear.

'Are you implying that Mr Paige had a motive for lying in court?' the younger officer asked.

'Of course he had a motive. He wanted me to be his mistress. He hated Reuben – he was jealous of him.'

'Not jealous enough to kill two people just to put the blame on your fiancé?'

'I don't know. I can't believe anyone would do that.'

Florid Face said: 'Kingswell claims he wasn't there when the explosion took place. He says he was with a Mrs Carmichael. Do you know anything about that?'

'Yes, Mrs Carmichael has confirmed it in a letter. She is still away but you could ask her daughter.'

'Has she got the letter?'

271

'No.'

'Then it's hardly likely to stand up in a court of law.'

'May I see him again?' Meg needed to reassure herself, to explain to him. His bad opinion of her was like acid. Aloud she said stupidly: 'When I ran away I didn't know all this would happen.'

'I'm sorry, ma'am. As you'll appreciate the, er, case for the murder of Amos Mew remains unchanged.'

'You don't mean they'll still ...' She felt herself grow cold. 'How long?' she managed to ask.

'In a few days.'

'But what I've told you ...'

'It makes no difference to the charge of killing the old man.'

She stared angrily at the two men. 'You're crazy! Reuben is innocent of any crime. I'm going to prove it.'

The officers stared impassively back and she knew that they did not believe her.

'Will you at least give him a message?'

'I don't see why not.'

'Then tell him, please, that everything will be all right. I'm going to discover the truth.'

'We will.'

Under her breath, she added: 'And tell him that I love him.'

Chapter Forty-Three

Meg could not afterwards recall the journey from the prison back to her shop. Her mind was in total chaos and, whichever strand of worry she tugged at it seemed to lead nowhere.

Once inside, she bolted the door, then lit the fire and made herself a cup of tea. Without Declan the place seemed cold and empty. She felt alone and vulnerable but at the same time she was glad that her child was safely away. Slowly she was coming to an unavoidable decision.

The main witness at the trial had been Bartholomew Paige. To an outsider he might seem a pillar of society but Meg knew that he would stop at nothing to get what he wanted. He had wanted her and now Reuben was fighting for his life.

The thought of what she had to do made Meg tremble. She knew that she had let Reuben down and inadvertently her actions had led to a near tragedy. Now, whatever it cost her, she must find a way to put it right. It struck her as an irony that she should now be the one to seek out Bartholomew Paige when for the past months she had been running from him. She did not know where the brick master lived but the fact that they shared the same solicitor should make it possible for her to find out.

Changing her clothes and making herself presentable, she set out for Mr Simpson's office. She feared that perhaps professional loyalty would prevent him from telling her where to find her enemy, so on the journey she prepared her story.

Mr Simpson had a client when she arrived but she was permitted to wait in a large withdrawing room. The place was tastefully furnished and the ornaments and pictures were pleasing to the eye. She soon became lost in contemplating her surroundings.

'Mistress Foggarty, a pleasant surprise. Would you like to come through?'

It was Mr Simpson himself who came to greet her. She stood up and held out her hand.

'Mr Simpson, it is kind of you to see me at short notice. I wanted to discuss something with you.'

'But of course, dear lady.'

Meg placed her gloves and fichu on the table and sat upright, resting her hands in her lap, gripping them together to stop them from shaking. When the solicitor had seated himself at the other side of his imposing desk, she said: 'I am thinking of selling my business and moving back to the Isle of Wight.'

'The Isle of Wight?'

'That's where I lived before.'

He frowned, looking at her intently. 'You couldn't be the same Meg Foggarty ...'

I'm afraid I am. I have only recently discovered what happened.'

'I heard.'

Meg thought quickly. It was now possible that Mr Simpson would make a connection between herself and Paige.

'When I lived on the island I made the acquaintance of a charming lady, Mrs Paige,' she said, hoping to forestall him.

'Mrs Edith Paige?'

'Yes.' She hoped that it was the right one.

Mr Simpson looked troubled. 'These are sad times,' he started. 'You have not heard?'

'Heard what?'

'About the accident.'

She waited, wondering what Paige might have done now.

'A terrible business. Mrs Paige has been widowed, just yesterday.'

'Widowed?'

'By a tragic misfortune. The family had gas lighting

274

installed. There may have been some fault, or some care-lessness on the part of the staff. Mr Paige and one of the maids were killed outright.'

It was too much to take in. 'You mean Bartholomew Paige is dead? But I ...' She could not believe what he was telling her. Paige was invincible, a ruthless force that could never be wiped out. Somehow she stopped herself from saying how recently he had visited her shop and warned her away from the man she was striving to save.

'Such a dear lady.'

Meg realised that he was talking about Mrs Paige. 'Yes.'

With a sigh he got up and went to a bureau. After a moment he returned with a piece of paper on which he had written an address. 'That's where you'll find her. She will no doubt be glad of a friend's support at a time like this.'

'Thank you.' Meg had no use for the address now but she put it in her fichu. Her hands shook so that she could barely fasten the clasp. Unsteadily she got to her feet.

'Thank you, Mr Simpson. I ...'

'Was there something else you wished to discuss?'

She shook her head, then remembered the pretext on which she had come. 'Oh. Yes, about selling the business. Well, perhaps we could leave it until another time.

'Of course. You must be upset by the news. Would you wish me to get you a carriage?'

'If you please.'

Sitting in the cab a few minutes later, Meg tried to make sense of this latest twist of fate. Bartholomew Paige was dead. No longer did she have to fear that he would come to threaten her. Now Declan was safe. One weight was lifted but in its place came another burden. If Paige was dead, then who would tell the truth about Amos Mew?

She opened her fichu, took out the piece of paper and, leaning forward, called to the cabbie: 'I've changed my mind. Please will you take me to this address ...'

The house was large, prosperous-looking and immediately recognisable by the boards and scaffolding along one side. In the front garden a pile of charred furniture rested on the lawn.

Meg dismissed the cab and walked up the drive. Fighting down her butterflies, she pulled an ornate iron rod that caused a distant bell to tinkle.

'My card,' she said to the maid, holding out one of her own *cartes de visite*. 'Please will you ask your mistress if she could spare me a few moments?'

Edith Paige received Meg in her drawing room. It was a large room, heavily furnished, and undamaged by the recent explosion. The widow appeared calm, with no sign of recent tears or distress. Meg noticed that she was dressed in russet brown and not mourning black. She took the plunge.

'Mistress Paige, please forgive me for calling at such a ... sad time, but it is a matter of some urgency.'

'Please be seated.'

Meg accepted the invitation and swallowed down her fears. Finally she started. 'I have come about a very delicate matter. I don't really know how to begin.' She stopped and looked into the pale, serious eyes of her hostess, hating the idea of hurting her. 'It concerns your husband.'

Edith blinked and Meg could see her grow tense. She forced herself to continue. 'I know that this must seem indecently hasty, but your husband was chief witness at a trial. He said that the accused had asked him for bullets so that he could kill his master. I ... I don't think that can be true.' Edith remained silent and after a moment Meg added: 'I was engaged to the accused, Mr Reuben Kingswell. I knew your husband, too. I used to work for him. He provided me with a cottage ...'

'You are Meg Foggarty?'

'Yes. They thought I was dead. Your husband – '

'There's no need to go on.'

'I'm sorry.' Meg willed her to understand, to forgive her for unwittingly behaving so foolishly.

Edith said: 'You weren't the first one. How did you know where we lived?'

'Through Mr Simpson.'

'Ah.' Her expression softened and she shrugged as if throwing off some burden. 'My husband liked his own way,' she said neutrally. 'I must confess that I had doubts

276

about this trial but I tried not to dwell on it. What is it that you want to know?'

'If there is anything that might throw doubt on Mr Paige's testimony.'

'What makes you think that he was lying?'

Meg struggled to find the right words. 'I don't wish to distress you but it seems that perhaps your husband formed some sort of attachment for me.'

Edith looked down at her hands, which were folded in front of her. When she looked up her face was composed. 'What you have just said is more important than you can know. All our married life I have tried to pretend that it was otherwise, but in my heart of hearts I knew.' She flushed guiltily. 'I didn't love him, you know.'

The confession shook Meg. She had assumed that this woman would want to protect his memory, keep her illusions intact.

For a while Edith seemed lost in thought. Then she said: 'Until recently I had assumed that all marriages were like this. Then, well, I realised that I had been mistaken.'

'If I don't find out the truth, Reuben will die,' Meg blurted out, her self-control ebbing away.

'You love him?'

She nodded.

'But you ran away?'

'I ran away from ... someone else.'

'I think I understand.' Edith sighed. 'A wife cannot testify against her husband but there is something that you should have. I can't believe that things have turned out as they have.' She went to a large sideboard that almost filled the opposite wall and opened a drawer, taking out a document. She turned and held it out to Meg.

'We are all guilty, my dear. Bartholomew left this in his desk. He must have written it some time ago and then thought better of it. It is, as you will see, addressed to his solicitor, but when he died I opened it.' She pulled a wry face and repeated: 'We are all guilty in our way.'

277

Meg took the paper, unfolded it and began to read. It was undated.

Simpson,
I wish to discuss a change to my will. As you know, my wife seems unable to give me children. I cannot accept this situation and intend to rectify it by trying elsewhere for an heir. In the event of my premature death I need to make provision for any child that may be born to me, even out of wedlock and even if that birth occurs after my demise. I intend to take a mistress for the express purpose of achieving this end. I have chosen one, by name Meg Foggarty, who presently works under my protection. Should she conceive a child that is born after my death I wish him to be raised as my true heir. If, as I hope, a child is born before my demise, I will then make further, more concrete arrangements for his future.

I do not think that it is necessary to discuss this with my wife until such time as a child is born. She will in any event concur with my wishes.

Draw up any documents that you feel are necessary and present them to me for signing.
Bartholomew E. Paige

Meg gazed at the letter. She felt curiously ashamed, seeing herself through this man's eyes. How could she have been unaware of his thoughts, the calm, premeditated nature of his plans?

She looked up to find Edith watching her. Her hostess said: 'It isn't I who can't have children, it was he. His doctor told me that he had the mumps when he was in his twenties. He tried to tell Bartholomew but he wouldn't believe him.' She shrugged. 'If necessary I will affirm that I gave you that letter but I hope that I shall not need to. I haven't told Mr Simpson about it and he might be hurt to think that I hid it from him.'

Some intuition made Meg hesitate. 'Mr Simpson is a very kind man,' she said tentatively.

'He is.' Meg saw that Edith Paige was blushing. 'I ... I should prefer not to give him a bad impression of me.'

'I understand. Thank you, ma'am.' On impulse Meg kissed

her. 'I'm sorry – ' she started, but Edith shook her head.

'Why should you be sorry? Bartholomew was a bully and a brute. I of all people should know. Get your young man released from prison and use the letter if it helps.' She walked Meg to the front door and formally shook hands. 'Goodbye, Mistress Foggarty. I wish you good luck. I shall listen out for news of you.'

'Goodbye, Mrs Paige. I don't know how to thank you.' On the doorstep, Meg added: 'And I hope you find happiness in the future.' As she walked from the house she wondered if it would be with Mr Simpson.

Meg drove to the prison and asked to see the governor. Her request was refused. Permission to speak to Reuben was likewise denied. She stood helplessly at the gate, unable to leave without having made some progress.

'Does Mr Kingswell have a lawyer?' she asked the warder, who still barred her entrance to the gaol.

'I think he's represented by a man called Mason. Got an office in Jewry Street.'

'Thank you. Er, do you know if a new date has been set for ...?'

'Day after tomorrow, lady, day after tomorrow.'

Meg found Mr Mason taking tea in his chambers. He was a small man with the appearance of being weighed down by the burden of his cases. The pipe he was smoking exuded a pungent stench which permeated not only his room but the approaching corridor.

Quickly Meg spelled out her business.

Mr Mason sat back on his desk and puffed thoughtfully. 'Heard about your reappearance,' he observed. 'Gave it some thought but I can't see that it changes anything. It was Mr Mew who Kingswell was actually accused of murdering. In cases of multiple crime like this, we usually take one charge as a sample, usually the most obvious one.'

'But I've got new evidence,' Meg said, resisting the temptation to open a window and let fresh air into the room.

'Such as?'

She told him.

He pondered what he had heard, biting audibly on the

stained stem of the pipe. He drooped his lips and nodded to himself. 'Could be something here, but it will need the Home Secretary to stop it now and he won't want to waste his time on trivialities.' As Meg went to object, he began to count on his fingers. 'Now, what do we actually know?'

'One, that you aren't dead, although some other woman is; two that you personally don't believe Kingswell had a motive to commit this crime; three, that your friend Margery claims the chief witness, who is now dead, had a fight with the accused before the accident; four, that you claim the same chief witness had a motive for not wanting you engaged to the accused because he wanted you for his mistress; five, that the accused was possibly with this Mrs Carmichael at the time of the explosion, although that's still only hearsay.'

He sighed and scratched his thinning hair. 'On the other side, this Paige wanting you for his mistress could equally be a good reason for Kingswell to try to get rid of him – and you. Perhaps Kingswell meant to blow up you and Paige and got two other people by mistake.'

'That's ridiculous!'

'That's supposition, madam, same as your account.'

'I've got evidence – Mr Paige's letter. His wife will affirm that it's genuine.'

'So she might but it doesn't actually prove anything, does it? Except that this man had some strange ideas about what he might or might not do.'

Meg looked at him incredulously. 'Are you saying that none of this helps?' she asked. 'It must do, surely. Perhaps if we could prove who the other woman is?'

Mason shrugged.

'Well, have you tried to find out?' His calmness infuriated her. 'Don't you realise, they're going to kill someone who is worth ten times any of them – and certainly ten of you!' She could no longer contain her anger and frustration. This man simply did not care. Fighting down her desire to shake him, she asked as calmly as she could: 'Mr Mason, what could stop this happening? What would you need to go to the Home Secretary?'

The man pondered for a long time, then shook his head. 'Well, if Mr Mew were to suddenly turn up – but at the moment, dear lady, I can't think of anything.'

Crying inside, Meg asked: 'Could you at least help me to see him? Please?'

He considered her words with the same lack of urgency that he had given to everything else that afternoon. Finally taking his pipe from his mouth, he laid it aside on the oak desk and again pursed his lips thoughtfully. 'I don't see why not,' he concurred. 'If you come to the gaol tomorrow at ten o'clock, I'll be there and, if Kingswell wants to see you, I'll take you in.'

Meg barely slept. The hope of seeing Reuben again, the nightmare of the fate that hung over him, the fear that he might refuse to see her and worry about how Declan may be coping without her, all kaleidoscoped in her mind. She was glad to see the first wisps of dawn lighten her bedchamber.

Meg washed thoroughly, brushed her hair until her arm ached and then dressed with great care in what had once been her best gown in those far-off days in Freshwater. Reuben had always complimented her when she wore it. Today of all days she needed every bit of confidence that she could find.

The minutes dragged so slowly that once or twice she was convinced that it was earlier than it had been when she had looked out of the window at the town clock five minutes before. When she could wait no longer, she left the shop and walked to the prison. She stated her business at the gate and was allowed inside into a small, bare room where she waited stiffly in the presence of a gaoler until Mr Mason turned up, accompanied by a second uniformed man.

Meg was almost fainting with emotion. Her legs would hardly carry her as she followed Mason and a warder along the labyrinthine corridors to Reuben's cell. She had to hold her breath to prevent her fears from running away with her. It seemed to take an eternity for the man to unlock the door, and as it swung open she gazed in at the prisoner seated by the bare wooden table, dreading what she might see. As he saw her, Reuben stood up and waited for her to come in.

'Reuben!' In spite of her attempts to be calm, the anguish bubbled over and she could not stop herself from moving towards him.

281

'Meg.' His voice was muted. He held her to him, his cheek resing on the crown of her head. Captured in his arms, she felt that the rest of the world receded. This was the only reality she could conceive of.

Too soon he stood back.

'I owe you an apology,' he started. 'The shock of seeing you last Friday, on top of everything else ...'

'Of course.' She felt distanced from him again. Her smile was false, polite.

He sat down on the bunk that served as his bed and she could feel his awkwardness. The presence of the solicitor and the warder was intrusive.

'Is Declan well?'

'He's in good health. I've left him with Mrs Dore.'

Reuben nodded and there was silence. Finally Meg took the plunge.

'I have to explain to you, everything.'

'There's no need. As long as you are well ...'

'Please. Let me tell you. Please.'

He listened in silence as she recounted everything, from the meeting with Paige, his crazy proposition, his assault upon her and her subsequent flight. She told him about Arthur and his inn, about her modest success with her dark box, Arthur's death and her inheritance and the fact that Bartholomew Paige was now dead.

He listened attentively, showing neither shock nor approval. 'You've suffered,' was all he said.

'We've got to get you out of here.'

He shook his head. 'The worst thing was when I couldn't resign myself to it. I didn't want to go to my grave not knowing what had happened to you and what had become of Declan.'

'But —'

He interrupted her. 'They won't let me out of here now, it's too late. But I didn't kill Amos.'

'I know that.'

'Or any young woman.'

'I know that, too.' She added impatiently: 'You must try and help yourself. I've got all kinds of little things to go on but your solicitor' — she glanced disapprovingly at Mr

Mason – 'says it's not enough. Isn't there anything you can think of?'

Reuben shook his head.

'Tell me about Mrs Carmichael, everything you can remember. Perhaps someone saw you?'

Unwillingly Reuben recounted the day. It was clear that he thought it a waste of time. As he started to tell her about sheltering in the barn, he finished: 'My main worry was what you were thinking, and what old Amos was up to.' He suddenly drew in his breath and his eyes grew wide. 'I've just remembered something else. Oh, God, I think I know who that woman was!'

'Who?'

'There was a girl, a sort of halfwit. She'd been hanging round the forge for several days. I'd been leaving food out for her and I remember thinking that she might be sleeping in the forge. Oh, my God! Poor little lass.'

Meg looked away in respect for his feelings and the memory of a poor halfwit girl. 'It might solve a mystery,' she said quietly. 'But it doesn't help your case.'

Now Reuben looked up at her. 'Meg, I want you to do something for me.'

'Of course.'

'No. You don't know what I'm going to say.' He hesitated and there was sadness in his tired hazel eyes. 'I want you to go now. Seeing you has been good. I've got something precious to remember.'

She began to protest but he waved her objections aside. 'While I've been here I've died, mentally, a thousand times. The reality has no fear for me. Knowing that Paige is dead, and in such a manner, makes it even easier, it could almost convince me that there is some kind of justice.' He was silent and she had no words to put her case. Finally he said: 'You're a lovely girl. I want you to look after yourself and Declan. It is a relief to know that you have money of your own. Don't spoil your life by trying to change the unchangeable.'

'Reuben ...'

'I'm going to die, Meg, tomorrow – no, don't cry. Just, please promise me that you'll stop fighting against impossible odds. Promise me.'

283

She bowed forward under the weight of her tears and he got up to comfort her. 'Hush, now.'

Again she was cradled in his arms, but they were the arms of a father, a brother, not a lover. She clung to him wanting his love back, wanting never to let him go. Gently but firmly he took her hands and pulled them away from his neck. He gazed into her eyes.

'You gave me a life,' he said. 'Whether it lasted a year or a day, a month or for ever, it was the best thing that any man could have.' He twisted the gold band around her finger. 'See, these links go on for ever and ever, till death us do part.'

Chapter Forty-Four

Meg did not remember how she left the prison, and had no recollection of travelling back to the shop. At some point in the day she knew that she should go and fetch Declan but she could not remember where to find him. Those treacherous minutes that had dragged their feet that morning now careered with insane speed, spilling out her life as she sat helplessly in her large, lonely drawing room.

Unable to bear the inactivity, she got up and began to pace around. She traced Reuben's name over and again on the rain-spattered window. Something final was happening and she had to do something about it but she couldn't remember what.

Some time in the middle of the night she awoke to the sound of Declan crying. She went to look for him but he wasn't there. His bed had gone and so had her mantel shelf with her precious pictures on it.

'Where are you?' she called out but there was no answer.

Reuben. She started to write his name again but then she couldn't remember how to spell it. She had started it with a B. Bruben, Breuben, Breuden, Brenden. That was it, Brendan. He was so drunk, always drunk. So beautiful, except on that last day ... Reuben. She wrote it large on the windowpane. Blood pounded in her head so loud that she could not hear above it. It was almost as if somewhere in the distance somebody was hammering to get in.

She jerked again into wakefulness, only to discover that there was an impatient thumping on the front door. She stumbled out of bed and down the stairs. Through the curtain she could make out the outline of a figure dressed in scarlet. Clumsily she unlocked the door and the apparition strode into the room.

'Meg Foggarty! We've been looking all over the city for you. My goodness, girl, you look absolutely dreadful. You need a good stiff drink!'

Meg wondered when she would wake up. There was something she had to do but she still couldn't remember what.

A glass was pushed into her hand and she obeyed the injunction of her companion to drink. The liquid startled her mouth and burned its way down her throat. She recognised it as brandy from the time she had welcomed in the New Year at the Bear. She had no strong liquor in the house and guessed that her visitor had carried it with her.

'That's better. At last there is a touch of colour in your cheeks.'

Meg looked at the woman in disbelief. 'Mrs Carmichael? I thought you were in India.'

'A good job for you I'm not. All this nonsense while I've been away.'

Now it was all back, the awfulness of the last day, the passage of time, a new dawn.

'It's Reuben, they're going to kill him!'

Mrs Carmichael tutted and pushed her back onto the bed.

'I heard about it as soon as I got back. I've been on to the Home Secretary myself, went up on the steam train and back again. I soon made him see sense. 'Gotthard,' I said, 'the law's like a mule when you're in charge. It won't budge even when you put dynamite under it. All this foolishness about my farrier killing people. He was with me, man, and anyway, he's far too decent a sort.' Such nonsense!'

'Mrs Carmichael, is Reuben ...?'

'He's still in that awful place. It will take several days before they sort out all their files and portfolios and dot their i's and cross their t's.' She sighed. 'In the meantime you had better come along home with me. I'm sailing across to the island this afternoon.'

'What time is it?'

286

Mrs Carmichael looked out of the window at the clock. 'Half past eight.'

Meg gave a little gasp. While she had been sitting there in that terrible, lonely daze, the time had come and gone when Reuben should have been taken from his cell and hanged by his neck until the life was squeezed out of him. She began to shake.

'There, girl. No need to take on. He's safe now. Just you come along and drink this nice brandy.'

'I want to see him.'

'Not today. For now you are coming back with me to the island. No arguments. You are going to be looked after and when you are fully recovered you can think about the future.'

'I let him down.'

'Paige wronged you.'

Meg looked away, trying not to remember. After a while she asked: 'Did you tell him that he should marry me?'

'Kingswell?' Mrs Carmichael looked surprised. 'Good Lord, no. You should know him better than that.' Taking Meg by the arm, she chivvied her towards the bedchamber to pack her valise. 'Come along now, we've got to get going.'

As Meg began listlessly to push a few things into her bag, her escort said: 'He isn't the sort of man to be told what to do. One way or the other, he'll always make up his own mind.'

Chapter Forty-Five

On the morning of 19 June at eight in the morning, Meg stood across the road and watched as the huge gate of Winchester gaol was pushed creakily open. A solitary figure appeared, dwarfed by the size of the walls behind him. He took a few steps and then stopped, uncertainly looking up and down the road.

'Reuben!' Meg began to hurry towards him. He looked at her but registered no pleasure at her presence.

'I didn't expect to see you.'

She suddenly felt awkward. 'I've hired a cab to take you back to Lymington, to get the boat.'

He did not move, and his face was troubled. For a moment he glanced away, then said: 'Thank you, but I'm not sure I'm going back. There are too many reminders.'

She felt shocked by his statement and embarrassed by her assumption. 'I simply thought ...'

'It's good of you, really, but ...'

'Perhaps the cab can take you somewhere else?'

He shrugged.

She took a package from her fichu and held it uncertainly out to him. 'This is just a little something to tide you over.'

He shook his head. 'I don't want anything. I'll find my own way, when I've had time to think.'

She dropped her hand, the package hanging like a fetter. Mrs Carmichael's words came back to haunt her. As calmly as she could, she said: 'You must have had plenty of time to think while you were in there.' She nodded towards the ominous building behind him.

288

He shrugged. 'Then I didn't think past the rope, and revenge. Now it's all different.'

Her heart was quaking. This was not how she had imagined it. She thought painfully of the homecoming she had planned, the Dores all waiting to greet him, Mrs Carmichael organising the builders to repair the forge.

'Everyone is looking forward to seeing you.'

The disbelief showed in his expression. 'Everyone thought I was a murderer.'

'They didn't! No one believed it.'

She stood there helplessly, not knowing how to stop him from drifting away. Finally she asked: 'Do you want your ring back?'

'Ring?'

She began to pull it off her finger but he stopped her hand. 'Please Meg. Don't push me. I know you mean well but I'm not the man you knew. I don't know who I am.'

She looked down at the eternal links. Finally she said: 'I'll understand if you can't accept what happened between me and Paige.'

'It isn't that.' He paused. 'You must see that it's different now. I hear you're a successful woman. You've made a way for yourself. I'm glad about that. I might be free but people are always going to wonder. Besides, who's going to want to bring their horses to me now?'

She shook her head impatiently. 'People don't think like that and anyway, what I've got has been through good fortune. It would help to ... '

Again he shook his head.

Suddenly she could hold back no longer. 'You said till death us do part! Well, it isn't death that's parting us, is it, it's pride!'

He did not move.

Pushing the money into her bag, she stepped back. 'Goodbye then, Reuben. I'm going back to the island. Declan is there with Mrs Dore. I ... I wish you luck with whatever it is you want.'

In a daze of pain and disappointment she turned and walked to the cab. All the time she hoped to hear his footsteps behind her but there was only silence.

'Lymington,' she told the driver. As the horse turned and began to trot away from the gaol, she caught one quick glimpse of a lonely figure standing outside the gate. He did not wave.

Meg was too numbed for tears. The cold disbelief at Reuben's rejection closed her off from the needle-sharp wind that swung round from the east and now buffeted the steamer on its way towards Yarmouth. Every crossing she had made had been filled with different emotions. This time it was despair.

In all her sufferings, in every fearful moment since she had learned of Reuben's fate, she had never seen beyond rescuing him, restoring him to his old life.

Somehow she had lost sight of the fact that she had committed the unforgivable sin of fornication. Because of what had happened to her, Reuben had withdrawn his love. It must happen every day that poor girls were used by rich men, then abandoned by the poor men they might have married. Foolishly she had hoped that he would be different, but he wasn't.

He was the only man she had trusted with her happiness and he had shown that he was mortal, not the ideal constant lover who would stick by her, come what might.

The boat gave a lurch and for a second Meg remembered where she was. Before long she would be back on the Isle of Wight, Reuben's island. It was here that her child had been born, and here that she had encountered a new world through Mrs Carmichael. In the village she had discovered the simple honest friendship of the Dores and known the fleeting joy of her betrothal. She glanced down at her left hand. Reuben's ring still encircled her finger – some love token!

Angrily she tried to pull it off to cast it into the frothing turmoil beneath the steamer, but it would not budge. She had never noticed before that it had become tight, yet now it refused to be removed from the third finger of her left hand.

She sank back and tears of hopelessness mingled with the salt spray. Whatever the future held, wherever she ended up, she knew that Reuben Kingswell's keeper still held her fast, binding her to the promise she had given him. Only now it was he, not she, who had run away.

Trying to keep her mind on her own options, she vacillated between the wisdom of settling in Winchester or returning permanently to the bay. Both made sense. Neither made sense. In Winchester she had a successful business but she was alone. On the island she had friends but no means of support. The island was where Reuben belonged. If he did not want her, then there was no place for her there. On the other hand, if he was not coming back, she need not deny herself the comfort of her friends.

She looked across the hazy expanse of water. The outline of the Needles rocks was not yet visible. She leaned back and breathed the sharp, clean sea air, thinking: If I can see the Needles before I count to one hundred, then I'll go back to the island to live. She started to count.

By the time she reached fifty-three, the rocky outcrop came into view.

Chapter Forty-Six

'I have come to a decision,' said Mrs Carmichael. 'I shall no longer torment my visitors by using them as photographic subjects.'

Meg smiled, keeping pace with her friend and benefactress as they started the steady ascent from Freshwater Bay to Simla Lodge. These morning promenades were becoming a habit.

'You aren't giving up photography?'

'Gracious, no! On the contrary, I'm helping Lord Alfred to illustrate his new poetic work.'

The sun was behind them and its summer warmth on her back gave Meg a rare sense of wellbeing. Ahead of them Declan dragged a stick along the dusty path, stopping occasionally to poke at the bushes.

'Snails, Mama!'

Meg nodded and the inexhaustible affection for her child welled up. Such a bright little boy! Brendan O'Neill's eyes regarded her, curious and innocent.

'I can't believe that you have been back six months,' said Mrs Carmichael, puffing slightly. 'How time flies! I think you did the right thing in coming back.'

'So do I.' Meg thought briefly of her studio in Winchester, which was now sold. Her new place at the bay had not been quite as successful, but in the city she had been alone; here she had her friends.

The two women continued in silence to the gate of Simla and there parted company. Meg and Declan retraced their steps back down to the rocky bay. Meg had photographed it many times, morning and evening, summer and winter, crowded and deserted. She never tired of its stark, savage beauty.

That morning she intended to go to another bay, at Totland, and from there to photograph those rocky promontories, the Needles. While the few affluent families who stayed throughout the year came to her for portraits, it was mementoes of their holiday that summer visitors sought, pictures of the bays and the cliffs, to take back as souvenirs.

As they walked into the yard behind Meg's house and studio, Ginny the mare puffed her friendly greeting from the loosebox, her short ears erect with welcome. Meg was touched by the merest droplet of pain when she looked at Reuben's horse.

'You needing a mount, mistress?' Alfred Cheke had asked her, soon after she arrived on the island. 'I got Reuben's mare here. I don't really need her but he wanted her took care of.' She had accepted gratefully.

Grazing behind her was Blanco the donkey. He had been part of her inheritance, like the Bear and Arthur's money. Now he was Ginny's boon companion. The two animals struck her as bizarre forms of keepsake.

'Me drive!' Declan begged, dragging open the door and reaching fearlessly for the horse's collar.

'In a minute.' She thought that he was a natural horse man. Even at this young age he seemed to have an understanding of how they thought and felt.

It took her only a few moments to harness the pony and store her camera and plates in the back of the governess cart. She sat to one side as Declan held the reins. Blanco brayed his protest at being left behind.

'Ged up!' Declan ordered and the mare obliged. 'Shall we go this way?'

'No.' Meg didn't want to go past the skeletal forge, rebuilt but still deserted. These days people still complained at the loss of amenity and took their horses down to Norton Village, some three miles away.

But Declan had already driven into the narrow lane towards the sheepwash and could not turn round. Meg bit her lip. Ginny began to trot, her ears pricked. Meg reflected sadly that perhaps the mare thought she was going home. As they neared the forge, she slowed down.

'G'wan,' Declan ordered, flicking her with the whip, but she tossed her head and stared in at the open doorway.

'Here, give her to me.' Meg reached for the reins. Then she realised that something was different: a wisp of black smoke rose from the narrow pipe of a chimney. Suddenly there was a loud ringing sound as a hammer made contact with hot metal against the bridge of an anvil. Her grip on the reins slackened and Ginny walked forwards into the yard.

At the sound of their arrival, the man inside came to investigate. In disbelief Meg saw Reuben step out, still holding the great pincers he used to hook the shoes from the fire. He gazed at Ginny in amazement and slowly his eyes turned to her.

'We didn't mean to come in,' she heard herself say. 'The horse brought us here.' She was aware that she sounded cold, defensive. Inside another voice kept repeating: I don't believe it, it's not true!

He patted the mare's head and stood back to cast a practised eye over her. 'Knew your way home, did you, gal?'

'I didn't know you were back.' Meg struggled to be natural.

'I hardly know it myself. I arrived last night. Er, won't you get down?'

She hesitated for a second, then stepped shakily from the carriage. Declan was already inside the forge, expressing his approval at everything he saw.

'I can't believe that's the lad,' Reuben said. 'He's so big.'

Meg looked at her former lover. He had changed: he seemed older and grey flecked his shaggy black hair. He was leaner, too, and his brow was creased as if from a habitual frown.

He followed her inside. The forge glowed and the same black kettle sang over the fire. For a moment it was as if he had never been away.

'Are you back to stay?' she asked as casually as she could manage.

'Yes.'

294

She tried to keep her voice casual. 'The villagers'll be glad. They've missed the forge.'

He acknowledged her remark and, putting the pincers down, turned to make tea. His back to her, he said: 'I couldn't write. I didn't know where you were.'

'That's all right.'

'No, it's not.' Steaming water jetted into the old pot. Above the noise he said: 'Letting you walk away that morning was the stupidest thing I ever did. You must think I'm pretty worthless.'

Again she couldn't think what to say. It was he who broke the silence.

'I was coming to see you, this afternoon. I saw Margy in the village. She told me where you were. She said she looks after Declan for you when you're at work.' As he stirred the contents of the pot with a blackened spoon, he continued: 'I've had the damnedest letter, from Paige's wife. She's just got married, and she's put some money in a trust for me. I can't take it but it was a kind thought.'

'You should take it. You must be entitled to compensation for what Paige did to you.'

'Perhaps.' He handed her a battered mug. She guessed that it had been there before the explosion and the thought of those deaths cast a pall over the place.

'I'm on my way to Totland,' she told him. 'I take photographs to sell. People like to have them.'

'Have you photographed the old beacon?'

She shook her head. She couldn't tell him that her heart would not allow her to go to such a sacred place. Instead she said: 'The camera's too heavy.'

'Perhaps I could carry it up for you some time.'

'Perhaps.'

He looked at the ground, then up at her. His eyes were different now, the laughter had gone but the same steady honesty remained. 'I'm sorry. I didn't know who I was. I'd lost all sense of self-respect.'

She took a sip of the tea and its smoky flavour was like a long-lost friend. Gazing back out through the doorway she saw Declan climbing onto a farm wagon leaning drunkenly because of a missing wheel.

'Get down!'

'He won't get hurt.'

She could feel his presence across the few feet that separated them. Her chest was taut and her hands threatened to betray her with their shaking.

'Where have you been?' she asked.

'Just wandering. I worked as and when I needed to. I guess it's taken me six months to go full circle.' Looking away he said: 'There's never been a day I haven't thought of you.' A sad smile touched his lips. 'You haven't found yourself someone else?'

'No.'

'You must hate me.'

'It was my running away that started it all.'

'It was Paige.' He looked across at her again. 'That's the burden of being beautiful, Meg. You attract all manner of people.'

She said nothing. After a moment she asked: 'Who did Mrs Paige marry?'

'A man called Simpson.'

She smiled.

Serious, Reuben added: 'I guess I'm not the only one who's wanted to marry you.'

She hardly dared to trust her ears or her heart. Involuntarily she twisted the band of gold on her finger. Reuben looked down at her hand.

'You still wear my keeper.'

'It won't come off.' She didn't know what she meant to imply, what she wanted him to think.

'I'm sorry,' he said again. 'It will take me a while to work up my business but soon as I'm settled – that is ...'

She thought that he had finished but he added: 'I'd like to ask you to walk out with me, proper, above board, proud.'

Before she could answer, Declan came running to her carrying a horseshoe. 'See, Mama, this is just the size for Ginny. She needs to be shod.'

The tension was broken. Reuben accompanied the child back outside, and Meg followed. She watched as they approached the horse and Reuben picked up her near

296

foreleg. With their dark heads close together they could have been father and son.

'You're right, she does,' he said. Letting her go he stood up again. 'Would you like to help me sometimes?'

The child's eyes sparkled. Over his head Reuben looked across at Meg. 'Seems like I've found myself an apprentice.'

'Perhaps you have. It's too early yet to tell.'

'Aye, too early – but not too late?'

She shook her head and suddenly tears brimmed over, splashing unchecked down her cheeks.

'Meg!' He reached for her then, holding her gently, comforting. She had found once more the haven that had so long been denied to her.

Gently Reuben rocked her, crooning words of endearment; 'My beautiful lass, my poor sweet girl.' Holding her away for a moment, he looked into her eyes. 'Give me an answer, won't you?' She felt the slow stirring of his groin.

'The weakness of men,' he said not moving away. His gentle grin was back. He raised his eyebrows and in answer she gave a single nod of her head.

He sighed as if a burden had been lifted. 'You've given my life purpose again.' With a hug he released her and turned to Declan, who was regarding them with amazement. 'Come along then, lad. If you're going to be my apprentice you'll have lots of work to do, but for today we're going to take a holiday. Let's put that fire out.'

Declan glanced briefly at his mother for confirmation, then back at the blacksmith.

'Where we going?' he asked.

'Why, first we're going to take your mother to Totland, to photograph her rocks, and then we're going to shoe this horse, and then – well, I don't know what then but whatever it is, we'll do it together.'